P[...]s danger.

Swordplay and combat practice with the other soldiers had never felt life or death, but this…*this* felt viscerally real. Graham had invited her onto the battlefield, where she had promptly engaged him in battle. What happened next could determine whether they—

He flipped her so swiftly and so easily she did not even register his movement until she found herself pinned beneath him, her spine against the soft grass, her breath vanishing from her lungs in a whoosh powerful enough to rustle the curly black tendrils tumbling over his forehead.

Now it was his body pressing into hers. Wide shoulders, slender hips, muscular thighs—and perhaps a hint of mutual interest pulsing between them.

A proper miss would be shocked right into a swoon.

It was a good thing Kuni wasn't the least bit proper. Not only had she *started* this, she intended to savor every second of it.

Praise for Erica Ridley and The Wild Wynchesters

"Erica Ridley is a delight!"

—Julia Quinn, *New York Times* bestselling author of the Bridgerton series

"Erica Ridley's love stories are warm, witty, and irresistible. I want to be a Wynchester!"

—Eloisa James, *New York Times* bestselling author of *My Last Duchess*

The Perks of Loving a Wallflower

"The holy grail for Regency fans: like Georgette Heyer, but with sex . . . a feminist fairy tale readers will rejoice in."

—*Publishers Weekly,* Starred Review

"Funny and sexy. The lead characters' identities are realistically nuanced. Completely enchanting."

—*Kirkus*, Starred Review

"An exquisitely written, utterly transcendent romance that perfectly captures the joy of being loved for who you truly are . . . pure reading bliss."

—*Booklist,* Starred Review

"This clever novel will delight readers."

—*Library Journal*, Starred Review

"A plot full of mystery, high jinks, and tender personal revelations."

—*New York Times*

"A sapphic Regency romp that radiates all the good, fuzzy feelings readers want in a romance."

—*BookPage*

The Duke Heist

"This entrancing Regency . . . is a knockout."

—*Publishers Weekly*, Starred Review

"Schemes, heists, and forgeries abound in this charming series starter. This unconventional and quirky Regency will have readers falling for the plucky family and rooting for Chloe and Lawrence to buck tradition."

—*Library Journal*

"Ridley's motley crew of Wynchester siblings is as charming as it is unforgettable, signaling more great romance ahead. *The Duke Heist* is everything a Regency romance fan hopes for."

—*BookPage*

Nobody's Princess

More books by Erica Ridley

The Wild Wynchesters

The Duke Heist
The Perks of Loving a Wallflower
The Governess Gambit (novella)
The Rake Mistake (novella)

The Dukes of War

The Viscount's Tempting Minx
The Earl's Defiant Wallflower
The Captain's Bluestocking Mistress
The Major's Faux Fiancée
The Brigadier's Runaway Bride
The Pirate's Tempting Stowaway
The Duke's Accidental Wife

Rogues to Riches

Lord of Chance
Lord of Pleasure
Lord of Night
Lord of Temptation
Lord of Secrets
Lord of Vice
Lord of the Masquerade

The 12 Dukes of Christmas

Once Upon a Duke
Kiss of a Duke
Wish Upon a Duke
Never Say Duke
Dukes, Actually
The Duke's Bride
The Duke's Embrace
The Duke's Desire
Dawn with a Duke
One Night with a Duke
Ten Days with a Duke
Forever Your Duke

Gothic Love Stories

Too Wicked to Kiss
Too Sinful to Deny
Too Tempting to Resist
Too Wanton to Wed
Too Brazen to Bite

Magic & Mayhem

Kissed by Magic
Must Love Magic
Smitten by Magic

NOBODY'S PRINCESS

A Wild Wynchesters Novel

ERICA RIDLEY

FOREVER
New York Boston

Forever
Hachette Book Group
1290 Avenue of the Americas, New York, NY 10104
read-forever.com
twitter.com/readforeverpub

First Edition: July 2022

Forever is an imprint of Grand Central Publishing. The Forever name and logo are trademarks of Hachette Book Group, Inc.

The publisher is not responsible for websites (or their content) that are not owned by the publisher.

ISBNs: 978-1-5387-1958-9 (mass market), 978-1-5387-1957-2 (ebook)

Printed in the United States of America

OPM

10 9 8 7 6 5 4 3 2 1

To anyone who has ever
yearned to stand out

And to Roy, for everything

Acknowledgments

As always, this book would not exist without the support of many wonderful people. My fabulous editor, Leah Hultenschmidt, who is always willing to hop on a call and chat things out. The team at Forever—including Jodi Rosoff and Dana Cuadrado in publicity, and Daniela Medina in the art department—for the times you went above and beyond. My brilliant agent, Lauren Abramo, for your wisdom, encouragement, and friendship.

My utmost gratitude to Rose Lerner, who makes every book better. Erica Monroe and my early reader crew: thank you so, so much for your feedback and enthusiasm. Enormous thanks go to intrepid assistant Laura Stout (aka mami), my right hand in the United States handling everything I cannot from Costa Rica. All the cowriting dates with Alyssa, Mary, and Coven—you guys keep me on task, and I love you for it. Thanks go to Darc, Jean, Jenn, Lace, Lenore, Pintip, Susan, Tracey, and Team #1k1hr for the texts from the trenches and all the mutual support.

Muchísimas gracias to my dashing Roy Prendas, who dons full Regency attire on cue and makes every single day our happy ever after. *Te adoro, popolote*.

And my biggest, most heartfelt thanks go to my amazing, wonderful readers. You're all so fun and funny and smart. I love your reviews and your Bookstagrams, and adore chatting together in the newsletter VIP List, on social media, and in our Historical Romance Book Club group on Facebook. Your enthusiasm makes the romance happen.

Thank you for everything!

Nobody's Princess

1

April 1818
London, England

Graham Wynchester turned away from the carriage window. "Are you certain you won't need me?"

Beside him on the seat, his sister Tommy sent him a flat look. "It's a simple infiltration and recovery. We've done it a thousand times."

Across from her in the carriage, Miss Philippa York didn't look up from the mountain of books open on her lap. The toes of her half boots played with Tommy's beneath the lace of Philippa's gown. "I'm fairly certain I've memorized every word written on the topic."

"Righting a miscarriage of justice isn't something you read," Tommy teased as she smoothed the distinctive red waistcoat of her Bow Street Horse Patrol uniform. "It's something we *do*."

"These aren't gothic novels," Philippa protested. "They're Graham's intelligence albums on the building, owners, and staff. Each one is incredibly thorough."

Graham grinned at her. His reconnaissance was always useful, but Philippa was the first to cling to his compendiums as though she adored the journals just as much as he did.

If all went well, that would soon change. A week ago, one of Graham's informants had learned that an important foreign dignitary would be visiting London and had requested the Crown provide documentation disclosing potential security concerns at all the significant places a royal guest would be likely to visit.

Graham was *made* for a task like that!

The Crown hadn't requested his intervention. The Home Office had begrudgingly accepted Graham's offer to submit his own report…after he pointed out that he wouldn't even be *aware* of the project, were it not for clear holes in security that Graham knew of and the Crown did not. The Prince Regent would see Graham's talents firsthand. In the meantime, he was sworn to secrecy about his involvement in the upcoming diplomatic preparations.

After a lifetime collecting other people's secrets, Graham finally had a delicious one of his own. And if all went very, very well, he might even achieve the dream he'd cherished since he was a child: acknowledgment by a royal.

"Someone can help *me*." Graham's sister Elizabeth sat across from him, sheathing and unsheathing three different sword sticks. "Which deadly blade should I wield? The one with the serpent handle, the one shaped like a raptor, or the one Marjorie painted with daisies?"

He pointed at the innocuous-looking cane covered in flowers and festooned with ribbons. "They definitely won't anticipate a rapier through the heart if you sally in with that confection."

Philippa looked up from her reading, alarmed. "Do you really think—"

"He's bamming you." Tommy adjusted her beaver hat. "Elizabeth will *pretend* to be violent, which will distract the inn's proprietor. You'll slip in and out undetected whilst I detain my sister after a prolonged and dramatic tussle."

"I don't have to pretend," said Elizabeth. "I could poke a few of them, just for flair. *They're* the villains who stole..."

While Tommy and Elizabeth bickered over the appropriate bloodiness of a staged altercation, Philippa met Graham's eyes.

"What about you?" she asked. "Do you need help with your mission?"

Bursting into sisterly laughter, Tommy and Elizabeth ceased their row at once.

"Help with... a wild-goose chase?" Elizabeth said in disbelief.

"It is nothing of the sort." While performing reconnaissance for his government, Graham had stumbled across a mystery—one that gave him the perfect cover for going out on research expeditions in person, rather than relying exclusively on his network of spies. There was legitimate work to be done. "A woman is in grave danger, and I am going to save her."

"You don't know that she's in danger," Tommy said. "You stumbled across a series of personal advertisements in the newspaper implying a 'package' was being tracked and subsequently went missing."

"He didn't stumble across anything," Elizabeth said. "He reads every word of every advertisement and every column in every publication. It's where half his intelligence comes from."

"Twenty-three percent," Philippa said helpfully. "His network of spies are also quite informative."

"And so is my own personal reconnaissance," Graham

reminded them. "Such as today. Just think! Perhaps I shall finally rescue a princess."

Elizabeth scoffed. "How would someone lose a princess? We'd *know* if someone lost a princess!"

"This is your second day looking for her," Tommy added. "Have you considered you might be misreading the situation, and no one is missing?"

He waggled his finger at her. "You're a doubting Thomas, both of you. You'll see."

"Graham's right." Philippa closed the albums on her lap with care. "My ladies' reading circle independently studied the obfuscated messages and reached similar conclusions."

"See?" Graham told Tommy. "They're the experts. Philippa and her friends solved a centuries-old enigma and designed a military cipher. If *they* say I'm right about this..."

Philippa nodded. "It does seem that two or more individuals are attempting to capture a woman, for reasons unknown. She has gone missing. Whether she escaped or was abducted by those hunting her, is also unknown."

"Exactly what *I* said. Two dozen clever bluestockings agree with me. But not my own sisters!"

Elizabeth smacked him with her cane. "You said 'princess.'"

"My darling expert," Tommy stage-whispered to Philippa. "What are the chances the missing woman is a princess?"

"Unknown," Philippa whispered back. "But unlikely."

Graham lifted his nose. "It doesn't matter. Wynchesters rescue anyone who needs rescuing."

"We usually wait until a client invites us to intervene," Elizabeth reminded him.

"Not Graham." Tommy poked his shoulder. "If he even senses an injustice, he springs into motion like a freshly wound clock. There's no stopping him...or his imagination."

"One day, I'll scale a tower to save a princess," he informed them. "I'll rescue her standing atop a noble steed with a rose between my teeth." He pantomimed the pose.

"Those are not things that people do," Elizabeth said. "It makes no sense. Why carry a flower in your mouth? And why should anyone stand on a horse?" She turned to Philippa. "What percentage of Graham's 'reconnaissance skills' comes from the circus?"

"Ninety percent," Philippa replied. "Mayhap closer to ninety-five."

"Bah." He tapped the panel behind him and the carriage rolled to a stop. "I'll see you spoilsports at dinner, and we'll *see* who has had the more exciting day. I'll wager five quid it's me."

"Ten quid!" called Tommy as Graham leapt from the carriage onto a cobblestone street just outside of Mayfair.

He brushed a barely perceptible wrinkle from his new mazarine-blue frock coat. He did not know which country the expected dignitary would visit from, or when he or she was to arrive. In the event the missing woman was indeed a stray princess, he wanted her first impression of him to be favorable. Like all his clothes, this afternoon's elegant ensemble was specially tailored for ease of movement, should he suddenly need to scale cathedrals or leap across rooftops. One never knew when one would need to perform daring feats for a damsel in distress.

This day would be full of adventure. He could feel

it. Graham had fathomed out the pattern in the covert advertisements.

She, or her captors, possessed a copy of *Boyle's Court Guide*, and was systematically appearing outside each aristocratic residence in the exact order they were listed in the guidebook.

Graham hadn't the least notion *why* the sightings followed this pattern. Following a popular—if outdated—tourist guide was a baffling manner in which to conduct a covert abduction...and an equally baffling manner in which to evade capture. But Graham *was* certain which homes were next on the list. He owned every printing of the guidebook and had determined the edition his quarry was following.

He picked up his pace.

Two refined ladies heading toward him on the pavement startled and clutched their reticules to their bosoms as they edged to one side.

Oh, for the love of...Keeping his gaze straight ahead, Graham clenched his teeth and maintained a carefully cordial expression as he passed. His Schweitzer & Davidson waistcoat cost more than both their ensembles combined, but his skin was darker, which meant he was obviously a dastardly miscreant out to rob them.

His sisters and sister-in-law need not withstand such daily insults, because their skin was white as milk.

The ladies liked to tease their bachelor brother for holding out for a princess, but the truth was, Graham didn't just dream of rescuing a royal. He wished he *were* one.

No one would snub him if he had a crown.

As recently as 1759, an African prince had been fêted by the ton and welcomed with open arms into the beau monde and all its amusements. He'd even received a standing ovation from the audience at Drury Lane. But one needn't look to the past to see the intangible advantages of royalty. Queen Charlotte had distant African ancestry. Her son, the Prince Regent, was an absolute disaster, and he would be fawned over the rest of his life.

If Graham were a prince, he wouldn't squander his position on gluttony and bad wagers. Just think how many more good works could be accomplished if he could influence the entire country! Having been raised in the glare of footlights until the age of ten, Graham was used to commanding attention. What he lacked was social standing. Playing ringmaster to a network of equally lowborn informants did not make him king, but at least he was using his gifts to help others.

Such as the missing woman.

He drew to a stop across the street from a large, terraced home. Was she here? Was she frightened? Was she still in danger?

There were too many people walking up and down the pavements, too many carts and carriages crowding the street. He would not be able to spot her from the street.

He needed a bird's-eye view.

There was no convenient aerial rope like the one he'd used in the circus, but Graham had long since learned how to use his surroundings to launch him higher. He ducked back in the direction he had come, found the first empty alley, and began to run down it as quickly as he could.

He launched himself into the air and touched his right foot to a wooden crate, then his left atop a dusty barrel. The toe of his right boot grabbed purchase along a slender doorframe, his left a particularly jutting brick. With one final leap, his hands gripped the edge of a cornice, and he swung himself atop the roof. All without ripping a stitch in his well-tailored coat.

Hunching low to the roof, he traced his steps back, this time with the advantage of two stories' height. He could see over the river of pedestrians, over the slow moving sludge of London traffic, and into the grand residence opposite.

The gardens were empty of everything but grass and meticulously tended flowers. The doors and windows were shut, but the curtains had been parted to let in sunlight. No terrified faces peered from the glass. No hulking villains dragged their captive through the roses.

Graham crouched on his heels in frustration. How was he supposed to save the missing woman if he couldn't *find* her?

There was no sign of—

Wait.

There, on the corner diagonally opposite from his perch, across the street from the terraced home. A beautiful woman stood in shadow, scribbling furiously in a small book.

It didn't just look like a surveillance operation. He recognized the pretty young lady. She had been amongst the passersby the *last* time he'd gone looking for his soon-to-be client.

This could not possibly be a coincidence.

From this angle, the brim of her bonnet blocked his view of her face, but he remembered it perfectly from the day before. The bonnet's ribbon was an unusually bright purple-pink, but that wasn't what had caught his attention. He'd walked past her—then did so again, slower—because of her beauty.

Soft, flawless skin in a rich, smooth brown. Wide-set

eyes as dark as the black hair disappearing beneath her bonnet in elegant braids. Curling black lashes. A mouth that pouted adorably, lost in concentration on whatever note she was jotting. Tall, for a woman. Well-formed. Sturdy and capable, as though she spent her days jousting, or some other equally improbable venture.

She had intrigued him so thoroughly the day before, he'd forgotten his mission for a full five minutes before he recalled himself. He'd spent the afternoon scouring the grounds of the next residences listed in the guidebook, in hopes of finding his quarry.

She was the one, Graham was sure of it. He had found her at last!

He had no idea what difficulty she was in, but he was here to solve it. He turned and raced back across the roofs to the alley where he had ascended.

"Fear not, fair maiden," he called as he leapt through the air to the empty alley. "Your devoted knight has come!"

2

Kunigunde de Heusch would not permit anything to stand in her way.

Not the oppressive gray skies threatening rain overhead. Not the harsh language the Londoners spoke in too many accents, either speaking too fast to comprehend or mumbling too low to pick out any words at all. Not this huge, overwhelming city with houses scrunched against each other and crowds of people so dense one could be carried along for a hundred meters without one's boots scraping the ground. She definitely would not allow herself to be cowed by the two Royal Guardsmen hunting her down to cart her back home.

Kuni rubbed her arms. She had never felt more out of place than in the moment she'd stepped off the boat and onto the pier. Everything was so different! The sights, the smells, the weather, the architecture. Things were new when she expected old, old when she expected new, big when she expected small, small when she expected big, bright when she expected sedate, and dull when she was hoping for a splash of color.

And *she* was different from everyone else. Years of practicing grammatically perfect upper-class English could not fully erase her natural accent. When she opened her mouth, she received one of two reactions. Either an exclamation of *Ooh, where are* you *from?* or else, *Netherlands! I met a fellow from Amsterdam once! He's called James. Perhaps you know him?*

Balcovia wasn't part of the Dutch empire, and hadn't been for over a century, not that anyone here seemed to care about those details...or much of anything. The London sky was sooty, the streets dirty, people and livestock darting every which way in front of horse-drawn carriages without a single care for their lives or for Kuni's constantly pounding heart.

How she missed Balcovia's wide, open vistas, its rolling hills and endless fields of green grass or yellow tulips, and its brilliant orange and pink sunsets! That was her view from the tower. Until this past week, Kuni rarely left the vast royal grounds for more than a few hours, unless it was to travel from the Winter Castle to the Summer Palace in a luxurious carriage fit for a princess.

Here, she was on foot. On foot! It sounded so simple. Kuni trained in every spare moment—blades, combat, maintaining stiff military posture for hours on end. At court, she danced until dawn. And yet her feet had never been in greater agony than now. The muscles of her thighs and calves twitched in protest whenever she paused, begging her to stop this madness and spend a few days reclining on plush cushions with nothing more pressing to do than sip chocolate by the fireside.

She could not indulge such slothful whims. Kuni had precisely forty days to achieve the impossible, and she'd used ten of those days already. Time was against her.

So were Balcovia's two best Royal Guards. Several times, they'd almost caught her. She'd managed to evade them purely by luck.

"Not luck," she muttered in Balcovian. "You're just as talented as they are. That's why you're here."

"What's that?" said an unkempt red-haired man with uneven whiskers, whose fetid breath smelled like some sort of alcohol that would *never* be served in a royal castle. "Are you lookin' for some private company?"

"N-no," Kuni stammered. "Carry on, good sir."

Good sir? Was that how one greeted leering drunks who propositioned strangers in the street? She was beginning to think her tutors had no actual experience traveling abroad.

And how should they? Neighboring France had been at war since before Kuni was born. Fifteen years ago when Napoleon had begun to seize power throughout the continent, Balcovia's military had joined a European coalition to fight back. All pleasure travel had stopped. It was too dangerous. Whatever information her tutors knew about England or France was many years old.

The intoxicated man leaned closer. "Give us your name, girl."

Kuni bristled. The thought of being spoken to in such an insolent, familiar manner! By a person such as this!

But she was trying to remain unnoticed. Causing a scene of any sort would be the fastest way to catch the eye of the Royal Guardsmen hunting for her.

She clutched her thick journal to her chest as though it were a Bible.

"I am Sister Mary Smith," she replied in her best, most repressed English accent. "Please carry on with your day elsewhere."

The whiskered man looked confused, but he tottered away.

Kuni sagged farther into the shadows in relief.

Even if the strange man hadn't unsettled her, she would have been tempted to give a false name. The English didn't even try to pronounce *Coo-nee-goon-deh* before laughing and asking what people *really* called her instead of Kunigunde.

To which she always replied with her full name and honorific, "Juffrouw Kunigunde de Heusch."

After all, none of *them* ever shortened their interminable, tongue-twisty "Right Honorable Miriam Darlinda MacMontague-Hargreaves, Dowager Marchioness of Brambleborough-on-Featherfettle" names to something like "Bambi" for *her*.

For the most part, Londoners looked right through her, especially dressed as she was now. It was not a phenomenon she was accustomed to as a member of the royal retinue—and she could not help but harbor mixed feelings about it, even if the anonymity was useful.

Still, she had work to do. If that meant wearing the oldest, plainest castoffs from her lady's maid, Kuni was more than willing to do it.

She was on a mission to outperform Balcovia's own Royal Guard.

In anticipation of an upcoming royal visit, her king had sent two of his Royal Guardsmen on a forty-day scouting expedition to identify strengths and weaknesses of English traditions and architecture, and ascertain which security measures should be put in place.

Unfortunately, the king's two best Royal Guards were also Kuni's brothers.

Floris and Reinald laughed at her for daring to dream

herself capable of becoming a Royal Guard. This was her sole chance to prove herself as capable as any man. No—better than an ordinary man. By providing the most useful intelligence herself, she would illustrate her true worth and at last be granted the title and uniform she longed for in the most elite infantry regiment in all of Balcovia.

Her brothers were Royal Guardsmen. Their father had been a Royal Guardsman. Their grandfather. Their great-grandfather. All the de Heusch men for generations had been chosen and honored by their king.

Kuni had trained with her brothers since she could toddle. Spent every spare second copying the royal soldiers' movements with military precision. Threw a knife before she could write her name. Stealth and skill gave her the edge in one-on-one combat. With throwing knives, the enemy needn't even sense her presence before Kuni's blade struck true.

The power royal companions wielded was invisible. Secrets, access to protected areas, influence over the princess.

Kuni wanted to be *visible*. To fight on the front lines, not hidden behind doors. To *guard* the princess, not embroider handkerchiefs beside her. To train with the soldiers, *as* a soldier. She would not rest until she wore the Royal Guard uniform with pride.

She intended to compete for a place in their ranks this summer along with the other aspiring soldiers. But the king would never allow a woman to join the competition unless she gave them a reason... such as being the hero of this mission. She had already penned her observations on two dozen residences. Shoddy security at each—honestly, the *English* would do well to hire her—and Kuni was well on her way to finishing on schedule.

Perhaps there would even be a spare day or two to take in the sights, such as... Who was *that*?

Kuni's exhaustive knowledge of her London guidebook vanished from her head. Although she was generally unimpressed with the men she'd met thus far, she had just caught sight of a man who had passed by her the day before. An absolutely exquisite gentleman with tawny golden skin, a stunningly handsome face, a well-tailored English coat, buttery buckskins that showed his muscled form to perfection, and an *exceedingly* arrogant stride.

Good God, for a man like this, a woman would happily learn all twenty unpronounceable words in his title.

She dipped her head lower before he could catch her staring. Her bonnet's brim cut off her view at his wide shoulders, which allowed her to drink the rest of him in without the risk of meeting his eyes. His easy pace exuded confidence and a lethal grace, as though his prey would not sense his approach until it was too late. But... *she* had noticed.

The attractive man was not walking in her general direction. He was striding straight toward *her*.

3

Kuni stepped back toward the shadows. Her heel scraped the brick wall behind her. There was nowhere farther to duck, no place to hide.

She had somehow caught this magnificent gentleman's eye and would have to send him on his way without so much as a word. She could not risk drawing attention to herself with an altercation. No scenes. No fuss. Invisible.

He stopped directly in front of her, dangerously close.

She lifted her head until his face came into view. Her breath caught.

He was even handsomer than she'd first thought. Strong jaw, wide mouth, black curls tumbling into breathtaking golden-brown eyes. It was truly unfair to have so much beauty stuffed into one man. Englishwomen no doubt crossed the street at a run to "accidentally" swoon into his embrace.

She gestured for him to go away.

He didn't move.

She made emphatic get-out-of-here arm movements that were impossible to misconstrue.

He tilted his gorgeous head. "Who are you running from?"

Kuni pressed her lips together. Attractive gentlemen were the hardest to be rid of. They couldn't imagine a woman not wanting them around.

Yet she dared not give him a scalding setdown. If her brothers were in earshot, the sound of her familiar voice would give her away. A dramatic scene would be even more likely to draw them in her direction.

Instead she pointed at her throat and shook her head vehemently, as if she were mute. There. That would shoo him off.

To her surprise, he appeared delighted by this development, and immediately began moving his hands and fingers in a series of rapid, meaningful gestures Kuni couldn't follow in the least.

Sign language. This angelic male specimen was fluent in *sign language*. He was too perfect to be real.

If this had been Balcovia, any of the princess's companions would have faked a swoon into his arms.

"Please go," she hissed in her best English accent. Two syllables. Easy.

His chiseled jaw fell open and his golden-brown eyes widened in shock. "You're *Balcovian*?"

What? How? Why?

Kuni glared at him in consternation. *She* was the trained soldier on a secret mission, yet he kept quickly and casually outperforming her every maneuver. Perhaps her reconnaissance report ought to recommend that the king's Royal Guard should employ *this* character along with herself.

"I beg you to be gone, you great snuffling rose blossom!"

He genuflected. "I am here to save you."

She yanked him back up before anyone saw him bowing at her. "I forbid you from saving me. I command you to be gone."

"You 'command' me?" He frowned in befuddlement. "What kind of person gads about 'commanding' other people—" He stared at her and lowered his voice to a whisper. "Are you a *princess*?"

"I am not a princess," she said quickly.

Too quickly.

Something in her tone or her face made him think his guess was not too far off the mark. He brightened as though she'd given him a gift he'd been waiting for all his life.

He tilted his head toward the sun. "I knew this day would come."

She took advantage of his inattention to hurry past him.

He was at her side before she'd completed her first step.

"How did they lose you?" he asked in wonder. "I can barely tear my eyes from you for even a second. I fear no other woman will ever look as fine."

She refrained from acknowledging she felt much the same way about him. In another context, she might have let him have a waltz or two. Perhaps even steal a kiss beneath the moonlight. But she was not here for flirtations.

"No one *lost* me," she informed him, walking faster. "I *evaded*. Now, as charming as you think you are, I hereby fully and irrevocably decline this and all future offers of assistance. Good day, sir."

He hesitated, visibly confused. "You *are* on the run?"

She blinked at the unfamiliar phrase.

"Fleeing capture?" he clarified. "Attempting to escape from the two hunters who have been stalking you?"

All right, yes. That was exactly what she was doing. How *he* had guessed her circumstances, Kuni hadn't the slightest clue. But the more time she spent chatting with him, the greater the likelihood one of her brothers would be lucky enough to fall with his nose in butter, as they say. Once they heard or glimpsed her, they'd—

She gasped and flattened herself against the nearest wall.

Her knight blocked her protectively as his fingers hardened into fists. "Who is it? Tell me where to look."

Floris and Reinald were two hundred meters away. Though she couldn't see their faces, the uniforms were unmistakable. They hadn't found her—yet. But they were heading in this direction. She had minutes. Perhaps seconds. If she made any sudden movements, they would spy her all the faster.

"Two gentlemen," she mumbled to her knight's smartly tailored back. It really was a nice coat. A rich blue superfine that begged to be touched. If she got out of this... "Tall, burly, skin a deep chestnut like mine, dove-gray coats—"

"I see them." Her knight's low voice rumbled into her fingertips.

She was touching his coat? When had she started touching his coat? Kuni snatched her hand from his hard, warm back.

"You cannot allow them to see *me*," she whispered.

"That will be tricky," replied her knight. "The closer they come, the less I can block you from view. Unless we pretend to be lovers, engaged in a passionate kiss..."

"Of all the blistering rumpwhistles," Kuni snapped. "You shall not kiss me."

Her muscles tensed, preparing for a fight. Why had her brothers stumbled across her *now*? Her fingers itched for the blades strapped to her thighs beneath carefully concealed slits, but she did not reach for them. The crowd was too dense, and a distraction of that nature could prove dangerous.

"If it wouldn't offend your sensibilities overmuch," her knight said presently, "might you rescind your earlier injunction and allow me to save you? Just this once?"

She considered her options. "You said you couldn't block me from view."

"Always have a contingency plan, princess. You run in the opposite direction. Take the first left, then the alley on the right. Go in the unmarked door twenty feet from the next street. It's the servants' entrance to the Puss & Goose. Tell them Winifred Winklemeyer sent you to reserve a north-facing room for one."

She stared at him. "What?"

"Meanwhile, I'll deal with these two. Are you in agreement?"

"Do not injure them." She doubted anyone outside the Balcovian Royal Guard *could* gain the upper hand, but this Englishman was full of surprises. "They are my—"

"I'm not going to harm them," he assured her. "I'm going to *lose* them. What's your name?"

"This is not the moment for formal introductions!"

"And I do hope to have that moment when we're through. I need your name to give them a reason to chase me. If they think I know where you are, they'll follow *me* rather than look about for *you*."

Oh. Her cheeks burned. "My name is Kunigunde de Heusch. But you can call me—"

He took off so quickly, he seemed to vanish into thin air. By the time she managed to spot him, he was almost to her brothers. He must have shouted something, because Reinald immediately gave chase.

Her knight narrowly evaded him, darting across the street. But Reinald was swift. He reached out to grab the back of her knight's handsome blue coat, only for the Englishman to...scale a sheer wall with his bare hands? Reinald looked just as thunderstruck as Kuni felt—and just as startled when her knight dropped back down from nowhere, one meter behind her brother.

Floris started forward to help, then jerked around to rake his gaze through the bustling street. He left Reinald and the Englishman to their own devices and pushed through the crowded street toward Kuni.

"Not today, you suffocating saffron." Kuni sprang into action, sprinting in the opposite direction.

Floris hadn't glimpsed her yet—he often operated on a Royal Guardsman's intuition—but his long legs would gain on her with every passing second.

She had to remain one step ahead.

4

Kuni replayed her knight's calm instructions.

Run in the opposite direction. That, she was doing. Or trying to do. So many pedestrians crowded London's busy streets, she half expected a parade to bear down at any moment. *Take the first left.* Yes. Kuni was already on the left side of the street and tearing around the corner.

Then, an alley on the right. Narrow. Fetid. Littered with broken bits of heaven-knew-what and bisected by a dirty trickle whose origin she had no wish to investigate.

An unmarked door twenty feet from the corner. Her tutors had told her other nations still used this measure, and that its length differed from country to country. Twenty of her brothers' enormous leather boots? Twenty of Kuni's half boots? Her knight had failed to specify on the right or the left. The end of the alley opened into a loud bustling street overflowing with horses and carriages like herrings in a barrel—

There. A door so nondescript one almost didn't notice. That had to be it. Even if it wasn't, it went *somewhere*. Floris could reach the alley at any second. There was no time to dither.

Kuni wrenched open the scuffed wooden door, flung herself inside, and slammed it closed behind her. It had a lock! And a thick crossbar! She rapidly engaged both and sagged against the sturdy barrier.

As her heart regained a less frenzied pace, she cursed herself—and her knight. Her newfound autonomy was not off to a fine start.

This could also be a trap.

She was in a silent, shadowy corridor, standing exactly where she'd been sent by a total stranger. Floris and Reinald were formidable Guardsmen—and diabolical brothers. They would absolutely send their sister a Trojan horse in the shape of an attractive man.

Or perhaps this had nothing to do with the Royal Guard at all. What *was* this place that she had been sent to? Puss & Goose? What did that mean? Had she escaped one danger only to fling herself headlong into another?

Luckily, Kuni never left home without a pair of daggers strapped to her thighs and twice as many throwing knives hidden just inside her spencer—and another small blade tucked along the busk of her stays.

She crept forward, exiting the corridor toward an open area bathed in sunlight ahead. She stepped into a cozy room with a thick door on one side and stairs on the other.

An older woman with pale cheeks and a cloud of white hair stood behind a wide counter. She whistled beneath her breath as she tied a brown paper package with a length of twine.

When Kuni approached, the older woman looked up, startled—but not scared. An odd response to a stranger emerging from the servants' entrance.

The old woman gave Kuni a sunny smile. "Why,

good afternoon, dear. Welcome to my inn. How might I help you?"

"Uh..." said Kuni eloquently. What had the Englishman said? She used her father's memory trick of a donkey's bridge. "Winifred... Winklemeyer... sent me to reserve a north-facing room for one?"

"I reasoned as much." The proprietress pushed her package aside and leaned over the counter with avid interest. "That is a charming accent. Where are you from, dear?"

Kuni sighed and relaxed. She was not in danger of anything besides the monotony of reliving the exact same conversation as ever with yet another clueless stranger.

"The Netherlands," she responded politely. Truthful, but vague. "Netherlands" could mean one of several principalities.

The older woman's face lit up.

"We had a guest from Amsterdam just last year! He was called..." The proprietress leafed rapidly through a large book lying open on the counter, then glanced up in victory. "Mr. Janssen."

"Mr. Janssen and I have not had the pleasure."

"Pity. You did say 'north,' did you not? You must be in a hurry, and here I am prattling on." The proprietress emerged from behind the counter and placed the brown paper package in Kuni's hands. "Here, take this nuncheon. It was for a different guest, but I'll have the kitchen prepare another. Come with me, dear."

Without waiting for a response, the proprietress hurried up the narrow stairs, pausing on the first landing to verify Kuni was following her.

"Oughtn't I to pay for my room?"

The proprietress laughed. "Of course not. That room is on a perpetual lease to the Wynchesters."

Wynchester. Kuni finally had a name for her knight—a name she recognized. During her ten days of reconnaissance, she had overheard mention of the Wynchesters in conjunction with good works enough times she had written it down in her intelligence journal.

"Do you mean the same Wynchesters known for acts of philanthropy?"

The proprietress beamed at her. "Indeed I do. You will never find more kind and generous souls. Which you must already know, if they are helping you."

Kuni did not want anyone's help, no matter how kind and generous their souls. Yes, Mr. Wynchester had come to Kuni's aid. But she hadn't asked him to, and did not like the idea of being beholden to him.

The lack of liberty to choose her own hiding place also rankled.

"What if I want that room instead?" She pointed at a random door.

"You could have it if you insist, but you still couldn't pay for it. All the rooms on this floor are on lease to the Wynchesters."

"Is there any bed in this inn I could pay for myself?" The words came out sharper than intended.

"The second floor is already full of guests," the proprietress said doubtfully, "but I suppose…there might be a spare cot in the basement."

Kuni gritted her teeth. A servant's cot in a damp cellar? If she took it, she'd be doing so to spite herself, which was the exact behavior her family accused her of—wanting to be independent at all costs.

But proving them wrong about her character meant accepting meddling Mr. Wynchester's arrangements and help—thereby proving her brothers *right* that Kuni was unable to manage on her own. She rubbed her face with her hand.

"Please continue," she said quietly. "I shall take the room you meant to give me."

The proprietress beamed at her and hurried up the stairs...to the very top.

It was an attic. Kuni had declined being relegated to a dank basement in exchange for being tossed into a hot, stuffy attic instead. *Hoera.*

She was a long way from her castle. This cramped, odd-shaped room was even smaller than her private water closet on the royal ship.

A cot with no pillow and a threadbare blanket listed unevenly against one wall of the narrow room. On the other was a shallow, flimsy wardrobe that looked like a strong sneeze would send it flying to pieces.

No space was left over for anything else. No dressing table. No thick carpet leading to a wide marble balcony with an unbroken view of bucolic pastures and fields of flowers. She couldn't even stand upright without her bonnet scraping the low, pitched ceiling.

"Uh." Kuni masked her reluctance. "Thank you."

The proprietress was not paying attention. She walked past the cot to the rickety wardrobe. Rather than open one of its badly hung doors, she reached around it and gave a great tug.

The wardrobe swung inward to reveal a hidden room.

5

With an expansive gesture, the proprietress beckoned her inside. "Here you are, love."

Kuni ducked through the opening and took three steps down into a large, bright chamber with sunny windows dotted along its slanted roof. Now this really broke her wooden shoe!

The bed was not as grand as her four-poster at home, but more than respectable and covered with soft, clean blankets. A trio of plush armchairs encircled a handsome round table. Spanning the wall behind it was a long sideboard, filled with plates and glassware of all types, and half a dozen bottles of wine.

Opposite the bed was a huge dressing table with three mirrors. It overflowed with creams and cosmetic pots, and items whose use Kuni couldn't begin to guess.

"What on earth..." She turned back toward the proprietress.

The wall to the other room had closed. The old woman was gone.

In alarm, Kuni dashed to where the opening had been and shoved.

The secret door swung open easily. She wasn't locked inside.

Relieved, she resealed the access point and turned back to the room. It was far more spacious than the garret on the other side of the wall, and considerably warmer. Kuni pushed open a few windows to allow in fresh air and gazed about the well-stocked room in awe.

To the left of the dressing table was an absolutely enormous wardrobe of sturdy oak. She strode forward and pulled open its doors to see if it was another hidden compartment. Inside was a plethora of clothing for both men and women.

Once again, Mr. Wynchester was full of wonderful surprises. If only she didn't resent him for it!

Kuni did not want her day saved. *She* would do the saving of days, thank you very much. The entire point of this mission was to prove how capable she was on her own without help, especially from a man. An Englishman!

But here she was, safely hidden, thanks to Mr. Wynchester. After barely escaping her brothers for the sixth time.

Perhaps Kuni wasn't as competent as she believed.

No. She would not lose her confidence now. Despite her brothers' skill at tracking enemy soldiers and anticipating battle stratagems, they had not managed to capture her. When else had the two best Royal Guards failed to apprehend their prey? She could do this. She *would* do this.

She had come so far. Braved *water*, despite the sea having stolen her mother years before.

For a woman whose feet had always been planted firmly on solid earth, climbing aboard a boat had been terrifying. Not the stowing part—Kuni and her brothers had played at hiding from each other since they were small. The royal ship had so many empty chambers it had been absolutely nothing to sneak aboard with a trunk and a lady's maid.

But the water! There was *so much of it*. Moments when the only things visible from Kuni's window were endless sea and endless sky. Like her mother, Kuni could not swim. Entrusting her life to a fancy wooden bucket had caused all those old memories to flood back in a rush. She had been relieved to escape her clandestine cabin.

The Balcovian ship would remain docked here for thirty more days. When it set sail, Kuni had to be on it, regardless of her terror of the open seas.

Methodically, Kuni took inventory of the secret room, starting with the wardrobe. Walking dresses, riding habits, evening gowns, overcoats for every weather. She peered under the bed to look for any more surprises, and only found a clean ceramic chamber pot.

She crossed to the sideboard and sniffed the package the proprietress had given her. The paper opened to reveal a large hunk of bread, a smaller hunk of cheese, half a browning pear, and several slices of cold meat. Not exactly a meal fit for a princess, but those days would soon be gone.

In Balcovia, the color of Kuni's skin was less of a hindrance than her sex. Like England, Balcovia had been home to Black people for centuries. But unlike England, Balcovia had shunned slavery and been appalled at other countries' attempts to colonize the world. Abolition efforts had been one of the main reasons Balcovia had seceded from the Netherlands over a century ago.

Black people had rejoiced at becoming citizens of an abolitionist nation. The king's family had felt betrayed—

as did the rich aristocrats who prospered from slaves toiling in the Dutch colonies. There had been several attempts on the king's life. One almost succeeded.

Almost. Kuni's great-great-grandfather Willem had thwarted the attempt, earning a bullet to the shoulder for his trouble. The abolitionist king offered Willem a position as a Royal Guard that very day. An enduring partnership that grew stronger with each new generation.

Her *male* family members, that was.

Kuni turned her investigation to the dressing table with its many pots and decorative boxes. More cosmetics than she had ever seen—most of which would not work on dark brown skin—and boxes stuffed with varying shades of hair in the mutton-shape of English whiskers.

She could walk out of this room a man, if she wished. But Kuni wanted a uniform, not a disguise. Hers was a lifelong calling, not a lark.

Kuni slipped a hand into her spencer and unpinned the military insignia she kept just above her heart. She ran her fingers over the narrow, ten-centimeter-long strap, touching the familiar thickly embossed crown above a chevron and the soft golden fringe beneath. The distinctive shoulder epaulet was the official symbol of the Balcovian Royal Guard.

This insignia had belonged to her father. He'd removed the epaulet from his uniform himself and placed it in Kuni's hand, curling her fingers about it. He'd expected to retrieve it when the war ended, but in the meantime had not wished his daughter to doubt for a moment that she was important and loved. Before he left for Waterloo, he'd told her he was proud of her, and had no doubt she would wear the insignia, too, one day, as their ancestors had done for generations.

Kuni wasn't chasing a dream just for herself. She was fulfilling a promise to her father, too.

She replaced the insignia next to her heart and rose from her chair. Birds sounded outside the open window. She turned to investigate the cause of the commotion—in time to see a lithe male form in a dapper blue coat drop through the attic window and land lightly on his feet to make a grand bow.

Mr. Wynchester had returned.

6

Graham beamed at the princess.

She glowered back at him.

He swept an extravagant bow. "Mr. Graham Wynchester at your service, Miss de Heusch."

At least, he *hoped* she was a "Miss" and not a "Mrs."

Her black eyes stared at him. "Did you vault into a locked room through the ceiling, you great ruffled tulip?"

"Er... yes. I thought that was clear. You appeared to be watching whilst the event was unfolding."

How he adored her lovely accent! The "Vs" almost soft enough to be an "F." The hard "th," not even attempted, replaced by a "D" instead. She sounded just like his father, except even *more* so. Bean had spent two decades in England and eventually lost most of his old accent. Graham had not expected to ever hear so musical a voice again.

"You cannot just materialize wherever you take a notion," she protested.

"*I* can." He bowed again. "It is one of my hobbies."

Her hand twitched, and for a brief moment he feared she might send his favorite vintage of wine sailing straight at his head.

"Of course it would be a hobby of yours." The princess narrowed her eyes at him. "How are my brothers?"

"Your..." Graham feared he goggled unbecomingly. "Those highly trained deadly assassins were your *brothers*?"

"'Were'?" She staggered backward. "They still are! They *must* be. If you—"

"They're alive and well," he assured her. "And more than a little confused. I didn't kill them. I lost them, as I said I would. They chased after me for a full mile before I doubled back over the rooftops."

"You *think* you lost them. They are not stupid."

"They did not appear to be," Graham agreed. "They were also well armed. I have never seen someone take a holiday with quite so many blades and pistols hidden upon their person. My compliments to their tailor. I had thought their suits merely ill-fitting, not concealing an entire armory."

The princess was not attending to his fashion commentary. "Floris and Reinald may return this way, if they have not already. They are intelligent enough to retrace their steps."

"Don't worry," he told her. "We shan't set out again on foot. I can summon a hack."

"'We'?" the princess repeated in offended hauteur. "I can manage my own conveyance."

"Am I wrong to suppose you've never rented a hackney carriage before?"

"Until this voyage, I had never rented anything. That doesn't mean I cannot. Though it's true things have always just been purchased for me. I feel like a pumpkin in a gooseberry patch." Her sharp gaze snapped to his. "Is that why you noticed me? Because I was so conspicuously out of place?"

"Ah. No." He settled into an armchair and motioned for her to do the same.

For a moment the princess looked as though she might refuse on principle, but she settled into the seat across from him.

"I noticed you," Graham explained, "because I was looking for you."

"You did not know that I was here!"

"I didn't know you were *you*," he acknowledged. "But I had been following the clues most assiduously. I realized someone was being tracked and had managed to escape her hunters."

She frowned. "Clues?"

"Advertisements," he clarified. "Written in cipher and printed in *The Times*. A newspaper. Your brothers may be lethal and fearsome, but I'm afraid they have no future in cryptography. I and two dozen of my sister-in-law's closest lady friends were each independently able to work out the meaning in less than a fortnight."

"What did the messages say?"

"You didn't read them?"

"I was not available for correspondence. I am far too busy attending to my duties to waste time reading English newspapers."

"Reading English newspapers *is* my duty," Graham said solemnly. "One of them anyway. Though these messages were for you. First, letting you know you'd been spotted at this place or that, and then quickly becoming more threatening lest you fail to surrender yourself to your hunters."

"Well, that sounds like my brothers. I thank you for your unsolicited intrusion and must now be on my way. I do not need your aid to summon a carriage. Good day, Mr. Wynchester."

"Well," Graham echoed.

He had hoped for a touch more effusive praise and perhaps an impassioned plea not to leave her side.

"I am at your service, Princess," he tried again.

"I do not require a guard. I *am* a guard." Her pretty eyes flashed. "And I am not a princess."

"But you do need my help."

"I do not need your help."

"I literally *just* saved you," he pointed out. "Moments ago. An unplanned rescue is still a rescue. Some might even say the action is ongoing."

She did not look impressed. "I am uninterested in leaping from one set of men who 'know best' into the protection of another."

"What if it's not protection?" he suggested. "What if I am the Sancho Panza to your Don Quixote? The Peaseblossom to your Titania? Benedick to your Beatrice?"

"Pease what?" Her eyes went wide. "Titania who?"

"Literature." Graham waved this away. "I have never met royalty before. What mischief are you here to make?"

"It is not mischief," she said. "It is a mission, which I will be completing on my own. That is why I left my maid aboard the ship—"

"You stowed away with a lady's maid?"

"I cannot arrange my hair properly without her," the princess explained. "And she was the one who fetched food so that I could remain hidden. But I cannot ask her to leave the protection of the royal vessel. Not to spend forty days cringing about in some inferior accommodation in a large, dirty city with no amusements to speak of—"

A string of consonants rattled from Graham's mouth before his electrified brain could find words to defend his home from this slander. "I'll have you know London is a fine city. A great, powerful, beautiful, thriving metropolis full of the best entertainments and the most elegant of…" He tilted his head. "In which specific inferior hostelry has your highness taken shelter?"

"I am not a princess. I am Kunigunde. *Coo-nee-goon-deh.* And my rooms are in the Pull…the Pult…in the Pick…"

"The Pulteney Hotel? In Piccadilly?" he said in disbelief. "The same noble establishment that hosted Alexander, Czar of Russia, and his sister the Grand Duchess Catherine four years ago? The Pulteney is the finest accommodation in all of London."

"And," said Kunigunde, "it is your only establishment with modern water closets, according to my guidebook."

Water closets. She was definitely a princess, no matter what she claimed.

"Are you carrying enough finery for a place like that?" he asked.

"I brought a single valise containing weapons, a few changes of clothes…the usual. And some jewels I could sell for pounds sterling. You must know the rest of the world does not use your currency. I find the English system both confusing and inconvenient."

"Couldn't you have exchanged your country's money?"

"Not without calling attention to the fact that I am from Balcovia. You were the first of your countrymen to divine the truth. Instead of exchanging currency that might have caused unwanted attention, I sold my least-favorite earrings. Diamond-sapphire castoffs from a friend."

"What sort of friend has *diamond-sapphire* castoffs?"

"My dear friend Princess Mechtilda. Unfortunately, the jewels were too heavy to wear comfortably in combat situations."

"Diamonds and sapphires," he repeated. "Do not even tell me how much blunt you traded them for. Even if I beg to know the details with my last dying breath, do not even hint at what you thought was a fair trade for bejeweled earrings belonging to a Balcovian princess."

"I know exactly how much they are worth and received every penny. I then registered with the hotel under a false name whilst pretending to be a lady's maid. The proprietor did not even question it." She added under her breath, "I was both proud and offended."

"Welcome to England," Graham said. "Our natural condition is proud and offended."

"In any case," said Kunigunde, "you can see that I no longer need you."

"On the contrary. You need me more than ever. If your brothers haven't found your rooms yet, they will. Even if you change hotels, it should not be much bother to bribe the right parties to discover your presence."

Graham would be mortified to take over a week to find a family member if he knew in which city to begin looking. The only wonder was that the search had taken the guards *this* long.

Perhaps the saving grace was that her brothers were just as unfamiliar with London... and, apparently, they had underestimated Kunigunde's determination and resourcefulness.

She nibbled on her lower lip. It was a distractingly appealing action.

Graham was *absolutely* going to be mentioned in every gossip column in England once news of the royal presence spread. Now that he'd met Kunigunde—and two Balcovian Royal Guardsmen—he was only one step removed from having met royalty himself. Perhaps he would be invited in appreciation of his outstanding service to his own king.

The next time the papers mentioned Graham Wynchester, it would not be in the usual pejorative terms. It might read: *Graham Wynchester, provider of critical intelligence to the Crown, as well as bosom friend of Kunigunde de Heusch, practically a princess…*

She gazed about the room. "If hotels are no longer safe…"

"Then you must come home with me," he finished firmly, and flashed her his most brilliant smile.

Her eyes narrowed to slits.

He held up his palms. "The Wynchester residence is truly the last place your brothers would look for you. We are unconnected to royalty and are just as resourceful as your Guardsmen. I can also ensure carriages and cohorts at your disposal for the duration of your stay."

"I do not want your carriages, and I do not need your cohorts."

"Do as you wish. You can walk back and forth from Islington if that's your pleasure. Spin a few yarns. Reenact *Canterbury Tales*."

"The *what*?" She stared at him. "Are you still speaking English?"

The truth was, Kunigunde's presence addressed several of Graham's preoccupations at once: his desire to help others, his obsession with royalty, and his long-held yearning to learn more about Balcovia, where his father had been born. Bean had told them dashed little. His recent history had been a sad time in his life, Bean had said. He would start a new future, with them.

But now that Graham had met Kunigunde, Balcovia seemed more magical than ever.

England, for all its wonderful features, held to deeply rigid demarcations of class and station. While London was home to twenty thousand free Black people, none of them sat in the House of Lords. Rising up through the social classes was almost impossible. Slavery was still legal throughout the rest of the British Empire.

Graham could not imagine what it must be like to be Kunigunde. To live in a country where Kunigunde could *be* Kunigunde. To have such a close relationship with a royal princess that she could receive bejeweled baubles as a casual gift from one friend to another.

He could not understand why anyone in her position would leave idyllic Balcovia. But for as long as she remained here—Kunigunde would be his princess, and Graham her faithful knight. It would be like living in a fairy tale.

"Think of our home as a travelers' inn of sorts," he coaxed.

"I work alone," she said flatly. "And I do not know you."

"Do you know the owner of the Pulteney Hotel?"

"Their accommodations were effusively recommended in my guidebook. I did not see your name anywhere."

"That is an embarrassing oversight. I have associates at every newspaper in London, but not at a single publishing house...yet. You want flowery praise? Try next year's guidebook. An entire chapter will be devoted to 'The Wonderful Wynchesters.'"

"Wonderful according to whom?"

"To whomever we can help. Our clients come from all over the city."

"You are unarmed. How can you defend them?"

"How can you tell I'm— Have you been admiring my fine, athletic form?" He waggled his eyebrows.

"I had not noticed," she said quickly. But she did not disagree with his assessment.

"I would not blame you if you choose to walk away from my offer," he admitted.

She arched her brows. "Since you are such a superb seeker, wouldn't you just *find* me again?"

"I *could*...but I shall vow to refrain, if that is your wish. It was not my intent to frighten you, or make you fear for your safety."

"Fear for my— I do not fear any Englishman!" she sputtered. "I could have sent a dagger through your heart before you first approached me. Besides, although your name fails to appear in the guidebook, gossip is not limited to the printed word. I have overheard murmurings since my arrival."

"You've *heard* of me?" he said in delight.

"Of your family as a whole. I do not know individual names or any detail, but the members of your family are said to be great philanthropists to the downtrodden. I assumed a pair of wealthy aristocrats who made conspicuous donations to charities."

"Well off," Graham agreed, "and frequently conspicuous. The rest is...best seen with one's own eyes. Would Your Highness like to perform firsthand reconnaissance on the matter? The offer of lodgings still remains."

She tilted her head, clearly considering the offer.

"We can retrieve your belongings from the Pulteney on our way to Islington," he offered. "My siblings will be delighted to meet you. And if you tire of them or me, we shall gracefully accept your goodbyes without fuss."

Graham's princess met his eyes in silence for a long moment, then took a deep breath. "Very well, determined knight. But only for a short while."

7

Kuni stared out of the window as the hackney turned onto the gravel drive of a pretty three-story residence. The Wynchester home was not a palace, but it was wider and more beautiful than the celebrated hotel where she'd been staying.

Instead of the cramped terraced houses she'd observed huddled about a single shared square in Mayfair, Mr. Wynchester's home in Islington was a pretty, freestanding residence amidst a sprawling garden. It looked like the sort of home indolent philanthropists might reside in.

Nonetheless, she kept her hands near her hidden daggers just in case.

Seated across from her, Mr. Wynchester nudged her boot with his own, his light brown eyes sparkling. "What do you think, Princess?"

"Is that the caretaker's cottage?" she asked innocently.

Dismay contorted his handsome features for only a moment before he burst out laughing. "Now I *know* you're bamming me. I would install you in a castle if I could, but for now you must make do."

From the moment Kuni had agreed to this temporary

arrangement, Mr. Wynchester had either treated her like royalty... or he treated her to moments of such unguarded familiarity one could almost believe she'd known him her entire life.

The latter was not what she was accustomed to. Even as a Black woman, Kuni rarely found herself in a situation at home requiring interaction with someone of lower status. When she did, they would bow or curtsey from a respectful distance, and would certainly never dream of nudging her boot to get her attention. Even on the few occasions on which she visited her own brothers, their training kept them silent and distant rather than warm and gregarious.

Unpredictable Mr. Wynchester was entirely unsuitable for a mission like hers. Nonetheless, Kuni could not help but find his unflagging cheerfulness and unchecked enthusiasm infectious.

He leapt from the carriage before his servant could open the door and reached up to hand Kuni down himself.

"Vulgar manners," she informed him as she placed her hand in his. "A Balcovian gentleman would never exit a carriage before a lady."

"I'm neither Balcovian nor a gentleman," he assured her, giving what she supposed was meant to be a lewd leer. The effect was spoiled by his irrepressible grin. "I've spent all afternoon devising a ruse to touch you. I'll be damned if I hand this opportunity to my tiger."

"Flatterer," she scolded, but could not hide her amusement.

Kuni had danced in the arms of countless men during royal balls, but none would have dared to speak to her in such an openly flirtatious manner. They would have been tossed out of the castle by their ears.

She supposed Mr. Wynchester would have simply dropped back into the ballroom from the ceiling.

He placed her hand on his forearm and led her up a very pretty path to the front of the house, where the door was already opening to reveal a portly older man with white skin, impeccable if subdued attire, and a polite manner.

Mr. Wynchester murmured, "Mr. Randall, our butler, will take your coat and bonnet."

"And my hand shoes?" she whispered back. "Or is it your custom to leave them on indoors?"

He stared at her. "Your what?"

"My..." Her cheeks heated.

Great gamboling cabbage, she'd got the words wrong! How she despised her lack of eloquence in this country. After a life of ease and high status, it was humbling to be so often in the wrong. She lifted her palms mutely.

"Oh, your *gloves*," Mr. Wynchester exclaimed. "Are they called 'hand shoes' in Balcovian? That is the most delightful thing I have ever heard. I cannot wait to learn all your other sayings."

Kuni desperately hoped she would not make any further embarrassing misstatements.

She handed her...*gloves*...and her spencer to the butler without a word. It would be harder to put one's foot in one's mouth if one's lips were closed.

Her tutors had insisted the trick was to think in the foreign language, which was all well and good when conversation was limited to *How do you do?* and *Might I have this dance?* Now that she was actually here in England, Kuni had quickly discovered she didn't have words for many of the new sights and situations, and even the ones she thought she knew were not always accurate. It was much easier to think in Balcovian.

Footsteps thundered down the wide marble stairs to the entryway. Her eyes widened in some shock at discovering their source: Not a herd of rampaging elephants, but a tiny slip of a woman with pale skin and flyaway blond hair bearing smudges of green paint.

As Kuni handed over her bonnet to the butler, the woman gasped as though she'd been struck with an arrow. She darted forward and snatched the bonnet right out of the butler's hands.

"It's Balcovian amaranth!" she squealed, cradling Kuni's bonnet to her chest as though it were her long-lost infant. "Grown only in the royal gardens! These flowers have one of the rarest hues of pink in existence!" She spun around in dizzying circles. "Do you see what this is, Graham? This ribbon was dyed *thirteen times* to reach this hue!"

Kuni barely had the chance to process that "Graham" must be Mr. Wynchester, before the blond will-o'-the-wisp spun away and dashed back up the stairs, vanishing along with Kuni's bonnet.

"She'll be back," Mr. Wynchester said with unconcern. "Probably."

He handed his hat to the butler. "Mr. Randall, one of the footmen will bring Miss de Heusch's valise. Please prepare rooms for her, and summon my siblings to the front sitting room."

The butler inclined his head. "You will find Miss Elizabeth already present, in repose on her sofa."

"Splendid." Mr. Wynchester escorted Kuni down a corridor. "My sister either won't look up from her pile of pillows or she'll challenge you to a duel out of boredom."

Kuni stumbled. "What?"

They had already crossed the threshold of an airy,

sunny salon filled with sofas and armchairs at one end, and boasting an enormous table covered in books and documents on the other.

Upon one of the sofas, a pale, plump, soft-looking woman indeed lay in repose amongst a veritable mountain of plush cushions, eyes closed. A florid cane rested at her side.

Mr. Wynchester stepped forward. "Elizabeth—"

The woman flew off the sofa, removing a wicked rapier from its deceptively innocuous housing mid-flight. She landed beside her brother in a fighting stance, the blade thrust toward Kuni.

Mr. Wynchester sighed and turned around. "She's only bam—"

He blanched to see Kuni's twin daggers already in her hands, deadly sharp and pointed straight at his sister.

"Where did you get daggers?" he asked hoarsely.

His sister grinned at Kuni and sheathed her sword. "I love her. She can stay."

She flopped back onto her pillows and closed her eyes as if nothing of consequence had interrupted her idle afternoon slumber.

Kuni's fingers were still clenched around the handles of her daggers.

"Please don't murder my sister," Mr. Wynchester whispered.

"I'd like to see her try!" said Miss Elizabeth without opening her eyes.

"I'll sell tickets," came an amused voice from right behind Kuni.

Kuni lowered her daggers and returned them to their scabbards through the ingeniously hidden slits sewn into her gown.

Striding into the salon was a slender gentleman the same height as Kuni. He had white skin, short, tousled brown hair, and twinkling brown eyes.

"I see you won the wager." He slapped a banknote into Mr. Wynchester's palm. "Ten quid it is."

At the gentleman's side stood a pretty, plump, blue-eyed woman with golden ringlets and a gown composed of a truly prodigious quantity of lace. *She*, at least, had the good sense to glance at Kuni askance, as though ladies drawing blades upon each other in a parlor was not at all the done thing, even in England.

Last to enter was a handsome, broad-shouldered gentleman with soulful brown eyes and gorgeous dark brown skin, who *might* be described as well dressed, were it not for the scuffed leather apron tied over his otherwise fashionable frock coat…and the bright-eyed weasel perched on his shoulder. Its spindly little whiskers twitched as it sniffed in Kuni's general direction.

"Have you seen Tickletums anywhere?" he asked the man who had lost a wager.

"Is that the peahen or the ocelot?" the slender gentleman queried.

Miss Elizabeth rose from her cushions. "Hedgehog. Tickletums is my very favorite of all the hedgehogs, and I wish you would let me have him."

"I'm *trying* to *train* them," the aproned man replied in the tone of someone who has been forced to repeat the same explanation time and again. "But we'll discuss Tickletums later." He turned and gave Kuni a curious but welcoming smile. "Do we have a guest or a client?"

"A guest," Kuni said quickly.

"An honored guest." Mr. Wynchester beamed at her. "Miss Kunigunde de Heusch of Balcovia, may I please have the honor of introducing my rude and disreputable but extremely kindhearted siblings?"

There was nothing to do but nod. Especially since he'd done an admirable job of pronouncing her name correctly. The word "Balcovia" seemed to garner as much interest as Kuni herself.

"You met Elizabeth first." This was the deceptively soft-looking woman with the deadly rapier. "Next to enter was my sister Tommy . . ." He gestured at the brown-haired gentleman, who winked. ". . . Along with my sister-in-law, Philippa." That was the polite puff of lace. "This is our brother Jacob." The gentleman wearing an apron and a weasel. "And here comes Marjorie."

The tiny blond woman from earlier skidded into the room. Kuni's bonnet was now clutched in Marjorie's fingers, each of which was flecked with varying pinks and purples.

"We're the Wynchesters."

8

Kuni stared at the Wynchester family in wonder. They gazed back at her with equally frank expressions of curiosity and friendliness.

"Oh!" The lace snowflake—Philippa—dipped an elegant curtsey. "*Welkom*, Juffrouw de Heusch."

All the others turned to look at her.

"Did you just call her...*Jeffrey*?" Tommy whispered.

"I memorized Balcovian salutations after joining your family," Philippa muttered back. Her eyes met Kuni's. "I hope I didn't butcher the dialect *too* much."

It had been intelligible—and correct usage.

"Who *are* you all?" Kuni said in awe.

Mr. Wynchester went through the names again, but that hadn't been what Kuni had meant. This family was unlike any she had ever met.

She'd always felt being subjected to two siblings was rather a lot, and she and her brothers rarely spoke anymore. There were *six* Wynchesters, each of them intriguing and unusual and so physically different they could not have come from the same two parents.

In the quarter hour since she'd walked through the

door, she'd had her bonnet stolen and her life threatened. She'd taken second place to a missing hedgehog, then been curtseyed to prettily and welcomed in near-perfect Balcovian.

"It's lovely to meet you," she told Philippa in Balcovian, and gave her a curtsey in return.

The others quickly echoed the welcome in English, then began talking over one another, making it impossible to keep up. Kuni tried to listen to one at a time.

"You really found her." Jacob nuzzled his weasel beneath its chin. "I can't believe it."

"I am offended you should say so," Mr. Wynchester replied. "I would have found her sooner—and indeed, I did so. But I didn't realize she was the woman I was looking for until today. We had to outrun a pair of Balcovian Royal Guards—"

"Royal Guards!" Elizabeth's eyes brightened. "Were they armed?"

"Very," Kuni said. "They're also my brothers. It is a long story."

"Mrs. Halberstam kept our guest safe in that secret room we installed at the Puss & Goose after the time Chloe kidnapped Faircliffe—"

Kuni started. "What? Who?"

Tommy grinned. "Our sister mistakenly abducted a duke when she meant to steal a...never mind. We have long stories, too."

"Another sister? How many Wynchester siblings are there?"

"Eight, counting Faircliffe," Elizabeth answered. "He and Chloe will be at Parliament tonight, but I imagine you'll meet them tomorrow. You *will* stay the night, won't you?"

"She's staying indefinitely," said Mr. Wynchester.

"Not indefinitely," Kuni corrected. "My ship returns to Balcovia in thirty days, and I have a mission to complete beforehand."

"A mission!" Elizabeth clapped her hands. "May we help? Oh, please say that we can. I've been ever so bored."

Philippa slanted her a look. "We just finished our last mission an hour ago."

"And I would have expired from ennui in the meantime, had Miss de Heusch not graciously answered my blade with her own, and—" Elizabeth stopped. "Is it not 'Miss' de Heusch? Philippa, what was the word that you said? *Juff*... I want to get it right."

"Juffrouw," Philippa replied, sending Kuni another anxious look.

"That is accurate. But you may call me Kunigunde."

Kuni rarely gave permission to use her first name to anyone but close friends, like Mechtilda and the other companions. Not that Kuni's traditional Balcovian name would be any easier for foreigners. She waited for the inevitable confusion.

Their smiles simply grew larger.

"Welcome, Kunigunde. Please, you must call me Jacob."

The other siblings responded in kind.

"Tommy."

"Philippa."

"Elizabeth."

"Marjorie."

Mr. Wynchester bowed deeply. "And Graham at your service, Your Highness."

"He would be," Elizabeth said. "Graham is obsessed with royalty from all countries. It has long been his life's dream to rescue a princess."

"I am not a princess," Kuni said quickly. She wished she could also negate that she had required rescuing.

"Graham no doubt already knew that, too," said Tommy. "He knows everything that happens in England, at least. You might *think* the wall of books behind me is a library—"

"I certainly jumped to that conclusion," Philippa said.

"—but these and the albums upstairs contain the intelligence Graham has gathered from every corner of London."

"I had help," he said modestly. "My files would not be half so thorough without an equally dense network of spies and informants. I would also have a book on Balcovia if any of us had ever visited."

"Or if Bean had talked about it," Marjorie added. "I wish he would have taught us more than a few phrases."

"Graham will create an album about you next, Kunigunde," Elizabeth warned. "If he hasn't already."

Graham tilted down the edge of his lapel. The corner of a small, thin journal peeked out.

"We *all* want to know about Balcovia." Marjorie pressed her paint-streaked hands together. "I have a hundred questions, which means Graham must have thousands."

Kuni swallowed nervously. Following the Wynchester siblings' rapid-fire conversation was enough to make her head swim.

"Let's give our guest a chance to acclimate first, shall we?" Graham smiled into Kuni's eyes. He lifted his hand, and his fingertips lightly brushed her arm.

Kuni felt the effect of both all the way to her core.

"I don't mind." A Royal Guard would not fear a simple conversation. "I can try to answer a few questions."

"At least sit." Graham motioned toward the crescent of chairs and sofas.

She looked at all the siblings, then all the chairs, then back to Graham.

"Sit next to me?" she whispered impulsively, then wished she hadn't. A Royal Guard did not depend on someone else. She was a perfectly capable, solitary soldier.

His gaze heated. "I am yours to command."

She glanced away, embarrassed at her momentary show of weakness. She hurried to one of the sofas. Graham joined her.

The rest of the siblings quickly took seats as well.

Elizabeth curled her hands over the handle of her cane and rested her chin atop it. "What is your mission? Does it involve bloodshed?"

"Not at this time. I am to join the Balcovian Royal Guard like my ancestors before me. My elder brothers are also Guardsmen, here to scout potential security concerns for an upcoming royal visit."

Graham straightened, his eyes sparkling as though she'd just confirmed some long-held wish.

Elizabeth wiggled the handle of her sword stick. "Balcovia has Royal Guardswomen? But that's lovely!"

Kuni winced. "I would be the first. A new crop of soldiers will be inducted into the training regiment at the end of this summer's annual competition. For me to be considered a viable candidate, the report I present to the king must be undeniably superior to my brothers'. If I can best them, I will earn the chance to compete against the other hopefuls in the combat trials."

"Well, that's simple enough," said Tommy. "If you need information about London, you're sitting next to the person most likely to have it."

Graham tensed, then nodded.

"And if you need something that's not on those shelves,"

Jacob added, "Graham can have the answer for you before suppertime."

The other siblings voiced their agreement.

Kuni stared at them. Not one of the Wynchesters had so much as blinked when she'd mentioned competing against men in combat trials.

Floris and Reinald had laughed themselves silly at the idea—despite Kuni regularly trouncing young men who *were* eligible to compete. Yet all six Wynchesters appeared to accept that Kuni's fighting and defensive talents were the equal of her competition's. The only question was compiling the report.

Their unexpected, absolute faith in her skills and worthiness was so heady, tears stung her eyes for a horrifying second. Kuni was forced to avert her gaze and blink to collect herself.

She straightened her spine. "Thank you, but no. The point of the mission is to prove *myself* worthy, not to pass off someone else's efforts as my own."

"I respect that," Philippa said.

"Although Graham wouldn't mind," Tommy added. "It's not stealing if you have permission."

"Not that I think you need help," Graham said. "The guards they sent are clearly amateurs. I wouldn't even have known to look for you if it weren't for their inadequately coded communications. I've no doubt you can easily outmaneuver your competition."

"Thank you. No one in the Royal Guard considers me worthy of a chance. Not because I lack any of the necessary skills, but because I lack a... That is, because of my gender."

Sounds of outrage and commiseration came from every woman in the room.

"It's not that I don't appreciate the sentiment," Kuni explained. "It's that I cannot accept any help. I must remain above reproach at all times in order to avoid accusations of being unworthy later. Idle rumors claiming I was unable to perform my duty without outside assistance will sink any possibility of me being chosen for the post."

"Either way," said Elizabeth, "I recommend running naysayers through with the closest sword."

"I will get that chance," Kuni said with a chuckle. "When I win the competition..." And she *would* succeed. Her father had believed in her. Soon the king would too. "I will be the first Royal Guardswoman."

The first, but not the last. Once other young women saw Kuni in uniform, they'd know that they, too, deserved an opportunity to prove themselves capable of anything they wished to achieve.

"I had hoped it was different in Balcovia," Elizabeth said wistfully. "One place on earth where women were considered more than useless decorations."

"You would be a dreadful guard," Tommy informed her. "I have never seen you stand still for longer than a minute."

"There's very little 'standing still' in active military," Elizabeth replied dreamily. "Just think if I'd been at Waterloo. I'd have a statue erected in my honor."

Kuni touched the spot above her heart where she kept her father's epaulet. She could not erect a statue in his honor, but she would become the respected soldier he'd always believed her capable of being.

From that moment on, the de Heusch *women* would be a full part of the family legacy, too.

9

Kunigunde doesn't need a plaque for people to know she's important," Graham said. "She *lives* in a castle."

"What?" All the siblings started talking over each other again. "Graham practically *did* rescue a princess?"

"I told you so," he said arrogantly.

"Actually..." Kuni hesitated. She wanted her words to do Balcovia justice.

The siblings leaned forward, listening eagerly.

"There are two principal royal seats. A beautiful Gothic castle to the north and the modern palace to the south. Although I am not royalty, I was born in the Summer Castle. As companion to the princess, I spend most of my time there and in the Winter Palace."

"Born in a castle," Jacob repeated. "Companion to a princess."

"*And* she carries knives," Elizabeth added.

"Graham will never let you go," Tommy teased. "He probably considers himself royal by proxy."

Graham's cheeks flushed. "You laugh, but it's true. We're now only one step away from actual royalty. We know someone who knows a princess!"

Jacob rolled his eyes. "If one could sit about all day watching royals live their lives, Graham would choose that over attending a play with substance."

"Why would I want to watch fiction, when there are endless true things happening at every moment?" Graham said reasonably.

While the brothers bickered, Tommy leaned toward Kuni. "What is it like in Balcovia? Do hangers-on like Graham plague you at every turn, or do your peasants not give a flying fig what the royals do?"

Hesitantly, Kuni did her best to explain the stratified classes, and how most ranks did not mix except during parades and festivals, and even then, the royal family held themselves apart.

Graham staggered as though he had been hit with an arrow. "Dash it! There go my dreams of meeting Balcovian royals in the flesh."

Kuni laughed at the idea. The princess would be far too well guarded to rub shoulders with commoners.

"What are the festivals like?" Jacob asked.

"And the food?" Tommy added.

The Wynchesters listened to Kuni's replies with rapt attention, never once making Kuni feel self-conscious about her accent or any grammar mistakes. They let her answer their questions in her own way and at her own pace, without interrupting when she paused to think of a word or to rephrase her answers. It was so different from how they behaved with each other, she was surprised to be treated with such patience. Perhaps it was the subject matter, not her.

Kuni so adored speaking about her beloved country, that it wasn't until she'd been answering queries for nearly an hour that she realized an obvious question *she* should have asked in the beginning.

She turned to Graham. "How did you recognize my accent as Balcovian?"

His brown eyes softened. "Because that's where my father is from. The great and noble Baron Vanderbean."

"Simmering snickersnees!" Kuni reared back in the sofa, away from him. "Thank heavens you did not mention that to my brothers. They would have chased after you for an entirely different reason if they had believed you an *eligible* bachelor."

Graham blinked. "I...don't know whether to be flattered or gravely wounded."

"Both," Tommy suggested. "Also Bean was my father, too."

"And mine," echoed all the others but Philippa.

"Bean—that is, Baron Vanderbean—was our adoptive father," Jacob explained. "And as white as any English aristocrat."

Graham added, "The only exception is Queen Charlotte and her children, whose features and distant African ancestry are gossiped about relentlessly. Is it really that different in Balcovia?"

"Very. Because Balcovia was founded on abolitionist tenets, one can find diversity of color not just amongst the soldiers and Royal Guard, but also the companions to our royal princesses. And companions often marry members of the lower nobility and younger sons of the highest titles."

Kuni herself had parried interest from two lords and a prince.

Graham and Jacob exchanged amazed glances.

Nobility was not the life Kuni was looking for. She did not expect them to understand.

"Did you ever meet Baron Vanderbean?" Marjorie asked eagerly.

"Of course not," Elizabeth said before Kuni could respond. "How old do you think she is?"

"Bean brought us together and made us a family twenty years ago this summer," Graham explained.

"Well before my come-out," Kuni said. "I would have been five years old at the time."

Marjorie perched on the edge of her chair, her hands clasped together. "What fabric did you wear? What were the colors? Tell me everything!"

"We all wore Balcovian amaranth," Kuni said with a grin. "It is the official royal color. You can keep my hat ribbon, if you like it."

Marjorie clutched her pink-stained hands to her chest and gurgled incoherently with joy.

"Marjorie feels about colors the way Graham feels about princesses," Elizabeth stage-whispered to Kuni.

"Speaking of which," Graham said pointedly. "Shall we allow ours to see her rooms and have a moment to herself? I can arrange a lady's maid to your specifications while you settle in."

Kuni had no intention of unpacking her valise. She wasn't here to stay. A soldier should always be ready to march. But she wouldn't mind spending a few days with Graham and his wonderful family.

He smiled at her. "Are you peckish? I can ring for a repast or have tea sent up to your chamber. Or if you're feeling up to it, we'll dine *en famille* in about two hours. Though I must warn you, our meals are not a formal affair."

Kuni didn't doubt that in the least.

"I will wait to dine with you," she said, feeling suddenly shy.

Compared to stilted royal functions with all their pomp

and rules, the Wynchesters were overwhelming in the best kind of way. Instead of being forced to make small talk with whoever was seated on her right, she suspected she could sit and watch them for hours without ever knowing what they might say or do next.

Graham rose to his feet and offered her his arm.

She took her leave of his siblings before accepting his arm and allowing him to lead her out of the salon.

"This way, my princess," he said grandly. "Allow me to direct you to the foreign dignitaries wing."

"You have a foreign dignitaries wing?"

"No." His eyes laughed at her as they neared the entryway. "But we have several connecting guest rooms, if you want to combine two of them into one."

"You are incorrigible," she muttered. "I am not that spoilt."

"You said the Pulteney was a hovel," he protested.

"I did not say 'hovel'! I said 'barely tolerable.'" She gave him her haughtiest look, but could not hold it for long.

He burst out laughing. "You liked it?"

"I adored it," she confessed. "It restored my faith in the notion that Balcovia is not the only nation with some degree of good taste."

"I hope you like your guest chamber here half as much." His soft gaze warmed her. "If there's anything you need... or desire..."

They had stopped moving. This section of the corridor was out of sight from both the butler in the entryway and the siblings in the salon behind them.

He was not flirting with her, Kuni told herself.

All right, yes, he was flirting with her. But that was all it was. Graham wasn't going to *kiss* her. The strange sparks between them were just a silly reaction to being alone with a man for more in one day than ever before in her entire life.

Or maybe Graham *wasn't* flirting with her. Maybe Kuni just wished he was. Maybe *she* was the one leaning too close, gazing up at him for far too long.

This wasn't real. It was just another rebellion. She wasn't interested in any Englishman. It would be both pointless and disastrous. She had mapped out her future, and she would let nothing get in its way.

"My private chamber," she croaked. "Where is it?"

He nodded and led her out of the corridor, the strange electricity gone. "Just up these stairs and to the—"

Before she could take the first step, a sharp breeze ruffled her skirts and the entryway filled with voices.

"Please," begged a scratchy voice. "We need to speak to the Wynchesters. We have no other hope."

Graham strode forward. "What's this?"

She hurried after him.

An older man and woman stood in the doorway. Their clothes had faded with age and had clearly been mended many times. Their skin was a yellowish gray, as if they were ill—or perhaps very exhausted. They clung to each other as though letting go would cause them to crumple where they stood.

"Please," said the woman. "We are in dire need of aid."

"I'm Graham Wynchester." His voice was so warm and kind, it was no wonder the elderly couple looked at him as though the sun had peeked from behind the clouds. "You've come to the right place." He turned to the butler and lowered his voice. "Have a repast sent to the sitting room at once."

The butler assented and hurried in the opposite direction.

Graham looked almost startled to see Kuni still standing there. "I am so sorry. I'll send up some chocolate, and a maid will escort you to your chambers. Or if you like, go around these stairs and down the other wing, where you'll find a library at your disposal on the left. I don't know if we'll be free for supper—"

"Can I help?"

Kuni regretted the question as soon as she'd asked it. Of course she couldn't help. She'd asked her brothers that same question every day for nearly every one of her five-and-twenty years, and the answer had never been yes.

Nor would it be today. If Graham wanted her assistance, he would have asked for it—not sent her off to read a book or to sip some chocolate while the Wynchesters attended to important matters. Only when she won the king's respect and became a Royal Guard would people cease underestimating her.

"I'm sorry," she mumbled. "I did not mean to insert myself in—"

"Of course you can help," Graham answered. "Every client deserves our very best."

10

Graham led the elderly couple into the sitting room. His family was busy with their usual pursuits: Tommy sketched out a map. Philippa cataloged a tower of books. Elizabeth polished the blade of a sword stick. Marjorie inspected every thread of her new ribbon. Jacob coached a wriggling weasel in the delicate art of… well, one never knew with Jacob.

But when they caught sight of the visitors, his siblings mobilized at once. Gone were the map and the sword and the ribbon. Even the weasel disappeared into a ventilated basket. All five siblings were on their feet at a respectful distance, quietly awaiting instruction.

Graham offered the couple the most comfortable sofa. As they lowered themselves onto the cushions, maids entered the salon with platters of sandwiches and a variety of hot drinks. He smiled to show his appreciation for their promptness. All the Wynchester staff was an essential part of the team. They returned his smile before stepping back.

He turned to the new clients. "There is no rush. If you're hungry or need a moment to collect yourselves before discussing how we can help, we have all the time you need."

"Thank you so much." The older woman and her companion reached for triangles of sandwich with gnarled, shaking hands.

Graham retrieved a fresh journal and a handful of sharpened pencils before seating himself on the sofa closest to the visitors. When he glimpsed Kunigunde hesitating in the doorway, he flashed her a smile and motioned for her to join him.

She eased down next to Graham and folded her hands in her lap. Her posture was impeccable. Somewhere on her person were at least two daggers. He could see no sign of the blades, but knew they would appear in her hands like magic at the first sign of danger. But at the moment, she appeared calm and attentive. Her head angled toward the visitors and slightly downward, allowing her to regard them without staring, and to listen without distracting.

It was not at all difficult to imagine her as an exemplary Royal Guard.

Soon, the guests set down their plates, patted their mouths with their napkins, and began to speak.

"We are Mr. and Mrs. Goodnight," the older man began. "We apologize for arriving uninvited to impose upon your hospitality—"

"No, we aren't sorry," his wife interrupted, her strong voice determined. "We're here because we've nowhere else to turn. It has been a grueling journey—"

"Three long days in the basket of a mail coach, stuffed on top of the roof with the luggage—"

"—and we must return to our family posthaste." Mrs. Goodnight's pale blue eyes were haunted. "How I fear what might happen if..."

"We live outside Manchester," Mr. Goodnight explained. "Tipford-upon-Bealbrook is a small town without much to speak of, save the local cotton mill. The Throckmorten manufactory employs hundreds of laborers. Sometimes it feels as though we all work there."

"That is, we *did* work there," his wife corrected him. "We've since grown too old. Our fingers shake, and our eyes aren't what they used to be. It is our daughter-in-law Adella who works there now. Our son Ned worked at the manufactory, too, but…" Her voice caught.

"He was injured in an accident at one of the machines," Mr. Goodnight said gruffly. "His wounds became infected. Adella is a widow now…and six months pregnant."

His wife took a deep breath. "Poor Adella is our family's only source of income. It is barely enough, and there will be no coin at all once she gives birth. That is why our grandson Victor took a post at the factory the morning after we buried his father."

Graham's heart ached for the young boy who had lost a parent due to the callous negligence of an employer. It was visceral. It was *personal.* But he did not talk about his past. Not even with clients.

"How old is Victor?" he asked quietly.

"Little Victor is eight." Mrs. Goodnight swallowed. "But there are children who are even younger."

"Whenever possible, Mr. Throckmorten requires his employees' children to work beside their parents for negligible pay. To decline this kind offer is to lose one's post—yet, to accept is to put one's child in danger."

Mrs. Goodnight nodded. "Victor is small for his age, so he is one of the unlucky ones sent inside the machines to make adjustments and repairs, often with the machines still running."

"It's how our son was injured." Her husband's voice grew thick. "One of our neighbor's children got caught in a moving machine, which tore her arm from her body. When our son leapt in to save her..."

"It happens all too often," said Mrs. Goodnight. "In every cotton manufactory. Most of the workers are women and children. We are hardworking people who take pride in a job well done, but the hours are grueling."

"A decade ago, we worked fifteen hours a day. Mr. Throckmorten now demands sixteen hours or more, six days a week, with only one short respite at midday."

Mrs. Goodnight's eyes were pleading. "Small children aren't meant to be worked like pack animals from the moment they open their eyes in the morning until they finally stumble home to bed. There's no time left for children to be *children*."

"We worry not just for our own family, but for our neighbors. We are all in these wretched circumstances together. The constant exhaustion is how fatal mistakes are made. Every person in the manufactory is at risk." Mr. Goodnight's Adam's apple bobbed. "Such as Molly, the poor little girl who lost her arm. And our son Ned, who lost his life by saving Molly's."

"With our daughter-in-law Adella in a delicate way... It's too much." Mrs. Goodnight wrapped her arms about herself and shuddered. "Mr. Throckmorten won't see that we're not out to cheat him. All the local families have begged him to allow half days for children. Eight hours of work in a hot, dangerous environment is surely enough for a child of as many years, is it not?"

"The blackguard won't hear of it," Mr. Goodnight said angrily. "He says, 'Those who wish to work, shall work the full schedule without complaint, or find employment elsewhere.' "

"For most of us, there *is* no elsewhere!" his wife burst out. "There is only Mr. Throckmorten, and he knows it."

"Adella has been with child thrice before. Only Victor survived. She asked Mr. Throckmorten if she could work fewer hours at a reduction in wages until this babe is born safely. He said if she made so much as an unauthorized visit to the chamber pot, she'd be out on her ear."

Kunigunde's mouth fell open. "How cruel!"

"In Tipford-upon-Bealbrook, Mr. Throckmorten is like a god. His mill employs most of the town. None of the workers can afford to leave their posts—or to anger Mr. Throckmorten. Several years ago, there was talk of a strike. Mr. Throckmorten found out and dismissed every worker sympathetic to the rebellion."

"It hadn't even happened yet!" Mrs. Goodnight said in disgust. "Lately, there have been rumblings of organizing again, of making a complaint or taking some sort of action. But there's no one to complain *to*, and none of the families can afford to lose a single day's pay, much less their posts. It's a dangerous game. With your help, mayhap it needn't come to that."

"I have money," Kunigunde blurted out from beside Graham. "I could give you—"

Mr. and Mrs. Goodnight straightened in affront.

"We are not beggars come crying for alms," Mr. Goodnight said stiffly.

"I know, but—"

Mr. Goodnight's cheeks flushed. "We are respectable people, happy to work for our due, and we wish only for a master who respects his dependents as fellow humans. We did not come to line our own pockets, but for you to put a stop to this horrible practice for all of our neighbors."

Mrs. Goodnight turned to Graham.

"If you could talk to Mr. Throckmorten." Her voice was hollow. "Even minimal concessions for children and expectant mothers...It would help not just our sweet Adella and little Victor, but dozens of others as well."

"I understand," Graham assured them softly. "We want to help everyone in the mill who needs it."

"It won't be easy. Mr. Throckmorten will not allow anyone outside of his employ on the manufactory grounds," Mr. Goodnight said.

"Of course they can manage a conversation," Mrs. Goodnight said. "They're Wynchesters. Whether their words shall have any effect, on the other hand..."

"Because he has no heart, we tried to appeal to his pocketbook," Mr. Goodnight explained. "Fewer accidents means less time lost—and more profit for Mr. Throckmorten."

"He won't hear of it," Mrs. Goodnight said. "What does he care if some urchin loses an arm or some devoted husband his life? There are plenty of indigent souls who would eagerly take their place. We're as interchangeable as spools of thread."

"We haven't the power to convince him, but you might. Half days for children under ten," her husband repeated, his gaze firm. "And reduced hours for women in Adella's delicate condition. Are we asking for a miracle?"

Perhaps, Graham acknowledged privately. But Wynchesters performed impossible feats every day.

"We will do everything in our power," he assured them. "Come, you must be exhausted. You cannot have slept riding up in the mail basket, with all that wind and racket. Honor us by consenting to be our guests tonight."

The Goodnights exchanged glances.

"We'd be in your debt," Mrs. Goodnight said at last. "But we must be on our way before dawn if we're to catch the next mail coach to Manchester."

Graham touched her shoulder. "Please allow my family to return you to yours in one of our coaches. The gesture is not alms, but a symbol of our commitment to aiding your daughter-in-law and your grandson. We know what it is like to lose a loved one and are deeply sorry for your loss. Meanwhile, my family will work to rectify this matter for all your neighbors."

"Thank you." Mrs. Goodnight held Graham's gaze, her pale blue eyes shimmering. Then she threw herself into her husband's wide chest and burst into tears.

He stroked her thick gray hair. "It'll be all right now, my love. You'll see."

Philippa and Marjorie hurried to their sides.

"We'll show you to your rooms," Philippa said softly. "You can have some privacy."

The Goodnights nodded and followed Marjorie and Philippa from the sitting room.

Kunigunde turned to Graham, her face stricken. "I'm sorry. I should never have interrupted—"

"We listen to our clients." Graham kept his tone even, but firm. "When they finish relaying any information they wish for us to know, we help them in the way *they* want. For many, like the Goodnights, their desires have never been given consideration before, much less attended to. We empower them by honoring their wishes, whatever they might be."

Kunigunde nodded jerkily.

Elizabeth flopped into the next seat, her eyes kind. "I know what it is like to want to leap in at the first sign of trouble. It is my personality, as well. I would much rather run Mr. Throckmorten through with a rapier than attempt to *reason* with him."

Tommy pulled her chair closer to Graham. "*Is* that the plan? Is this monster someone who can be reasoned with?"

Jacob dropped into the armchair next to Tommy's, his weasel back in his lap. His brown eyes locked on Graham's expectantly.

Graham swallowed his unease.

For almost twenty years, it had been Baron Vanderbean who had listened to the clients and devised the plans. Since Bean's death two years prior, the siblings had struggled to find a new system. Their eldest sister, Chloe, had seemed the natural leader, but when she married the Duke of Faircliffe and went to live with him in Mayfair, the Wynchester hierarchy had been thrown into disarray once more.

As the head of a network of informants, Graham was used to commanding others, so he was unsurprised when his siblings looked to him as the new leader. Unsurprised, but not always ready.

Particularly when he bore bad tidings.

"I don't yet have a plan," he answered Tommy. "Almost all the cotton mills in England are run in similar conditions. Perhaps even worse."

"*Almost* all," Jacob repeated. "Which means there is a chance that we can help the workers at this manufactory."

"If there is a way, we will find it," Graham agreed. He turned to Tommy. "Can you send a note to Chloe, and have her meet us here after breakfast tomorrow?"

Tommy nodded. "Just Chloe, or she and Faircliffe both?"

"Both," Graham answered. "I suspect this case will require all hands on deck."

11

Despite her new guest chambers being every bit as luxurious as her suite at the Pulteney Hotel, Kuni spent most of the night tossing restlessly on the soft mattress. She was embarrassed for having interrupted when she should have stayed silent.

A Royal Guardswoman did not *interrupt*. During ceremonial events, Royal Guardsmen stood facing forward with perfect posture and impassive expressions, no matter what non–life-threatening events transpired an arm's length away. The trick was to appear as motionless and soundless as furniture until and unless her royal charge required physical protection.

She had *practiced* this. For most of her childhood. How many birthdays had she spent standing as straight as a sentinel, never flinching when her brothers destroyed her new doll piece by piece and ate her cakes right in front of her, one delicious crumb at a time?

And yet, at the first true opportunity to prove herself, she had offered coins to grieving parents so they could save themselves, when what they had wanted was to save *others*.

It was a lesson not just in humility, but in presumption. Kuni wasn't a Wynchester or a Goodnight or even a citizen of this country, and she'd thought she knew best.

Listen to the clients and then take the action they request.

So simple. So obvious. Wasn't that what Kuni had been fighting for all her life? To be listened to. To be taken seriously. To be allowed to pursue the future *she* wished, not the one forced upon her by a well-meaning third party.

She wanted honor. Of course the Goodnights would, too.

Graham and his family had been magnificent. Kind, competent, and compassionate. Even the kitchen staff had managed to produce a tray of sandwiches before the guests had finished seating themselves.

If anyone could solve the unsolvable, it would be the Wynchesters. She'd seen the variety of costumes in the wardrobe of that inn's secret room. Who knew how many tricks and tools they had stashed around the city? Little wonder the desperate traveled for miles to place their lives in the siblings' hands.

* * *

When dawn came, Kuni gave up on sleep.

The gowns she wore to royal functions required extra hands to stuff Kuni inside and lace her up. She'd left those at home. These traveling dresses with hidden apertures for daggers were specifically designed to pull on and off with ease. The new maid Graham arranged the night before had tended to Kuni's hair, leaving little else to do in her toilette.

She assumed she wouldn't see another soul for hours. Princess Mechtilda and her siblings never rose before noon; therefore, their companions rarely did either, giving Kuni plenty of time to train with the soldiers. She assumed wealthy Englishmen slept just as late. But by the time Kuni's boots were halfway down the marble stairs, the pleasant din of voices and plinking silverware reached her ears.

She hurried toward the noise to find the guests of honor and all the Wynchesters—minus the weasel—seated about a large dining room table. A few of the chairs were piled with newspapers, but there were plenty of seats to spare.

Graham's eyes were the first to meet Kuni's. His welcoming smile warmed her skin and brought a smile to her own face.

He gestured to the fragrant food lining the closest wall. "Help yourself to anything on the sideboard that pleases you, then come and join us."

Kuni lifted the topmost plate from a stack and made her way down the sideboard, piling item after item onto her plate. Some she recognized and some she did not. Breads, fruits, fish.

She was determined to sample everything she could while she was abroad. Princess Mechtilda was counting on Kuni to report back on every aspect of her experiences in England. The princess said it would feel as though she had been on adventure, too.

There was no free seat next to Graham, so Kuni chose a spot between Jacob and Marjorie. The Wynchester siblings smiled at Kuni and did their best to include her and the Goodnights in their rapid volleys of half-told stories and familial teasing.

When the Goodnights finished their meal, their faces were full of hope.

The Wynchesters piled onto the front garden to see them off as though the Goodnights were their own grandparents. They tucked their clients into a comfortable hired carriage with plenty of food and blankets for the trip north.

After the coach pulled away, they lost their easy humor and looked at each other with troubled eyes.

Philippa's hands twisted in the lace of her gown. "I keep thinking about the child whose arm was wrenched off in a moving machine."

Marjorie swallowed. "I can't stop thinking about Adella Goodnight."

"We'll find a way to help," Graham said firmly. "We're only waiting on—"

A gleaming coach-and-four pulled to a stop in front of the house.

"Right on time," said Jacob.

At Kuni's quizzical look, Marjorie explained, "Chloe's here. And her husband, the Duke of Faircliffe."

The door to the coach flung open and out bounded a brown-haired woman wearing a striped orange-and-yellow morning gown and the ugliest bonnet Kuni had ever seen. It bore mountains of flowers, a stuffed bird, and clumps of ribbons tied at odd angles. Behind her emerged a tall, elegant gentleman wearing a perfectly normal black hat.

"Where is the princess?" demanded the duchess with the ugly bonnet.

"Not a princess," Kuni said automatically.

Graham made the new arrivals a fabulous leg. "Your Graces, Duke and Duchess of Faircliffe, it is my great honor to present Juffrouw Kunigunde de Heusch of Balcovia."

Kuni's mouth parted in surprise. He'd included her correct honorific!

He grinned at her and whispered, "Philippa helped me."

The duchess ran up to Kuni with open interest. "I am dying to know every word you have said about Balcovia. But if I know my brother, he's already recorded each syllable into a fresh journal for just that topic."

Graham slid a slender book out from under his lapel and handed it to his sister.

"Miss de Heusch, I would love to come to know you better once we've resolved the current matter," said the duchess. "That is, if you're amenable?"

Kuni nodded. "I would like that, Your Grace. Please, call me Kunigunde."

"In that case, I am Chloe, and there's no need to 'Your Grace' me. On the other hand, this is my stuffy husband, His Very-Much Grace, the Duke of Requiring Formal Pretension Even When It Is Obviously Unnecessary—"

"*What?*" blustered the duke. "That's the last time I make you a bonnet!"

"'Faircliffe' for short," finished the duchess, linking her arm with her husband's. She raised her eyebrows toward her siblings. "All hands to the Planning Parlor?"

12

The Wynchesters jostled each other across the garden, into their house, and up the stairs to the next floor in their enthusiasm.

Kuni, trailing behind, could not keep up with the mix of conversations. Just as she reached the top of the stairs, the siblings filed through an open doorway into a room with a strange black floor.

Before she could follow them into the room, its door swung closed, cutting off their raucous chatter so abruptly, it was as if they ceased to exist. *Verdomme.* She was left with her mouth full of teeth, as her mother would say.

Kuni reached for the handle, then paused. The message could not be clearer. "All hands" did not include her.

She placed her ear to the door. Nothing met it but silence.

Kuni stepped away before she could be humiliated by a servant stumbling upon her behaving in such a fashion.

Not being wanted was nothing new. It might not even have been on purpose. How many times had her brothers simply forgotten to include her? They hadn't *meant* to leave her out of absolutely everything interesting they ever did. She simply didn't cross their minds.

Why would the Wynchesters be any different from her own siblings? This family had only met her yesterday. She wasn't one of them.

But for a bittersweet moment, she could not help but wish she were.

As there was nothing left to do in this hallway, Kuni took herself back to the ground floor.

The salon was empty of people now but brimmed with curiosities. She walked the perimeter slowly, taking in everything she could without touching, as though visiting the priceless objects on display at the Balcovian royal palace.

The long table was strewn with maps. Not the normal kind, perhaps of the countryside, but of strange routes through neighborhoods and the interiors of various buildings. This was where Tommy had been working before the Goodnights arrived. Next to the maps, a handful of romantic novels lay atop a daunting five-volume set entitled *A Short History of Europe*. That was Philippa's pile.

The far wall was also full of books, none of which bore a title. These weren't novels, but some of the albums Graham and his siblings had referred to. There were dozens of them. Hundreds! Kuni could not imagine knowing this many things or having this many questions that needed answers.

When the Wynchesters had offered to help Kuni compile an exhaustive report, it seemed they had not been overstating their means and ingenuity. This salon was less like a parlor for receiving guests and more like the sort of command room she imagined generals using when they conspired to stop Napoleon Bonaparte.

If she needed to infiltrate a hospital or a prison or St. Paul's Cathedral, the plans and routes and diagrams were all sitting right here.

But Kuni could not cheat. Royal Guards were honorable. If she couldn't complete the assignment fully on her own, they would say she didn't deserve the title. She dare not let gossip of perceived weakness ruin her chances. By personally compiling thorough and useful intelligence, she would prove her worth to her family and her king.

And maybe also to the Wynchesters. Who did not need her interference in their mission, just as she did not require theirs in hers.

Kuni glanced at a tall-case clock scrunched between the bookcases. Nine o'clock in the morning was a far later hour than usual to set off on her daily reconnaissance. If she intended to join her ancestors in becoming the best of the best, she would not accomplish the feat by moping about someone else's parlor.

She was almost to her guest chamber to retrieve her own intelligence journal when a door swung open behind her.

Noise burst out at once, followed by all eight Wynchesters, who disappeared down the stairs without noticing Kuni hovering awkwardly farther down the corridor. All of them except Graham. He was the last out of the room.

It was dreadful how attractive she found the man.

She had meant to mind her distance from him, but one glance at his sparkling brown eyes, tumbling black curls, and exquisitely tailored frock coat...There was no hope of going anywhere.

After securing the door, he glanced over his shoulder and caught sight of Kuni. Rather than follow the others—

or motion for her to join them—he strode down the corridor to meet her.

He was easily the handsomest rogue she had ever seen. Who could blame her if her pulse skipped and her heart beat a little faster whenever that quick mind and intense gaze concentrated solely on her?

"How did you do?" she stammered before she could start drooling lustfully down his tasteful waistcoat. "Is everything sorted?"

"I hope so," he said, surprising her. She hadn't thought of any solution to the Goodnights' problem. "At least, it could be very soon."

"That is wonderful! I didn't think there was any hope of teaching Mr. Throckmorten to show a hint of empathy."

"Neither do we," Graham answered. "So we're not going to waste our time trying. Chloe says the reformation of labor practices in cotton manufactories has come up several times recently in the House of Commons, but the topic always fades because there's never a strong enough catalyst for change."

"You believe the Goodnights are that strong catalyst?"

"I wish I did," he answered dryly. "If the MPs won't listen to each other, they certainly won't heed a pair of penniless grandparents."

"Will they heed anyone?"

"Perhaps they'll listen to *many* voices. A team of us are leaving for Tipford-upon-Bealbrook right after nuncheon."

That was less than three hours away. Kuni was not surprised they could be ready so swiftly.

"We shall draft an official petition for restricting the hours of labor in this particular manufactory and gather as many signatures from the town and adjacent villages as possible."

She frowned. "Will that stop Mr. Throckmorten?"

"It will illustrate that there is a profound problem and that the representatives' constituents are demanding change. Philippa's father, Mr. York, is a leading MP. Philippa can convince him to bring the petition to the floor. Then, once new regulations pass the House of Commons, Faircliffe will ensure it does the same in the House of Lords. In any case, a Wynchester makes no plans without a—"

"Wait." Kuni wished she understood the English legislative and judicial systems better. "You're saying the reason Mr. Throckmorten is getting away with exploiting his workers, is because he's not doing anything illegal."

"That's unfortunately correct."

"So instead of trying to convince a blithering gubbins like that to change, you will simply make such working conditions illegal—thereby improving them not just in one town, but in all manufactories everywhere?"

"Exactly." Graham grinned at her. "Want to come along?"

Kuni's chest constricted and her breath caught. She *was* invited. He had just invited her!

But of course she could not go. Graham did not speak for the rest of his siblings, and more importantly, Kuni had a mission of her own to complete.

The royal vessel would set sail in twenty-nine days. She and her unimpeachable report needed to be on it.

She shook her head. "My mission is here in London."

"Or," he replied, "you could use whatever you need from the intelligence I've already collected and be done by the time our coach is readied."

"I am perfectly capable of conducting my own research," Kuni said sharply. She had *explained* this. "I do not need your help to do my job."

He shrugged. "Well, I won't mind if you help me with mine. I wish we could get one of our princes' signatures on the petition. The more important the names on the paper, the faster the bill will fly through Parliament."

"How long will it take?"

He made a face. "The MPs might take action on the first day, or they could form committees and take weeks to debate every detail. Faircliffe and Philippa's father will do their best to hurry things along, but it is not as simple as 'Abracadabra.'"

Kuni had no idea what an "abracadabra" was, but she didn't doubt the Wynchesters could do it.

"I hope they pass the law before I leave," she said. "I would like to be here when you and the Goodnights celebrate your victory."

Graham's fingers touched hers. "I would like that, too."

His voice had gone husky.

Kuni could pull her arm away from his soft touch...if she wished to.

It was the last thing she wanted.

The sparks between them had returned in full force. She longed to splay her fingers on his strong chest, to feel the hardness of his taut muscles, the breadth of his shoulders. And then lock her hands behind his neck and kiss him.

Not because he'd rescued her. But because he was letting her decide if she wanted to be rescued.

"I'll return in six or seven days." His heated gaze held hers. "Just in time for a romantic supper for two, if you're interested."

"Six or seven days?" she echoed in dismay.

Kuni only had four weeks left in England. She had looked forward to stealing a few moments of his company when she returned from her reconnaissance each day.

Spending even a day of it without him would cast a long shadow. Though she liked the sound of a romantic supper.

"You can come with me, princess," he coaxed, his eyes twinkling. "If there's no room on the seat, you can sit on my lap."

His voice was teasing, but Kuni had never been more tempted. Not just by the novelty of being included in something actually important...but the thought of being that close to Graham.

Touchably close.

Kissably close.

She licked her lips, then forced herself to shake her head. "I shall not distract you from your mission."

The corner of his mouth curved. "Or allow me to distract you from yours."

He perhaps understood her better than she'd guessed.

Like Kuni, Graham's priorities were things outside of himself. His role was to watch over those who most needed to be guarded. Was there anything more noble?

She touched a fingertip to his lapel, then jerked her hand away.

It didn't matter how much she liked their flirtations. How much she liked *him* and his odd, utterly delightful family.

Her future was in the Royal Guard.

She would be stationed in Balcovia...hundreds of kilometers away.

13

While the Wynchester clan prepared for their trip, Kuni returned to her guest chamber to stay out of their way. After smoothing a bit of cream into her dry skin, she cleared a large space for wide movements and began her morning standing stretches before launching into her more intense strengthening routine.

It didn't take long to feel energy coursing through her blood. Practicing the movements she had learned with the Royal Guardsmen was difficult when limited to a bedchamber—even one as spacious and well appointed as this—but the morning was brisk and cloudless. Perhaps opening the window for a bit of sun and fresh air would let her close her eyes and imagine she was training with the Balcovian soldiers, not as a hanger-on but as a fellow guard.

When she moved the curtain aside, movement caught her eye below. Sun filtered through the spring-green leaves to reveal Graham Wynchester emerging below, between the house and a stone wall dividing the Wynchester property from their neighbors.

Her breath caught.

It was both like and unlike all the afternoons she had watched the soldiers from the castle window when she could not leave Princess Mechtilda. Then, Kuni had longed to be part of the guards' ranks, not the companions'. The men tolerated her training with them in the mornings when she could slip away, but they did not miss her when she was gone or pay any particular heed to how she was progressing, year after year.

Graham must have finished packing for the trip north. He was performing stretches similar to the Royal Guards' routine, but he did not look like a soldier. Nor did he look like a gentleman. His black curls were rumpled as though he had freshly risen from bed. His legs were clad in form-fitting buckskins, and his strong shoulders and muscled arms were hidden only by the thin cambric of a white shirt, tucked loosely into his waistband. No coat. No waistcoat. No cravat. Just delicious, decadent dishabille.

He glanced up and caught her staring at him with hunger.

Kuni's face flamed with heat in mortification.

He smiled as though he'd been hoping she would spy on him. He motioned for her to come down and join him.

Her pulse skipped. She forgot all about her embarrassment and tapped her chest with eagerness instead.

"*Me?*" she mouthed.

Graham scooped his arm through the air in an even larger come-hither motion, then began bending and twisting in much the same way Kuni had just done beside her bed.

He was going to train! And he wanted her to join him!

She dropped the curtain and hurried to her trunk. All her clothes were still folded neatly inside. She had not allowed the maid to place them in the provided wardrobe.

If a guard needed to leave quickly, there was no time to waste packing up luggage. Besides, Kuni knew exactly where everything was.

She reached for her outdoor training dress. It had a Balcovian amaranth bodice with several hidden compartments, and a billowy, overlarge skirt she had sliced up the center and sewn into two pantaloon legs, both of which were equipped with easy access to the daggers strapped to her thighs.

When standing still, it would look like she was wearing an ordinary gown, but the split legs allowed her to ride a steed astride like a man—or perform a complex series of jumps and kicks to and fro across a battlefield, just like the soldiers in their sharp military uniforms.

She raced through the silent house and out the servants' entrance to the rear garden where she had glimpsed Graham.

He was next to a row of brightly colored spring irises, his body parallel to the ground as he pushed up with his arms and slowly lowered himself back down. Upon sight of her, he started to rise to his feet.

Kuni motioned for him to continue. She was more than familiar with press-up exercises. She sprinted lightly over to him and dropped into position at his side, lowering herself down and pressing back up, keeping time to his rhythm.

His eyes widened in obvious surprise.

"What?" she asked archly. "You thought the English were the only ones who know how to exercise their muscles in this way?"

"Knowing how to do a thing and actually doing the thing are not at all the same thing," he answered. "Every person in my household has *seen* me do this. You're the first to do it *with* me."

She pressed up in silence, inordinately proud of her years of training and the strength of her body. It was worth it. Even before she'd been anywhere near the battlefield practice sessions, her brothers would tease her at the drop of a feather to stop whatever she was doing and show them five of these maneuvers with perfect posture. Or ten. Or twenty. She could do over a hundred now without a respite.

Before she was even halfway there, however, Graham sprang to his feet and held out his palm to her.

Ah! She knew what came next in Balcovia. After strength-building was hand-to-hand combat.

She placed her hand in his, gripping tight, then yanked her elbow backward. Graham's body jerked toward her in surprise, which was all Kuni needed. She used his forward momentum to tumble him past her and onto the ground on his back. Even as the breath whooshed out of him, she was already dropping atop, her palms flat against his, pinning him beneath her and covering the length of his body with hers.

"Wh-what?" he managed hoarsely.

"Was hand-to-hand combat not the next step in your routine?" she asked innocently. "That's how we do it in Balcovia."

His eyes shone. "I adore Balcovia."

Graham's lips were close enough to kiss, not that she would do any such thing. It was enough that her body pressed its full weight scandalously against him. Her bosom to his waistcoat-less chest, her hips to his, their thighs mashed together.

She should probably roll off and set him free.

Soon.

Any moment now.

Or not. Her limbs were frozen in place. All right, all right, her limbs were anything but frozen. *Molten.* Her limbs were molten. Her body had melted against him, molded itself to him, melded them into one.

She wasn't even conscious of the weight of her limbs anymore. He was the life raft supporting her amidst an ocean of green grass and frothy flowers. Despite the danger inherent in pressing one's curves against a man's hard body, she felt oddly safe with him.

Perhaps it was more that she *wanted* to taste a little of this danger. Swordplay and combat practice with the other soldiers had never felt life-or-death, but this...*this* felt viscerally real. Graham had invited her onto the battlefield, where she had promptly engaged him in battle. What happened next would determine whether they—

He flipped her so swiftly and so easily she did not even register his movement until she found herself pinned beneath him, her spine against the soft grass, her breath vanishing from her lungs in a whoosh powerful enough to rustle the curly black tendrils tumbling over his forehead.

Now it was his body pressing into hers. Wide shoulders, slender hips, muscular thighs—and perhaps a hint of mutual interest pulsing between them.

A proper miss would be shocked right into a swoon.

It was a good thing Kuni wasn't the least bit proper. Not only had she *started* this, she intended to savor every second of it.

Quickly, she took mental inventory, just as she'd been taught to do before engaging in a skirmish or approaching enemy territory. Instead of scanning her environment for weapons and foxholes, she noted the angle of Graham's cheekbones, the curling length of his eyelashes, the amused quirk of his firm mouth, the hardness of his muscles, the strong forearms not only trapping her in place, but propping his chest up slightly so that her bosom did not bear the full brunt of his weight.

A mistake, that. The battlefield was no place for chivalry. His gentlemanly gesture gave her more than enough space to flex out of his embrace and spring into fighting stance, a dagger in each fist, before he could even begin to scramble to his feet.

But why on earth would she want to interrupt a perfectly scandalous snuggle for that?

"A proposition," he began softly.

She shut her mouth tight before she blurted out, *Accepted!* without any idea what she might be agreeing to.

Perhaps *that* was why missish young ladies swooned. It was not the rakes whose intentions they doubted, but their own will to resist seduction.

"You're only in England for four more weeks, correct?" Graham asked.

Kuni nodded.

"And I have no intention of ever leaving London. So there. That's our ending sorted. We've already had quite a memorable beginning. All that's left to decide is our middle."

"Middle?" The word made her think not of the midpoint of her mission, but rather the midsection of their bodies, which were still plastered together, hip to hip, belly to—ahem.

This was *not* wishful thinking. This gorgeous man with the ability to scale any heights and enter anyplace he pleased...wanted to be right here with her. And was leaving the choice in her hands.

"A temporary flirtation," he said, his voice as smooth and intoxicating as a glass of sweet advocaat. "Only while you're here. No expectations, no demands, no betrothal… just two people enjoying each other's company. Wherever our togetherness might lead."

"No courtship," she managed.

"No wooing of any kind," he agreed. "I will never abandon my family or our clients, and you would never defect from the Balcovian Royal Guard. An impasse…if we were worried about the future. But we already know we part ways in four weeks. The only question is how we spend the time that remains."

"A temporary flirtation?" She echoed his earlier proposition, tasting it on her lips. A proposal as decadent and irresistible as fine *boterkoek*. Very tempting indeed.

"If you're amenable." His clear brown eyes were hot on hers. "If you would rather spend your time some other way, I shan't bring it up again."

"And…if I *were* interested in such a development?"

He grinned at her. "I am shocked by your brazenness, Juffrouw de Heusch. If you hope to steal a kiss from this English gentleman, you'll have to catch me first."

Her mouth fell open. "If *I*— Of all the presumptuous—"

But he had already sprung off her, as lightly as the wind whisking away the seeds of a dandelion.

In the split second it took her to leap to her feet, he had launched himself up the roots of an enormous tree, onto a low branch, and atop the edge of a stone wall no taller than Kuni, with a width she could span with her hand.

His grin only widened at her disgruntled expression. He made a come-this-way-if-you-can gesture with his hand and scampered backward along the uneven, narrow wall, paying absolutely no attention to where his feet might fall, and somehow managing to step perfectly in the center without looking.

She tried to follow his trajectory, starting first with the protruding tree roots. She launched herself from the tallest root toward the lowest branch with as much power as she could—and did not even come close to landing atop it.

At the last second, she was forced to grab a taller branch and swing herself up onto the one he'd used. The rough bark scraped her palms. Luckily, the skin did not break. She trained often enough that her skin had lost its baby softness years before.

But she hadn't trained like *this*. Now she was on her feet on a tree branch...hunched awkwardly beneath several other protruding branches. How the devil had he managed to spring *up* from here, and leap onto the stone wall? If she attempted to jump, she'd either hit her head and shoulders on one of the branches, or fly face-first into the gray stone wall without reaching any altitude at all.

She expected Graham to laugh, or perhaps to make a smirking comment about women who believed themselves capable of being soldiers, as her brothers and the other royal guards would have done.

Instead, he ran back toward her, his steps light and sure despite his gaze being fixed solely on Kuni. As he neared the tree, he crouched down as he ran, then took a flying leap, sailing over her head to a branch on the other side, pausing there barely long enough to tremble the leaves before dropping to the ground just beneath her.

He held out a hand. "You want to start from the beginning? I'll show you."

Her heart knocked into her ribs. Graham wasn't going to mock her ignorance. He was going to *train* her to follow his moves.

He wasn't the only one with *moves*. Two could play at this game.

She reached for his hand. Instead of daintily leaping down, as soon as her fingers locked around his palm, she pulled him forward and off-balance. As he straightened, she flipped head-over-heels from the high branch, pulling her daggers from her thighs as she spun to land in a crouch, blades at the ready.

Kuni smiled at his confounded expression. "Teach me yours, and I'll teach you mine."

"It's a deal." He held up his palms in supplication. "No need to impale me with knives."

Kuni made them vanish as quickly as they'd first appeared. She blinked at him innocently as she held up her own empty palms. "What knives?"

14

Graham could not help but be impressed. No one ever got the upper hand on a Wynchester. Kunigunde had managed to turn the tables on him twice.

He now suspected that when he had pinned her beneath him against the grass...he had actually not done any such thing at all. She had allowed herself to *seem* pinned beneath him. If she'd wanted to be free, she could have arranged it in the blink of an eye, with or without the appearance of her daggers for extra flair.

Her pretty black eyes shone with enthusiasm. "Show me how to leap onto the wall."

If it had been anyone else asking, Graham would have hesitated. Most people, regardless of sex, did not purposefully attempt Graham's unorthodox method of climbing trees or scaling walls.

Kunigunde, he suspected, not only wouldn't let the occasional bump or scraped knee slow her down, but actually have the maneuver committed to memory before noon.

"Let's start with the tree," he said. "I'll show you how to pick the best branches."

Her smile lit her face so bright, it warmed him from the inside out. It was as if he'd offered her a treasure chest full of gold and diamonds, rather than the quickest path to scraped hands and a bruised backside.

"I'm watching." She stood beside him, her limbs relaxed but ready.

He pointed out not just the "good" branches, but also the "bad" ones, explaining in which circumstances each was useful, and when it would be best to select another.

"The key," he explained, "is being able to make the calculation midair. Sometimes you won't know until you're halfway up an alley wall that the ledge you'd *hoped* to spring off would crumble from the weight of a flowerpot. You'll often have less than a second to make a decision that will determine whether you continue up or land on your arse."

She looked at the tree doubtfully.

"Good. You should look at every surface just like that. Never trust anything to be sturdy or solid. In most cases, you won't even need it to be. You're just tapping your toe long enough to change direction or launch yourself a little higher."

"A tree seems full of unnecessary obstacles and easy-to-snap twigs."

"It's also close enough to the ground that you won't injure yourself overmuch if you fall from it. And it's a great opportunity to learn for yourself which branches make better jumping points, and why."

"*When* I fall, you mean."

"Anything worth doing starts with falling," he said cheerfully. "Don't worry about the wall—that's an entirely different lesson. Start with getting to that branch of the tree." He pointed.

She took a step back and lowered her center of gravity. "Ready."

He stepped aside.

Without so much as a fortifying breath, she raced forward, taking the protruding tree roots like stair steps. She leapt for one of the lowest branches—and missed it by inches.

Instead of falling, her hands grabbed two other branches and hoisted herself into place. Rather than pause, she sprang immediately to the second branch, and then the third, and then the fourth and final—

Not quite. *Now* she was falling. Not with a screech and ungainly flailing, but the controlled descent of someone who had tussled with gravity on countless prior occasions. She did not land with her back over a tree root, but on all fours in a patch of grass to the side.

She was in that position for less than a blink. She sprang up and spun about, then sprinted forward to try it again.

On the seventh try, she made it.

On the twentieth try, she'd made it four times in a row. She beamed down at him from the branch parallel to the stone wall.

"Perfect," he told her. "Stupendous. Now do it using the *wrong* branches."

"What?"

"This tree is perfect for breaching that wall. Most environments you find yourself in will not be so obliging. You'll have to make it all the way up anyway. Try it with one 'wrong' branch at a time until you can get to the top exclusively using the very worst choices."

"Show me how *you* do it."

"No."

She glared down at him from the tall branch.

He gave her an unapologetic shrug. "If you're chasing a criminal or fleeing a villain, there won't be a helpful mentor conveniently located to scout the best surfaces and demonstrate the proper path. You just have to try. You'll either make it...or not."

She nodded once and leapt nimbly to the ground, her lips set in a stubborn line. Graham knew that look well. His mother had always said he'd worn a very similar expression while learning a difficult and daring new trick for the circus.

Kunigunde gave a running start and made it to the second branch before it cracked beneath her feet, sending her to the ground.

"Don't hesitate," he called out. "It would've held for a split second, but not for any longer."

She tried again and again, her touch-points faster with each new attempt. Occasionally, a hand flung out for balance, and she would start over, even if she hadn't fallen.

When she finally made it to the top using exclusively terrible branches for purchase, Graham let out a war whoop. "You did it! I knew you could!"

She stared at him as though she couldn't quite credit she had actually beaten the course. "You thought I could all along?"

"You doubted it?"

Her expression was incredulous.

Oh. She hadn't doubted *herself*. She'd assumed *Graham* had doubted her. That he was standing aside for sport, expecting to watch her fail.

Exactly what kind of support had she received from her siblings? None at all?

"Anyone can see that you have the athletic build and necessary mental fortitude to learn any skill you please," he told her. "The question was never *if* you would make it to the top, but *when*. Now that we have the answer..."

"...I do it again?" she guessed.

"Until you can make it three times in a row," he confirmed. "After, we can practice jumping onto narrow surfaces without falling."

She climbed down with good cheer and sprinted back up the tree, not stopping until she'd managed it five times in a row without the slightest wobble in her balance. She beamed down at him from the tall branch.

He could not help but be impressed. "I don't know who is in charge of the Balcovian Royal Guard, but if they have any brains in their head, they'll give you all the special training at their disposal."

She snorted. "I'll tell Floris and Reinald you said so."

"Your brothers? They shouldn't need me to point out the obvious. You're gifted and tenacious, the perfect qualities for any aspiring acrobat."

"Don't you mean 'soldier'?"

"Do I?" He motioned her down from the tree and over to a section of soil with several humps of protruding roots. "As before, we'll jump onto completely inappropriate surfaces from a distance easy to recover from if you fall. Once you can do it with perfect balance, we can talk about the wall. But I warn you—this bit is deceptively tricky. It can take weeks or months to master a high beam."

Or never, in most cases. But, as Graham was rapidly learning, Kunigunde wasn't like most *anything*. If anyone could learn to leap atop a narrow beam during the free moments of a four-week reconnaissance mission in a foreign country, that person would be Kunigunde.

"Tell me about your information network," she said as

she practiced hopping onto an uneven narrow tree root. "Do you have spies on every corner?"

"Almost every," he said with pride. "It took years to build up contacts in so many places. I won't bore you with the details."

"Bore me," she begged. "I'm fascinated."

He narrowed his eyes. "Are you going to copy my espionage techniques, too?"

"I'd try if I thought I'd have any success at it," she admitted without any shame. "I'm much better at tossing daggers into people than I am sweet-talking information out of them."

"Hmm, I don't know. It seems to be working with *me*."

She batted her eyelashes at him before jumping onto a tree root.

As she practiced, he gave her a brief overview of where a few of his informants were located and how they passed him information, expecting her eyes to glaze over at any moment. Instead, she gazed at him with rapt interest, impressed enough that she kept forgetting she was meant to be jumping on top of things.

Soon, they were seated hip to hip on a low, thick root, having given up on acrobatics entirely in favor of giving their full attention to their conversation and each other.

Graham's siblings considered his fact-gathering missions a useful addition to the Wynchester wheelhouse. Kunigunde understood in a way he had never previously been able to verbalize.

She didn't just want to belong to the Balcovian Royal Guard. She wanted to be invaluable. Indispensable.

That was what Graham wanted with his family. He never wanted the show to go on without him. He wanted to be the *star* of the show. To have an act so essential to the whole, there would be no performance without all the pieces working together.

His wish to become a star had inadvertently come true when his sister Chloe married the Duke of Faircliffe. Without Bean as head of household—and without Chloe, who had briefly taken over—the role had fallen to Graham.

He could never take Bean's place. Nor could he attempt to replace Chloe. But Graham could—no, *did*—lead his family on their missions in the best way he knew how. Which meant practicing his acrobatics, expanding his network of informants, compiling detailed compendiums containing every bit of information he gathered...and staying right here in London, directing the entire spectacle from his home.

His face was no longer on playbills, but his family's fame grew day by day. Soon, thanks to his current clandestine assignment, his name would appear on the front pages of the newspapers he scoured so voraciously. He would be important not just to his siblings, but to his entire town. The whole country.

Graham Wynchester, indispensable. Protector of London. Local hero.

Perhaps one day, personally recognized by royalty.

15

After nuncheon, Kuni tried not to stare at the Wynchesters in abject envy as they made their goodbyes. Four of them were going: free-spirited Tommy, bookish Philippa, softhearted Jacob, and dashing Graham. No matter who they might meet, one of the four was bound to be able to coax the next signature.

This afternoon was completely unlike the day when each of Kuni's older brothers set off to join the Royal Guard and left their little sister behind, and yet she had the same foolish twisting ache in her belly.

Her brothers had never allowed her to accompany them because they thought girls were useless. Not only had the Wynchesters invited Kuni, but it was also clearly not a case of only the men of the family being deemed important. There was no doubt Graham's invitation to join him had been sincere.

Nor was he leaving Kuni all alone. The duke and duchess were at their home in Mayfair or off in Parliament. But observant Marjorie and bloodthirsty Elizabeth were staying behind just like Kuni.

The butler entered the salon where all of them had

gathered to make their goodbyes. "The coach is ready and waiting."

Philippa tied her bonnet while Tommy and Jacob put on their hats.

Graham strode up to Kuni looking more handsome than ever. Gone was his earlier dishabille. His wide shoulders were now shown to perfection in a sharp coat of olive green. The white of his cravat sat in gorgeous contrast to the golden bronze of his skin. His soft black curls tumbled over his forehead artlessly, giving a casual air to his impeccable demeanor.

"Last chance." Light brown eyes met hers, his voice low and inviting. "There's still room on my lap if you want to come."

"I do not wish to take part," Kuni lied. "I have an important mission of my own to complete and must make the most of the few weeks that remain."

It wasn't a lie. It was true. It just *felt* like a lie, because every particle of Kuni wanted to launch herself into his carriage to go and protect someone today.

But she had made a vow to her father and their ancestors. Generations of de Heusch guards had served the king as his favored and most trusted soldiers. Her great-great-grandfather had shown the way to unity and freedom. Thanks to her relative's timely protection of a king who chose people over profit, slavery had been abolished. Every de Heusch generation since had done their part to serve the king and secure more freedoms. She would not break her family's noble tradition at any cost. It was her destiny.

"As you wish, princess." Graham set his hat on his head at a rakish angle, his intense gaze never straying from Kuni.

Elizabeth bounded up to them, an innocent-looking cane held out in each hand.

"Be kind to my swords," she told her brother.

"I don't need your swords," he replied. "We're collecting signatures, not heads."

"But if the opportunity presents itself," she insisted, "run through as many blackguards as you please, starting with the owner of that cursed cotton mill. Then bring the blades back in good condition."

Graham embraced his sister without taking the swords. "What if I loan the blades to Jacob?"

Elizabeth pulled back, appalled. "Jacob won't harm a fly. Literally. Whilst you're collecting signatures, he'll be in the manufactory collecting arachnids and releasing them out of doors. Or he'll train them to attack in deathly swarms." She brightened. "That's not a bad idea. I shall ask him what he knows about training killer insects." She hurried off to catch Jacob before he slipped out through the door.

"Killer insects?" Kuni said skeptically.

"You scoff, but half the feats Jacob has accomplished with animals are because one or more of the siblings wagered that it could not be done. I should intervene before Elizabeth plants the idea into his head."

But he did not move.

Neither did Kuni.

All the other Wynchesters had embraced or kissed goodbye. A loud, teasing bustle of activity that Kuni had watched from the rear of the room, in the shadows. She did not know them well enough to partake in such affectionate displays.

Or rather, she did not know how to display or receive affection. Her family was not demonstrative.

It had been an age since the last time she'd been

embraced. She touched the soft muslin of her gown where her father's epaulet hid beneath. He had never hugged her before that day, as far as Kuni could remember.

Her brothers never touched her, except to pull her braids or to give her a playful shove. She barely remembered her mother and had no reason to expect softness from anyone else. It was as though, the day her father hugged her goodbye, he had suspected it was the last time he would ever see her.

So, no. She would not take her leave of Graham that way, even if they had been the best of friends and had known each other since birth. Embracing felt like gambling with fate. Like shouting up to the heavens, *Here, this is a thing I care deeply about. I dare you to take it from me.*

Fate always won the wager.

Graham reached forward. Not to pull her to him, but as though he wished to run his thumb over the back of her hand or the bare brown skin of her arm. He stopped before his finger made contact.

That might have been the end of it, had Kuni not flinched. Sort of flinched. And sort of maybe accidentally pushed her arm that final half-centimeter to feel Graham's thumb against her skin.

It was not an *embrace*. This was nothing. Just a four-week temporary flirtation. Meaningless. Forgettable.

Yet her heart pounded as though she had ventured too close to the edge of a boat in the middle of a sea.

The other siblings had left the house. Jacob, Tommy, and Philippa were outside in the carriage. Marjorie and Elizabeth were in the front garden to wave them off. They were waiting for Graham. He ought to hurry.

Not gaze smolderingly at Kuni as though the only mission on his mind was the possibility of stealing a kiss.

A very low possibility. Very, very low. She absolutely, positively, probably would rebuff him if he tried.

Maybe.

Or…she could let him kiss her, and prove to both of them at once that the strong pull between them contained nothing of substance. Nothing she would miss when she went home to Balcovia. Nothing she would think about every second of every day while he was gone.

He rubbed the pad of his thumb against her bare skin.

Just once. Lightly. Reverently. As if savoring the soft warmth of her skin to take with him on the long, cold ride north. He tilted his head toward her.

She lifted her chin defiantly. Or perhaps raised her lips invitingly. It was a bit of a mix. She was certain he could improvise. Nothing seemed to stymie him. Not scaling a tall building with his bare hands, and clearly not the fear of starting something they could not finish. A kiss would only complicate matters. If they were wise, they would leave their flirtation at mere words.

Their mouths drew close.

Footsteps sounded. "Master Graham?"

They jumped apart before the butler reached the threshold. Either that, or the butler had already spied them almost kissing, retreated quietly, and then stomped back extra loudly to give them the opportunity to compose themselves before he officially interrupted.

"I'm going." Graham lifted an eyebrow at Kuni. "Are you coming outside to see us off, Princess?"

"No," she said. "I am very busy. I shall not even notice you're gone."

He grinned at her as if this tart speech was tantamount to a soppy declaration of love. Her heart thudded. He tipped his hat, then strode out the door and down the corridor without saying goodbye.

She rushed to the closest window and peeked through the curtains.

The carriage set in motion the moment Graham stepped from the house. With one hand holding his hat, he caught up easily and swung himself in through the door, his face alive with laughter.

Kuni touched her fingers to the cool glass, then yanked them back.

She was being ridiculous, and Royal Guardsmen were never ridiculous. Who cared if the last person she'd watched ride off to battle evil had never returned home? This wasn't her home, and Graham wasn't hers, either. Kuni was just passing through.

She was to keep her mind on her mission, not devilishly attractive men. Especially not one particular rogue she definitely was not going to miss.

When Elizabeth and Marjorie reentered the salon moments later, Kuni was well away from the windows and busy reviewing the notes she'd gathered thus far.

"The princess is too busy to wave goodbye to her hosts?" asked Elizabeth.

"I am not a princess," Kuni replied instantly, then realized she hadn't corrected Graham the last time. Perhaps she wanted him to think so highly of her. Or perhaps she liked having a pet name.

Or maybe what she wanted was the safe distance that being royal provided. Courtship between a commoner and a princess was laughable. It took the matter out of Kuni's hands. This was the way the world worked. Princesses on one side of the wall and knights on the other. *She* wasn't rejecting Graham...or running away.

And if it just so happened that he could scale the wall between them…

"Don't tell Graham you're not a princess," said Marjorie. "There's nothing he adores more than royalty."

Meaning he cared less about Kuni because she was not a real princess?

"Gossip," Elizabeth said. "Graham might be addicted to gossip slightly more than royalty."

"*Royal* gossip is his favorite," Marjorie agreed. "His primary obsession."

Elizabeth rubbed her hands. "Better yet, Graham adores appearing in the scandal columns…in royal gossip about *himself*."

Marjorie wrinkled her nose. "That's never happened."

"But he wants it to," Elizabeth shot back. "Why else has it been his life's dream to rescue a princess? And now that it's happened, no one even knows. How he must suffer."

"I am not a princess," Kuni said again. "And I would have got on just fine without him rescuing me."

Mostly fine.

"It's not just princesses," Marjorie said. "He saves women to make up for…" She shut her mouth tight, then blurted out, "He can't save everyone, but he'll die trying."

"He's the most daring Wynchester," Elizabeth agreed. "Next to me, that is. He yearns to appear in one of his breathless gossip sheets. As a figure of awe, rather than ordinary, scandalous Graham."

"Your brother is far from ordinary," Kuni said, indignant. "He certainly does not require royal connections to prove his worth."

"You're new to England. Here, high-ranking connections determine a person's worth. Where would Brummell have been without Prinny's patronage?"

"Who?" asked Kuni.

"Beau Brummell." Elizabeth poked her canes toward the bookshelves. "I'm sure there's a three-volume compendium detailing the dandy's every pithy word and perfect fold of his neckcloth if you want to bore yourself unconscious for a few hours."

"I would rather not."

Elizabeth nodded approvingly. "Leave the gentlemen to high starched collars that prevent their handsome heads from turning, and to their tailored coats and champagne-shined boots they cannot even pull on and off by themselves. Some men are *so* helpless. What would they do without fierce, blade-wielding women like you and me?"

"Sleep," Marjorie answered without hesitation. "Graham always says he cannot rest at night because we'll be forced to flee to France if you go on a murderous rampage."

"It's not murder if the villain *deserves* to have his blood spilled," Elizabeth protested.

"Pretty sure it is," Marjorie murmured.

"Just wait until *you* need to be rescued! I'll stand idly by sharpening my sword, perhaps saying to the scoundrel, 'Oh no, my dear, I shan't harm you. Marjorie prefers I invite all despicable villains to a spot of tea first.'"

Kuni rather agreed with Elizabeth's methods.

"The tea plan might work." Marjorie shook a finger at her sister. "One should always attempt polite conversation first."

"Pah," said Elizabeth. "You're as bad as Jacob. Never say you've started writing poetry, too?"

"My paintbrushes make my poems for me," Marjorie answered. "And we've only Jacob's *word* that he writes poems. He may listen to others at those poetry salons he attends, but Graham says Jacob never shares his own. He's certainly never shown any to me."

Elizabeth leaned forward on her canes, her eyes sparkling. "Then what do you think he's writing? Letters to a secret lover? Gothic novels for Minerva Press?"

"Maybe he writes the gossip columns that Graham likes to read," Kuni suggested.

Both Wynchester sisters stared at her.

"Jacob would *never*," Marjorie breathed.

Elizabeth practically bounced with delight. "I should love it above all things if that were true! Just think—Graham's life's work, sending scouts to every corner of London to collect information and subscribing to every newspaper in town to be the first to read words his own brother was writing abovestairs."

"Surely he cannot cover *every* corner of London."

"He has countless informants." Marjorie grinned. "It's not your fault he found you. It was inevitable."

"Fate," Elizabeth agreed.

Kuni shivered and pretended she hadn't heard the dramatic pronouncement.

"Graham tips them well for their service," Elizabeth explained. "Some don't seek gold but would rather be owed a favor. Street children, crossing sweepers, maids, guards, tavern owners, surgeons, flower girls, opera singers, hackney drivers, disgruntled footmen... You cannot imagine how many scrapes his spies get into that require professional extrication."

"Maybe she *can* imagine," Marjorie suggested.

"She can't," Elizabeth said firmly. "She's a princess who lives in a palace. Her Highness hasn't the least idea what gaming hells and Blue Ruin and the Dark Walk *are*, much less what sort of trouble they might bring to someone of weak character."

Kuni wanted to argue, but the message was clear.

Graham's spiderweb was so large, he probably couldn't even remember all the names of those who had tangled in it.

With contacts and connections in every corner of London, was it really Kuni who interested him? Or was "princess" the final item to tick off a very long list? If you built a big enough web, you could catch anything.

Kuni would not be a trapped fly, trembling in place as she awaited his return. She had her own web to weave. The king's approval to capture. A princess of her own to defend to the death.

It was time to go to work.

16

Graham tore his gaze from the carriage window only after the house faded from view. He turned toward his siblings, who were already deep in a discussion about acquiring signatures for the petition.

"How do you think it's going back home?" he interrupted with an air of affected casualness.

Tommy arched her brows. "We've been gone for fifteen minutes."

"Exactly." Graham looked at Jacob. Surely his brother would understand the risks.

Jacob inclined his head. "Fifteen minutes is plenty of time for mayhem. Marjorie—"

"I'm not talking about Marjorie," Graham said in exasperation.

Philippa tilted her head. "Then which of our two fierce, armed warriors are you worried about?"

All four of them stared at each other for a moment before saying in unison, "*Both.*"

"Can you imagine if they joined forces?" Philippa whispered. "Dangerous on their own, but together…"

"It's a big house." Tommy glanced out the window.

"Not that Kunigunde will be moping around it anyway. She has her own mission."

"Everything will be fine as long as they keep out of each other's path," Jacob said with confidence.

"That should be simple enough," Tommy assured Graham. "Kunigunde doesn't want help, and Elizabeth doesn't like people. They'll never see each other."

Philippa and Jacob exchanged silent glances.

"Mayhem," Graham muttered and turned his gaze back to the window.

* * *

After the maid refreshed her braids, Kuni stepped out of the Wynchesters' home and into the brisk April sunlight. A footman stood at the ready.

Asking the Wynchesters' butler, Randall, to summon a carriage had felt strange. Kuni wasn't used to having to ask for things.

The Wynchesters were friendly with their staff, but she couldn't recall Princess Mechtilda addressing a servant with anything but a direct order. The princess could name few maids or footmen. However, she and her companions recognized many of the handsome Royal Guardsmen by name. Those elite infantry soldiers in their distinctive amaranth uniforms commanded universal attention and respect.

Soon, Kuni would wear that uniform, too.

Wheels crunched on gravel and a clean black carriage pulled up to collect her. It was not as fine as the Balcovian royal family's ridiculously ostentatious coach, but would serve just the same.

She ignored the odd emptiness in her chest at entering

an empty carriage by herself instead of preparing to trundle along hip to hip with Graham. Silly to miss a sensation she'd never known.

A footman opened the door.

Kuni started forward, only for the shaft of a bejeweled cane to swing up and block her path.

She shoved the cane away and turned to face Elizabeth Wynchester. "I am *not* going to sit around your house sewing decorative samplers."

Elizabeth stared at her. "Why would anyone pick up a needle when they could pick up a sword?"

Kuni felt much the same way. And would indeed carry a sword when she became a Royal Guard. "I have limited time. Please let me pass. Your brother gave me permission to borrow any of the coaches I please, but I am happy to pay for the favor."

Elizabeth waved this away. "I don't give a button about your money. I'm going with you."

"I do not require anyone's assistance."

"Oh, I'm not going to *help* you," Elizabeth assured her. "I'm going to *guard* you."

Fury rose within Kuni. No other words could offend her more. "I do not require a guard. I *am* a guard."

"Well...you require one a little bit," insisted Elizabeth unrepentantly. "You wouldn't be a guest of the Wynchester family if you hadn't needed Graham's protection, and *I* wouldn't be a Wynchester if I let you run off unprotected."

"I am not 'running off,'" Kuni pointed out through clenched teeth. "I am taking a carriage staffed by a driver and a footman. It would also be my prerogative if I wished to set off on foot, alone."

Elizabeth opened her mouth.

Kuni forestalled her. "I know what this is. You are one of your brother's spies. He's keeping a book about me, and whatever you observe will find itself in those pages."

"Well," said Elizabeth. "Your wild accusations aren't... *inaccurate*. But they are—"

Kuni crossed her arms. "What?"

"—*incomplete*," Elizabeth finished. "Marjorie's up in her third-floor art studio and the rest of my family is gone. I'll be bored if I stay here. The least you can do is let me poke holes in anyone who looks at you sideways."

"That makes no sense," Kuni burst out. "If you wanted adventure, why not join the others?"

"I can't," Elizabeth replied matter-of-factly. "My body would not last cooped up in a coach for two straight days, no matter how fine the squabs. I'd either slow down the others by forcing the journey to take a week, or end up unable to move my limbs for a fortnight once we arrived."

Kuni's lips parted in surprise. "I thought you were the strongest of them all!"

"You've never seen me without a cane, yet assumed I wasn't helpless?" Elizabeth linked arms with her. "I would take a bullet for you."

Kuni snorted at the absurd idea.

"I hope we get in a violent skirmish," Elizabeth continued dreamily. "The bullet shall graze my sword arm and the villain will think that he's won, only to discover too late that I am equally deadly with the other arm." She pantomimed a vicious jab with her bejeweled cane.

Kuni extricated her arm and leapt up into the carriage.

Elizabeth bounded in behind her.

Kuni sighed and accepted her fate. "What would I be doing in this Gothic scenario?"

"Being weak and helpless," Elizabeth answered decisively. "Princesses need saving. It's knights who do the rescuing. And the occasional knightess."

"I am not a princess. I am a soon-to-be Royal Guardswoman."

"And I'm *your* Royal Guard," Elizabeth answered cheerfully. "Except not royal. And I'll only guard you if there's reason to be violent. I hope you'll be kind enough to start a riot."

Perhaps her uninvited companion was a boon, Kuni decided. For one, her brothers were searching for a solitary stowaway, not two ladies out for a stroll.

And for two... Being utterly overwhelmed by someone else's eagerness to tag along was an unfamiliar sensation. Perhaps a hint of how her brothers might have felt, whenever Kuni insisted on joining them to train or to shoot or to throw daggers. She didn't have a sister, but if she did, Kuni imagined she would be very much like Elizabeth Wynchester.

Kuni and her imaginary sister would have wanted each other's company. Trained together on purpose. Helped each other voluntarily. Perhaps become Royal Guardswomen together. The long fight wouldn't be nearly so lonely a prospect if she didn't have to battle alone.

"Tell me about life in the castle." Elizabeth leaned against the squab. "Is it all wine and gluttony and dancing?"

"In the evenings. Daytime is much quieter."

Princess Mechtilda slept through most of the sunlight. Companions were expected to be present when she awoke, which meant that by the afternoon, Kuni could no longer be outside with her knives or practicing moves and marches with the soldiers. All she could do was watch by her window and train her muscles as best she could in her fluffy, luxurious bedchamber.

The soldiers thought of her as something of a pet. They knew her family history. How her great-great-grandfather had become a Royal Guardsman after saving the life of Balcovia's first king. How every generation since had given birth to new and formidable Guardsmen. And of course no soldier wished to slight the sister of Floris and Reinald, the great and feared fighting masters.

Kuni wanted to show all those doubters that she was worthy. Not just the insignificant relative of those who had come before her.

Elizabeth leaned forward on her cane. "Will you still be invited to fancy balls once you're a Royal Guard?"

"No."

Technically, Kuni wasn't invited now. But even if attendants weren't announced by name, Kuni was part of the royal retinue. As long as she held that status, no door would be closed to her.

Through the window, the center of London drew ever closer. The carriage rolled over a bump and she shifted in her seat.

Elizabeth's green eyes sparkled with curiosity. "Will you miss all that merrymaking?"

"I shall not have time to," Kuni answered. "Royal Guards hold their positions for twelve hours a day."

This wasn't entirely true. Standing stiffly beside a gate or a doorway during ceremonial events gave one nothing *but* time to think about all the things one wasn't doing.

But Kuni would be glad to be done with frivolous nonsense. As a Royal Guard, she would fulfill an important role, on and off the battlefield, not fritter her time away with silly dances.

"Royal Guards begin training in young adulthood and

take posts for life, or until physically unable to maintain the role."

"Are companion positions supposed to be for life, as well?"

"No, the post only exists for as long as the princess requires companions."

Elizabeth's brow furrowed. "What does that mean? She could wake up one day and decide to be rid of you?"

"It means it is not up to her. Not really. When she marries—her future husband to be determined by the king, unless Princess Mechtilda has her way—Her Highness will become mistress of a new household and must leave the old one behind."

"You mean, 'leave the old one unemployed'?" Elizabeth asked, her tone caustic.

Kuni nodded. "Princesses' companions begin work when they are about eight years old. We're all within a year or two of the princess's age."

"How old is Princess Mechtilda?"

"Twenty-four. One year younger than me. It is unusual for a Balcovian princess to remain unwed for so long, but she is the youngest of several sisters, the others of whom have already been married off to form strategic alliances. The king has his eye on the Duke of Cambridge for his final daughter. It is the reason for the family's upcoming visit."

"Prinny's brother?" Elizabeth said in surprise. "I fear it's too late. Graham says the duke is rumored to be courting Princess Augusta of Hesse-Kassel."

"That is because His Grace has yet to meet Princess Mechtilda." Kuni stretched her feet out before her. "It has long been an open secret that Her Highness is hoping to fall in love. Not strategically, but passionately. If not with

His Grace, then with someone else. She has threatened to follow her heart, no matter where it leads."

"Graham adores all the intrigue with the royal dukes and their paramours. He has entire journals of how *he* wishes the royalty of England and Europe would unite. When we were younger, he had Marjorie paint little portraits of his favorite imaginary pairs." Elizabeth waggled her brows. "Always *Graham* beside all the young, pretty princesses, of course."

Of course. Kuni smoothed her jagged nails.

"Later, when the Duke of Clarence left his long-term mistress to hunt for a proper heiress, it was all we could do to stop Graham from penning a long letter full of unsolicited advice on whom to wed."

"*Did* you convince him not to?"

"Probably not," Elizabeth said with a laugh. "Whatever you do, don't tell him Princess Mechtilda dreams of a love match. Graham will be waiting for her on the dock with an armful of posies."

Kuni did not laugh. The unbidden image caused her insides to roil uncomfortably. She did not wish to examine the reasons why.

She did not believe in such flowery stuff as "love at first sight" or "tumbling head over heels." She followed her ancestors, not her emotions. When she was ready for a husband, she would choose a mate with the same care and calculation as the years she'd spent training to be a Royal Guardswoman. It would happen on her terms or not at all.

Elizabeth sobered. "If the princess does marry soon, that means you have a matter of months before you never see her again."

"Not as a companion. But I will be a Royal Guardswoman in the highest infantry unit in Balcovia. Princess Mechtilda and I made a pact years ago. She will request the king assign me as her personal Royal Guard."

Marjorie frowned. "Even if she marries an English prince?"

"Then she will request it of her husband."

"What if he refuses?"

"If I cannot guard Mechtilda as planned, it will be my honor to remain in Balcovia to guard my king."

"What will the other companions do?"

"It is not unusual for a princess and her companions to all wed within a year of each other. Often to a lord—or higher."

In fact, her brothers had already selected the aristocrat they expected Kuni to wed. Riches, respect, a lofty title *other* than Royal Guardsman. They could not understand why marrying "well" wasn't accomplishment enough.

"I don't know which part sounds worse," said Elizabeth. "Bowing and scraping to a princess, or marrying the first nob who asks, just to avoid being tossed in the street on someone else's wedding day."

"Royal companions enjoy access to almost every corner of the royal residences. We have significant influence with the princess, and are well paid for our service. We also have small fortunes by the time we retire from our posts, which is part of what makes us attractive brides for aristocratic suitors. But I agree with the sentiment. I would rather be a soldier than a coin purse."

Kuni returned her gaze to the window. The fashionable Mayfair district was approaching. Large terraced homes built in crescents around small, trim squares. Nothing at all like the countryside in Balcovia.

"The life of a Royal Guard must be dreadfully exciting."

"Floris and Reinald say it's not, for regular Guardsmen. As fighting masters, my brothers are always busy, but they claim everyone else has been idle and bored since the end of the war." Kuni rolled her eyes. "Then again, they would say anything to keep me from participating in our family's legacy. On the few occasions we see each other, the first question from their mouths is when I'll be married and off their hands."

"Is there a third possibility?" Elizabeth asked. "Could you use your fortune to live independently?"

Kuni shrugged. "I suppose. I have never considered it, because to me there has always only been one choice: the Royal Guard. My father was a Royal Guardsman, my grandfather, my great-grandfather... The Royal Guard is where I belong. It is a family, both literally and figuratively."

"I understand." Elizabeth's voice was soft. "Family is more than blood and means everything. My siblings and I followed in our father's footsteps, too. We wouldn't have it any other way."

"Baron Vanderbean took on clients and had adventures?"

"Heroic ones and legally dubious ones and every kind in between," Elizabeth said with pride. "Wynchesters are like guards ourselves, but with no uniform or glory. We're under no one's orders but our own. We do what's right because it's honorable, and that's enough."

"Because you found the right family, they welcomed you with open arms." That was all Kuni wanted. The carriage rolled to a stop. "Ah! We have arrived."

"Arrived where, exactly?"

Kuni pulled out her guidebook and showed her a marked page. "We're performing reconnaissance on these two aristocratic residences. Weaknesses in security, unguarded entrances—not just doors, but windows and any other openings. How many servants are visible, whether they remain at their posts, if they are dressed in any particular livery…"

"Before you get angry with me for what I'm about to suggest, I think you and your plan are brilliant. You'll be a wonderful guard. It would simply be remiss of me not to point out that we *have* all this information at home, in neatly penned journals accompanied by detailed drawings and maps."

Kuni shook her head. "I must prove I am capable of determining, finding, and collating the information myself. A guard must be able to read her surroundings—not just someone else's notes. Cheating would dishonor my ancestors, and the gossip would disqualify me for the post."

"Then we do it your way." Elizabeth gestured with her bejeweled cane. "After you."

To Kuni's pleasure, Elizabeth proved herself a marvelous surveillance companion. She and her flamboyant cane deflected any glances sent in their direction, and she had a keen eye for precisely the sort of details Kuni was gathering for her report.

Granted, Elizabeth might have already seen that information in Graham's books or Marjorie's drawings or Tommy's maps, but to her credit, Elizabeth only pointed out details Kuni could observe with her own senses, gamely doing her best to play along on Kuni's terms.

Listen to the client. Then take the action they wish.

Fortunately, Kuni didn't feel like a client. Elizabeth was too gregariously bad tempered for the outing to feel remotely professional on her part. Despite her droll misanthropic commentary, Elizabeth was enjoying herself immensely and made no attempt to hide it.

A strange sensation unfurled in Kuni's chest. She couldn't recall a single time her brothers had offered to help her achieve her aims. Nor could she recall a moment they'd seemed pleased to be in her company.

For Kuni, joining forces with Graham to evade Floris and Reinald had been the first endeavor of its kind. The morning she'd spent training with him in the rear garden had been magical. Now she was repeating the two-heads-are-better-than-one experience with Elizabeth. Kuni was forced to admit she enjoyed working as a team more than being on her lonesome.

It was not a circumstance she could allow herself to become used to. In peacetime, shifts as a Royal Guard were inherently solitary. Even if she and one of her brothers were posted on opposite sides of the same door, they would face straight ahead without speaking. Afterward, unmarried guards retired to the barracks. She could be one meter away for twelve hours and still not *see* them any more than she did now.

Not that Kuni would become a ceremonial sentinel. She would be Princess Mechtilda's right hand and personal Royal Guardswoman. Hand-selected by the princess herself, with her blessing. They'd been planning their lives together ever since they were children acting out their future roles with dolls.

As the first female guard, Kuni doubted her quarters would be with the men. Perhaps the king would give her a small room in the castle, as he'd done for her mother. Far away from the camaraderie of the Guardsmen.

But she wasn't joining for her brothers, Kuni reminded herself. In addition to keeping a vow to her ancestors, she was repaying a princess for the long hours spent training instead of earning her wages as a proper companion. She owed Mechtilda a great debt. The princess was counting on her.

Just as importantly, once Kuni was accepted into the most elite infantry unit in the land, other little girls would see her. Their future now held *choices*. The next generation of Balcovians could look very different. What could honor her country and the de Heusch legacy more than that?

When the sun started to set, she closed her guidebook. She would resume reconnaissance in the morning when the light was better.

What about Floris and Reinald? She opened a folded paper containing the copy she'd secretly made of her brothers' required appearances as Balcovian diplomats. This evening, they were to meet with the Prince Regent. By now, they would already be in the castle. Kuni ignored the pang in her chest. Next time, she would be an honored ambassador, too.

She tucked the itinerary back inside her reconnaissance notebook and turned to Elizabeth. "Shall we return to your home?"

"Must we?" Elizabeth lifted her cane. "I have good days and bad days. On bad days, I can't move. On good days, 'tis the villains who had better step out of my way. This is a good day. I don't want to waste a moment of it."

"What do you want to do?"

Elizabeth's eyes danced with mischief. "What if I said I knew the location of some brigands that upstanding Guardswomen like ourselves ought to defend helpless citizens against?"

"Do you?" Kuni said warily.

"Are you armed?"

Two daggers on her thighs and six throwing knives just inside her pelisse. "Always."

"Then we're ready for Bond Street." Elizabeth linked arms with Kuni and changed direction. "This is going to be so much fun."

Kuni narrowed her eyes. "Is this where you intercept a bullet meant for me?"

"Oh, those cocky loungers *wish* they were bold enough to try!"

"Those... what?"

"Arrogant, villainous loungers. Dreadful, ill-mannered, self-important blackguards down from university. They stroll Bond Street at twilight three or four abreast, in order to force hapless passersby off the pavement and into the muck. Oh, how they laugh!"

"What clapperclawed dung beetles!" Kuni could not imagine any such thing happening in pretty, polite Balcovia. "They sound as horrid as your filthy streets."

"Worse. They drink their spirits and swing their walking sticks and try to cause as much trouble as possible—"

"So they *are* armed."

"Armed!" Elizabeth scoffed. "All they use those sticks for is to trip better-dressed dandies and lift the skirts of mortified young women. They're armed with nothing but too much self-confidence and a complete lack of conscience. To those ruffians, boorish behavior is an amusing jest."

"Then what is our recourse?"

"Do unto *them*," Elizabeth said with a hard smile. "Trip them and force them into the muck, as they do to others. The trick is to look helpless so that they sally forth with their little sticks and big laughs. And then"—several sudden sharp swipes with her cane—"we give them a taste of their own medicine."

Kuni could find no fault in defending innocent passersby against such yellow-hearted antics, but something about Elizabeth's zeal sent the back of her neck tickling with suspicion. "Were you one of the loungers' victims?"

"I?" Elizabeth goggled at her as though Kuni had spouted *appelstroop* from her ears. Then she glanced away and sighed. "Marjorie did not hear them come up behind her. Deuced unsportsmanlike. If I had been there, I should have poked holes in every last one of them."

"Marjorie?" The tiny blond woman was barely bigger than a goose feather. "What cowards! I suppose the existence of such habitual bullies is yet more proof of England's inferiority."

"Pah," scoffed Elizabeth. "If you never leave the palace, how do you know your peasants aren't dealing with far worse?"

Elizabeth hunched suddenly, her grip on her wobbling cane unsure. Because their arms were still linked, Kuni's own posture was thrown off-kilter.

"What—"

"*Shh*," Elizabeth hissed. "Look helpless. Here they come."

Up ahead were four young bucks, bold with drink. The smug quartet formed a barrier across the entire pedestrian pavement, forcing hapless women doing their shopping to ruin their gowns by stepping into the gutter or risk darting across the street and getting struck by a carriage.

As Kuni watched in outrage, they indeed swung out their sword sticks to trip passersby who ventured too close or to lift the skirts of a fleeing maiden with tears on her face. This was celebrated with hoots of laughter loud enough to be heard over the din of horses and carriages.

"I shall deal with this," Kuni whispered. "I have a throwing knife for each of their shriveled hearts."

"I cannot believe *I'm* about to be the voice of reason," Elizabeth whispered back, "but Graham strongly advises against capital crimes on public streets. Wait until it's self-defense, but don't kill them. It will be more satisfying to see the shock on their whiny faces."

The two women crept slowly up the pavement as if oblivious to the whooping, self-congratulatory bucks. When Kuni and Elizabeth could go no farther without running headfirst into one of their dramatic neckcloths, one of the Bond Street loungers slid out his cane to trip Kuni at the same time his puffed-up crony lifted the hem of Elizabeth's skirts.

Both women sprang into action at once.

In a blur of motion, Elizabeth whipped her rapier from its bejeweled sheath and set about slicing their great clouds of neck linen into ribbons. While they attempted to defend themselves against this unforeseen threat, Kuni knocked them one by one into the muck-lined street, using her twin daggers to slice the tails from their coats as they fell.

"Now you are marked coming and going." Kuni glowered at the fallen bucks, her hands fisted around the hilts of her daggers. "Tell your friends not to pick on the helpless again, lest they wish for public humiliation."

The loungers' mouths gaped. "Where are you *from*?"

"Islington," Elizabeth snapped. She sheathed her sword and looped her arm with Kuni's. "And I have more sisters."

A cheer erupted from the gathering crowd.

"We'll be watching you." Elizabeth and Kuni held their positions on the curb, arm in arm, facing down the red-faced men in the gutters.

The loungers exchanged sheepish glances and scrambled away, trying unsuccessfully to scrub horse droppings from their yellow buckskins with their monogrammed handkerchiefs.

"There," Elizabeth said with satisfaction. "Now you have a taste of what it's like to be a Wynchester."

Kuni did not miss the murderous looks the fleeing university bucks sent over their shoulders. "I suspect we have not seen the last of the Bond Street loungers."

Elizabeth grinned. "Which means *they've* not seen the last of us. I can't wait to do it again."

17

Kuni and Elizabeth arrived back at the Wynchester home in high spirits.

A sword had arrived for Elizabeth, who immediately rushed upstairs to find a spot for her new blade.

Now that their adventures together had ended, Kuni went to her guest chamber to shrug out of her knife-lined pelisse. She tucked her surveillance notebook into her valise for safekeeping. She wished Graham were here, so she could tell him about everything that had happened. And train with him again in the rear garden. And... maybe to take that kiss they had almost shared.

The handsome rogue was everything she never thought she'd find. Fearless and talented, a force to be reckoned with, who required no aid from anyone... and wanted her beside him anyway. As an equal. As a team. Perhaps even as a lover.

Unfortunately, he was also an Englishman firmly anchored in ugly London. And Kuni... would be wherever Mechtilda was. In Balcovia, if they both were lucky. Frigid Russia, if they were not. But Kuni's place was at the princess's side, just as she'd trained for all her life. No longer would the childhood friends need toy dolls to act out a fantasy. As long as Kuni's performance in England remained above all possible reproach, the life they'd schemed and struggled for together would soon be theirs at last.

When she stepped back out of her guest chamber, Marjorie was visible on the landing, her face tilted up at the stairs, lost in thought.

Kuni strode up to her, heedless of the clatter of her boots against the floor. A Royal Guard's steps were silent, but she wasn't on duty as a Royal Guardswoman at the moment, and she wanted to catch Marjorie before she disappeared back into her studio.

After such a splendid day with Elizabeth, Kuni suspected Marjorie must be just as much fun. And, if Kuni was honest, her chest twisted longingly at the hope of spending companionable time with siblings—even if they were not her own.

These short weeks would be her one chance for such interactions. She didn't want to miss a minute of it.

Marjorie was still staring off into nothingness when Kuni approached her from the left.

She kept her voice light and low, so as not to startle Marjorie. "I had a lovely day tossing ruffians into the street with your sister."

There was no response.

Kuni tried again, louder. "I said I pummeled brigands with Elizabeth."

Marjorie didn't even blink. She continued to stare straight ahead as though Kuni were less consequential than a gnat.

As far as cuts went, Kuni had suffered this one far too many times for it to still be able to wound her. One of her brothers' favorite childhood tricks was pretending their sister wasn't right in front of their faces, begging to be noticed, to be important, to be needed.

She would not humiliate herself like that again. If Marjorie preferred to abstain from Kuni's company, then maintaining distance would be best for them both. Princess Mechtilda needed her. Kuni would be valued again soon enough.

She turned away, intending to slip past Marjorie and down to the ground floor.

Marjorie let out a high-pitched "Eep!" and stumbled back against the wall, one hand clutched to her chest.

Kuni raised her brows. "You did not hear me speaking into your ear?"

"That's the one that doesn't work right." Marjorie touched the opposite ear. "This is the good one."

"Oh." Kuni's neck and cheeks heated. It hadn't been a slight after all. Kuni was the one who owed the apology. "I am sorry for startling you."

Marjorie shook her head. "I could have warned you earlier. I do hear in that ear a little, but not when I am in noisy places, and I'm afraid you caught me in the noisiest place of all—lost in my own imagination."

"I'm sorry," Kuni said again.

This must be how mere loungers had managed to sneak up on her. An unfair advantage she was sure *they* wouldn't be sorry about at all. Kuni was doubly glad to have tossed them in the muck.

"If you want me to accept your apology, then don't act awkward about it. The reason I didn't warn you is because so many people then change how they speak, and begin talking too slow or too loudly or exaggerating their lips, all of which makes it harder to understand. As long as I'm looking at you and you're speaking normally, neither of us will have a problem."

"Sign language." The pieces fit together. "When I first

met your brother, he thought I was deaf and tried to talk to me using his hands."

Marjorie nodded. "The entire family can sign. Bean—er, Baron Vanderbean—sent me to a special school so that I could learn. The whole family learned it with me. Even some of the staff."

"Why did they, if you can hear?"

"Mostly hear," Marjorie corrected. "A childhood bout of smallpox damaged the inside of my ears. Bean wanted us to be prepared in case my hearing worsened. Luckily, it has stayed the same. And signs have proved a useful tool to have."

"I can imagine," Kuni said. "Or rather, I *cannot* imagine what trouble you Wynchesters get into that requires sign language to get you out of."

"Lots of trouble." Marjorie smiled. "Many, many times."

"Can you teach some to me?" Kuni asked eagerly, then winced. "Is that a gauche request?"

"Not gauche," Marjorie assured her. "Common. But most people haven't the patience to learn more than a sign or two, or perhaps the alphabet. I'd wager *you* would put in the effort necessary, but I fear you wouldn't find the results useful after you leave."

"Would you teach me some signs anyway?"

"That depends." Marjorie flexed her fingers as though preparing for battle. "Which words would you like to learn?"

"The ones you would suggest most useful to know."

Marjorie grinned. "In that case, yes. I should be happy to. Come upstairs with me. You can practice whilst I paint."

Kuni started to ask a question as she followed Marjorie up the stairs, then held her tongue until they were facing each other again.

Marjorie's art studio was awash in color and canvases and easels, with barely enough free room to walk or sit—save for a plush green chaise longue. Kuni wasn't certain if that was where models and visitors were invited to repose, or where Marjorie collapsed in exhaustion after spending all day and night painting. Perhaps both.

"Before we begin..." Marjorie turned to Kuni. "Signs are just as regional as spoken languages. Why learn English sign language, if the Balcovian version will be completely different?"

"It has nothing to do with Balcovia. I haven't the least notion what it must be like not to hear well, but I do know what it is like not to fully understand the conversations going on around me. Ever since I stepped off the boat. Even meals with your siblings can be impossible to follow. Sometimes I cannot make any chocolate from your fast words."

It was Marjorie's turn to look contrite. "Oh, I am so sorry. I'll tell them to—"

"Please don't," Kuni said. "It will get better. I do not want them to talk to me like I'm a baby. It *would* be easier if only one person spoke at a time, but the rest of London will remain noisy and chaotic. I want to be able to follow along. In English, and in sign language."

"It's not easy," Marjorie warned. "The grammar is distinct."

"I do not expect to become fluent overnight," Kuni promised. "I want to be able to communicate with all of you at all times. And I am not afraid of hard work."

"No, I suppose you're not." Marjorie lifted her hand and gave a decisive shake to two of her fingers.

Kuni tried it. "What does it mean?"

"'Again.' You can use this sign to ask me to repeat

something you didn't understand. And you can also interrupt my siblings to ask them to repeat themselves in English. Now it's your turn."

Obediently, Kuni made the sign for *again*.

"Not that," Marjorie said with a laugh. "Although you did very well. How do I say 'again' in Balcovian?"

"*Opnieuw*," Kuni answered. "Why?"

"You're not the only one who likes to learn new things." Marjorie's blue eyes sparkled. "And it will delight me to have a secret language even my siblings don't know. Before you leave, we must flaunt it in front of them obnoxiously."

Kuni laughed. "Then we have a trade."

"Agreed." Marjorie held out her hand.

Kuni shook it. "What are you working on up here?"

"Something to hang in the empty wing of the house we've finally started using again. So far it only hosts the Lusty Literary Ladies' reading circle—"

Kuni made the sign for *again*.

"*Opnieuw*," Marjorie said. "Philippa's bluestocking society, though she claims they don't have an official name. Do you know what a— No? All right. 'Bluestocking' means 'unfashionably bookish female,' although the term originates from literal blue stockings once worn by a man...to a woman's intellectual salon."

Kuni snorted. "At least they were not called the Powdered Wigs or the Graying Whiskers."

"Philippa doesn't care what others say. She loves books and learning, and so do her friends. She put in a library on the ground floor of the west wing, and they fill it up with noise and laughter every Thursday afternoon. The rest of the rooms are empty, and all the walls are blank. For now."

"What are you painting?"

Marjorie rocked on her heels. "A wonderful, nostalgic, only mildly embarrassing then-and-now series featuring each of my siblings."

Kuni's mouth fell open. "Show me Graham's only mildly embarrassing portrait at once."

Marjorie grinned and led her to one of the easels. "I kept all the sketches I made over the summer of 'ninety-eight, when Bean adopted us. Even if I hadn't, I would never forget my first look at each of my new siblings. I'm still working on it, but you'll get the idea."

Kuni stared at the portrait in wonder. A strong countenance gazed back at her, defiant and vulnerable.

The same flyaway crop of soft black curls, the same golden bronze skin, the same quick brown eyes in a face that looked barely nine or ten years old. His clothes were unpainted and the background was indistinct, causing his hopeful-yet-wary expression to stand out all the more.

"That is incredible." Kuni could not tear her gaze away. "I can imagine him just like this."

"Here's Chloe's." Marjorie pulled her to a pair of canvases. "Her before-and-after is complete."

Kuni could not suppress a grin. Young Chloe's clothes had been painted in, as had the background, but with a monochromatic palette of cream and tan and beige. The effect should have been blurry and forgettable, but instead served to highlight Chloe's pretty face and the startling intensity of her sharp gaze. That was then.

In her "now" portrait, Chloe was a veritable kaleidoscope of color. She also wasn't alone. The Duke of Faircliffe stood beside her, his puppy-love eyes only for his wife.

"I'm working on Tommy and Philippa's now," Marjorie

said. "You and I can teach each other words as I paint. Hand me the puce?"

Kuni's eyes widened. She made the sign for *again*.

"It's a brownish-pinkish-purple version of Balcovian amaranth. And I was just testing to see if you remembered the sign. I'll arrange my own palette. You can sit on the chaise longue and tell me how to say 'color.'"

"Kleur."

Marjorie's eyes lit up. "But that's easy!"

"Do not worry," Kuni assured her dryly. "The rest of the words won't be."

An hour passed in a blur of English and Balcovian and sign language.

Kuni hadn't known it was possible to spend happy moments indoors at home like this, until the Wynchesters welcomed her into their circle. They made her feel like a unique and whole person in a way she never had with her own family. The way Kuni longed to be welcomed into the Royal Guard by her brothers.

"So," Marjorie said as she swiped her brush across the canvas. "You and Graham..."

Kuni almost choked. "No," she protested quickly. "Nothing scandalous is happening."

Mostly not. He *might* have kissed her, and she *would* have kissed him, had the butler not spoiled the moment. And she *had* lain on top of him in the garden, then allowed him to do the same to her. But mutual interest did not imply more than a temporary flirtation. This would lead nowhere.

"Why not?" Marjorie crossed her arms. "Is something wrong with Graham?"

"Nothing at all," Kuni said with feeling. "But I return home in four weeks and he will remain here. There is no sense starting an affair that cannot last."

"So you've thought about it." Marjorie turned and daubed paint against the canvas. "Interesting."

"No—I mean—" Kuni took a deep breath. "I might marry one day, but it will be to a fellow Royal Guardsman, who keeps similar hours and sleeps in the same barracks."

"I never mentioned marriage," Marjorie said. "More and more interesting."

"No... I..." *Must change the subject at once.* "I want the next generation of girls like me to be able to follow in my footsteps," Kuni babbled. "Balcovia is very forward-thinking in many ways, but the sexes have not reached parity. Once I'm a Royal Guardswoman, that will change forever."

"Mm-hmm," said Marjorie. "So when I ask about my brother, your first two thoughts are marriage and children."

"No—" Kuni tried again. "Those are the first two thoughts put in every Balcovian female's head. The only thoughts we're instructed to have. In my specific case, my brothers expect me to toss my wooden shoe after an actual royal."

"Because they are proud of you?"

"Because they would be done with their duty," Kuni replied flatly. "If I outrank them, they could wash their hands of me. They wouldn't think me important unless I were a princess... or become their equal."

"Which is why you want to be a Royal Guardswoman? So that your brothers are forced to acknowledge and respect you?"

"No," Kuni said automatically. "The Royal Guard is Balcovia's most elite, noble, and prestigious—"

"But mostly because of your brothers, right?" Marjorie

added a flourish to the canvas. "How certain are you this plan will work? I don't mean becoming a Guardswoman. If you want to be one, I'm certain that you will. But will it do the trick?"

"Do you mean, will my brothers see me as an equal or just their sister in a costume?" Kuni asked tightly.

When the *king* found her worthy, everyone would have to respect her. Even her own family. Besides, there was no longer anyone's attention to fight over. Mother had died long before. Father, three short years ago. He had been alive to see Floris and Reinald achieve their rank. Her brothers had nothing to prove anymore. It was Kuni who had not been given the same opportunities and support. After she did it anyway, making the Royal Guard all on her own, Floris and Reinald would be forced not just to acknowledge her talent, but also the potential of all the other aspiring Guardswomen. The de Heusch legacy would double overnight.

"What about you?" Kuni asked. "You're not following the usual path, either. You are how old and unmarried?"

"Almost thirty," Marjorie said with pride. "I will *never* get a vaunted Almack's voucher."

"What," Kuni asked, "is an Almack?"

"An exceedingly boring place where everyone always does exactly what's expected of them. It has more rules and traditions than your Royal Guard."

"I shall take pride in undertaking my noble task day after day," Kuni said stiffly. "I can think of no better future than one spent dedicated to guarding the princess, as I have promised."

"Can you not?" Marjorie swirled her paintbrush in turpentine. "I wonder."

18

Because Graham and his brother sat in the carriage facing backward, he could not watch their approach into Islington without twisting around and craning his neck. He attempted neither. Graham already received sufficient teasing from his siblings about his fear of missing something interesting…and the implication that who he was missing was Kunigunde.

After a long week, the four were almost home, and they brought a petition with well over a thousand signatures. They ought to be tired, but the success of the mission filled them all with energy. After a quick bath and something to eat, they would be off again—this time, scattered in different directions.

Tommy and Philippa would head straight to Parliament to give Chloe the good news. The Duke of Faircliffe and Philippa's father were already recruiting MPs with influence to talk to their voters about staging an event to bring awareness to the cause. Now Mr. York could present a motion for immediate change in the House of Commons. Jacob could not wait to visit his barn.

As for Graham…He'd promised Kunigunde a romantic

supper for two. He hoped she planned to accept his offer. Before he'd left, Graham was certain they'd almost kissed. He'd been looking forward to another chance ever since.

Graham was already out the door before the carriage rolled to a stop. There was still an hour of sunlight left, and his limbs were tired of sitting still. He stretched his arms as he jogged to the front door. He would have climbed the exterior wall straight to his bedchamber for a bath, but could not resist the temptation to poke his head into the sitting room to see who might be home.

Elizabeth reclined on one of the sofas, surrounded by a mountain of cushions, two sword sticks, and a pitcher of arrack punch. His chest tightened with sympathy.

"How are you feeling?" He walked closer to get a better look at her.

Sometimes her bad spells were only for a few hours. Other times, they lasted for days. All the doctors could do was prescribe rest, laudanum, and bloodletting.

Elizabeth refused to allow anyone to spill a drop of her blood, but she had no choice about having a rest. Her body would let her know when it was ready to be active again.

"Ugh," she said. "I've been prostrate since last evening. I hate missing all the excitement."

His blood quickened. "Do we have another case?"

"No."

He waited for more information, but it was not forthcoming. "Was there some sort of adventure?"

"Adventures all week." She shifted on her pillows to reach for her glass of punch. "How was your mission? Did you collect signatures from every living creature in the region?"

Jacob, Tommy, and Philippa arrived in time to hear the question.

"Almost," Philippa answered with pride. "Some of the

ones still employed at the manufactory were afraid to sign, lest they lose their livelihoods, and of course we did not take signatures from small children."

"And large children?" Elizabeth asked.

"If they're old enough to be eligible for employment, they're old enough to have an opinion on the exploitation of their labor," Jacob said. "We let anyone sign who was willing to. Previous employees need not fear retribution and were all eager to sign."

"Whilst Graham led the reconnaissance," Tommy said, "Philippa arranged for a team of dozens to knock on every door they could. She has done this sort of thing for her father before and was brilliant at leading the charge."

Philippa smiled. "Thank you. Most petitions never reach more than a few hundred names, even here in London. The population of Tipford-upon-Bealbrook is fewer than six thousand."

"How many people signed the petition?"

Tommy grinned. "One thousand five hundred."

Elizabeth looked impressed. "Brilliant work!"

"We'll take the petition to Chloe as soon as we've freshened up." Philippa linked her fingers with Tommy's. "Shall we?"

Whatever Tommy whispered in her ear had Philippa's cheeks blushing pink, and they disappeared from the salon without delay.

The other siblings grinned at each other.

"Lovebirds." Elizabeth shook her head. "If I didn't have a heart of stone, I should find it deeply romantic."

"You do find it deeply romantic," Graham assured her. "You just don't want to admit it."

"What are the next steps?" Elizabeth asked as if he hadn't spoken.

"Faircliffe will meet with Philippa's father in the morning," Jacob said. "After that, its speed depends upon the House of Commons."

Elizabeth's lips twisted in frustration. "Is there nothing we can do in the meantime?"

"Spoken like someone with a soft heart," Jacob whispered to Graham.

Elizabeth glowered at him.

"Unfortunately, not at the moment," Graham answered. "Most workers are terrified of retaliation by Mr. Throckmorten. At the slightest sign of disloyalty or insubordination, he won't hesitate to eject an entire family from their posts."

"We'd give every worker enough gold to avoid cotton mills for generations if we could," Jacob said. "But there are hundreds at this manufactory and thousands more just like it. England needs bigger change than we can implement on our own."

"Then I hope Parliament moves swiftly," Elizabeth said fervently.

"As do we all." Jacob glanced down at his wrinkled clothing. "If you'll excuse me, I must visit the barn before my bath arrives and goes cold."

Graham waited for his brother to leave the sitting room before asking Elizabeth the question that had been burning in his chest from the moment he arrived home.

"Where's Kunigunde?"

Elizabeth harrumphed and leaned back against her pillows. "Probably with Marjorie. They're thick as thieves now. All full of private jests and giggles."

Graham blinked. He could not imagine Kunigunde giggling, or quiet Marjorie spending hours in chatty conversation. But most of all, he had never witnessed his sister Elizabeth ever once express a wish to become close friends with a non-Wynchester.

"You're not...*jealous*, are you?" he asked carefully.

"Jealous!" She shot up, grimaced, then sank back into the pillows, glaring at him as though this lapse was his fault as well. "*I* spend more time with Kunigunde than Marjorie does. They have only the evenings together, whereas Kunigunde and *I* spend all day in armed reconnaissance."

"You do?" His muscles stiffened. "I thought she didn't want help."

Elizabeth stared at him as though he were dotty. "I don't *help* her. Why would I help her? She can do anything."

The opposite of a forlorn princess in want of a knight or a more lasting flirtation.

"I don't doubt her ability to achieve her mission. But it will take every minute of her time here." Time that she wouldn't be able to spend with Graham—or even enjoying England. "It's an inefficient use of her limited resources when we've got the answers she seeks over there on the wall."

"That's what I thought," Elizabeth said. "But it isn't any faster. Nobody but you can fathom the method to your madness. Except maybe Philippa. She made a wonderful filing system for Tommy. You should ask her to do the same for you. It would take me years to sort through all those journals, but Philippa could probably finish by Friday."

He glanced at the tall shelves of thick albums. Between a lifetime of recordkeeping and his clandestine mission for the Crown, the information Kunigunde needed *was* in there. But Elizabeth was right. Useful details were buried amongst thousands of pages of intelligence unrelated to Kunigunde's needs.

"Here's the situation," Elizabeth said. "You want to help her, and she doesn't want your help. There's only one way for you both to win."

He stepped back in surprise. "There *is* a way?"

"You create the report you're dying to build," his sister answered. "You're the only one who knows where to find the information. Begin a new album—you know you love to—and prepare the most comprehensive compendium the King of Balcovia could ever desire."

Graham was already halfway finished with the compendium he was to deliver to his government. Making a copy of the most salient points for Kunigunde would not take much more effort.

"And then I give it to her?"

"And then you *don't* give it to her. She doesn't want or need it. But the reason Balcovian envoys are here is because their royal family is visiting in the near future. *That's* who you might impress."

But not Kunigunde, apparently. "I would have better luck impressing the King of Balcovia?"

"You know better than anyone that reconnaissance is not a onetime task, but an ongoing process. When His Balcovian Majesty arrives, his information will be out of date. And you will just happen to have the solution."

"You think I should create the same thing Kunigunde is…but not tell her," he repeated. "Then later, I bring my intelligence to her king, and somehow become a Balcovian favorite in the process?"

"Exactly!" Elizabeth beamed at him. "If anyone can do it, it's the man who knows everything and can infiltrate anything. You'll just pop in with the exact information His Highness lacks. He'll have no choice but to officially recognize the undisputed brilliance of Graham Wynchester."

At which point...Kunigunde might recognize his worth, too. "I can't tell if your advice is brilliant or cork-brained."

She nodded sagely. "That's how most of my advice goes."

"She asked us not to help," Graham reminded her. "And I wouldn't want Kunigunde to think I was trying to upstage her with her own kingdom."

"Even at the cost of potentially meeting those royals in person?" She stared at him. "You're not falling in love, are you?"

"Anything worth doing requires falling first," he said. "But I am far too nimble to take such a tumble."

"No falling for me. I will sit right here, drinking punch and gin."

Graham grinned at her, then bounded up the stairs to his bedchamber. He was tempted to peek into Marjorie's studio to see if she really was giggling with Kunigunde, but he wanted to look his best first.

He bathed, shaved, and selected fashionable evening attire: a coat of gray superfine and a waistcoat of celestial blue. As soon as his neckcloth was tied to perfection, he hurried upstairs toward his sister's studio in search of Kunigunde.

Marjorie was alone...and acting strangely. When she saw him approach, she threw a tarp over an easel and ran to close the door until only one blue eye peeked through.

"I'm busy," she said through the crack.

"Have you seen Kunigunde?" he asked before Marjorie could slam the door in his face.

"Not since breakfast. She finished the grand houses days ago and started surveillance on other locales. No, I haven't seen the Balcovian royal family's confidential itinerary. Kunigunde could be anywhere from Piccadilly to Brighton and likely won't return until well after nightfall. Goodbye."

The door closed.

Well. That was more information than Graham had previously had, but still disappointing. It did not sound as though tonight was the night for a romantic dinner after all.

He trudged back down the stairs. To be fair, it wasn't as though Kunigunde should be waiting around for him. He hadn't even known exactly which day he would return. And he *had* known she would be busy.

But he had too much pent-up energy to relax. Perhaps he would practice his acrobatics. It had been an entire week since the last time he climbed the outside of a building or performed flips on horseback. Such restraint had been torture. Perhaps he could string up one of his high ropes from the house to the barn and—

"There you are!" Jacob caught up with him halfway down the stairs. "Just the man I was looking for. Do you want to go on a rescue mission with me?"

"*Yes*," Graham said with feeling, then immediately grew suspicious. "To rescue a 'who' or a 'what'?"

"To rescue little Ralphie," Jacob answered with far too much innocence.

"And what," Graham asked politely, "is Ralphie?"

"An...antbear," Jacob admitted.

An *antbear*. It sounded simultaneously very large and very small.

"He's incarcerated in the Royal Menagerie," Jacob explained in a rush, "and mistreated even worse than the other animals. Most of the inmates don't last above a few years, even when normal life expectancy is in the decades.

Remember how that monkey died after only six weeks behind bars?"

Graham closed his eyes. "You want to rescue an antbear called Ralphie from the Tower of London."

At least it was a castle. Perhaps there would be a princess inside in actual need of rescue.

"There's only one keeper of the menagerie," Jacob continued. "You know what a clueless, self-absorbed rotter he is. After all the lion maulings, the visitors are meant to stay on the other side of the rail from the animals, but he lets everyone poke through the bars with sticks. He has neither the inclination nor the least idea how to keep an antbear alive, much less healthy."

"And of course you do."

Jacob's eyes shone. "Of course. There are actually multiple different types of antbear. The first is also known as an 'aard-varken' or 'earth-pig'..."

Graham stopped listening.

He'd known before asking that Jacob could present a four-hour speech on the care and feeding of antbears at the drop of a feather. He would have suggested his brother simply take over the post of Keeper of the Royal Menagerie, if it weren't for Jacob's aversion to the entire practice.

Graham also knew exactly what his brother was about to say to rope him in.

"...and I know you feel the same as I do about living creatures held captive against their will," Jacob finished. "I'm going regardless, so it's up to you if you wish to miss out on the adventure."

A perfect one-two punch. Graham would rescue the lions and the tiger, too, with that argument.

"All right," he said. "But I want to be home at a reasonable hour for supper."

Jacob grinned. "Then grab your tools. I've already called for a carriage and fresh horses."

In less than an hour, they were at the Tower of London. The menagerie closed at sunset, which meant the gates should shut at any moment.

As soon as the last family left, the guard locked the iron gate and retreated from sight. Graham and Jacob waited another quarter hour, though caution was likely unnecessary.

For gatekeepers of public attractions such as these, the duty period ended after the last visitor left each day. Staff enjoyed room and board on a different section of the property, and wasted no time heading to the refectory for a hot meal and a few pints of ale. A sole guard remained to walk the grounds. The interior corridors would be empty until morning.

Nonetheless, the brothers had no intention of entering where they might be seen. There was a long stretch of wall left unguarded between the menagerie gates and the Jewel House. Graham scaled it easily, then tossed a rope down to haul up his brother.

"Tell me more about your supper plans," Jacob said. "Do they involve a certain Balcovian warrioress?"

Graham had made the mistake of confiding Elizabeth's ungifted intelligence journal scheme in the carriage, and that Graham was still searching for a way to woo Kunigunde openly.

"If I'm lucky, I'll eventually have that romantic dinner," he answered. "I don't suppose you'd pen a few lines of poetry for me to sweeten the offer?"

Jacob looked horrified. "Never pass someone else's words off as your own. I am fully on Kunigunde's side in this matter. Besides, you're already writing her a poem."

Graham stuffed the rope back in his satchel. "I am?"

"You are if you take Elizabeth's advice. What else would you call an album crafted with such care? It's poetry in *your* words. You never loan your journals out of the family. You're giving your jealously guarded intelligence to *her* king. That's practically a lover's-eye locket with a curl of your hair inside."

"But she wouldn't know I was doing it," Graham reminded him.

Jacob snorted. "Do you think all poetry finds itself into the hands of its inspiration?"

"A fair point," Graham said. "I guess it would be a poetry album of sorts, then. But I'm not doing it. Kunigunde's king would judge her—"

He flung out an arm to halt his brother and pulled him into a shadowy recess of the stone wall.

Soft footsteps were coming in their direction.

"I thought you said all the interior guards go for an ale in the staff refectory after visiting hours conclude," Jacob whispered.

Graham elbowed him in the ribs to be silent.

This corridor should be empty until morning. But of course, even the most meticulous reconnaissance could only track the way things *normally* were. Anything could happen. And now an out-of-place guard was going to pass within inches of them.

Perhaps the Jewel House visitors had lingered after sunset. Perhaps the black panther had escaped entirely on his own. Perhaps—

A woman stepped into view. "What are *you* doing here?"

"Kunigunde?" Graham said in disbelief.

19

Kuni stared at Graham in wonder. There in the alcove, he looked unspeakably dashing in a soft gray coat that molded to his muscles, accented by a silk waistcoat as blue as a Balcovian sky. Oh, his brother was there, too, and almost as handsome, but it was Graham who had consumed Kuni's every thought whenever she didn't have Marjorie or Elizabeth to distract her—and even sometimes when she did. Ever since Kuni had let him pin her to the grass in the garden instead of breaking free.

Graham had that effect on her. He made her feel like she was the center of his attention. Like there was nowhere he'd rather be, nothing he wished she was doing, other than sharing her breath with him. As though having her near him was enough. Like *Kuni* was enough.

He made her want to stay right where she was. On her back. In his arms.

Then there was that moment, right before he left. The moment when she was certain he had been about to kiss her.

The interrupted kiss had hung between them ever since, stretching from Islington all the way to Manchester. Taut and invisible, binding her to him no matter how hard she tried to shake free.

And now here he was. Hiding in a dark hollow of a shadowy castle, dressed in evening attire almost fit for a royal outing—save for the leather satchel draped across one shoulder. Not that it detracted. He looked rakish and dangerous, and delicious enough to lick. Either her memory had not done him justice or absence had made the charming rogue even handsomer.

"What are you doing here?" she asked again.

"We're on a rescue mission," he answered.

"For poor little Ralphie, who is counting on us." Even in the dim light of a sconce, Jacob's gaze looked distant and tortured. "He should never have been taken from his home. He's barely three years old and must be confused and frightened. We *have* to transport him somewhere safe."

Kuni didn't realize until she'd heard their explanation that a silly little part of her had hoped Graham had come in search of *her*. Of course he hadn't. The Tower guards didn't even know she was here. How would Graham? He was so freshly bathed, his hair was still damp. They must have come straight here after arriving home to find another client waiting for them.

Leave it to a Wynchester not to pausc for a moment's rest between a week of battling the country's laws and rescuing a small child in danger.

But Graham's eyes were only for her. "What are *you* doing here, Princess?"

"Testing the Tower's security. I entered through the Jewel House behind a group of visitors eager to see the Crown Jewels. Your guards should all be replaced. They should not have let me wander off."

"Were there multiple guards?" he asked with interest. "Usually there's only one."

"Exactly. How is he to keep a proper eye on anything?

He could scarcely keep the crowd back from the jewels. Did you know that insubstantial little rail has only recently been installed? Three years ago, someone just walked up and calmly destroyed the State Crown!"

"I did know," Graham said. "I conducted an extensive interview with the woman who did it. She wasn't the least bit calm."

Jacob sent his brother a pointed look. "We're on a rescue mission. Not a teatime chat."

"Right." Graham's eyes sparkled at Kuni. "Want to help?"

Her breath caught. Or perhaps that was from the intoxicating scent of his freshly bathed body, scant centimeters before her. She yearned to touch the silk of his waistcoat, to feel his hard muscles beneath the soft superfine covering his arms and shoulders.

And...she *did* want to help. More than anything. She yearned to be an important asset, but was never asked to be part of the team—until Graham. He made her feel valued. With him, she didn't have to prove herself. He wanted her fighting by his side. Was fully confident anything he could do, she could learn to do, too.

This time, she had no excuse to reject the offer to join him. She'd already confirmed what she had long suspected: British security was horrid. If Kuni could sneak off through the tower, so could a villain. Or a stampede of wild bison. She'd watched from an arrow-slit as the guard closed the gate and left. He wasn't even *looking* for a missing guest.

"Well?" Graham asked softly. "Do you want to be part of the team, if only just this once?"

Her heart galloped beneath her hidden epaulet. "I do. Very much. Thank you for inviting me."

"Follow me." Jacob stepped out of the alcove and turned down the stone corridor.

Kuni didn't move.

Neither did Graham.

This felt like the moment they'd shared before, when they might've kissed goodbye. It felt like a second chance.

Kuni bit her lip. "Before your brother turns back or we get interrupted again..."

How could she possibly resist him?

He saw her. He invited her. He wanted her, even if he didn't need her. He found her capable... and desirable.

She flung her arms about his neck and kissed him.

His strong arms enveloped her at once, pulling her even more snugly against him. A thick leather strap ran crosswise over his chest, and the starchy explosion of linen at his throat crumpled against her, but she had never felt more at ease than in his arms.

No matter how much her brain warned her that this infatuation could go nowhere, she felt as though she'd rather the fortress tumble down around them than end this sweet kiss.

It was Graham who pulled away, with clear reluctance. "We have to follow Jacob. I don't know what they've done to Ralphie."

"You? Not know something?" she teased, her heart beating far too fast.

"No one could know more about Ralphie than Jacob." He took her hand in his.

They raced down the stone corridor in search of Jacob and the small child in danger, keeping their footfalls as silent as possible.

"This way to the menagerie." Graham motioned to an opening so narrow, it almost looked like a boarded arrow slit.

Instead, it was a little pocket that ran parallel to the corridor, then divided in two directions.

They crept along the outer edge sideways for about a hundred meters before the crevice widened again. They were now above a wide, ill-lit chamber full of large iron cages and the unmistakable scent of animal dung.

Graham tugged her hand. "Stairs are over here."

Jacob was *inside* one of the cages, its iron door ajar behind him. He was lifting a small...large...Well, there was no way to judge its appearance when Kuni hadn't the least notion what she was looking at.

The creature appeared to be some sort of cat-sized rat thing with furry legs, a bald head and back, long pointy ears, and an even longer and pointier snout with pig nostrils at the tip.

"What does that thing have to do with Ralphie?" she asked.

Graham cleared his throat. "Er...it *is* Ralphie."

"What?"

Jacob pressed the cat-rat-pointy-pig-thing to his waistcoat. He began to wrap an enormous scarf around them both, swaddling the creature to his chest.

"Ralphie...isn't human?" Kuni managed weakly.

Jacob glanced up from his swaddling. "Ralphie is an antbear."

"Well, now I've bought a cat in the bag." She spun toward Graham. "I thought we were rescuing a child!"

He held up his palms. "I said 'menagerie'!"

"I don't know what a 'menagerie' *is*!"

She took a longer look around her. Her guidebook mentioned a display of wild beasts in the west tower. She'd paid little attention because there was no chance of the royal family visiting livestock. She couldn't imagine what the Wynchesters were doing here, either.

"Ralphie needs us," Jacob said. "What could be more defenseless than a baby antbear who—"

"Of all the waggish flummery..." Kuni pointed at the odd-looking creature. "That thing is not a client!"

"We help the helpless, full stop. No living thing in need is undeserving of aid."

She turned her disbelieving gaze to Graham, whose lips were clamped shut as though to hold back a tide of laughter.

His eyes showed his amusement. "If you find Ralphie peculiar, I have bad news for you about all the other animals living on the Wynchester estate."

"Oh, very well," Kuni said. "Which way do we go?"

"Back the way you came?" Jacob suggested.

She shook her head. "There is no getting back into the Jewel House. The guard was responsible enough to secure the door I slipped through. I checked for weaknesses. How did you two enter?"

"Scaled the wall," Graham answered.

Of course he had. She could see how doing so in reverse with an antbear clutched to one's chest might prove difficult.

"We can go out through the west entrance." He gestured at a bag of tools strapped to Jacob's side.

She raised her brows. "Won't we risk being seen?"

Jacob removed an oversized woolen cloak from his leather satchel. "I'll wrap this about myself. Hunched over with my face hidden, I can pretend to be Graham's pregnant wife. If anyone sees us, I moan alarmingly, he looks appropriately panicked, and we scurry out in the confusion."

"That is a ludicrous idea," Kuni said.

"We've done it dozens of times," Graham assured her. "Nothing scatters grown men faster than the thought of witnessing a strange woman giving birth."

"And we're Black," Jacob added. "The browner your skin, the less inclined people are to help you."

"What a dreadful country. In Balcovia—"

"—only white kings rule," Graham finished dryly. "Your country was founded by abolitionists, which is enviable, and you are practically royalty yourself, which is...frankly, also enviable. But can you honestly say the color of a Balcovian's skin does not affect how they are treated?"

A thousand overheard comments and "politely"—as well as *impolitely*—worded slights flashed in her memory. Usually from visiting dignitaries...but not always.

"Of course she can't say Balcovia is a perfect utopia," Jacob said. "She lives in a palace. She has no idea what life for common folk is like."

"But I do know what my life is like," Kuni said quietly. "And you are right. Both of you. It's a terrible truth and a feasible plan. I will do whatever you need."

"Thank you."

"It is my honor." In fact, her blood was already rushing at the prospect of *doing* something to help another. Not standing sentinel in silence but diving in headfirst as her great-great-grandfather Willem had done all those years earlier. "Who shall I pretend to be if we're stopped?"

"You can be the midwife," Graham said. "I have no idea what we'd all be doing visiting a menagerie when my dear wife ought to be resting—"

Kuni tried not to picture him doting on a pregnant wife. She wouldn't be here to witness it. Some Englishwoman would be the one to welcome children into Graham's life. Kuni would be glad to miss the happy tidings.

"Well, my baby is coming early," Jacob said. "The midwife insisted I exercise my legs, and I have a fondness for animals."

"Will the antbear stay calm?" she asked.

"Ralphie's asleep already. He'll be as quiet as a—" Jacob moved away from them and hurried toward another cage. "Look what they've done to Lady Leonatus!"

"No," Graham said. "We are not taking an eagle with us."

"They clipped her wings," his brother said in outrage. "Clipped an *eagle*. She lives to hunt and fly! And she's stuffed into a cage the size of my armoire. We cannot leave her behind to wither and die like this."

"And you cannot strap a bird of prey to your chest," Graham said.

Jacob already had tools in hand to open the cage.

"Stop him," Kuni hissed.

"It's a lost cause," Graham whispered back. "He adores birds and is always rehabilitating and releasing injured ones. There is no chance of Lady Leonatus staying here."

"But she will eat Ralphie if they are strapped next to each other," Kuni protested.

Graham sent her an expectant look.

"No. You are an unmitigated parsnip if you think for one second..." She swung her gaze toward his brother.

Jacob gazed back at her plaintively.

"Oh, all right," she grumbled and inched closer to the open eagle cage. "Give me Ralphie, and you take Lady Leonatus under your cloak. We are Wynchesters, here to help the helpless."

Which was how Kunigunde, companion to the princess and future noble Royal Guardswoman, found herself creeping out of a British fortress after nightfall with an antbear strapped to her chest.

They were spotted only after unlocking the gate. The trio took off running down the dark street, a lone guard trailing far behind.

A groom leapt down from an unmarked carriage at the corner. He made rapid hand signs. Graham answered in kind. Grinning, the groom rushed forward to bundle Kuni inside the coach. Graham and Jacob were beside her before she could blink.

The carriage tore down the cobblestones at speed.

Safe with their feathered and furry clients, the trio looked at one another and burst into laughter.

"Put it in your report," Graham suggested. "'Security so lax, I entered the Jewel House and walked out of the Tower of London with an eagle and an antbear.'"

She chuckled. "No one will believe me. *I* don't even believe me."

"Have Marjorie sketch a picture of you to immortalize the moment," Jacob offered. "Something to remember today by."

"I don't think I will ever forget today," Kuni answered. She sneaked a glance at Graham.

His fingers brushed against hers. He knew exactly which moments she would relive whenever she thought back. Not the eagle. Not the antbear.

Training together in the garden. The kiss they'd finally taken. The heat of his embrace.

She swallowed hard and forced herself to pull her hand away. She could not fall for him. She *could not*. As he'd pointed out repeatedly, they already knew when and how their flirtation would end.

They could never share more than kisses.

20

Although Kuni ostensibly spent most of the next day in reconnaissance for her report to the Balcovian king—then at her escritoire, filling intelligence albums with pages of detail—her mind would not stop replaying the events of the previous night.

Not just her mind. Her entire body remembered how it felt to have Graham's mouth pressed against hers.

She also relived how boggled she had felt to discover the abducted child was a baby antbear, and to rescue him anyway. How free it felt to flee across cobblestones with a sleeping antbear swaddled to her chest and tumble into the Wynchesters' carriage with all the humans bubbling over with laughter.

It was unlike anything she'd ever experienced before. And the opposite of being a Royal Guard. Instead of standing still, staid and stern, facing forward, spine straight, silent for days, weeks, months...It had been a full hour of nonstop fun.

She was no longer surprised. The Wynchesters were like that.

Every moment scouting estates with Elizabeth was

full of high jinks and hilarity, as were the long evenings sparring with swords. Marjorie was just as funny, with her secret projects and paint-streaked everything. Their many conversations ended as often as not with tears of laughter running down both women's faces. And every unforgettable minute she'd shared with Graham...

The problem wasn't that Jacob's suggestion to ask Marjorie to commemorate a favorite moment in a painting was a *bad* idea. It was that Kuni wanted to keep *all* the moments.

Like the one unfolding before her, for example. Philippa was currently hosting what she referred to as a "reading circle" but which appeared to be an excuse for two dozen ladies to set their books beneath their chairs and fill their hands with food and wine. There was even a plaque on the door that read:

THE AGNES & KATHERINE LIBRARY
FOR WOMEN WHO CAN ACCOMPLISH ANYTHING

The gathering was marvelous. Kuni had never seen anything like it.

When the ladies glimpsed her peering at them from the corridor, two of the women dragged her into the sunny library. A third handed her a glass of Madeira as if they'd been waiting for Kuni to join them all along.

The rest of the young ladies were seated in a large oval. Most appeared to be aristocratic, white, and wealthy, like Philippa, although there was one whose skin was a beautiful tawny brown. They were all clearly delighted to be in one another's company. There were so many conversations going on at once, Kuni gave up on following the threads and just watched.

This, too, was the opposite of the formal gatherings Kuni accompanied the princess to. Oh, to be sure, Princess Mechtilda had a naughty streak and a wicked sense of humor, but she wasn't allowed to display it publicly. Kuni suspected the princess would have sold her best tiara to spend a single afternoon in company such as this.

The fashionable young lady with the pretty brown skin and freckled cheeks bounded up to her. "I'm Florentia. Where's your *Vindication*?"

"Uh," Kuni stalled. "My what?"

"*A Vindication of the Rights of Woman*, by Mary Wollstonecraft."

Kuni cleared her throat. "Mary . . . who did you say?"

The conversations closest to them hushed.

Florentia looked horrified. "Mary Wollstonecraft. Who wrote the most important political and philosophical treatise of female education in the past century."

Kuni's face heated. "I . . . seem to have missed that one."

"We will solve this at once," Florentia assured her, and held out an open hand behind her. "Who has a spare *Vindication*?"

Half of the room leapt up to be the first to offer Kuni their copy of the book.

Her cheeks flushed again, but for a different reason. Her ignorance didn't matter. The friendly bluestockings had no intention of rejecting her as an outsider for failing to recognize their esteemed author of the month. They wanted her to feel welcome. To have access to what they had. To know what they knew. To be part of their group.

Just like Graham.

"It's all right," Kuni mumbled. She waved away the books and handed back her glass. "Thank you for the wine. I cannot stay."

She ran from the room before they could tempt her with tea cakes and friendship.

Because Kuni *couldn't* stay. She was a de Heusch—a future Guard. The best of the best. Princess Mechtilda needed her, and Kuni had a legacy to fulfill.

It was going to be hard enough to walk away from the Wynchesters. She was doing her best not to dwell on the impending moment when she must say farewell to Graham forever. Just the thought filled her belly with a deep ache.

The most foolish thing she could do would be to collect even *more* people she could not keep.

She hurried up the stairs toward Marjorie's art studio, which had lately become a refuge for Kuni, too. But when she reached the first-floor landing, she heard Marjorie's voice from down the hallway.

Kuni turned toward the sound of lively conversation. Bright sunlight and laughter spilled into the corridor. The door to Tommy's dressing chamber was wide open. Marjorie said the room often doubled as an impromptu theater, as the siblings loved to watch her transform into someone else.

Was another mission afoot?

Intrigued despite herself, Kuni casually—if as slow as a shield toad—began to stroll toward the open doorway. After all, her bedchamber was down the hall. It was perfectly unexceptionable for her to walk past, and perhaps accidentally glance inside.

It wasn't as though she were angling to be invited on another adventure. She did not have time. They all knew it. She wasn't part of their family. They all knew that, too.

But yesterday had been so *fun*. Her blood had rushed with exhilaration, her strong arms and fast legs useful for something other than standing still.

Perhaps it was better if she didn't peep in on them. The Wynchesters' madcap exploits were just one more thing Kuni knew better than to get used to.

But it was too late. Marjorie was already motioning Kuni into the chaotic dressing room.

Only Marjorie and Tommy were inside. Well, Marjorie, Tommy, the large family cat—called Tiglet—and approximately five hundred articles of clothing, most of which appeared to have escaped their armoires and were now strewn haphazardly over the floor, the chairs, the mirrors, the dressing table, the windowsill, and every other surface.

Marjorie held out a plate of biscuits. "Tommy's cleaning her room."

"She...is?" Kuni accepted a biscuit and stared into the tempest doubtfully. "What did it look like before?"

"Overripe fruit," Tommy said. "All five wardrobes, full to bursting."

"Is that not what wardrobes are *for*, in England? To store clothing?"

"Oh, to be sure," Tommy answered. "But I have new things I need to fit inside and no room for them."

Marjorie turned to Kuni. "About once a year—or whenever there's more costumes than space—Tommy goes through everything she has and determines which items she no longer needs. We donate anything that makes sense for children to orphanages, and most other items to the Women's Employment Charity in St. Giles. Everything else goes to local theaters."

"Could you...purchase another armoire?" Kuni asked.

Tommy whirled toward her sister. "See? I told you it was a sound idea!"

"No," Marjorie told Tommy firmly, then turned back to Kuni. "Another wardrobe won't fit in this room. If Tommy were left to her own devices, she'd fill the entire *house* with costumes."

"I don't see why she couldn't," Kuni said. "Not the whole house, but what of the unused wing? The only thing in it is Philippa's library. Surely there is room for a wardrobe or two?"

Tommy dashed forward, only to trip over a pile of boots and sprawl face-first into a veritable mountain of livery and gowns. She extricated herself from tentacles of shirtsleeves and hair ribbons and took Kuni's hands. "Marry my brother so that you can have a vote!"

The air wheezed from Kuni's lungs at the thought of keeping Graham forever. She could not draw breath, much less make words.

Luckily, Tommy barreled on without pause. "So far, it's you and me and Philippa who think I should definitely have all the disguises I want. Graham might vote however you do, and since Jacob has an entire *barn* full of creatures—"

"That's a selfish motivation for matrimony," Marjorie scolded her sister. "Graham and Kuni should both be free to marry anyone they please, without being influenced by the fate of your costume collection."

"Think it over," Tommy whispered, and waded back through her piles of clothes.

Kuni would think of nothing else. Try as she might.

"My art studio is smaller than this dressing room," Marjorie reminded her sister.

"Paintbrushes are smaller than wigs," Tommy shot back.

"You could knock down an adjoining wall or two in the empty wing and build an even bigger studio for your art," Kuni suggested. "Unless you have an empty room upstairs next to the studio you already have?"

Marjorie stared at her. "Tommy's right. You should definitely have a vote at the family meetings."

Kuni knew they were teasing. There was no future between her and Graham—or between Kuni and this wonderful family at all. In three weeks, the boat would leave, and Kuni would be on it.

None of which she wished to contemplate at the moment.

"I'll sweeten the agreement." Tommy's eyes twinkled. "If you promise to vote in our favor, I'll make you an entire wardrobe full of Balcovian Royal Guard uniforms, and you can wear them whenever you want. Have Marjorie paint what the costume looks like, and I'll begin this very day."

Marjorie nodded. "All you have to do is marry our brother."

"'Royal Guard' is not a costume. It is my profession. Or will be. I will not wear the uniform until it is real and I deserve it."

"It's *clothing*," Tommy replied. "What you look like on the outside has nothing to do with who you are on the inside. Once you're the most decorated soldier in all of Balcovia, you'll still be a Royal Guardswoman even when you're in your sleep bonnet and night rail, won't you? Besides, you already 'deserve' it, and you know it. Isn't that why you're here?"

Kuni blinked at her.

"Tell me what your future uniform looks like," Marjorie begged. "I want to paint it."

Kuni crossed her arms. "I will not wear it."

"I just want to have a picture of you as a Royal Guard," Marjorie said. "Don't *you* want to see?"

The idea was very, very tempting.

Kuni had been surrounded by Royal Guardsmen all her life. She had imagined herself as a future Guardswoman ever since she was a child. But she had never *seen* what it would look like to be one of them.

Even when the king granted her petition, when Kuni indeed became the first female to join the elite infantry unit and the personal guard to Princess Mechtilda herself, the royal portraitist would not be commissioned to commemorate the moment.

"Very well," she said at last. Then inspiration struck. "Will you paint something else for me, too?"

Marjorie's eyes lit up. "You know I would. What is it?"

Tommy glanced up from a mountain of wigs, her eyes wide with interest.

Secret projects, Kuni signed to Marjorie.

I know signs, too, Tommy signed back.

Marjorie giggled. "Tell me in Balcovian. Maybe I'll understand."

They had definitely practiced these words. *"Een schilderij van—"*

Randall appeared in the doorway. "Supper is served for Princess Kunigunde."

"I am not a..." Kuni began, then gave up. Very well. She could be Graham's princess for one night.

"Unspeakably unfair," Tommy muttered. "The timely interruption *and* the secret language."

"Supper?" Kuni glanced at Tommy's clock, then turned back to the butler in surprise. "It is four thirty in the afternoon."

The butler bowed. "Master Graham awaits you."

21

Kuni followed Randall not to the dining room where the Wynchesters usually took their meals, but into the mostly unfurnished wing.

The reading circle was still in their library. Kuni kept her eyes firmly on the back of the butler's graying head to keep from peeking in at all the friends she could have made if she were here to stay.

At the end of the corridor was a bright corner room. Inside the large, otherwise empty room was a small table for two. No sideboard. No visible food. Just a beautiful little table in the center of an enormous room. Upon the tablecloth were two place settings, a bottle of wine, a posy of flowers, and two completely unnecessary lit candles.

It was utterly charming.

Graham stood to one side, hands folded behind him. At the sight of Kuni, his warm brown eyes shone with pleasure. He strode forward.

"Romantic supper for two, as promised." He pressed his lips to the back of her hand. "You probably thought I'd forgotten."

She'd hoped he had. Kuni liked Graham too much to

possibly keep her defenses intact when besieged by such a sweet gesture. But she would have to try.

Even though he was very good at breaching walls.

"Isn't it a little early for supper?" she asked lightly.

"It's absurdly early," was his cheerful reply. "But 'romantic snack for two' doesn't have quite the same ring. Since we're both under the same roof at the same time, I didn't want to miss my chance."

She was saved from having to answer by two footmen gliding into the room. One helped Kuni into her seat while the other opened the wine. After pouring a few centimeters into each goblet, the footmen melted back to a discreet distance.

Before, she would not have noticed the position of footmen. As the princess's companion, Kuni was so used to being waited on—or being the one waiting on Mechtilda—that the presence of maids or footmen registered about as much as the individual mullions on the windows. Without them, the whole thing would fall apart, but no one ever exclaimed in wonder at well-functioning mullions. Royals looked right through the painstakingly crafted glass to the view on the other side.

But once Kuni had taken her first step onto the dock in London, everything had changed. Ada, her lady's maid, remained on the ship. Starting then, Kuni was on her own. If she wanted to change her clothes or eat a meal, it had been up to her to make it happen. Graham had found her after only a week, but that had been more than long enough to put many of the privileges she'd long taken for granted into perspective.

Graham clinked his glass with hers. "To Princess Kunigunde."

"To the Wynchesters," she said quickly. "You are all

so kind to me. And to the Goodnights. How is the case going?"

There. That wasn't romantic. It was being a grateful guest. That should set the tone for their supper. Which she would remember forever, no matter the topics discussed.

"Mr. York has requested to bring the matter to the House of Commons. He'll have an answer soon." Graham waited until she'd tasted her wine before sipping his. "In the meantime, I have taken the liberty of selecting this evening's snack."

She frowned. "The liberty? Doesn't the man of the house always make decisions?"

"In England, menus are actually considered the responsibility of the *lady* of the house. But I haven't a wife. Besides, my family and I have always taken turns suggesting meals to the kitchen staff."

Scalloped sea wolves! If there was ever a role Kuni had not spent even a single moment preparing for, it was becoming mistress of an Englishman's household. Another reason to keep their flirtation light and temporary.

"I've found everything your chef has prepared to be delicious."

Graham's eyes twinkled. "I've decided to do something a little different tonight."

"It is all different to me," she replied. "Hardly anything you eat reminds me of home."

He leaned forward, his gaze interested. "Tell me what Balcovians eat. If you were in charge of a romantic supper for two, what would you serve me?"

Anything he wanted.

"You are assuming *my* ideal romantic supper would involve *you*." She was not quite able to hold a straight face.

He clutched his hands to his chest. "My heart…It is breaking audibly…"

"Or perhaps that's your wounded pride," she said with a laugh. "In Balcovia, I would never invite a man to a cozy dinner for two, much less be charged with determining the meal. I ate whatever was served, which was always rich and plentiful. At formal supper parties, one might find…"

Kuni was animatedly describing her favorite dishes when a windswept maid rushed into the room and handed a tray with a single domed silver platter to one of the footmen.

With much pomp and flair, the footman lifted the silver dome and made a flamboyant bow, bringing the uncovered platter to Kuni's side. "Madam."

She stared at the plate bearing four small pastries, then lifted her eyes to the footman.

He gazed back at her, deadpan, though the corner of his mouth gave a little twitch.

Kuni looked at Graham. "What are they?"

"Pies." He grinned at her. "From the pieman down the street."

He was joking.

He was *not* joking. While Kuni had followed the butler, one of the maids had dashed from the house to buy pies from a man in the street.

Kuni stared at Graham, wide-eyed.

A smile flicked at his lips. "Rather than try to impress you, I thought it might be better if you came to know who I really am. My family's love of cheap pies is all Chloe and Tommy's fault. When they lived at the orphanage, they used to pick pockets in order to buy halfpenny pies. These two rectangular ones are savory, and the two square pies are sweet. You can have one of each."

"All right." She waited for the footman to serve her.

He did not.

After an extended pause, Kuni realized the footman was never going to move. Awkwardly, she reached for her fork.

"With your hands," Graham explained with a wink. "Tonight, the cutlery is just for show."

"With my hands," Kuni repeated. But she reached for the pies and put one of each on her plate. The sweet one was cool to the touch. The savory one was hot, but not too hot to hold. The aroma was divine.

Keeping low, as if he were presenting the season's finest quail to a king, the footman turned the tray toward Graham, who placed the sweet pie on his plate and held the savory one.

His eyes were mischievous. "I asked myself, 'What can I possibly offer a person who has been catered to in a palace all her life?' The only logical answer was: common food. I wanted to give you an experience you might not have had otherwise, and I think it's fair to guess that not many people can boast being served halfpenny pies on a silver platter."

He would be right.

"You had excellent presentation," she told the footman, then picked up her savory pie.

She and Graham took their first bites at the same time.

The pastry was crisp and flaky, the meat tender. Her stomach growled, and her chest warmed. It was a very good pie. Not that she'd had many others to compare to.

"What do you call this?"

"Meat pie."

She lifted her brows. "Any particular type of meat?"

"Probably." He grinned at her. "Usually pork of some kind, though not always. Do you like it?"

"I do." She savored another bite. "I begin to think my king has been overpaying for his meals."

"I confess our Prince Regent is not known for restraint at his dinner table, either," he said. "The grand banquet he held at the Royal Pavilion last year featured one hundred and twenty different dishes."

"None of which were halfpenny pies?" she guessed.

"Not a one." Graham shook his head sadly. "The mark of an amateur."

"I suppose you got hold of the menu and have the list of dishes served written in a journal somewhere?"

"*Menu?*" he repeated, aghast. "I got hold of the *chef* and had him write down each recipe. If you're hungry, I can ring for the maid and have the kitchen duplicate the royal feast. Just think..." His expression turned dreamy. "I could serve you one hundred and twenty-*one* unique dishes."

"Maybe next time," she said with a laugh. "Pies are perfectly fine for a romantic snack."

His voice softened. "Would you like there to be more romantic moments in our future?"

Kuni popped an indelicately large final bite of pie into her mouth to avoid having to answer.

Graham did not appear fooled by her quick thinking, though he graciously finished his own pie rather than press the question.

While his mouth was full, she quickly changed the subject. "What is this empty wing supposed to be used for?"

"All the future Wynchester children," he answered promptly. "And whatever their hobbies might be."

Future children.

This was not the safe subject she'd been looking for.

He misread her expression. "Do you think it cruel to place offspring in a separate wing? It might surprise you to learn many families of means send their children off to be cared for outside the home until they turn three or four."

This did not surprise Kuni at all. Seeing her father had always been a special treat, too.

"But that is not what you intend to do?" she guessed.

"The separate nursery is to keep babies' cries from waking my siblings. But if any future Wynchester offspring belong to me, I shall relocate my bedchamber to this wing as well, in order to spend as much time with them as possible. I suppose that makes *me* strange."

Kuni didn't think him strange at all. What he was describing sounded splendid.

But Graham fathering children was also definitely not a direction she wished to steer the conversation.

"If Tommy doesn't wish to bear children, she should still be allowed a room or two to do whatever she wants," Kuni said instead. "Philippa's books are arguably *her* children, and she has a library in this wing in which to store them."

"You're right. That is a very good point." But his gaze was hot on Kuni. "Do you want children?"

"Uh..." Her eyes went wide and her cheeks flushed.

"It's all right if you don't plan to have any," Graham said quickly, seeing her discomfort. "Most English people would think a woman unnatural to hold such a disinclination. But my siblings and I will not judge. We were all orphaned or left behind. The world has plenty of children already, with not enough mothers and fathers to care for them."

She *would* like children. Had occasionally caught

herself daydreaming about it, particularly when she glimpsed a mother with a child. But she always shoved the thought away, because motherhood was not in her future.

"I cannot have any," she said stiffly.

His golden skin paled. "Oh—I'm so sorry. I should not have asked. It was an intrusive question."

"Yes. No. That is..." She took a sip of wine while she formulated a safe response. "As far as I know, everything works as expected. I cannot have children because I am going to be a Royal Guard."

He frowned. "Royal Guards can't have children? Didn't you say you came from a long line of Royal Guards?"

"A long line of Royal Guards*men*," she clarified. "If there has never been a female Royal Guard, the king certainly shall not employ a pregnant one."

"Oh," Graham said. "I see."

That was only part of it.

The truth was, Kuni wouldn't want to have missed her son or daughter's entire childhood because she'd worked through every moment, save for a half day here and there. Kuni knew what that felt like. She would not put another child through such loneliness.

Being a Royal Guardswoman would be fulfilling enough without adding the guilt of being a bad mother. Nor could she renounce the post of her dreams and risk resenting her children for the loss. That wouldn't be their fault, either. She would simply have to be an exemplary aunt.

Kuni downed the rest of her wine in long gulps as she fished for a safer subject.

Too late. Graham was faster. "If you had a spare chamber to fill with anything you liked, what would *you* do with it?"

The question made her dizzy. He refilled her wine. She stared at the goblet without picking it up.

Kuni had never had anything of her own. The Crown provided everything Kuni could ever want, but none of it was really hers.

The bedchamber she'd had since becoming the princess's companion would go to someone else when Kuni became Mechtilda's personal guard. Her father had lived in guard barracks. Her brothers had also moved to the barracks when they earned their uniforms. But even if the king built barracks for Guardswomen, it wouldn't be a place of Kuni's own.

After their years of active military service, older Guardsmen often took ceremonial posts. When they retired from that as well, they no longer enjoyed free boarding. Guardsmen weren't left on the streets—they amassed fortunes at their posts and usually settled in bucolic cottages with a view of the land and castle they'd helped to protect. It was a beautiful way to spend one's final years.

But it was a long time to wait for a permanent home that couldn't be snatched away.

"I've no need for an extra chamber," she told him. "The only thing I have ever wanted was to be a Royal Guard. Once I become part of it, the only rooms that will interest me are the ones I'll be guarding."

Graham gave her a long look. As if not just considering her words, but evaluating what he knew of *her*.

Perhaps someone who had *not* spent her whole life training to be strong and silent might have shifted uncomfortably under such prolonged attention. Kuni didn't even blink. Tourists loved to try and catch Royal Guards' attention, and it never worked. She had spent a lifetime trying to keep her feelings locked up tight, just like the men.

She didn't always succeed.

Graham dropped the matter. "Are you ready for the second course?"

"The sweet pie?" Grateful for the reprieve, she scooped it off her plate and took an exploratory bite from one edge.

Sugar exploded on her tongue. Fruits and…some sort of cream? She tried to peer inside the pastry. "Berries and custard."

He smiled. "What do you think?"

"I think I want yours, too."

He tried to hand it to her, and she waved it away. He deserved to enjoy his pie. Besides, the recipe for this delicacy must be in one of Graham's books. Kuni was absolutely going to put in her report that the castle kitchen should add this selection to its repertoire.

"The *only* thing you've ever wanted was to be a Royal Guard?" Graham asked.

Well, the only *achievable* thing. It wasn't as though she could make her brothers treat her like Graham's siblings did. Or guard a princess while being nine months pregnant, and then carry the baby around with her day after day, his padded bottom on one hip and her sword at the other.

But she *was* capable of being a Royal Guardswoman. A de Heusch forged new paths. *Better* ones for everyone. No matter what Floris and Reinald said, or what tradition had been until now.

"No one thinks I can do it."

He stared at her as though she'd turned into an antbear. "*I* know you can do it. Every Wynchester knows you can do it. Elizabeth hinted there are quite a few terrified bullies who know firsthand that you can do it."

To Kuni's horror, the backs of her eyes prickled. How

long had she yearned to hear words like that? To be believed, to be believed *in*, to be encouraged. She set down her pie and swallowed the lump in her throat.

Traveling to England had been like entering another world, but being here with him was like living another life. A life she'd never known was possible.

"Before they left Balcovia, my brothers laughed at me for wanting to be one of them. They said I couldn't even guard *myself*, much less a princess."

Graham's eyes flashed. "Arrogant ignoramuses."

She hid a smile. "By the end of this voyage, I'll have taken care of myself for more than a month. And they..."

"...will have failed to guard their own sister." Graham smirked appreciatively. "Elegant. I like it."

"It will also prove that I possess different skills, and a perspective they lack. I do not want to compete with them. I want them to see my talents complement theirs."

He nodded. "Stronger together. I understand completely. Celebrating talents that other people have devalued is very Wynchestery of you."

Kuni's heart gave a traitorous thump. She ignored it.

"Please do not judge Balcovia based on my brothers," she said quickly. "It truly is... a wonderful country."

He arched a brow. "I thought you were going to say 'the best country in the world.'"

"Well, I *was* going to say that," she confessed, "but *you* know that England is the only other country I've ever visited."

"I'm teasing you. I've no doubt Balcovia is as marvelous as you say. I've never left England. To be perfectly honest, I should love to take a short holiday and see it for myself someday." His eyes lit up. "Especially if the holiday includes a trip to wherever the royals are staying. I would spend hours staring indiscreetly from too close a distance, imagining what goes on inside."

"Well... I could explain exactly what happens?"

He leaned forward, his pie forgotten. "Tell me."

Kuni launched into an explanation of the protocols for the Grand Reception Hall in the palace versus the castle, and the customs in each. He was delighted by the differences in culture.

Yet her words began to feel forced. Was Graham actually interested in her, or Kuni's connections to royalty? Perhaps he hoped to use her to do some social climbing of his own. Why settle for a Guardswoman, when he could meet a princess like he'd always dreamed about?

22

Graham took a sip of his wine. The burgundy tasted bitter after the berry-and-custard pie, but he needed a moment to collect his thoughts.

His romantic evening—oh, very well, his *sunny afternoon*—with Kunigunde was going splendidly. She liked the pies, she had answered all his questions about Balcovia...but she seemed a little uncertain. He might be moving too quickly. While she was in Princess Mechtilda's employ, Kunigunde might not have suitors of her own.

"Are you unused to romantic attentions from interested parties?"

"You are the first gentleman I've been alone with, if that is your question. You are not the first aspiring suitor. I managed to hide both of the lords from my brothers, but now that there is a prince who...It doesn't matter. I will not marry."

"A prince," Graham repeated, the wine turning to vinegar in his gut. "A prince wants to marry you."

"A youngest son," she said. "Currently eighteenth in line to a throne. He'll never sit upon it. And his relatives disapprove of the match." She held up an arm. "Too dark."

"But *he* doesn't care about skin color. And if you *did* marry him..." Graham said slowly. "You would be a princess."

"*If* his grandfather confers the title upon me. The family wouldn't be obliged to give me the honor."

"But you would be *eligible* for the title. Either way, you'd essentially be a princess."

She inclined her head. "Yes."

The thought of Kunigunde becoming an actual princess did not thrill Graham as it would have nearly two weeks ago when he'd first met her. He had not merely been introduced to his princess. He had invited her home, prepared her a...romantic snack. But someone else was courting her. A *real* prince. With a *real* courtship.

"Prince Philbert has not asked for my hand," she said firmly. "He is just a flirt, that's all."

"Does he flirt with other people, or just with you?"

She closed her mouth and stared back at him in silence.

"Just with you," he said softly. "I see."

"I know you prize royalty above all. Please do not tell me to jump at my chance to be a princess," she warned. "I hear it enough from my brothers."

He had not remotely been about to encourage her to marry this flirty little prince whom Graham suddenly despised. As soon as this meal was over, he was going to set fire to every word of intelligence he had ever gathered about Prince Philbert and his royal family.

Graham was jealous twice over. Jealous of this wretched prince, for his ability to court Kunigunde. And incredibly envious that she enjoyed a world Graham had always dreamed of. An opportunity to *be* royal, in real life, not in fantasy. To *live* the fairy tale.

She let out a sigh. "The prince may be part of the royal

party when the family comes to visit London. Reinald and Floris think it the perfect opportunity for me to spend more time with him. 'Get him to finally say the words!' "

"So you'll be...together...often...on your next voyage here?"

"We would be if I came as a companion, rather than a guard. He's not a bad sort. It's in part my fault we dance together so often. I am fond of him, so it is hard to say no."

Graham would just bet. He clenched his jaw.

He did not even wish to glimpse this paragon of a prince, though there was likely no escaping it. Not now that he knew the scoundrel's name. Visiting royals were always highly visible. Going everywhere, being shown off by Prinny and the queen.

People would fill the streets, eager to catch sight of them. People like Graham...usually.

But the thought of seeing Kunigunde in cozy conversation with this dancing prince she was "fond" of—and who undoubtedly wished to marry her—soured Graham on the idea of being a spectator.

"I'm sorry for this prince," he said, "but you will not be his consort or anyone else's, because you're going to be Princess Mechtilda's personal Royal Guard, no matter what." He paused. "Right?"

"Right. Though Reinald and Floris think I should avoid explicitly rejecting his suit, as a contingency plan."

No plan without a contingency was the Wynchester motto.

There had never been a better time for an exception.

"No contingencies," Graham said. "You definitely don't need that prince. You'll be dashed busy as a guard. Don't forget you're welcome to borrow any of the albums in my collection, if they should prove helpful."

She frowned. "I do not need your help."

"I know you don't." And she didn't need that royal prince, either.

Not that Kunigunde-as-Balcovian-guard would put her any closer to Graham. For all he knew, the princess would be stationed in some far-flung turret somewhere and he'd never see Kunigunde again.

She waved a hand. "Let's not talk about Prince Philbert."

Right. Their intimate afternoon was veering off-course. They were discussing Kunigunde's other suitors, despite Graham having explicitly said the reason for this tête-à-tête wasn't to interview *her*, but to let her come to know *him*. This was not what he had done.

He'd spent years collecting private details about other people. Facts, without any emotion attached. When it wasn't your life, the past was simple. Just words on a page.

The one history he had never chronicled was his own. He had no wish to relive the dark parts of his early years—and no hope of forgetting them. For better or worse, they had made him who he was.

But she was here, before him, as he'd wished. Was he going to do as he promised, or not?

"I must say, being royal isn't everything." Kunigunde wrinkled her nose. "*I* would not choose it."

Graham exhaled. "That's because for you, it wouldn't be much of a change. And because you already had something *else* you always wanted to be, besides royal."

"Are you saying you always aspired to be…a prince? That doesn't make sense. Royalty is a lineage. The direct descendants of monarchs, past and present."

"Unless one has an *illegitimate* connection." He ran a hand over his curls and peeled back a layer of his past. "My mother was an acrobat in a traveling circus, and I never knew my father. Her skin was dark and beautiful like yours, but I came out this halfway color. Obviously my father was white, but who was he? Aristocrats had graced our performances. And since my father could have been anyone…"

Kunigunde's eyes were sympathetic. "Oh, Graham."

"I know," he said with a sigh. "Now, at the age of nine-and-twenty, I have a realistic idea of how I might have been sired. But when I was five, six, seven, my imagination was bigger than the stage I performed on. And I wanted a father. What if he came to a performance and recognized me? What if he were a prince and whisked me away to a palace? What if he married my mother, and she became a princess, too?"

"Did your mother know of your fantasy?"

Graham nodded, then motioned for the footmen to leave the room. He'd never talked of this to anyone except his siblings and Bean. If Graham was going to reopen old wounds again, it would be with only one person listening.

"Mama knew the possibility of being important made me happy. It also kept me performing, and performing well. The ringmaster dealt out harsh punishments to those who failed to take the stage or did not live up to expectations."

The ringmaster's whip wasn't what drove Graham. He wanted to make his mother proud. They were a team, and he had vowed never to let her down.

"I imagine you never gave a poor performance."

"It wasn't Mr. Schmidt's opinion I cared about. I spent every spare moment training in order to be the highlight of the show. If my father was in the audience, I needed him to notice me."

"To rescue you."

"Not exactly."

Graham wanted to be loved. If only by an audience of strangers, for forty-five minutes at a time. And if, somewhere in that audience, was the man who sired him…

"The circus was all I knew, so I had no idea what aristocratic life would be like. Everyone seemed to agree that royals had it best. If my father were a prince, he could restore me to my rightful place at his side. Give me the thing that should have been mine all along."

"A palace instead of a tent?"

"Recognition." He chuckled hollowly. "The circus was called 'The Splendiferous Schmidts,' not 'Graham and His Mama,' despite our feats of daring being the main attraction. Royals are recognized for nothing more extravagant than having been born, whereas my mother and I worked every hour of every day, flew through the air every night, and no one even knew our real names."

"Weren't you famous?"

"Famous and anonymous. We were all given fanciful stage names like Strongman Stu or the Flying Foxes. I hated knowing people looked at me all day and all night, but never actually saw *me*."

"But if you were Prince Graham, they would *have* to see you. Your name would be important. *You* would be important."

"Exactly. I thought I should make an *excellent* royal: I was used to attention, because I had been raised in the footlights. Used to pressure, to risk, to having to always do the exact right thing." He swirled his glass and watched the wine settle. "Of course, I was never discovered as the long-lost heir to a fairy-tale prince. Most likely, my father knew who I was all along."

"He did not wish to claim his own child?"

"Oh, I think he claimed me. I think I was one half of the act that brought him the most money from paying patrons. He was never going to let me go."

She winced. "How did you get away?"

"Bean." The name cracked when it came out. Graham took another long drink before trying again. "Mama and I trained with nets, but performed without them. Performers were always getting hurt. Sprained ankles, broken arms, gashes from tiger claws. But no one's act was half as dangerous as mine with my mother."

"I assume your routine was more than somersaults."

"Flips and tumbling can be quite impressive when done right. We began each performance on the ground, to show how high we could spring off each other, how flexible our bodies were. Then we took to the air."

"A high beam?"

"A rope, stretched across the entire tent with the ends over the audience's own heads. They loved it. My mother and I would climb poles on opposite sides of the tent. No hand- or toeholds. Just a long shimmy, straight up, to a thin wooden platform barely large enough for a pair of feet."

"My belly gave a horrid lurch just trying to imagine it. The idea makes me as dizzy as looking at the sea."

"I loved it," he said softly, his voice as far away as his mind. "I felt safer flying across the top of the tent than I ever did standing at the bottom. I was ten years old. I thought I was invincible."

"You found out you were mortal the hard way?"

"Not me." His throat tightened. "My mother."

Kunigunde sucked in her breath in horror. "No safety nets…"

He nodded grimly. "In front of a full audience. It made the front page of the London newspapers for two days. It was the only time my mother's name was ever mentioned. The Splendiferous Schmidts became even more popular. So many people in search of a thrill, my father doubled the price of admission."

"Did you save those papers?"

Yes. Graham saved everything he could, because he hadn't been able to save his mother. The one true princess in his life. He'd been saving people ever since. Collecting every piece of information possible, so as to never again feel as unprepared and helpless as he did that day. Religiously recording the lives around him, so that no one else need ever be forgotten.

"Bean helped me clip the articles, but I didn't read them. I didn't have to. I will never forget my mother flipping toward me across the rope... and the nauseating moment her toes did not quite gain purchase."

Kunigunde shuddered.

"I was too far away and there was no one to catch her. The sound of..." He closed his eyes tight and swallowed hard. "The show was over, of course. Mr. Schmidt had to clean up the stage for the next performance. Baron Vanderbean was in the audience. He found me and gave me a choice. The first choice I'd ever had."

"Stay or go," she said quietly.

Graham nodded. "The ringmaster claimed he had a contract. I had never signed one, but of course I wouldn't have. I was underage. Who knows what he'd coerced my mother to sign?"

"He would not produce a copy?"

"He didn't have to. Bean let the ringmaster name his own price, without any attempt to negotiate. He wanted there to be no future argument, no future claim. Bean drew up his own contract on the spot and had the ringmaster sign away any hold on me or my mother."

Kunigunde blinked. "Your mother?"

"Bean arranged for a proper funeral. I didn't want Mr. Schmidt there, so Bean made sure he wasn't."

"Baron Vanderbean sounds very considerate."

He nodded. "Though I doubt the Schmidts would have bothered to pay their respects. They didn't respect my mother when she was still living. Our fellow performers deserved to say goodbye, but only a few managed to sneak away. The strongman, the animal trainers..."

"Animal trainers," she repeated. Her eyes widened. "Was... Jacob..."

"Jacob's story is his to tell. The same goes for the rest of my siblings." He paused. "I suspect you already know Marjorie's?"

"A little." Kunigunde touched Graham's hand. "But we were talking about your mother. That is... unless you would rather not remember the details of her funeral?"

"I'd rather she'd never died at all." The words were raw. He cleared his throat. "The service was short and sparse. Bean would have arranged for enough pomp and circumstance to rival a king, but I couldn't bear for strangers to see my grief. After Mother was interred, we came home." He gestured with his hands. "Here."

He would never leave it. Not his home, not his family, not London, where he had finally become important on his own terms. Not as the star of a circus, but as the head of a family who saved people. This was where he belonged.

"It must have seemed as though you'd managed to find a palace after all."

"It still does at times," he admitted. "Bean said my life

was my own now. I need only leave behind the bad parts. I could train every day if that was what I wanted, or never leap through the air again. It was up to me."

"You chose to keep training."

"Acrobatics was all I knew." Graham started to shrug, then shook his head. He was here to show her his true self. "Acrobatics was the one thing I shared with my mother. I think you know what it is like to wish to honor a parent by following in their footsteps. By being the thing you know would make them proud."

Her eyes went glossy. "I do."

He knew she would. Kunigunde comprehended his need to be bigger than himself, to be the man his mother hoped he would be, to protect others, more intuitively than Graham could express with words.

"You might think Bean rescued me, but all of my siblings did, too. They gave me another reason to live. I no longer had a mother, but I had a wonderful new family." He could not help but smile at the memory. "Sometimes, someone else saving the day is the best thing that can happen to you."

"And now all of you spend your lives saving others."

She did not say *Like you failed to save your mother*, but he knew she understood. Everything Kunigunde did was in the name of family, from her deceased ancestors long ago to those who had not yet been born. She wanted to be a Royal Guard not just for herself, but for future generations of Balcovian girls.

Much like the reason Graham was London's protector. He wanted to save *everyone's* mother. And father. And child. And neighbor. He didn't want anyone to yearn for a rescue that never came. He would always be here to save as many as he could.

"My siblings and I know what it's like on both sides of the rescue coin. But we didn't start out being heroes. We were children. One of the first things Bean taught me was how to read."

"The papers," Kunigunde said quietly. "The articles you didn't read."

"I couldn't have done so even if I'd wished to," he agreed. "I still haven't, though for years I read every word ever printed about the Splendiferous Schmidts. But I didn't clip a single article about the circus. Mr. Schmidt has taken enough from me. He deserves no place in this house."

"Were you hoping God would strike him out of business? Or plotting revenge of your own?"

"I don't know. Maybe. I hungered for news, despite dreading the inevitable memories. I didn't miss the circus exactly, but it was my entire life for so long. It took a while to figure out who I was if I wasn't onstage."

"And the circus is where all the *good* memories with your mother took place. All of your performances were together, as a team. Of course you would miss that."

"I knew you would understand." He gave a crooked smile. "Once I learned to read, a whole new world opened up. *Everyone* had a story. Bean encouraged me to find articles that interested me—probably to keep me reading—but he needn't have bothered. I was hooked. There was even a time when I thought I might want to be a reporter for a newspaper."

"Until you decided to fight injustice another way?"

"Bean was already doing that on his own. I think it was part of why he adopted the six of us. To have a legacy, like you do with your family."

Kunigunde nodded her comprehension.

"Two years later, a woman came to the door with a problem. A young mother. This time, Bean wasn't certain how to find the answers she needed—but *I* knew. I had half of the information she sought upstairs in my bookshelf, and I knew just where to go to find the rest."

"You mean the newspapers? Information in journalists' notes that did not get published?"

He chuckled. "No. Through a fourth-floor window. A room only accessible from inside a secure building... unless you happened to have the ability to climb five stories of exterior white stucco in the dead of night with no rope or net."

"Were you nervous?"

"*Bean* was nervous. I was ready to make a new name for myself. Not 'the Flying Fox,' but Graham Wynchester. I wanted to be *useful*, not a novelty. I wanted to right wrongs."

Her eyes warmed. "And you saved the day."

He laughed. "*I* saved the day. It was the first time. I couldn't believe it." His chest swelled at the memory of helping to reunite a mother with her child. It had felt like reuniting with his own mother, if only for a moment.

"I imagine you couldn't wait to do it again."

"After that, I was addicted. To newspapers, to spying, to rescuing anyone and everyone. To me, these aren't 'adventures.' These are people's lives at stake. People like us, people different from us. People who need us."

She nodded slowly. "I understand that, too. Wanting to be needed, to be useful. Wanting to make a difference. Wanting to be recognized for a job well done."

"You *are* important, whether or not you join the Royal Guard. Don't lose yourself when you gain a uniform. It's just a symbol, like a playbill. Juffrouw Kunigunde de Heusch is already enough."

She stared into her wine but didn't reach for it. "Are you trying to save me, too?"

"I don't have to. You're one of the most capable women I know. The truth is simpler." He hesitated, then forged ahead. "I missed you while I was gone."

Her gaze flew to his.

"During our week apart, I thought of you every moment. Since our return, my esteem for you has only compounded. I am constantly reminded how special you are."

How important she was quickly becoming to *him.*

"Normally, I would not declare myself so soon. But the one thing we don't have much of is time, and I don't want to waste a minute of it. This 'romantic snack' was just an excuse. I didn't know what I could give you that you don't already have...so I gave a piece of myself that I've never shared with anyone outside of the family."

"I...How are you possibly still unwed?"

Graham chuckled. "I used to answer that question by saying I was waiting for a princess. But lately, real life has been better than fairy tales."

He rose to his feet and held out his hand for Kunigunde.

She bit her lip, then placed her hand in his and let him pull her to her feet. The skirts of her gown rustled against him. He could not bear for her to disappear forever in a few weeks.

"I like you," he told her softly. "I don't know yet where this is going. Maybe somewhere. Maybe nowhere. But I would like to find out, if you're interested."

She gazed back at him with her dark eyes. "I am trying very hard not to be interested, but you've made it impossible. No, do not look at me like that. It weakens my knees. We have no future, no matter how fond we are of each other. This won't ever be more than it is now."

He traced his thumb along the softness of her cheek. "Still temporary?"

"And I'm not gone yet." She wrapped her arms about his neck.

He kissed her hungrily. Not the hurried, first-time kiss they'd shared in the Tower, but a melding of souls. A vivid reminder of what he was not going to be allowed to keep.

She tasted like berries, but sweeter than any pie. Made all the more tempting by being a forbidden treat. He wanted to taste her everywhere. To kiss every inch of her skin. Wanted to lick deep within her, to sup on her until she exploded in pleasure around him.

But the lines she'd drawn were clear. This was temporary. Nearly three more weeks. Very well, then. He would take as much advantage as he could. Would let her take advantage of anything she wished.

He had no demarcation lines from which she must keep her distance. No more walls to break down. His only hope was to let her see everything that he was. If she liked what she saw, perhaps the rules would change.

And if he wasn't enough... Well.

At least his memories of her would be full of kisses like this one.

23

The intelligence album Graham was compiling for the Home Office was almost complete. He had not made any notes for Kunigunde, though his brother's framing of the idea was tempting.

"Poetry," Graham muttered as he affixed Tommy's copy of another of her maps. "Bloody Jacob and his bloody *poetry* that he never lets anyone read."

Graham had taken to working on his compilation before dawn, by the light of two large candelabra, while everyone else was still asleep. He needed the large table in the sitting room to spread out all his supplies and documents.

Kunigunde did not see a future between them. But maybe, when he proved himself useful to British royals, he could become a viable suitor for a certain Balcovian not-princess. And make their romance a little less temporary.

At least Kunigunde liked kissing him.

In the week since their intimate afternoon snack of halfpenny pies, they couldn't pass each other in the corridor without falling into each other's arms for a passionate embrace. A position Graham could never have enough of. His stomach clenched in trepidation.

The more time they spent in each other's arms, the harder it would become to let go.

He pushed the thought away. Well over a fortnight remained before her royal ship set sail back to Balcovia. A lot could happen in eighteen days.

Such as, whatever Kunigunde and Marjorie were up to.

Kunigunde often took Elizabeth with her on scouting expeditions, but with Elizabeth, one knew exactly what to expect. Mayhem, generally, but predictable mayhem.

Now that Kunigunde and Elizabeth had made post-reconnaissance strolls along Bond Street part of their routine, witnesses reported that bosky university loungers scattered on sight—if they dared put in an appearance at all.

But with Marjorie...One never knew with Marjorie. She could be quiet for days, until she wasn't. Or sequestered up in her studio for weeks, until she wasn't. Or seem a perfect angel for months, until you discovered she'd spent that time learning how to forge monarchs' signatures and seals from twelve different countries.

Graham pushed up his shirtsleeves, then turned to a blank page in the album. The maps were affixed with corner mounts so that they could be easily removed for study, but he pasted down a few other bits and bobs. Then he moved the album-in-progress to a spot atop the tallest bookcase to dry and set about cleaning up all evidence of his project.

When the salon had returned to its usual state, he glanced at the clock. The kitchen would begin breakfast preparations soon. There was time to style his hair and change into an unwrinkled frock coat before meeting Kunigunde in the dining room.

He hurried toward the stairs, but paused when he reached the entryway.

Kunigunde was descending the staircase, carrying what appeared to be a book wrapped in cloth. Normally, Graham would have immediately set to unraveling the mystery of the strange parcel, but whenever he was in the same room as Kunigunde, his mind emptied of everything but her.

She was dressed in a gorgeous, flowing morning gown. An overskirt of sheer white mesh set off the rich brown of her soft skin perfectly and allowed for tantalizing glimpses of a formfitting underdress in that brilliant pinkish-purple Balcovian amaranth color Marjorie loved so much.

The bodice sported a delightful flounce of lace, though he could only spy a sliver of it. An unbuttoned, taupe spencer covered her arms and upper torso. Likely concealing not just her lovely bosom, but a collection of freshly sharpened throwing knives to allow convenient access.

If only the blades were the greatest danger. It was her kisses that drugged him and her goodbye that would cause lasting damage to his heart.

When she reached the bottom of the stairs, he took Kunigunde's free hand and pulled her into the closest room in the empty wing.

"You look ravishing," he murmured.

Her black eyes twinkled up at him. "Are you sure you don't mean, 'I want to ravish you'?"

"I mean both things. Get over here." He hauled her against his chest.

It was a slightly less sensual embrace than their usual, what with Kunigunde holding the swaddled book out to one side, but any kiss from her was a kiss well worth taking.

Her mouth was familiar by now, her taste every bit as exciting as the first time. He would never tire of her lips against his, of their bodies pressed together, of his bare hands tracing the flare of her hips.

They did not break apart until they heard others' footsteps hurrying down the stairs in search of breakfast.

"I suppose we ought to put in an appearance at the table." He released her soft curves with regret. Nothing on the sideboard would be half as tempting as the woman in his arms.

She hesitated, which put all of Graham's nerves on edge. Something was wrong.

He cupped her cheek. "Are you all right?"

"I am fine," she said quickly. "It's... *Here.* This is for you."

She placed the large book into his hands.

It was so light, he nearly fumbled it. Not a book at all, but a canvas.

He carefully unwrapped the linen to reveal a painting mounted on a frame of lightweight wood. It was a painting of Graham.

And... someone else.

Not Kunigunde. An apple-cheeked blond woman wearing an elegant gown covered in ruches and ruffles, and an ostentatious gold crown sparkling with jewels of every color.

"Is this..." he breathed.

Kunigunde nodded. "Princess Mechtilda of Balcovia."

Graham was depicted in full court dress, genuflecting to the princess. Her Royal Highness inclined her head in acknowledgment, the very picture of elegance and grace. Literally a picture. In Graham's hands.

His eyes flew to Kunigunde's in delight. "I cannot *wait* to tell people this royal moment actually happened."

"Look closer," she answered.

Only then did he realize where the scene was located. In this house. In the Wynchesters' finest parlor. Every detail was captured, from the ivory-colored ceiling entablature to the intricate pattern of the carpet.

He stared at the image of his boyhood fantasy. "A painting of my fairy tale?"

"It shall not be fiction for long. I can make a meeting happen. The princess and I have known each other since we were small. If I tell her I'd like to introduce her to someone, she'll be eager to meet you. She will have to bring her Guardsmen, of course."

"Eager," Graham repeated. "To meet *me*."

He could barely think. The rest of the room disappeared, save for the painting in his hands. He was already imagining himself living this painted moment. Standing before an actual, honest-to-god princess. Bowing to her. Watching her personally acknowledge *him*.

No one was ever, ever going to believe this. *Graham* could barely fathom it. He couldn't wait for the scene to come true. Especially because it meant Kunigunde would be in London, too.

Her expression was guarded. "I take it you like your gift?"

"I adore it!" Was he *gushing*? Elegant, self-possessed gentlemen did not *gush*. But there was no better word to describe how he felt about this painting and his impending introduction to royalty. "A princess. A real princess. In my parlor. In front of my face."

Her lips twitched.

"How long can she stay? For tea? For dancing?" He swirled about the room with the painting, holding the canvas at an exaggeratedly formal distance as he waltzed.

He stopped when he caught sight of Kunigunde's face.

"Are you angry?" he said uncertainly. "That I like the gift you made for me?"

She schooled her expression. "No. I knew you would. I'm glad you like it. That's why I did it."

"I won't *really* dance with her," Graham said. Obviously. A formal introduction would be mind-boggling enough.

"I do not believe for one second that you would turn down Princess Mechtilda if she wished to waltz with you. Lord knows *I* have danced with most of the princes in Europe and even several from Africa. Countless times."

He lowered the painting and stared at her. "Like that flirtatious prince?"

She shook her head. "Philbert's attentions mean nothing."

"What about my attention?" Graham pulled her to him with his free arm and crushed his lips to hers.

She locked her fingers at the nape of his neck and pressed even closer.

This kiss had a different hunger than the others. One of frustration. Of desperation. Of possession.

And the knowledge that none of it mattered if he couldn't change her mind.

"I'm still leaving," she said when their lips broke apart.

This time, Graham did not answer, *I know*.

"I can't promise I won't try to convince you to stay while you're here," he said instead. "But I will promise that if you still want to leave at the end...I won't get in the way."

No matter what her future held.

24

By the time Kuni and Graham entered the dining room, the others were finishing their breakfasts. His siblings smiled in welcome, and politely declined to comment on her and their brother's delayed arrival and rumpled appearance.

Or perhaps they were not given the chance to opine. Graham brandished his new painting, circumnavigating the large table so everyone could see, without allowing anyone's fingers but his to touch his precious canvas. He did pause to press a quick kiss to Marjorie's temple for her part in the debacle.

Uh, *gift*. Kuni's very good gift that Graham liked very much, which was the reason she'd come up with the idea. A gift she absolutely had not begun to regret giving. That would be churlish. Completely irrational jealousy of a woman Graham didn't even *know*.

Yet.

But he would.

And Kuni would be the one to introduce them.

She thought she did very well at smiling appropriately at the many compliments tossed in her direction for such a perfect gift. What a rare and cherished opportunity she was giving Graham! Did she realize she had made his day? His year? His decade?

Yes, yes, Kuni *did* realize. Waltzing with the canvas as though he'd already fallen in love with Princess Mechtilda had been a good clue. As had his excited announcement to his siblings, followed by the painting's new—but temporary—place of honor against a rain-splattered window in full view of the table. Graham assured them he would hang it properly after breaking his fast.

Kuni tossed a few slices of toast onto a plate and took her seat at the table.

Tommy's eyes glittered. "We *all* are allowed to meet the princess, right?"

"You cannot meet her as Baron Vanderbean," Elizabeth scolded. "She will *know* you are not. You would've had to have been born before Bean left Balcovia."

Tommy just grinned.

"Yes, you shall all meet her." The words were thick in Kuni's throat, the toast too dry to force down, no matter how much she buttered it.

Graham quizzed Kuni about every detail Marjorie had painted. The princess's bejeweled crown, her hair, her eyes, her gown, her fingers.

Who cared about Princess Mechtilda's *fingers*?

Graham did, of course. He had been starry-eyed about princesses sight unseen, but now that he possessed a portrait of Mechtilda…

Kuni had known this was coming, and still it rankled.

Graham liked Kuni…but he loved royalty. She was just the bridge, leading him where he really wanted to go. If the king had his way, Mechtilda would marry the Duke of Cambridge—but perhaps not before she stole a commoner's heart.

His bright eyes latched on to hers. "You are utterly the best. Thank you again."

She nodded and took another bite of toast to keep from saying something she shouldn't.

The meeting was months in the future. It wasn't even scheduled yet. And already, she could see exactly how it would go.

Maybe Kuni should wait out in the coach.

Graham was never going to have a royal title through blood...but *marrying* into royalty was second best.

If Kuni could do it, why wouldn't he want to try, too? Princess Mechtilda dreamed of marrying for love. Graham was undeniably lovable. Kuni would not put it past Mechtilda to take one look at this handsome, charming, mischievous commoner and abdicate her crown to follow her heart.

Just as Graham had always imagined.

Kuni gulped her tea and wished it were strong *jenever* from back home.

It was silly to be jealous. Even if Mechtilda wanted to run away with Graham—which she might—Kuni had no claim on him. It shouldn't matter who he did or did not marry.

There would be no time to think about him. She would be very, very busy as a Balcovian Royal Guard. Too busy to even recall the long ago time she'd sailed to England. Busy protecting Mechtilda, as the king ordered. There would be no running off to elope on Kuni's watch.

A sudden flurry caught her eye.

Chloe dashed into the dining room in a dripping bonnet and pelisse. The duchess was pink-cheeked and out of breath.

Thank God. Something to talk about besides Graham and Princess Mechtilda.

Kuni hoped it was another case. She was ready to climb the walls herself.

"It's today." Chloe clasped her hands to her chest and gave a little twirl. "Mr. York has the floor to present our petition to the House of Commons tonight!"

Hoots and huzzahs erupted from all around the dining room, princesses apparently forgotten . . . for the moment.

"Finally." Elizabeth sagged back in her seat and pushed away her empty plate. "How I hated waiting for news."

Tommy twined her fingers with Philippa, who looked deservedly proud of her father.

"You've coached him on what to say?" Graham asked.

"Only a hundred times. They could appoint someone *today* to draft the new law." Chloe's eyes shone. "I'll be right there to watch it happen. Who's coming with me? The carriage is ready and waiting."

"Er . . ." Elizabeth looked around the table.

Graham glanced at his pocket watch. "*Now?* Parliament won't begin for another five hours."

"There's no dedicated seating for women," Chloe replied. "After I convene with the men, the ladies and I must save our places!"

"Literally no one will be waiting in that attic a second earlier than absolutely necessary," Tommy said dryly.

"Come on," Chloe begged. "I know you're as excited as I am. Who wants to watch the fruits of our labor unfold before our eyes?"

Silence fell. The siblings gazed at their empty plates as though wishing they still had the excuse of eggs and kippers. They sent shifty-eyed looks at each other, then all spoke at once.

"My swollen joints won't let me climb that many stairs."

"You *know* I hate that attic. I told you I'd never choke

on that dreadful chandelier smoke again. It's hot and cramped and uncomfortable, and they gab on until four in the morning."

"I have to reshelve all the books in the library."

"I have to clean my paintbrushes."

"I have to train a muskrat."

"I have to hang my new portrait of the princess."

That does it.

"I will go," Kuni said. Leaving before Princess Mechtilda could permanently gaze down at the dining table seemed the absolute best use of Kuni's time.

Besides, spying on British lawmakers sounded like an adventure. She had never been allowed anywhere near Balcovian legal proceedings and couldn't imagine what it might be like. This way, she could take notes for her report.

Chloe beamed at her. "Then grab your spencer. Though I suppose you shan't need it. The attic *is* a tad warm."

"Might need the throwing knives," Elizabeth suggested. "All those long, droning speeches...Not a single man knows when to stop talking. A knife to the chest should move things along."

"No murdering members of Parliament," Tommy said firmly. "Unless they deserve it."

Chloe waved a hand. "Spencer, knives, and an umbrella."

Kuni glanced out the window. She'd ignored it ever since Princess Mechtilda had been perched on the sill. "Good God, it's raining pipestems out there!"

Graham glanced away from his painting. "It's raining what?"

"Technically not stranger than 'cats and dogs,'" Philippa told him.

"We'll be here putting the champagne on ice." Tommy

leaned back in her chair. "Unless you'll be too tired at that hour to celebrate with us?"

"Oh, Kunigunde and I won't *stay* until the wee hours of the morning."

"You?" Graham said in disbelief. "Leave Parliament early?"

"We'll return by midnight, unless ours is the last topic raised. Once we have news, I won't be able to wait to share it. Even if they don't appoint an MP today to draw up the new law—"

"I hope it's Father," Philippa said. "He has a version started already."

"—the moment the House forms a committee to investigate, we're on our way." Chloe's eyes flashed. "Mr. Throckmorten will be forced to comply."

Philippa looked worried. "I hope the committee deliberations don't drag on longer than necessary. We might need to deploy our contingency plan."

"Parliament might not form a committee at all," Marjorie said. "Your father could present his draft of the new law today."

"Come on, come on." The duchess motioned to Kuni enthusiastically. "Let these slugabeds miss everything."

Kuni glanced at Graham. According to his siblings, his constitution made him fundamentally incapable of voluntarily missing out on any news or event. Perhaps he would join her.

He was too busy gazing in raptures at his new painting to notice her leaving.

The duchess hooked her arm through Kuni's and dragged her from the dining room. "We're off to the best show in town."

25

Kuni and Chloe climbed into the ducal carriage and set out toward Mayfair.

"I cannot believe we are the first to want to limit the exploitative conditions imposed on mill workers," Kuni said, then immediately blushed.

There was no "we." *Kuni* had not gone to Tipford-upon-Bealbrook to help the Goodnights. Everything that had happened, and was about to happen, was because of the Wynchesters.

The duchess did not seem to notice the gaffe. "We're not the first. Parliament cannot agree on how to accomplish reform, which often means accomplishing nothing at all. Besides 'houses of industry.'"

Kuni frowned at the odd phrase. "Those aren't in my guidebook, but I seem to recall... Is it involuntary service?"

The duchess nodded. "Workhouses. Beginning with children age four and above."

Age four.

"I didn't begin working until I was eight." Which had primarily involved playing with toys on plush carpets with a princess, their indolent days filled with frequent breaks for naps and chocolate. "Was...Graham forced to work at a young age?"

"I doubt he views it as 'forced' because he worked beside his mother, but yes. He was born into performative employment. Not me. I was abandoned as a baby. I met Tommy in an orphanage."

Abandoned. Kuni gulped in sympathy. "You didn't have to work until you were older?"

"Technically, I've never had paid employment. By a young age, I was an accomplished pickpocket, and provided for myself that way. We do as we must. Like you, I gather."

"Me? I rarely saw my parents, but the companion contract ensured I would be provided for throughout my years of service and beyond." Kuni hadn't been *abandoned.* Even if at first it had felt like it.

That was one of the reasons she would never have children. The king's command would always take priority. Kuni would rather sacrifice her chance at being a parent than not live up to the name. The other Guardsmen would be all the family Kuni needed.

The duchess tilted her head. "You were put into a situation you neither asked for nor wanted. And you immediately set about pursuing the life you *do* want, despite the obstacles in your way. I cannot imagine it was easy to be accepted by the soldiers."

"They tolerate me," Kuni admitted. "I am still proving myself. That is why I am here."

"No." Chloe gestured at the carriage around them. "You're *here* because you have a heart like a Wynchester. If all you cared about was being a soldier, you would not have given up a single moment of your limited time for *our* mission. Or to flirt with my brother."

"I...uh..." Kuni's face grew hot. She did more than flirt with the duchess's brother. Kuni and Graham threw themselves into each other's arms at every opportunity. Chloe was right. A future Royal Guard should be concentrating on her mission, not romance. "It's a temporary flirtation. It doesn't mean anything."

"Does it not?" The duchess looked skeptical. "Does Graham know it's temporary?"

"It was his idea," Kuni assured her.

"I can believe he said those words," Chloe allowed, "but I am less convinced that he meant them. Graham doesn't do *anything* temporarily. He's an acrobat for life, a Wynchester for life, the keeper of all London's secrets for life... When my brother looks at you, he must see—"

"—a Balcovian soldier," Kuni said firmly. "A woman who is *leaving*. I know where I belong as well, and it has nothing to do with England. No offense meant."

"None taken. England is far from perfect. That's why we're here. To battle for the people who have no one else to fight for them."

Kuni leapt at a small change in topic. Anything to avoid examining her feelings about her temporary flirtation with Graham. "What legal measures do your husband and Mr. York hope to achieve?"

Chloe's arched brow indicated she saw through the deflection, but she answered the question rather than probe deeper into Kuni's relationship with Graham.

"In 1802, the Health and Morals of Apprentices Act attempted to prevent injuries and protect labor in manufactories with twenty or more employees, or three or more apprentices."

Kuni sank back against the squab. "It didn't work?"

"Regional inspectors monitor working conditions, but

there are thousands of factories and very few inspectors. Worse, many mills are too small to be held accountable by the current laws. What we need is comprehensive coverage that applies to *all* laborers, regardless of manufactory size."

Kuni flexed her fingers. "Which is where *we* come in."

Er, the Wynchesters. Not "we." *Them.*

The duchess straightened her hat as the coach pulled to a stop. "Yes. England needs humane conditions for all workers. Small children, pregnant women, any laborer who cannot reasonably be expected to fulfill long hours…There are many allies in Parliament already. Dozens of MPs searching for a solution."

"And you're bringing one?"

Chloe grinned. "*We're* bringing it."

Kuni could not suppress a frisson of excitement at being included in the mission. Every muscle was tensed and ready to defend those who needed protecting.

Inside the duchess's terraced residence, her husband was in a cozy parlor decorated with pretty looking glasses, hunched over a low table piled with papers. Seated across from the Duke of Faircliffe was a portly white man Kuni did not recognize, with receding blond hair and a sheaf of papers clutched in his hands.

"I returned as quickly as I could," Chloe said as she and Kuni strode into the room. Both men stood at once. "Mr. York, this is my dear friend, Juffrouw de Heusch."

Kuni glanced at the duchess in surprise. Not only because she had done an excellent job at pronouncing Kuni's name, but because of the phrase *dear friend*. After Kuni set sail, they were unlikely to see each other again. Save for a short royal visit by Princess Mechtilda.

Her heart gave a pang. Leaving would not be easy, but

returning into the Wynchesters' lives two months from now for a short half-hour chat...that day would almost be worse.

"It is lovely to meet you, Mr. York."

"And lovely to meet you..." He glanced at Chloe out of the corner of his eye. "Er..."

"'Miss de Heusch' is fine," Kuni assured him.

Kuni normally preferred to be militant about her name, but this was Philippa's father. Kuni's *dear friend* Philippa, if the world had worked a little differently. As it was, there was no point wasting time in a pronunciation lesson when she would never cross Mr. York's path again.

"Miss de Heusch," he repeated, coming admirably close.

The duke was clearly distracted with the matter in hand, but he glanced up at Kuni, eyes crinkling. "Couldn't think of an excuse to avoid Parliament?"

Kuni grinned at him. "Didn't try."

The duchess ushered Kuni into an elegant armchair and took a seat on the sofa next to her husband. "Where were you, before we interrupted?"

For the next several hours, the trio argued, debated, refined, reflected, crossed out, crumpled up, and began anew. Kuni was spellbound.

When Chloe had claimed Mr. York had his lines memorized, she had not been exaggerating. They took turns playing speaker and opposition, never pausing for so much as a breath before firing off their eloquent responses.

Kuni watched it unfold in awe. She didn't comprehend half of the words or recognize most of the names mentioned, but it was clear all three possessed an encyclopedic understanding of England's laws and procedures.

Maids tiptoed in and out of the parlor, delivering refreshments and refilling drinks as though this were a perfectly ordinary domestic scene in this household. Perhaps it was.

Now Kuni understood why the other siblings had opted to stay home to put the champagne on ice. There was nothing Kuni could do to help. The men were more than ready. Mr. York would be able to convince even a radish-brained snood of their moral and rational position within a matter of minutes.

Kuni might not be present when the changes officially took effect, but she still felt as though she were witnessing history unfold before her.

Faster than one might expect, it was three o'clock and time to set out for Westminster. The duke would be watching from the adjacent Strangers' Gallery listed in Kuni's guidebook, while the duchess and Kuni peered down from the attic.

When they arrived at the House of Commons, the stairs to the attic were indeed plentiful, narrow and uneven.

The viewing portal was a large wooden octagon, rising from the floor to the rafters. Each of the eight panels bore a cutout just large enough to poke one's head through. Doing so invited a face-full of rising smoke from the chandelier, which hung in the center of the octagon, obstructing the view of the parliamentary chamber below. At least it had stopped raining and the small attic windows were open, allowing the noxious smoke to escape.

From what Kuni could see, the participants below were of a single type: wealthy, white, and male, their ages skewing older.

"The future of the Goodnights and all the other laborers in Tipford-upon-Bealbrook and elsewhere relies on... these men?"

"Trust me, *I know*." The duchess leaned her shoulders

against the wooden octagon. "The struggle is ongoing. But several men seated here today have confirmed they will fully and vociferously support any measure that addresses the underlying— *Shh.*" The duchess poked her head into the closest aperture. She popped back out only long enough to say, "They've called on Mr. York! It's *starting.*"

Kuni hurried to her post and peeked through the opening.

"The laborers are aware that a reduction in hours must bring a commensurate reduction in wages," Mr. York was saying. "That adjustment is an acceptable compromise. 'Tis better to employ two healthy laborers to split sixteen hours than to force the same on a single child. With exhaustion come mistakes. Mistakes cause increased danger for the workers and delayed or defective product for mill owners."

"The pocketbooks of wealthy owners like Mr. Throckmorten are not *our* concern," Chloe whispered. "But many MPs possess a financial stake in execrable manufactories. They have grown rich from exploiting the poor and the helpless and will not be swayed by appeals to ethics. The prospect of losing money, however, will not be borne."

Kuni watched, fascinated.

"Because the House values the trade of our country," Mr. York continued, "it must not fail to feel for the suffering of such workers. We must consider the plight of those whose trade has sustained our heavy purses."

"Hear, hear!" shouted several MPs.

Excitement bubbled through Kuni's veins. It was working!

The Speaker of the House bade Mr. York to read the petition in full.

After doing so, Mr. York concluded by requesting a

limit of ten and a half hours of hard labor per day, with an allowance of half an hour for breakfast and an hour for dinner.

This time, the cries of "Hear, hear!" were muffled by a loud roar of dissent.

A gentleman with an enormous cravat sprang to his feet. "The House condescended to form a select committee upon this very subject two years ago. Their report indicates that the workers in manufactories are *not* overworked. This petition is none of our concern."

"Not overworked?" Kuni said in disbelief.

"Mr. Curwen," the duchess muttered in disgust.

"It is not the House that should act as children's protectors, but their parents. Such oversight is simply not a matter for the government. If parents do not like to see their children in cruel conditions, then they are the ones best positioned to remove them from it."

"Such rubbish!" the duchess fumed. "As if an otherwise penniless family forced to work at the only employment in their district would have any *choice* in the matter! He means for their only options to be exploitation or starvation?"

Kuni was flooded with gratitude for the men and women who tended the picturesque hills of flowers she loved so much. The farmers and fishermen and dairy maids without whom the palace could not supply their long, lavish meals. She could not help but wonder what the lives of laborers in her home country must be like.

An ally stood. "Once I was made cognizant of the injurious nature of my factories' previous mode of regulation, I took immediate action to correct it. Pursuit of profit and good Christian values need not be enemies. I am most anxious to concur with Mr. York's proposed remedy."

"Sir Robert Peel," Chloe whispered.

"Gentlemen!" A new man rose to his feet. "These arguments are unnecessary and immaterial. The petition brought to us by Mr. York is signed *not* by the allegedly exploited laborers themselves, but by uninterested parties in their community. Therefore, the document and its topic bear no grounds in this chamber."

"What hypocrisy!" Chloe sputtered. "This twaddle is nothing more than a flimsy, barefaced excuse to discount the opinions of—"

Mr. York leapt to his feet, but was interrupted by the Speaker of the House, who called for a summary vote.

When the vote was through, Kuni frowned at an unfamiliar rebuke. "What does 'ordered to lie on the table' mean?"

Bleakly, the duchess's head disappeared from the aperture. "It means no."

Kuni jerked her head out as well to stare at Chloe. "It means *no*?"

"It means they won't amend the laws. They won't even create a new committee to consider it. They don't think it merits their time."

Which meant everything the Wynchesters had done... was for nothing. All those people whose hopes—and lives—depended on that petition...

"But the men agreed to the facts," Kuni stammered. "Small children. Long hours. No respite, even for food. And dangerous conditions."

"Sometimes, two sides can agree on the facts of a matter, without agreeing whether those same facts sum up to good or evil."

"How could it be good?" Kuni sputtered. "The imbalance of power is laughable. People with no other options rely on the manufactory for survival, whilst the owners can simply employ new workers. Their pockets stay lined with gold, no matter what path they take."

"Aha," said Chloe. "You have discovered why the other side does not find it evil."

"How can they sleep at night?" Kuni burst out.

"On very, very comfortable beds," the duchess answered wearily.

Kuni's body ached with disappointment. Her chest was hollow, and her stomach churned with acid at the realization that nothing was going to change.

"So that's it?" Her vision was blurry. "We just leave those poor people to starve…or be mangled…or die?"

"Not at all. We tried to bring reform through proper channels, but Wynchesters never make a plan without a contingency." Chloe's chin rose. "If a clean fight cannot happen, then we'll just have to get our hands dirty."

Kuni's breath hitched. "You mean…there might still be a way?"

"There's always a way." Reverently, the duchess touched her hand to her chest and lifted her fingers toward the rafters.

Kuni tilted her head. "I don't recognize that gesture."

"Oh…of course not. It's something only Wynchesters know. We do that when we feel something deeply, and mean with all our heart whatever it is we just said."

Only Wynchesters. And the duchess had just shown Kuni.

"We *will* find a way to help Mr. and Mrs. Goodnight. I will see to it personally." The duchess rolled her shoulders and gave a slow, terrifying smile. "Heartless and miserly Mr. Throckmorten is our problem to solve. Would you like to be part of the solution?"

Kuni's chest tightened. Her situation had not changed. She was not here to help the English people, she was here to aid the Balcovian king. She was a Royal Guard, not a Wynchester.

But what kind of person was she if she did not use her talents and limited time to defend those who could not defend themselves? The king was not helpless. Reinald and Floris were two of the best. Kuni's report might be incomplete, but it still contained valuable insights.

Who did the laborers have on their side? Certainly not their government. Was she like these "gentlemen" who believed the plights and deaths of children were none of their concern? Was Kuni like her brothers, who believed royalty, not peasants, were the ones worthy to be guarded?

Or was she going to do whatever she could to improve this untenable situation while she was still here? Even if a less-than-impressive report risked the role she'd spent her life fighting to achieve?

Decided, Kuni snapped her heels together and stood at attention. She could not stand back and allow others to suffer.

"All right. I'm in. Teach me how to fight dirty."

26

While Chloe and Kunigunde were at Westminster, Graham worked on his secret album of painstakingly compiled intelligence. Dusk had fallen hours ago, and the book was almost finished. Once the newest pages were dry, he would place the book in the bookcase. It was his commissioned intelligence, not a spare copy, but all the same...Perhaps the volume might catch her eye as she was browsing past. His efforts could be helpful to both their missions.

Meanwhile, more than a fortnight remained of their flirtation right here in his home.

Plenty of time for ravenous kisses to turn into a hunger for something more. Perhaps even for something permanent. He was courting her, no matter how few days remained. Whether Kunigunde could be convinced to consider his suit, on the other hand...

Carefully, he copied in the essence of his interview with a footman who no longer worked for the Prince Regent at Carlton House.

He could not help but wonder what questions Kunigunde might have asked the man. Her Balcovian perspective meant she could see things in a way he might not. Notice details he could otherwise have overlooked.

There was nothing Graham liked better than collecting other people's perspectives. With Kunigunde, there was an extra layer of longing. He wished his clandestine assignment and her mission could have been done in partnership with each other. He saw no need for both of them to duplicate effort in solitude.

He wanted to work at her side, together.

It would be a welcome change from his usual. Marjorie was upstairs in her studio. Elizabeth was off practicing her voice impressions. Jacob was outside rehabilitating Lady Leonatus. Tommy and Philippa were snuggled together on a couch in the library, Philippa with a tome on God-knew-what, and Tommy sewing gold buttons onto a pink costume.

Graham was here, alone in the salon with his books. He held the last interview up to the light. The ink had dried. It was safe to turn the page. He enjoyed cutting and pasting and transcribing—he was proud of every single volume in his collection—but the work would be much improved with a partner.

The right partner. Kunigunde. It was *her* he wished were seated beside him. He could imagine laughing together about this factfinding escapade or that. Perhaps debating whom to interview or what maps to include or which newspaper articles deserved a place in an album.

The thought brought a smile to his face. Then again, he always smiled when he thought of her.

This was it. The final page in the album. The last opportunity to provide critical information. He thought for a second, then dipped his pen in the standish and added a few lines of text. The album would not be complete without mentioning the presence of—

"What are you working on?"

Kunigunde.

He barely refrained from making an undignified *Eep!* of surprise. Why was she back so early? Where was Chloe?

Graham slammed the book closed—*shite*, the wet ink!—and tossed as many blank sheets of paper as he could over the incriminating evidence, without attempting to seem like he was actively covering up the scene of a deception.

It did not work.

Amused, she brushed away the blank pages to lift the cover of the journal. "Are you hiding bawdy etchings of…"

Buckingham Palace. Extremely lewd…architectural illustrations of room configurations. Bawdy measurements of…each door and window.

Her eyes snapped to his. "Tell me this isn't for me."

"It isn't for you," he said quickly.

She snorted. "Then who is it for?"

Shite. "I cannot answer that question at the present moment."

"I'll bet." Her lips tightened. Kunigunde swiped the loose pages away to reveal the album he'd spent all this time compiling.

She flipped through the pages faster and faster.

Maps. Interviews. Timetables. Samples of livery. Lists of servants.

Her shaking finger tapped on a newspaper clipping detailing planned modifications to the accommodations the Balcovian royals were most likely to use.

"You're lying," she said tightly. "For who else would you be compiling an album of maps, customs, and security measures for an upcoming royal visit?"

"It's not for you," he repeated. "Though I may have thought... if you happened to find my work useful... It would be like poetry."

"These are not poems," she said flatly.

"It's a metaphor," he muttered, then blinked. A *metaphor*. It *was* poetry. "All I wanted to do was—"

She slammed the book closed. "Why must it be what *you* want to do? Why can't you respect how *I* wish to conduct my own life?"

A fair point. One to which he did not have a ready defense. He'd known she didn't want outside interference, and it looked as though he'd gone ahead anyway. If only Graham weren't sworn to secrecy about his own intelligence-gathering assignment!

"You—" The word exploded from her as though it were the start of a probably well-deserved tirade. But the recrimination went no further.

She visibly turned into a blank statue of herself. Spine tall, shoulders stiff, chin up, expression neutral. Dispassionate. Indifferent.

Her Royal Guard face.

"*No.*" Graham leapt up from his chair. "If you want to yell, then yell. You don't have to be stoic. Not with me. I want to know you. I can deal with emotion."

"I am guarding *myself*," she burst out. "*From* you. I thought you listened to me. But nodding along when I talk does not mean you hear my words. You are just like my brothers. You don't see me as an equal, but as a silly little girl in need of your protection and superior wisdom and oversight."

"I don't think you... I..." Graham tried to think. "I was never going to force my intelligence album upon you."

"Were you not?" Her chin was still high, her dark eyes

blinking rapidly. "You're seated at this big table piled with journals and ink and paste, out of consideration for my wish that you *cease* all attempts to insert yourself into a mission I must complete alone?"

"I'm sorry," he tried again. Kunigunde was one of the most amazing women—one of the most competent *people*—Graham had ever met. He happened to be creating the same thing. He'd fantasized that working together would lighten the load for each of them.

But instead of helping her, he'd hurt her.

"I swear I never meant to—" He stopped, made a wry expression, then shook his head. There was nothing he was at liberty to say. "An apology isn't an apology if it's mostly excuses. And I am probably only digging my hole deeper."

Her dark eyes begged him to understand. "If you did believe in me, then you would have believed your efforts superfluous. If you had faith that I could achieve my aim with my own abilities and on my own recognizance, there would be no need to do my work for me. Our conversation would have been: 'I plan to be a Royal Guardswoman.' 'Go on, then.' Full stop."

Graham fundamentally did not agree that competent people should never accept the aid of other competent people. His king was employing him, just as she hoped hers would employ her. His family comprised eight extraordinarily competent individuals who dedicated the majority of their time to helping one another achieve countless things.

But Kunigunde's point was that she *wasn't* him...or part of his family. If she wanted to drink cold tea and ride a horse seated backward, that was up to *her*, not him.

Which meant Kunigunde would not simply reject his

assistance in *this* circumstance. She was unlikely to ever want his help. Not in this or any other thing. She wasn't looking for a partnership.

Graham's gut twisted. That he *could* help wasn't in question. Her objective was to accomplish it on her own. His meddling directly undermined that. Undermined *her*.

"What I've been searching for all my life is recognition of my *own* worth. Not you flaunting yours," she said quietly.

"I'm sorry," he said again. "Though I have my reasons, I cannot explain them at this time. You are within your rights to feel both angry and offended. I am truly sorry to have disappointed and hurt you. I cannot destroy the album, but I can ensure it remains out of your sight."

Her eyes looked tired. "Don't bother. Make a million such albums if you wish. It is not my book. I don't care what happens to it."

He walked around the table but did not reach for her. Kunigunde's stiff posture and beaten expression indicated she would not let him hold her.

But he did not want to leave matters like this. "Will you come and sit with me?"

27

Graham gestured toward the U shape of empty sofas and armchairs on the other side of the salon, far from the offensive album. "Please talk to me. If you want to. I'm ready to listen."

Indecision flashed on her face. Then she crossed the room and took a seat. In an armchair, not a sofa. So that his body would not be next to hers. But she was still here, with him.

He sat in the next chair. Within arm's reach if she wanted him...which did not appear to be the case.

"Before meeting my father, my mother was a lady's maid to one of the queen's companions," Kunigunde said at last. "It was one of the highest positions a maid could reach, short of serving royalty directly. Until she married a Royal Guardsman. When she no longer needed to be a servant, her social status rocketed skyward. As the wife of a Guardsman, Mother was allowed to keep small but comfortable rooms at the castle. My maternal grandmother increased her own standing the same way."

She looked down at her hands, then smoothed an invisible wrinkle from her lap.

"Enviable matches, all of them." Her gaze snapped to Graham. "But the women were never respected in their own right."

"I thought you said the marriage improved your mother's social standing?"

"The wife of a Royal Guardsman enjoys far more prestige and opportunities than most commoners' wives. But it doesn't come with a uniform or a title. Or power of any kind. The post is his, the money is his, the wife is his. Possessions he can collect, to show off his own worth. Not hers."

"It wasn't a happy marriage?"

"It wasn't a *marriage*. Not in any way that mattered. The Royal Guard requires long hours and months of travel. Even when my parents were on the same grounds, Father was more likely to collapse in exhaustion at the guard barracks than to spend his scant free hours coming to see her. Mother used to say the only times she ever saw him were when he was begetting another heir."

"It... doesn't sound cozy."

Her smile was wistful. "I worshipped him. As did my brothers. When we were young, we believed Father had come to visit *us*. Perhaps he did. That was what he told us, anyway. How we relished those hours. Each time, a competition to be the best-behaved child. To be the one he liked most. To be a reason to come home." She rubbed her face. "I never won."

"It sounds... lonely."

"It should not have been. My brothers and I had Mother. We gave her the same consideration she got from anyone else—which is to say, none at all. We ran to the fields whenever the soldiers were practicing and pretended we were training with them. Reinald was first to cease pretending."

"Because he was grown?"

"Much earlier. Before one is old enough to join the military, there is a program for youths, starting at age eight. It is every bit as demanding as the training for adults. How well you perform as an adolescent can determine your opportunities once you are eligible to be part of the real military."

"Your brothers are both Royal Guards. They must have acquitted themselves well."

"Of course they did. They would rather have died than be anything less than the best. It's part of being a de Heusch. They hoped that being in the military also meant they could see Father. Or rather, that he would keep a watchful—and hopefully proud—eye on *them*."

"I assume this military apprenticeship is not available to girls?"

She snorted. "I was sent off to be a companion. My mother wanted me to make a good match, too, and this was my best chance to achieve it. If I applied myself, I could even reach higher than she had."

"But you didn't want to be a companion."

"Not even for a moment. I would have traded all the dolls and lace in the world to be out there on the field training with the soldiers."

Not just with the soldiers, Graham realized. With her *family*.

"I had to hike up my skirts to achieve the proper range of motion. It is why I slit my underskirts to just above the knee whenever I wear a knife strapped to my thigh, or even just to march with my hands and arms in their proper positions instead of holding up a long skirt. Gowns can be very inconvenient."

"How much marching can be done from behind a window?"

"Not much. That is why I sneaked away at every opportunity. From dawn to noon, I was usually with the soldiers."

"You weren't dismissed from your post for insubordination?"

"Princess Mechtilda was my coconspirator. There was not much supervision once we were out of the schoolroom. Guards roamed in the corridors, of course, but were not in our rooms with us. If a minder stuck his nose into a room containing the princess, she would send him scurrying away with frigid imperiousness."

"She knows you're here now, and why?"

"We planned it together. She told the king she had sent me on a special mission and implied it had to do with vague womanly concerns so that he would not ask too many questions. Not that he would. Companions are for children. Now that Mechtilda is of marriageable age, her father hopes she will dismiss her companions in favor of taking a husband."

"So the princess always knew you planned to be a Royal Guard."

"She will ensure I am assigned to her specifically. That was our pact. Becoming her personal Guardswoman is my honor and my duty. After all, the Balcovian Crown has essentially been paying me to train for that role all of these years. This is how I pay her back."

"Even if the princess hadn't asked you to, it sounds like you and your brothers would've joined the Royal Guard to be close to your father."

"We want to honor our ancestors. They have all been Royal Guardsmen fully committed to protecting people like Princess Mechtilda. My great-great-grandfather Willem was born a slave, and became the very first Royal Guard. He set Balcovia on a path to freedom. Each new generation strives to live up to that heritage. *All* of the royal guards exist because of my family."

"It sounds like something to be proud of. And a lot of responsibility."

"My brothers and I fully realize what we're signing up for. No one has fewer illusions about life in the military than a child of a soldier."

"Your mother," he said in understanding. "Have Reinald and Floris married?"

She shook her head. "They say they would never live apart from someone they loved, unlike our father and his before him. Which means they'll either leave their posts prematurely in order to start a family, or remain bachelors until they retire and marry in the last years of their lives."

"Those... aren't great choices."

"They are lonely choices. We were all elsewhere when my mother died. She and a few other Guardsmen's wives had taken an afternoon trip on an oyster boat. My mother fell over the railing and was caught in a current. By the time they found her..." Kunigunde trembled. "I got word whilst taking dancing lessons with Princess Mechtilda. My brothers were practicing routines on the battlefield. By nightfall, Mother's rooms belonged to someone else."

"I'm sorry," he said softly. "It is not easy to lose a mother."

"I am so glad that you *knew* yours." Her dark eyes were mournful. "Not spending any more time with her than our father had is my greatest regret. It helped me to see what kind of life I did not want to have—and what kind I do."

"Do you not want to marry...anyone at all?"

"I saw my parents' marriage. If I wed, I want many happy years with my husband. For that, I need to be on an equal footing. There can be no betrothal, no courtship, until I am a Royal Guard. Then he cannot think he is elevating me with his attentions or talk down to me like I am his inferior in intelligence and worth."

Graham swallowed. His would-be poetry album had not painted him in the best light. He had never broken a vow of silence, even to his siblings. But how could he leave Kunigunde in pain, over such a mundane misunderstanding?

"I don't know if this makes it better or worse," he said haltingly, "but it wasn't actually for you. Not directly. I would have given it to you if you wanted it, but since you did not...The truth is, I was commissioned to create that album before I'd met you."

Her eyes narrowed. "Is that true?"

"I swear on my own mother."

She nodded. "Then it is true. And so is the part where you hoped I'd stumble across it because you believed I needed assistance. You still do not believe in me, after all this time."

"Not so," he said quickly. "My siblings are very talented and I have full faith in all of their skills, but each of us has *different* strengths. Mine is intelligence-gathering. Yours is being a guard. Being employed to exploit my own abilities does not mean that I doubt yours. I was and am certain you *would* be part of the royal entourage, as a Guardswoman."

"If that's true, you're the second person to believe I can do it."

"Who was the first?"

She reached into her bodice and pulled out a fringed epaulet in the shape of a stripe beneath a chevron. "This was my father's. He gave it to me just before he left for Waterloo."

"He must have suspected he wouldn't be coming back."

"One out of three soldiers at that battle never returned home. Seventeen thousand on our side, and something like thirty thousand on Bonaparte's. That's more deaths in total than the entire population of Balcovia. Our army's losses were immense."

What she didn't say aloud was that *her* loss had been immense. The one man who had not only believed she could do anything she set her mind to, but that she should. That she *would* succeed, come what may.

She stroked the epaulet. "He gave this to me for two reasons. First, to promise me that he would make it back. When the war ended, Father was going to sponsor me before the king.

"Princess Mechtilda has requested my inclusion in the training squadron many times, but her wishes alone are not enough to sway the king. Even the express desire of a royal princess must first be corroborated by the opinions of a man."

"Your father agreed you would make a superb guard, but chose to wait to give his approval?"

"He wanted me to *be* a guard. Not a frontline soldier against Napoleon. He feared I would face…exactly what happened to him." Kunigunde's fingers worried the epaulet. "He might have been right."

"But once the war was over, with his support, you would have been allowed to compete with the other aspiring guardsmen."

"Father had no doubt I would succeed. After all, I was

hand-selected by Princess Mechtilda herself. What better post could there be? We were to celebrate together when I won the right to train alongside future guardsmen." But it hadn't happened. She'd lost her chance *and* her father, all at once.

"I'm so sorry. For everything." Graham wished he could fold her into his embrace. "You said he gave you the epaulet for two reasons. What was the other reason?"

She stared down at the epaulet. "To let me know that he carried me always in his heart." Her voice broke. "I have carried it next to mine ever since."

Quickly, she slipped it back inside her bodice and swiped at her cheeks. "I should go. I..."

Graham rose to his feet and reached for her. Slowly. Gently. So that she knew taking refuge in his arms was something she could do if she wished, but that his embrace would not be forced upon her.

She held herself still for a moment, then fell against his chest.

He held her tight for as long as he could. When she broke away, her cheeks were dry again, her composure restored.

She gave his lips a quick kiss. Just long enough to convey that he hadn't ruined everything completely.

He felt the relief all the way to his bones.

You are already important and capable, he wanted to say. *You don't have to prove it.*

But of course it wasn't as simple as that. She *would* have to prove it, if she wished to have any hope of being accepted into a man's world as a woman—and as an equal.

She turned away.

"Wait." He frowned and reached for her hand. Parliament

had barely begun and would not finish for several more hours. Chloe had said not to expect them until midnight. "What are you doing home so early? Was the attic too much to bear?"

Kuni gripped his hand tight. "Those malodorous powder-melons…"

"The… what?"

"It didn't work. Not the petition, not all of the carefully constructed arguments… In the end, they threw the topic out because it hadn't been brought by the affected parties."

A strangled sound erupted from Graham's throat. "What poppycock! That isn't a rule. They just don't give two flying figs about—"

"I know. Chloe knows. She went home to think, and said she'll be over tomorrow."

He rubbed his temples. "The laborers were talking of organizing a protest, but that must remain a last resort. If Mr. Throckmorten punishes his employees for daring to beg fewer hours for small children, he certainly will not forgive a transgression like that. A man with that much power in his small community can wreak worse vengeance than merely rescinding employment."

"We cannot let down Mr. and Mrs. Goodnight. Or their pregnant daughter-in-law, Adella. Or their little grandson, Victor. Or the new baby…"

"All is not lost. There is always another option," he said firmly. Kunigunde had never experienced poverty, but Graham and his siblings remembered exactly what it was like to be poor, and helpless, and out of hope. "A Wynchester makes no plan without a contingency."

The corner of Kunigunde's mouth lifted. "Fight dirty?"

"Absolutely." They could not fail the Goodnights, and

the hundreds of families just like them. "I'll call a family meeting for tomorrow. You...can carry on with *your* plans. Royal Guard, no contingencies. You have important matters to attend to. We shan't bother you."

"*No*," she blurted out. "That is...I want to do my part. If you'll let me."

28

The next morning, Kuni sat at the escritoire in her guest chamber. She shoved away the journal she'd been filling with encyclopedic details since arriving at the Wynchesters. Today, she cared not about royalty, but ordinary citizens. Stomach tight, she began to pen two letters she hoped she need never send.

One was to Princess Mechtilda. The other was to her brothers. Both letters explained why she was doing what she was doing…which was not reconnaissance for the Balcovian Crown.

These letters would be entrusted to Randall, the butler, in the event the upcoming adventure with the Wynchesters proved a bit *too* adventurous, and Kuni ended up incarcerated or otherwise in need of emergency aid. Randall would deliver the letters to Reinald and Floris in person.

If her brothers—or, God forbid, a royal princess—were forced to take action to extricate Kuni, she would not only never hear the end of it…She would also never be a Royal Guardswoman. She swallowed hard.

Her future wasn't the only one on the line. Hundreds of exploited laborers depended on what unfolded next.

A knock sounded on her door.

"Planning Parlor, in fifteen minutes," came Elizabeth's voice.

"I'll be there," Kuni called back.

She held the letters above a candle to dry them faster, then folded and secured each using a special seal Princess Mechtilda had given all her companions long ago to mark their notes to one another. The design was decorative, not postage—a lark for little girls—but now it would serve as a mark of authenticity. If a courier delivered a missive from England bearing this seal, the princess would know it was from Kuni—and that things had not gone to plan.

She found Randall polishing silver belowstairs. He took possession of the emergency missives and promised to follow her instructions.

Contingency plan complete, Kuni hurried upstairs to the Planning Parlor. The rest of the Wynchesters were just arriving. She followed Tommy and Philippa across the threshold in awe.

Had Kuni thought the sitting room on the ground floor resembled a command room? She hadn't even been close.

The floor of the Planning Parlor was made of slate and apparently used as a blackboard. A chart was drawn here, a map sketched there. Tall windows let in bright sunlight. Map cases and bookcases covered every spare inch of the exterior wall. A long walnut table full of drawers stood on one half of the large room, surrounded by sculpted wooden chairs. This was not where the Wynchesters were.

The siblings were arranging themselves amongst the more comfortable-looking armchairs and sofas in a C shape before an unlit fireplace on the other half of the room. Above the mantel hung two paintings. One, a portrait of an older white man with kind eyes and a mischievous smile. The other, a forest scene of imps cavorting about a fire.

"Come sit," Elizabeth called out.

There was a spot on Chloe's sofa—the duke was still in the House of Lords—but Kuni did not sit with her.

She headed toward the empty armchair by Graham's side. As she eased into her seat, the backs of his fingers caressed her upper arm.

At first, she'd had difficulty forgiving him for compiling an intelligence journal after she'd explicitly asked him not to. He was the star of his own show. Why steal hers as well? But she believed his claim that he'd been commissioned for a similar project before he'd even met her. She had never heard Graham lie. Plus, he'd sworn on his beloved mother. That was not a vow he would take lightly.

Graham had not meant to hurt her or to undermine her. He believed in her ability to do the same job wholly on her own and recognized the risk of accepting any outside aid. If Kuni were disqualified from the post of her dreams because she'd delivered someone else's work instead of providing her own and proving her competence...

But her biggest concern at the moment was not the Royal Guard. It was Mr. and Mrs. Goodnight, who were lying awake at night, worrying about their daughter-in-law, their grandson, and the as-yet-unborn baby, whose survival was in jeopardy under the current conditions.

Unless Kuni and the Wynchesters achieved something extraordinary, even a successful birth would only doom the child to the same dangerous fate as the rest of her family and all the other children at the manufactory.

The siblings filled the Planning Parlor and looked expectantly at Graham.

"Before we begin." His voice was calm and controlled, as it had been the day the Goodnights arrived. "We shan't waste time lamenting unfair laws or the incompetence of Parliament. Many MPs were on our side. If they are not the answer, *we* must be the solution."

"I'm ready." Elizabeth removed her sword stick from its sheath. "Point me in the direction of Silas Throckmorten, and I will dispose of His High-Handedness personally."

"You may get your chance," Chloe said.

All heads swiveled in her direction.

"Elizabeth shall not kill him," she said quickly, "or slice off his hands. Graham and I put our heads together before breakfast this morning. We must return to Tipford-upon-Bealbrook. Not to collect signatures—"

"But to cut off *heads*," Elizabeth said with satisfaction. "I like it."

"—to visit Mr. Throckmorten and his cotton mill in person," the duchess corrected her firmly. "While we collected signatures, Tommy created and annotated extensive maps that will now prove advantageous, as we plot our assault. Bealbrook is the river that cuts through town. The property is bordered by both water and woods. But that's not how we'll enter."

Graham touched his fingertips together. "We need full access to the manufactory and its workers—without causing the Throckmortens any suspicion."

"How will we manage that?" Philippa asked. "We're still Wynchesters. Anything we do is highly suspicious."

Tommy's eyes sparkled. "We'll *all* be in disguise."

"All of us?" Marjorie's expression was skeptical. "In disguise as what?"

"Kunigunde gave me the idea," Chloe said.

Kuni sat straight up, startled. "I did? What was it?"

"We'll go as a royal entourage. No one—certainly not self-important scoundrels like Silas Throckmorten and his wife—would turn away a surprise visit from Princess Mechtilda of Balcovia."

"Small wrinkle," Kuni said. "Princess Mechtilda is still *in* Balcovia."

"No one else knows that." Graham lifted a pile of broadsheets. "The royal ship has been docked at port for twenty-five days. The scandal columns are rife with speculation of who is aboard and why they're here. I have seen so many outlandish theories that literally anything we come up with will seem reasonable by comparison."

"What reason *did* the royal family give for this visit?" Tommy asked.

"None," Kuni said. "It would not bode well for international relations if our king admitted sending a scouting mission because he did not trust your countrymen or the ability of *your* king to provide adequate security."

Graham folded a newspaper. "It doesn't matter. Princess Mechtilda could say she's visiting Manchester because she only visits things that begin with the letter 'M,' and it would be printed in five scandal sheets by morning."

"And we needn't pull off the ruse indefinitely," Chloe added. "Arrive, interview, investigate, leave. One night at most."

Kuni frowned. "Silas Throckmorten may be a barbigerous dottle, but he doesn't seem stupid. What would a royal retinue be doing in Tipford-upon-Bealbrook without the royal princess?"

"You're right." Graham cleared his throat. "Obviously this plan requires a royal princess."

"Or the appearance of one," Tommy said. "Philippa looks most like your painting."

"Absolutely not," said Philippa. "I could be a cowering lady's maid, but there is no chance anyone would believe me to be Her Royal Highness."

"You're *my* queen," Tommy told her. "Your beauty outshines them all."

Philippa blushed and shook her head.

Kuni looked at Graham. "Princess Mechtilda is tramping through cotton mills instead of taking tea with the queen?"

"First, there's no reason to suppose she hasn't *already* seen Buckingham Palace. It would not be unlike Queen Charlotte to host a visiting princess for an exclusive tea without extending any other aristocrats an invitation."

"Second," Tommy added, "not being part of the social whirl is a *good* thing. It lends credence to the idea that the princess is not here for pleasure, but for business. Average citizens have no idea what Balcovia's primary industries are—"

"Tulips and amaranth," Marjorie answered. "Both very pretty."

"And fish," Jacob added. "Lots of fish."

"But to anyone who has grown rich on cotton," Philippa continued, "it makes sense that Balcovia might wish to do the same. Why not tour successful manufactories in order to replicate their success back on the Continent?"

"The *most* successful mill," Elizabeth said. "They'll be so flattered at being considered the best in England, they won't look deeper. Their heads will be too full of all the ways they intend to lord this visit over their friends and competitors."

"Princess Mechtilda would never condone such practices," Kuni said. "Most raw cotton is imported from slave plantations."

"None of us condone it," Tommy said. "This is a role. We play whatever part we must to help our clients."

"Even if it means painting Balcovia in a slightly less-than-favorable light," Marjorie added. "The rest of us will know the truth."

Kuni sighed. "I don't like it. But all right. For the clients' sake, and all the laborers."

"It'll work," Tommy said. "The Throckmortens see nothing wrong with what they do. They will adore being singled out by royalty as a shining example of English superiority."

"There *is* the slight detail of a Balcovian princess needing a Balcovian accent," Jacob pointed out.

"I know where to find one." Chloe sent Kuni a meaningful look.

Kuni blinked in alarm, then turned to Graham.

He was also gazing at her expectantly.

"No," she said. "Under no conditions."

Tommy tapped her jaw. "I could alter a costume."

"Kunigunde would make a wonderful princess," Marjorie agreed.

"Kunigunde," Kuni said, "would get the guillotine."

"Pah." Tommy waved this away. "You don't have to impersonate an actual royal. Invent a new princess. The Throckmortens can't find Balcovia on a map. They won't have any idea what the royal heirs are called."

"Actually," said Graham, "it's best if we stick as close to the truth as possible. The scandal columns *have* mentioned the names of the royal family, but they have not published any likenesses or mentioned any descriptions."

"Because they don't have any," Marjorie said. "The Balcovian royal family hasn't been to England since before the war began. It's been almost two decades. Princess Mechtilda could be any of us."

Tommy leaned toward Kuni encouragingly. "It'll be simple. Just talk at them in Balcovian and look disdainful. We'll take care of the rest."

"I will not impersonate my royal princess," Kuni enunciated. "If it is so simple, why don't you do it?"

"I would," Tommy answered with feeling. "But I am dreadful at foreign accents."

"I will do it," Elizabeth said in a perfect Balcovian accent. "I've been destined to be a princess ever since my noble birth on the banks of Sint-Maartensdijk."

Kuni stared, impressed. Elizabeth hadn't copied Kuni's speech pattern. Her accent was more...*southern.*

"Are you certain?" Chloe asked. "It's a long carriage ride."

"I can keep my joints limber if the journey could take five days in each direction instead of two," Elizabeth replied, still using the Balcovian accent.

"Done." Graham brushed his hands. "Now, on to the question of—"

"Your accent is impeccable," Kuni blurted out. "How are you managing to—"

"This is our father's voice." This time, the tone was rich and deep.

"At least it was the summer we were first adopted," Graham explained. "Baron Vanderbean was recently arrived in England. His knowledge of the language was not nearly as good as yours, and his accent quite thick. As his English improved, his accent receded. By the end, one scarcely noticed."

"I can do all the versions," Elizabeth said. "But I think this expedition calls for Maximum Bean."

"Not Bean," Marjorie said. "Maximum princess."

Graham grinned at Kuni. "As long as Elizabeth is

everything they expect her to be—and more—they won't question a thing."

"What do they expect her to be?" Kuni asked suspiciously.

"Backward," Graham admitted. "You think your country is the greatest on earth. Our countrymen have the same opinion of our own. Most will have only heard of Balcovia from gossip columns, if at all. Balcovia is not a place one travels to for the cuisine, like Florence—"

"We have excellent food," Kuni said with indignation.

"—or copy their fashion, like Paris—"

"Balcovian amaranth is both rare and beautiful!"

"—or possess a long and storied history of philosophers, like Greece—"

"We are extremely intelligent!"

"—so they will be expecting untold quantities of peculiar customs and many breaches of good English manners."

Elizabeth rubbed her hands together. "This is going to be *so* much fun."

"It does not sound like Balcovia at all," Kuni snapped.

"That's what's perfect," Chloe assured her. "I will go along as myself, to lend credence to the story. Afterward, if need be, I can say that I was duped by a charlatan. As you've pointed out, records will show that Princess Mechtilda is *not* in the country. Balcovia's reputation will not be harmed."

"Even better," Graham told his sister, "you can claim you weren't there, either. We'll make the journey anonymously. Your presence in Tipford-upon-Bealbrook will be your word against the Throckmortens, who—if we do our jobs correctly—will be in no position to bring suit, because they will be facing charges of their own."

Kuni frowned. "What sort of charges? Their horrid treatment of children and their other laborers is perfectly legal."

"I don't know yet," he answered. "That's what we're going to find out. The rest of us will masquerade as maids and footmen. Staff is usually the most effective disguise. Servants are completely invisible to the affluent English eye."

And to the affluent Balcovian eye, if Kuni was being honest. Yet the idea of pretending to be servile did not fill her with ebullience. She tried not to wrinkle her nose.

"Or..." Tommy leaned forward. "Since you *do* have the right accent...How do you feel about being fake Princess Mechtilda's personal, full-fledged, acting Royal Guard?"

A visceral wave of longing rose in Kuni's chest.

"After the long journey, I may need to rely on my cane," Elizabeth said. "To the Throckmortens, I'll look especially vulnerable and helpless."

"And having a Royal Guard will make the visit seem all the more official," Philippa added.

"If my brothers hear of a Black Balcovian Royal Guardswoman up north," Kuni said, "they will know exactly where to find me."

"Pah," said Tommy, "that's nothing a false cleft chin and a pair of sideburns cannot cure. With the right cosmetics, you could strut in front of your brothers without them recognizing you. Besides, we'll be there and gone before the scandal columns get word of our visit."

"What do you say?" Elizabeth waggled her brows. "Want to see what guarding a royal princess feels like?"

Yes. More than anything.

But should she go this far?

"Good news." Tommy held up a map. "I've worked out the best places to stop for the night. Five days each way will work out perfectly."

"I'll create a false coat of arms," Marjorie said. "We'll journey in unmarked coaches and affix royal shields just before we enter Tipford-upon-Bealbrook."

"And," Graham said, his eyes shining, "the slower journey means we needn't switch horses at posting-houses. We can take our trained geldings!"

Kuni sent a suspicious glance toward Jacob. "Are they... messenger homing horses?"

"No." He smiled. "They're rescued circus horses, trained for acrobatic tricks."

"Why do we need... acrobatic horses?"

"You never know when you'll need circus horses," Graham said. "They could be our secret weapon."

"I'll take Hippogriff," Jacob suggested.

"No more hawks!" his siblings chimed in unison.

"Or mongooses," Elizabeth added.

"Is it 'mongeese'?" Tommy whispered.

Kuni had no idea. They had lost her again.

Graham took Kuni's hand. "I know where your priorities lie. You needn't come along if you don't wish to."

"She does want to," the duchess interjected before Kuni could answer. "I promised to teach her how to fight dirty."

Graham did not look at his sister. His eyes were on Kuni. "Maybe you'd like being a Wynchester more than you think."

He was not talking about the cotton manufactory. He was suggesting she give up her role in her family's legacy and shirk her duty to a royal princess. Abandon Kuni's family *and* her honor.

"I'm coming with you," she said loudly, then dropped her voice. "And then I *am* leaving."

His thumb traced soft patterns on hers. "I do want you to come. And I don't want you to go. But I had to try. You've less than a fortnight left. If all goes well, we'll be home with two days to spare. If our journey takes longer than expected..."

Kuni rubbed her temples. Yes, she had done those calculations as well, the very moment Elizabeth mentioned her need for at least five days of travel each way. But the Goodnights deserved protection.

"You can't keep me away. The inhumane treatment at the Throckmorten cotton mill must be stopped. *I* will be there to help you do it."

29

Kuni watched the Wynchesters assign tasks and volunteer for roles in rapid-fire succession. Over time, following their boisterous conversations was getting easier, even when they spoke over one another like this.

Jacob was quickly and unanimously voted to be in charge of interviewing laborers and neighbors. His calm and sensitive demeanor put even the most skittish of people at ease.

Graham was to discreetly document all intelligence, be it from interviews or the Wynchesters' personal observations.

While his existing albums centered on London and its inhabitants, as soon as they heard Mr. and Mrs. Goodnight's case, Philippa and her bluestocking friends had researched everything they could about cotton manufactories in general, and the greater Manchester area in specific. She would be sharing this knowledge on the journey north.

In addition to schematic maps, Tommy would take a trunk of costumes and cosmetics, should the need arise for one or more of the Wynchesters to suddenly become someone else.

Since being cast as princess, Elizabeth had not dropped her thick Balcovian accent. She intended to keep it from now through the end of their mission, so that she would not accidentally break character.

Marjorie would play one of the royal portraitists. She intended to start a new sketchbook filled with Elizabeth-as-a-princess's many alleged visits to notable London sights.

Chloe would be present as herself. She had held the title of Duchess of Faircliffe for a year. If the Throckmortens connected Chloe to the Wynchesters or her past, they would think her embarrassed of her low beginnings and eager to flaunt her newfound status. A nouveau riche upstart, just like the Throckmortens.

The Duke of Faircliffe would remain at home, in part because he was needed in the House of Lords, and in part to provide an alibi for Chloe, should she need to claim later that of course she had not traveled to Manchester with a fake princess. A duchess would *never* leave her duke's side during the height of the season.

And Kuni...could hold her future position, if she wanted. Or play a lady's maid, if she didn't.

"Well?" Marjorie asked Kuni. "What did you decide? Will you be a servant or a guard?"

Tommy cleared her throat. "I may have happened to coincidentally put together a Balcovian Royal Guard uniform in your size. If you want it."

Oh, Kuni wanted it. Longing shot through her, deep and sharp. And suspicion.

"You should not have!" She spun her head toward Marjorie. "That picture I helped you to paint. Was it for Tommy all along?"

Marjorie's angelic face was all wide-eyed innocence.

"It sounds to me like in the end, it turned out to be for *you*."

"*Please* come with me for a fitting." Tommy leapt to her feet. "Give me an hour and we can make your uniform fit you to perfection."

Equal parts excited and nervous, Kuni followed Tommy into her dressing room. The mountains of clothes and wigs were gone.

Tommy shut the door and strode to the center wardrobe. "Now, where did I put the...Ah, here it is!" She held out a neatly folded stack of cloth.

Kuni accepted the garments with trembling hands. The material was not as stiff as one of the real uniforms, but the colors were almost perfect. Coal-black trousers and a coat of rich pink, trimmed in gold with matching gold buttons.

Tommy bit her lip. "You didn't say you wanted a female, full-skirted version, so I tried to make the same uniform your family has worn since the beginning. Is it all right?"

The truth was, asking for a feminine version of the uniform had not occurred to Kuni. In her mind, this *was* the uniform.

She hugged it to her chest. "It's beautiful."

"Don't cry on it," Tommy said. "Or get it dirty. We can't wash it without risk of the color fading, and that coat used every drop of dye resembling Balcovian amaranth we could get our hands on."

"Guards don't cry," Kuni assured her. "I shall do my best to return the uniform to you in this exact condition."

"Keep it." Tommy smiled impishly. "I made one for myself, too. I'm just waiting on more dye to color it."

Kuni opened her mouth to reprimand Tommy for her

presumption, then realized she had no right to chastise her. For Tommy, it was a costume. No different from Balcovian children wearing their mother's slippers and shawls, and pretending to be princesses.

Even for Kuni, this was not the *real* uniform. It was a few hours of make-believe for a good cause, and nothing more.

In no time, Kuni was standing on a wooden stool, splendidly outfitted in an impressively convincing uniform. The sleeves and the ankles were unhemmed. Tommy bent over, pinning everything in place.

Pins poked out from Tommy's mouth. "Let's see where we need to make adjustments."

Kuni had never seen a woman in regimentals. Not until she caught sight of herself in Tommy's many tall mirrors.

And here she was. *Wearing* the uniform she'd dreamed about.

It took her breath away.

She couldn't look away from the mirror. Soon, her countrymen and -women would see her just like this. Her brothers, Floris and Reinald. Princess Mechtilda. The King of Balcovia. Little girls like Kuni had once been.

On that day, no one would be able to deny Kuni's value and worth. She wouldn't have to *prove* herself capable and important. It would be obvious, just by looking at her. Right hand to Princess Mechtilda herself.

"I have Grenadier Guard regimentals, too," Tommy said, pins poking from her mouth as she adjusted the trousers. "Which means I have a hat. Our guards stole the bearskin idea from the French in order to look fierce. I thought it was silly until I saw Marjorie's painting and realized Balcovia uses bear hats, too. Won't it be hot and heavy? The bloody thing weighs a ton."

"I won't mind," Kuni said. "It is a privilege to wear the uniform and an honor to serve the king. My comfort is secondary."

"If you say so." Tommy stood and rummaged in the wardrobe, emerging with a tall, black bearskin hat. "This still has one of the white Grenadier plumes, but it will do."

It took some maneuvering on both their parts to tuck Kuni's braids safely inside the tall hat. Tommy was right. It was awkward and heavy. Outside in the snow, its warmth would be welcome, but indoors at summertime, it wouldn't take long for a river of sweat to run down Kuni's neck and soak her linen undershirt.

She thought about taking the hat off—but if all went well, this would become part of her daily uniform. If she expected to wear it for twelve straight hours then, surely she could manage half an hour here with Tommy.

Besides, the uniform would feel right when it was real.

Her heart knocked against her ribs. Kuni had struggled not to cry when her older brothers joined the Royal Guard. Not out of jealousy—she'd never doubted she would one day march at their side. But because the fight was coming toward Brussels. Toward Balcovia. Her father had decades of experience, but her brothers did not. If they had been sent to the front lines along with him…She could have lost all three at once.

Her fingers reached for the talisman next to her heart.

Tommy swatted at Kuni's hand before she could touch the epaulet. "Don't move. I'm measuring."

Kuni lifted her chin and stood stiffly. A Royal Guard did not fidget or require a talisman to feel brave. If the king asked her to ride into battle with a bear on her head, she would do so with honor.

But the war was over. There was no more danger. From the sound of it, there wouldn't even be bullets for her rifle. Instead of being a pretty bauble on some prince's arm, Kuni would become a toy soldier for the king.

The thought made her chest feel hollow.

She was grateful she would not be the king's to command, but Princess Mechtilda's. The role would still be primarily ceremonial—Kuni did not anticipate any dramatic threats to the princess's charmed life. But she would be aiding a friend and inspiring an entire nation of young girls to demand change. A *very* de Heusch legacy.

And she was aiding friends now. The mission with the Wynchesters would be nothing like being a Royal Guard, her uniform notwithstanding. Instead of standing in place doing nothing, they were going to *go* and save lives.

How could Kuni say no to that?

"Graham told me you saw the album he'd been working on." Tommy squinted at a pinned hem and made some chalk marks on the fabric. "He says you wouldn't touch it."

Kuni closed her eyes. "It's not for me."

"What has that to do with anything?" Tommy pushed to her feet and slid the remaining pins back into their cushion. "Aren't we tailoring this uniform in order to help others? Why is it acceptable for you to assist the Goodnights, but Graham can't help *you*?"

"They *asked* for help." Kuni held Tommy's gaze. "Should I sneak in here while you're asleep and 'mend' all your hems for you? Perhaps I'm better at it. Would you thank me for sewing your clothing my way without giving any consideration to your wishes?"

Tommy shuddered. "Stay away from my costumes. You've made your point."

"I didn't want you to make this uniform, either," Kuni reminded her. "If it weren't for the Goodnights, I wouldn't wear it. And I will not be taking it with me."

"You're right. I shouldn't have done it against your wishes. And Graham would not have appreciated it if he discovered you'd replaced all of his albums with journals of your own, even if your arrangement of facts was better than his."

"It's more than that. Accepting aid undermines my efforts to prove myself as equal to the men. If I show any weakness, it will be blamed on my sex, and I will not be chosen."

Tommy winced. "A critical point, and the one I should have kept most in mind. We're so careful to give our clients autonomy, yet when it comes to friends and family, we often leap without thinking. Philippa has reminded me of this more than once. I see I have more work to do. I'll have a talk with Graham, as well."

"Please don't. Our relations should be between him and me."

Tommy tilted her head. "What exactly *is* happening with you and my brother? I saw him touch your hand. And your arm. And your cheek. I assume that is only the beginning. Is this… serious?"

Kuni's chest constricted. She took in a slow, unsteady breath. "No. It is not serious. It cannot be. I am going to leave and he is going to stay. The best thing for both of us is to guard our hearts. In two weeks, we say goodbye."

"Hmm, I suppose you could try that." Tommy's expression was dubious. "Well, guard away. Let me know how it goes."

30

Kunigunde slept on Graham's shoulder, her hands curled into her lap. He wrapped his arm around her, shielding her from the bumps of the carriage. And also because he liked the feel of her snuggled next to him. At the inns, he would have traded Jacob as a roommate in a second if there'd been any hope of Graham and Kunigunde sharing a bedchamber instead.

He slipped his free hand over hers. Her index finger held a faint ink stain. He slid the pad of his thumb over the small spot. He did not care if this small caress was visible to the other passengers in the carriage.

Not that Tommy and Philippa were paying any attention. They shared the forward-facing seat, and their eyes were only on each other.

Chloe, Elizabeth, Jacob, and Marjorie were in the coach ahead of theirs. Another carriage brought up the rear, filled to the brim with trunks and valises. Three carriages didn't quite look like a royal procession, but it would be impressive enough for their purposes.

"Graham, have the driver pause here," Tommy said suddenly.

He knocked on the connecting panel, giving the signal. Soon, all three carriages were somewhat hidden behind a copse of trees.

Kunigunde opened her eyes and turned her gaze toward the windows. The Pennine Hills had given way to flat countryside filled with leafy green elms and willows.

"This is Tipford-upon-Bealbrook?" she asked.

"It will be, in a few miles," Tommy answered. "The town is a tenth of Manchester's size, but densely populated. Plenty of traffic will clog the streets. This is our moment to ready the ruse."

Graham and Jacob pulled a valise full of pinkish-purple cloth out of the third carriage. In no time, they had the horses dressed in not-quite-amaranth.

Marjorie and Chloe fitted the doors on both sides of each coach with the false coat of arms. Elizabeth and Philippa handed colorful, faux-Balcovian sashes to each of the drivers, and a matching flower made of silk for their lapels.

Tommy gave them all a wicked grin. "Now it's our turn."

"I cannot wait to be Princess Mechtilda," Elizabeth said fervently.

"*I* cannot wait for Mr. Throckmorten to get his comeuppance," Kunigunde said.

"Oh, he will." Tommy led them to the carriage full of valises. "When he and his wife attempt to brag about a visit from a princess who's never stepped on our shores, the Throckmortens will be called liars. They'll become laughingstocks amongst their friends and their entirc town."

"How can you be so sure?" Kunigunde asked.

"Because it happened before somewhere else," Graham

answered. "Last year, a Princess Caraboo deceived gullible country gentry before being unmasked as a fraud."

Jacob nodded. "When the Throckmortens attempt to spread their Princess Mechtilda story, it will destroy their credibility and social standing as well. All the same, we never do anything without a contingency plan. In this case—"

"Enough delaying." Tommy handed out parcels of clothing. "Start dressing."

Quickly, Kunigunde and each of the Wynchester siblings disappeared into the thick trees to change into their disguises.

Graham shucked his cravat and frock coat and waistcoat in exchange for purple-and-gold livery. Pinkish-purple. Not Balcovian amaranth, but Marjorie insisted no one here would know the difference. They only needed to keep up appearances for today and tomorrow.

He emerged from the trees to find Jacob and Tommy wearing the same Balcovian livery. Philippa stumbled out next, wearing a long gray dress with a white apron.

Tommy stretched Philippa's blond ringlets into a severe bun and tucked it beneath a floppy linen mobcap. "You look adorable."

"I look like a chambermaid, I hope."

Tommy kissed her cheek. "An adorable chambermaid."

Graham couldn't see Marjorie and Elizabeth yet, but he could hear them arguing about which pose looked more royal in between what sounded like the whoosh of a sword snapping stray twigs from a tree.

Where was Kunigunde? Everyone else was ready. Had she become turned around in the woods? Did she need his help?

Graham slipped through the trees, nimbly dodging uneven branches and jutting knots of gnarled roots. The woods were utterly silent, save for the sound of his own breath and the distant calls of swifts and wheatears.

And then he saw her.

She was just fastening the final gold button.

His heart leapt into his throat. He had never thought woman-in-trousers was a particular fantasy of his. But now that he saw Kunigunde dressed as a Balcovian Royal Guard, all Graham wanted to do was to peel the uniform off and make love to her out here in the grass beneath the spring flowers.

Her eyes met his and she gasped.

"I just got here," he said quickly. "I wasn't... watching... you..."

Except obviously he was doing just that. Standing foolishly behind a leafy branch and drooling hungrily into his collar points.

"I arrived too late to see anything good?" he tried again.

She arched her brows. "You don't see anything good?"

He charged through the branches with the grace of a rhinoceros and pulled her into his arms. He had bumbled his words, but he could be eloquent with a kiss.

She wrapped her arms about his neck, careful to mind his white wig, and kissed him back as though she, too, was tempted to peel off his livery and make good use of the soft grass in the clearing. He wished they had more time together.

Graham could not abide the thought of Kunigunde leaving without giving him a chance to court her properly. She looked like a Royal Guard and intended to become one.

Whereas, *his* aspirations...

On the journey north, he had made a list in his mind.

A *real* romantic supper, a sunset promenade, a waltz, a moonlit garden, the fair, the opera, the sea at Brighton.

He kissed her with all the emotion she did not want him to confess aloud.

If she stayed a little longer, he might find the right words, perform the right feats. He could interview every love match in London and find the exact moment when the stars aligned, and then recreate every one of them for Kunigunde.

Except that there wasn't time. They wouldn't get to any of the items on his list. Just trundling along backward in a carriage for five days, a quick stop to save Adella and Victor from an unsavory fate, then five more days of bumping back home, arriving just in time for Kunigunde to repack her valise and set sail for Balcovia.

When was she supposed to fall in love with him during all of that?

This journey was Graham's one and only chance. He had been doing his best. They were always side by side in the carriage and at every meal, and pressed front to front in each other's embrace whenever they had a moment alone. They talked, they laughed, they kissed... but would it be enough?

Footsteps crunched twigs. He and Kunigunde drew apart just in time.

"Come on, lovebirds," Marjorie said. "We're all waiting."

Graham took Kunigunde's hand and hastened back to the carriages. Marjorie, in her Balcovian portraitist ensemble, entered the first carriage with Chloe, Elizabeth, and Jacob. Kunigunde and Graham joined Tommy and Philippa in the second carriage. The trunks were all packed up in the third.

He did not let go of her hand as the wheels began to turn. He never wanted to let go of her at all.

"You're still staring," she whispered.

"Now that I've seen you in your uniform, I'm imagining taking it off," he murmured back.

She elbowed him. "*Shh*, your family will hear you."

"So you're saying...if they *weren't* here in the coach with us..."

"Philippa and I can take a hack from here," Tommy said with a wink.

Kunigunde's cheeks darkened with embarrassment and she slid down into the corner of the carriage. "You can't see me. I'm invisible."

"You're in bright purple-pink," Philippa said. "I can't see you because your coat has blinded me."

Kunigunde shot up. "Amaranth is a lovely color. A royal color. My favorite color."

"Can you imagine facing an entire battlefield of soldiers dressed like that?" Tommy stage-whispered loudly. "Boney wasn't running away from their *cannons*."

"It's the hats." Philippa poked at the tall bearskin cap on the floor. "Those should frighten anyone off."

Graham picked up the hat. "It weighs as much as a bear *cub*. How does anyone fight whilst balancing a two-foot-tall pelt on their heads?"

"They don't wear them into battle." Kunigunde took the hat from him and placed it on her lap protectively. "It's part of the official ceremonial dress for Royal Guardsmen."

"Since this isn't a ceremony," Philippa said, "doesn't that mean you aren't required to wear it during this mission?"

Kunigunde stared at the bearskin hat in her lap, then quickly placed it back on the floor. "Pity."

Graham grinned at her. He couldn't help it.

That his siblings got on well with her was an understatement. Tommy wouldn't make a costume for someone she didn't approve of. Jacob had adored Kunigunde ever since she'd stolen an antbear for him. Chloe, ever since that day huddled above the House of Commons. Kunigunde and Marjorie had conspired together on multiple secret projects...that Graham knew about. And he half suspected what Elizabeth liked best about their long rests at inns was the chance to fence with Kunigunde until nightfall.

She was *practically* a Wynchester. Essentially, a *practicing* Wynchester.

Having her here next to him—joining his family as though she were one of them—filled him with a sense of rightness.

He hoped she felt it, too.

Surely Kunigunde would see that taking action to help those in need was better than standing guard next to those who needed no help at all.

And if that didn't work...she must see that she and Graham *did* work. On their long journey, the Wynchesters had switched carriages any number of times, to mix up the passengers and keep conversation lively. But Tommy and Philippa always stayed together—and Kunigunde chose any carriage with Graham in it. Surely Kunigunde agreed that theirs was a possibility worth exploring. That eight days—good God, how were there only eight days left?—were not enough.

He wanted forever.

31

The trio of carriages pulled to a stop in front of a wide two-story house with tall white columns and ivy climbing the wrought iron around the windows.

It did not look like the home of a greedy, cruel monster with no heart. But Kuni supposed exteriors did not always match interiors, and blackguards did not always realize they were blackguards. The palace did not make the prince.

Trees flanked both sides and the rear. There was not enough land to mimic an aristocrat's sprawling estate, but the plentiful trees prevented any view of one's neighbors, which gave the illusion of being on a grand property.

There were a few other buildings close by. A fine barn, which likely housed Mr. Throckmorten's horses and carriage. Through the trees, a much smaller barn stood next to a smaller cottage, which had once been a dower house—and if all went well, would soon host the Wynchesters.

Their plan was to impose on the Throckmortens' hospitality and stay in the guesthouse tonight, in order to easily slip out to interview witnesses and later inspect the manufactory when no one was watching.

But first, they needed to be *invited*.

Elizabeth and Chloe led the way, with Kuni striding imposingly on Elizabeth's other side.

She had left the tall bearskin hat in the carriage. Not only wasn't this a ceremonial occasion, the Throckmortens' door wasn't tall enough for Kuni to walk through wearing so much hat on her head. Carrying it under her arm would have spoiled the effect completely.

Chloe wore an elegant, but unostentatious traveling gown of subtle blue stripes with swansdown trim.

Elizabeth... well. She was decked in a little bit of every style, going back centuries. An enormous train filled with layer upon layer of bows and ruffles. Prodigious panniers jutted out from her hips, forcing her to navigate doors sideways. Leg-of-mutton sleeves, tight at the wrists only to balloon to impossible heights at the shoulders. An alarming ruff the likes of which Kuni had only seen in paintings, orbiting around her neck in a zigzag of starched lace. Her sword stick was festooned with bows and ribbons.

And all this in contrasting shades of bruised purple, garish yellow, and lurid pink. Even Elizabeth's plump cheeks had been rouged an unearthly pink, and her lips painted like plums.

Kuni would have been embarrassed to be guarding her. She did not look the least bit Balcovian.

Marjorie said this was the point. Tommy had designed "Princess Mechtilda's" ensemble to ensure the princess remained the only object of interest during the visit. The Throckmortens would be so busy staring at Elizabeth that they wouldn't notice a handful of unremarkable servants disappearing into the woodwork.

Chloe rapped the knocker.

An understandably startled butler opened the door.

"Why, good day, sir," Chloe said, as though it were the butler who was the unexpected surprise. "I am the Duchess of Faircliffe, and my esteemed companion is Her Royal Highness, Princess Mechtilda of Balcovia."

The poor butler's eyes widened with each word until they nearly fell out of his head. No sounds escaped his gaping mouth.

"We've come to pay a call on Mrs. Throckmorten. Is your mistress receiving today?" Chloe lifted the butler's limp hand and placed two calling cards in his gloved palm.

One was the Duchess of Faircliffe's actual calling card. The other, painted by Marjorie, was a florid riot of colors almost too decorative to make out Princess Mechtilda's name.

The butler stared at the cards as though they might grow wings and fly away.

"Come in," he gasped at last. "I will…I will see if my lady is at home."

There was no need. Mrs. Throckmorten had heard the commotion and was briskly descending the staircase to investigate.

"What is the meaning of this, McCall?" she demanded.

"It's a duchess," the butler stammered. "And a princess." He handed her the calling cards.

She took them and blanched at the rich, gold-embossed names. Then spots of color bloomed high on her pale cheeks.

"Oh—of course—I didn't realize—I—" She dipped a fawning curtsey, her head lowering almost to the floor.

"None of that," Chloe said cheerfully, striding forward to give Mrs. Throckmorten's hand a firm shake. "This is how they greet in Balcovia. Isn't it fun? Your Highness, come see how charmingly Mrs. Throckmorten shall shake your hand."

Elizabeth stepped forward, her frills and bustles and ruff almost blocking Mrs. Throckmorten from sight.

Chloe slid one hand behind her back.

Kuni palmed the pair of calling cards the duchess had just nicked from their hostess. She handed the cards to Graham behind her, who slid them into a pocket. Now there would be no physical record of their pretensions to royalty.

Chloe smiled at Mrs. Throckmorten. "I know our unexpected visit is a shock and an imposition..."

"No, no," Mrs. Throckmorten said. "Not an imposition at all. Come in. Stay as long as you like."

"In the beautiful, glorious nation of Balcovia," Elizabeth announced, "royal visits last for one night. Where do I leave my servants? A shack is fine. But something nicer to store our horses."

"Er..." Mrs. Throckmorten tried to glance over Elizabeth's towering sleeves. "I...that is...There's a guest cottage, if you'd rather they spend the night there. And an empty barn that you are welcome to use. You and the duchess shall of course enjoy the finest chambers in my home."

"And my Royal Guardswoman," Elizabeth said. "And my lady's maid. And my personal court portraitist."

Marjorie dashed forward and tilted her sketchbook toward Mrs. Throckmorten.

The open page showed Elizabeth in all her garish glory—sketched on the journey up—shaking hands with a freshly penciled Mrs. Throckmorten, looking prettier and years younger than her actual appearance.

Her sallow face flushed with pleasure. No doubt she

was already imagining this version of herself painted in oils and hanging in a palace's portrait gallery.

"Of course. Everything shall be just as you say." Mrs. Throckmorten swung her gaze toward the still speechless butler. "McCall, have a footman install Her Highness's... extraneous servants... in the cottage. And have a tea service sent to the parlor."

"At once, madam."

Graham, Jacob, and Tommy in their livery and Philippa in her mobcap stepped aside, to be led away by the footman.

Meanwhile, Mrs. Throckmorten took Chloe, Elizabeth, Kuni, and Marjorie to a well-appointed sitting room.

Elizabeth seated herself in the center of a sofa. Chloe took the armchair at its right, and Mrs. Throckmorten an armchair just opposite.

A duchess would normally be an item of great interest, but with a princess whose bustled hips barely fit on the sofa—and whose enormous ruff barely cleared the door—in one's parlor, one could be forgiven for not being able to tear one's gaze away.

Kuni stood in rigid perfection, arms at her sides, chin up, face forward, to the left of Elizabeth's sofa. This might not be the real Princess Mechtilda, but it *was* Kuni's first chance to practice being a Royal Guard in action. Or in *inaction*, rather. Her role was not to move a muscle unless the princess was in danger.

Marjorie darted about the room, madly sketching from all angles.

Mrs. Throckmorten folded her hands in her lap and looked from Elizabeth to Chloe, then quickly back to Elizabeth.

"To what do I owe the pleasure of Your Highness's

visit?" Mrs. Throckmorten asked. "Er, and also you, Your Grace. An honor."

Chloe smiled reassuringly. "This is all Her Royal Highness's idea. She has long thought cotton is common—"

Mrs. Throckmorten reared back. "Well! She... I..."

"—but after the war ended, she was able to procure *English* cotton, and has been completely won over by its superior quality."

"Oh," Mrs. Throckmorten said again, much relieved. "English cotton mills *are* rather special."

"In my country," said Elizabeth, "we have no manufactories. This is a shocking waste. Why should peasants frolic in the hills when they could be working for the king in a factory?"

"Er... yes." Mrs. Throckmorten smiled, gaining confidence. "My husband and I say something quite similar every day."

Chloe glanced toward the open doorway. "Is Mr. Throckmorten at the factory now?"

"Oh—not at this hour. The supervisor is in charge. My husband has a standing appointment every afternoon downriver. Silas will be disappointed to have missed—But he won't have missed you, will he? If you'll be staying until tomorrow morning, might you do my husband and me the great honor of also sharing a humble supper with us tonight?"

Kuni had no doubt whatever was served would be the finest menu Mrs. Throckmorten could imagine.

"We should love to," gushed Chloe, as though dining with the owners of a dangerous, exploitative factory was her life's dream, fulfilled. "But just you and your husband, if you please. The princess is paying *very* few calls outside the highest echelons of the aristocracy, and feelings get *so* hurt when minor lords feel they've been snubbed. I am confident we can trust in your discretion?"

Mrs. Throckmorten's eyes glittered. "Of course. I wouldn't dream of telling a soul."

Elizabeth gazed about the room with disdain. "In my country, beverages do not take so long to arrive."

"Oh!" Mrs. Throckmorten scrambled to her feet and dashed to the corridor to see if the maids were on their way.

Kuni risked sending Elizabeth an unamused scowl. "In my country, princesses *and* paupers possess better manners."

"That's exactly what she'll say to her friends when we leave," Elizabeth whispered back.

Chloe waved Kuni away. "The more outlandish Elizabeth is, the more improbable the story will seem when the Throckmortens try to brag about the visit."

Kuni resumed her stiff-spined post, as irritated with herself for breaking form as she was with the horrid portrayal of her home country.

A rattle of platters sounded in the hallway. Mrs. Throckmorten swept back into the room, followed by three maids bearing a tea service that could feed an army.

"How can my husband and I be of assistance to Balcovia?" Mrs. Throckmorten asked as she poured the tea.

"Her Royal Highness has decided to turn the tulip fields into cotton mills upon her return," Chloe explained. "Since there are no Balcovian experts in the industry, the princess wishes to glean insights from the best manufactories in England."

"*Oh.*" Mrs. Throckmorten preened. "That does sound like Silas and me. Our cotton mill is the most profitable in the country. We never waste a penny or a minute of time. Our output is second to none."

"In my country," Elizabeth said, "only a fool develops his own commercial enterprise, when he could copy someone else's."

Kuni gritted her teeth so as not to send the fake princess another glare.

"Anything we can do to help," Mrs. Throckmorten promised.

"Her Royal Highness was hoping to be given free rein to tour the manufactory," Chloe said smoothly. "When might we look around?"

"Oh." Mrs. Throckmorten glanced uncertainly at the clock. "Silas will very much wish to guide you himself. But he won't return until late, and those lazy wretches—not lazy! Very industrious! The most industrious workers in all of England!—are behind on production, and will work past sundown until they've caught up. I'm not certain this is a good time to visit."

"Can you send your husband a note to ask?"

"Oh no, I'm not to interrupt him while he's...His meeting is vital to the workings of the mill. Silas should not like to be...I really couldn't bother him. He's with a very important associate."

Chloe and Elizabeth exchanged frowns of disapproval as though to say, *More important than royalty?*

"I'll ask Silas when he returns tonight," Mrs. Throckmorten added quickly. "The workers will be back at their posts before dawn. As soon as Her Royal Highness has broken her fast, Silas will be thrilled to accompany her to the manufactory and answer any questions she might have about our processes or the laborers."

"Do you pay them?" Elizabeth asked.

"Er..." Mrs. Throckmorten stirred her tea, clearly trying

to ascertain the correct answer to the question. "Certainly we pay our employees."

"In my country, we don't pay anyone we don't have to, and the king needn't answer to anyone."

Mrs. Throckmorten relaxed. "Well, Silas is very much the master of our little kingdom. As I said, we do pay our employees, but we try to keep as few of them as possible. The rest are either apprentices contracted at minimal wages over many years, or the children of any of the above, who are happy to work for a pittance. I highly recommend the practice. One saves *so* much money."

"It sounds too good to be true," Chloe said. "Is it legal?"

"In my country," said Elizabeth, "the king's will is law."

"One needn't be royalty," Mrs. Throckmorten assured them with a little laugh, "although the way we live, it sometimes feels like it. There was a petition that went round...but the right coins in the right pockets, and that sort of thing goes away."

"There's no governance at all?"

"Oh, there's some sort of law about apprentices—Silas will know the details—but little covers employees, and there are no rules at all about minimum wages. We could staff the entire factory for a halfpenny if we wished to. But we do not. Silas and I are practically..."

"Philanthropists?" Chloe said dryly.

"One must give the right impression to one's community," Mrs. Throckmorten replied, with a conspiratorial roll of her eyes. "If I were queen, trust me: not a farthing would be spent on wages. The honor of working for royalty should be more than enough payment."

This lady! Kuni's muscles ached from vibrating in place. She longed to smack the self-satisfied smirk from Mrs. Throckmorten's face.

Chloe smiled. "Her Royal Highness is considering modeling the inaugural Balcovian cotton mill after one of England's own. With your permission, might her court portraitist also make a few sketches here and there to show the royal family how a manufactory ought to be managed?"

"Oh!" Mrs. Throckmorten set down her tea. "Of course. Anything you need. Her Highness's servants can sketch whatever the princess pleases. It would be an honor to know the Balcovian king modeled his mills after ours."

"It's not certain yet," Chloe warned. "But we will send you word as soon as it happens."

"In my country," said Elizabeth, "we reward loyal subjects with a token of gratitude. Would you prefer a gold brooch decorated with rubies or emeralds?"

Kuni thought Mrs. Throckmorten was going to swoon right out of her armchair.

"Either," she gasped, not objecting to being labeled a loyal subject of Balcovia. "Both. That is—I mean—"

"Noted," Chloe assured her. "I do hope our presence isn't a bother."

"Not a bother," Mrs. Throckmorten said quickly. "Anything Her Royal Highness desires, she shall have with our blessing."

32

As the night wore on, Mrs. Throckmorten grew in a tizzy, mortified at her husband's continued absence, but proud to be witnessed keeping "town" hours instead of "country" hours.

Kuni couldn't care less about the clock. She cared about the mistreated laborers toiling in the manufactory.

Mr. Throckmorten arrived home from his appointment visibly inebriated and barely in time to share a ten o'clock supper with the esteemed guests he hadn't known he was hosting. After supper, Chloe and Elizabeth entertained the Throckmortens for another hour or two before they, their Royal Guard, and the Balcovian portraitist retired into very pretty rooms to wait for the others.

Jacob, Graham, Tommy, and Philippa had spent their day in reconnaissance. They'd changed out of their servants' costumes and into ordinary attire that would blend in with this section of the country.

"Before we came the first time, I worried Graham and I *wouldn't* blend," Jacob told Kuni. "But there are several Black families in Tipford-upon-Bealbrook, and an even larger community in Manchester. We were able to do most of what we hoped."

"Starting with purchasing everything we could find at the local bakery and vegetable market," Graham said. "We spent all morning and afternoon going door to door, handing out any supplies people wished to take and listening to anything they wished to tell us."

Their stories were similar to that of Mr. and Mrs. Goodnight. Many local families had either lost a loved one to a machine or suffered the permanent damage that came with a serious injury.

None had a better choice. Anyone with enough money to move to a different town had already done so. Here in Tipford-upon-Bealbrook, there was no other major employer—unless laborers wished to walk ten miles to the big city or spend coins they did not have on hackney transit they could not afford.

It was the Throckmorten cotton mill or nothing.

Although the Wynchesters had wanted to interview the laborers themselves, the workers would only have a few hours' sleep before reporting back to the manufactory. The siblings hadn't wanted to rob them of their much-needed rest.

And…Graham wasn't certain he could bear to talk to Victor. Losing a parent in graphic fashion, in the same place that one worked, before one's very eyes, under the thoughtless command of a ringmaster who cared no more for his humans than he would a donkey…Graham would stay in the street. Gathering information was what he did best. There were plenty of others to visit the manufactory.

Later, Tommy's expression was full of anger as she described what they'd seen. "The sun had long since set by the time the laborers were permitted to trudge back to their homes."

Chloe's brows shot up. "I cannot believe the Throckmortens would waste money on illumination rather than simply allowing the laborers to work humane hours."

Tommy snorted. "They aren't spending much on candles. The workers are only permitted the tallow sort."

"Tallow?" Kuni asked.

"Made from animal fat," Tommy explained. "They're cheap, smelly, and smoky—and there are precious few to be found in the factory. One of the laborers caught her fingers in a spinning machine because of the poor lighting, and was delayed cleaning up the blood."

"'Carelessness' is grounds for docking an entire month's wages, even for apprentices," Jacob said. "The supervisor seems sympathetic to their plight—"

Graham consulted his notes. "A Mr. Yates."

"—but he's terrified of Mr. Throckmorten and of no help to the workers. Tommy provided more assistance than Yates."

"All I did was redress her wound to guard against infection after she left the factory."

"Like I said," Jacob repeated. "More than Yates. Mr. Throckmorten has the supervisor under his thumb."

"That changes tomorrow," said Chloe. "We're to have a tour of the mill first thing in the morning."

* * *

Kuni slept restlessly, her dreams full of children and accidents. She awoke long before the sun.

Nor was she the only one up early.

In the beautiful, glorious nation of Balcovia, royals

apparently broke their fast in the first moments of dawn. Kuni, Marjorie, Chloe, and the fake Princess Mechtilda were ready to leave for the manufactory tour within a quarter hour of the first employees' arrival. Or perhaps they were not employees, but apprentices, forced out of desperation to sign long-term, exploitative contracts.

But although the Wynchesters had risen with the sun, Mr. and Mrs. Throckmorten did not. They seemed to have no difficulty sleeping at night and were still snoring audibly at ten o'clock in the morning.

Kuni, Marjorie, Elizabeth, and Chloe stood impatiently in the dining room, awaiting their hosts.

Tommy went out to refine her maps. Jacob checked on the horses. Philippa in her guise as maid and Graham in his livery went to glean whatever intelligence—or gossip—they could from the servants.

It was noon before the Throckmortens were bathed and dressed and downstairs to break their fast and greet their guests.

"Town hours," Elizabeth muttered when the stairs finally creaked. "As if they'd been out waltzing until six."

Mr. and Mrs. Throckmorten did not seem to notice they had kept their guests waiting.

"Oh, look," Mrs. Throckmorten exclaimed with a laugh. "We've come downstairs at the same time!"

Kuni refrained from responding only because she represented the Royal Guard.

Finally, after the longest second breakfast of Kuni's life, Mr. Throckmorten escorted them down a winding road through the trees to the cotton mill.

It was every bit as repugnant as she had feared.

There were plenty of windows, which was both a blessing and a curse. During daylight hours when it was sunny, there would be no problem seeing the machines clearly. But because rain was always imminent and dirt could travel on the wind and damage the cotton, the glass was always kept shut. The sun's warmth amplified inside the large, unventilated room, beating down upon sweaty bodies hunched over tables or crawling between moving machines.

With the windows closed, the machines were even louder, their racket echoing off the dirty panes and the scarred walls. The poor laborers must work with their temples pounding from the noise and return home with a roaring headache every night.

Kuni glimpsed little Victor right away. His ruddy cheeks and orange hair were exactly as his grandparents had described.

His mother was just as simple to spot. Adella Goodnight's pregnant belly was the only protuberance on her slender frame. As her son scurried between the machines, she watched him so closely, her own fingers had several near misses with moving parts.

Mr. Throckmorten checked his pocket watch for a third time, as if bored by it all. Kuni had to step closer to make out his words over the noise.

Mr. Throckmorten was not nearly as impressed with Princess Mechtilda as his wife. He said he did not recognize any royalty but his own.

Kuni wasn't certain whether he was referring to England's monarch or to himself.

"Well, there it is." He straightened his waistcoat and patted his breast pocket to be certain it still contained its cigar. "I'm afraid I'm late for my appointment. If there's nothing else, you should return to the house and do whatever it is that ladies do."

"Might we stay a bit and look around?" Chloe asked.

"Don't go near the machines," Mr. Throckmorten advised. "If they catch your hem or a sleeve, that's it."

Chloe gave him her practiced smile. "Her Royal Highness thanks you for sharing your home, your hospitality, and your knowledgeable experience."

"Eh, a child could run one of these operations." He retrieved the cigar from his coat pocket and stored it in the corner of his mouth instead. "Just be sure to employ a trustworthy supervisor, or you'll catch the curs trying to eat at their posts instead of keeping their minds on their work."

"In my country—" Elizabeth began.

"Bavaria, you say?" The cigar bobbed as he spoke.

"Balcovia," Chloe murmured. "But close."

Kuni shut her eyes. Bavaria was a famous—and landlocked—kingdom within the German empire. *Balcovia*, on the other hand, was a beautiful coastal country known for—

"Bah." Mr. Throckmorten took another unsubtle peek at his pocket watch. "Never stepped foot outside England, and never will."

Never cared about anyone other than himself, more like. Not even his own employees in this very room.

Kuni had never felt so helpless. If she were a real Royal Guardswoman—if Elizabeth were the actual Princess Mechtilda—surely there would be something immediate they could do to help. She felt sick at so many desperate workers sweltering in dangerous conditions.

"In my country," said Elizabeth, "a well-bred host would offer his guest a refreshment to combat the heat."

Mr. Throckmorten sighed, and motioned the party over to a tall dais where the supervisor sat behind a small desk. He motioned the supervisor away. "Go inspect the cotton, Yates. We'll dock the pay of anyone who is behind schedule."

The supervisor's tortured eyes revealed his dismay at this command, but he nodded obediently and hurried off toward the machines.

"This is where I sit and enjoy a hearty lunch on the cooler days when I visit the manufactory." Mr. Throckmorten unlocked a wooden panel and slid it open to reveal, not papers, but two glasses and a bottle of whisky next to an odd clay pot the size of a large pineapple and shaped like a pig.

"I'd offer you the supervisor's perch, but..." He gestured at Elizabeth's wide panniers, which had no hope of fitting into the confines of the wooden armchair.

She stared back at him blankly.

"Lemonade would be better on a hot day," he tried again, his fingers twitching with impatience. "My wife has plenty of it back in the house."

"I should like to try English whisky."

"Scottish, I'm afraid." He poured her two fingers of golden liquid.

She picked up the glass and peered at the whisky as though it were an oddity.

Mr. Throckmorten returned the bottle to the desk and hefted the pig-shaped pot. It was clearly heavy. A square hole in the pig's back showed it was filled to the brim with coins and banknotes. He cradled the pig in the crook of his arm like an infant.

"Scottish?" Elizabeth set down the glass. "In that case, I require a taster. In my country, a small child always tests my alcohol to ensure it is not too strong for my delicate constitution."

What? Kuni stared at her.

"A redheaded child," Elizabeth added.

With obvious impatience, Mr. Throckmorten glanced about the room and caught sight of Victor just emerging from behind a cotton spinner. "*You*. Come at once."

The lad was clearly wary, but wasted no time hurrying to do as his master bade him.

They'd earned a respite for little Victor!

"I must make haste," Mr. Throckmorten repeated as he locked the desk. "Observe the mill as much as you please, though I recommend not above an hour. It will only get hotter in here."

A footman appeared at the manufactory door. "Your carriage is ready, sir."

"Finally," Mr. Throckmorten muttered. He cradled the pig and hurried out the door without a backward glance.

Kuni crouched on one knee to be eye-level with Victor. "We would like it if you sat a moment with us."

He sat down gingerly, as though afraid even the hard wood dais would be snatched out from under him.

Kuni sat next to the little boy. She remembered what it was like to yearn to be noticed and treated as seriously as an adult. "Victor, how many of the people in this room are apprentices?"

He looked thrilled to be included and held up one hand, the fingers splayed.

"Five?"

He nodded.

"And you all work the same hours, whether you're an apprentice or not?"

He nodded again.

Kuni's gaze shot up toward Chloe. "When we were discussing Parliament, didn't you say that was against the law? If a factory owner has three or more apprentices, he must limit their hours?"

"That's right. It *is* against the law...which happens all the time." Chloe cast her eyes around the room. "The regional inspector should report the circumvention when he makes his inspection."

Victor shook his head. "He doesn't inspect. He drinks whisky with Mr. Throckmorten."

Both men were circumventing the law for personal gain.

Kuni gazed about the crowded room. "Every one of these laborers needs a personal guard."

"Exactly," said Elizabeth. "That's who the inspector is *supposed* to be."

"The inspector is a Mr. Durbridge," Kuni recalled. "Tommy has his residence marked on her maps. Graham heard about their gaming habit."

Chloe's eyes shone. "We can't change each individual factory, but we *can* replace an incompetent inspector with someone who does his job. Mr. Durbridge must be in charge of inspecting dozens of mills like this one. Perhaps hundreds. All we have to do—"

Adella ran up to them, one hand curved protectively beneath her belly. "Is everything all right? Is Victor bothering you?"

"He's wonderful," Marjorie told her. "And I think things *are* going to be all right."

"Your parents sent us," Chloe whispered.

Adella's face cleared. "You're—"

Chloe nodded. "We understand the inspector withholds information from his report?"

"*Inspector*," Adella spat. "Mr. Durbridge is a criminal, just like Mr. Throckmorten. That's where he is now and every afternoon. A few miles down the river at Mr. Durbridge's house, gambling with wages that belong to *us*."

"He doesn't pay his employees' wages?" Kuni asked in disbelief.

"Often enough to keep us coming back," Adella answered. "But we're docked for every infraction. Injured? Lost wages. Killed?" Her mouth stuttered the word and her eyes filled with tears before she blinked them away. "My husband died the day before his monthly wages were due. Since Ned was no longer employed, Mr. Throckmorten kept the money."

"That putrid tufted turnip," Kuni growled.

Adella's eyes glistened. "Mr. Durbridge and Mr. Throckmorten both would rather lose our money at casino than allow us a farthing for funeral expenses. All the coin he's found a pretext to keep stays locked in his desk in a clay jar, just to taunt us with his power and our lack."

"We saw that jar," Marjorie said. "It's shaped like a pig. He took it when he offered us whisky."

"*He's* the knurly, pettifogging swine."

Adella made a face. "Mr. Throckmorten makes a dramatic production of holding up the pig whenever someone disappoints him, just to keep the rest of us too frightened to defy him. He's been winning at cards lately, he tells us. The jar is almost too heavy for him to carry."

"I reviewed the maps on our journey north," Kuni said. "If I recall correctly, the residence has some sort of shrubbery all around the house and garden, and a small exit behind the property."

"Rosebushes and a hedgerow." Adella looked impressed. "The rear access to the river path is marked with two large white posts and cannot be missed. But why does it matter where Mr. Durbridge lives? He'll be there gambling with Mr. Throckmorten until nightfall."

"With *your* coins," Marjorie said.

"Not just mine," Adella said grimly. "That money belonged to me and many others. Including the child injured in the same accident that killed my Ned. Our loved ones are gone forever, but if we could at least have all our lost wages back..."

Kuni exchanged a slow smile with Elizabeth. "Done."

33

Graham reunited with the others in Elizabeth's—ahem, Princess Mechtilda's—private guest chamber.

"How was Her Highness's visit with Mr. Throckmorten?" he asked.

"He saw *this*..." Elizabeth tried to look down at her bustled hips and enormous flounced skirts, but could not, because the jutting disk of her wide ruff blocked any view of her body. "... and thought I was *German*."

Tommy made a face. "Not the ensemble I'd wear to Oktoberfest."

"More importantly," Chloe said, "he's been withholding wages from his workers for years and gambling with the spoils."

Kunigunde curled her lip in anger. "Mr. Durbridge would rather wager stolen money on a game of whist than guard those he's meant to be protecting."

"Obviously we're stealing it back," Graham said.

"And then some." Chloe smiled. "Mr. Throckmorten has been winning lately, so his pot is particularly flush. He keeps the ill-gotten gains in a clay jar that looks like—"

Marjorie held up a sketch depicting the caricature of

a clay pig. A small square was missing from the top of its rump. The sides of coins and the corner of a banknote peeked out.

"Too much stolen blunt to fit in an ordinary pocketbook." Graham shook his head in disgust. "You'd need a reticule bigger than your head to carry that thing."

Tommy held up a finger and fished through Princess Mechtilda's costume trunk. She retrieved a thick canvas satchel, roomy enough to fit a few loaves of bread.

Elizabeth made a face. "Why would Princess Mechtilda own something so cheap and ugly?"

"It's not for you," Tommy answered. "You can't play highwayman and be Princess Mechtilda at the same time. You and Chloe entertain Mrs. Throckmorten whilst the rest of us sneak off."

Jacob frowned. "We cannot descend upon Mr. Throckmorten and Mr. Durbridge en masse without causing a scene."

"I love scenes," said Tommy. "But you're right. This requires subtlety. Two Wynchesters, at most. One to make the theft and perhaps another who can provide a distraction if necessary."

Before Graham could volunteer, Kunigunde said, "I'll do it."

Hope radiated throughout his chest. She did want to be one of them!

Chloe looked skeptical. "Have you *any* experience robbing, stealing, pickpocketing, pilfering, or any other manner of nicking objects undetected?"

"I abducted an antbear," Kunigunde offered.

Chloe arched a brow at Jacob.

"He was being oppressed," he explained. "We liberated him from captivity."

"I won't do the stealing," Kunigunde said. "But I did stow away on a boat and evade my brothers. More importantly, I am an excellent *guard*. I can deflect attention if necessary, and provide defense with pleasure." She slid a pair of throwing knives from beneath the lapels of her royal coat to illustrate.

"I'll go with her," Graham said quickly. "I can steal anything."

"I said the mission requires *subtlety*," Tommy reminded him. "Not a circus."

"I can be subtle," he protested.

"Kunigunde will be there," Marjorie said. "She'll maintain order."

"She'll also need to keep silent," Philippa said. "If anyone hears her accent, they'll know it's us."

"Or the Germans," Elizabeth muttered.

"Well, you can't go like *that*." Tommy gestured at Graham's livery and Kunigunde's royal uniform. "I'll dress you to blend with the locals."

"How far is Mr. Durbridge's house?" Chloe asked.

"A few miles," Kunigunde answered.

Tommy pulled out a map. "This is where we are... and that's where Mr. Durbridge lives. 'Rose Manor.' Two tall hedgerows separate his property from his neighbors. The primary access points are the main road, and the rear path through the woods."

Kunigunde peeked over Graham's shoulder. "The good news is, with all these houses and offshoots from the river paths, once the rotters lose sight of us, they'll have no idea where we've gone."

"They'll probably think we continued on to rob someone else," Graham agreed. "The likeliest explanation is a crime of opportunity. Two utterly foxed gamblers, wagering large sums every single afternoon, at a table on the ground floor, near an open window. Practically irresistible bait to a thief."

Jacob nodded. "If anything, the surprise will be that misfortune took *this* long to befall them. The entire town knows of the two men's standing appointment. They must be infamous all the way into Manchester."

Graham opened his intelligence journal. "There are no dogs on the property. There is one butler and a few maids, but all are cautioned to stay clear of the gamblers unless summoned by the bell. Tommy's maps indicate which ground-floor rooms are which. It will be easy in, easy out."

"Once we have the wages, will the coachmen be ready with our carriages?" Kunigunde asked.

"Not quite that fast. Whilst the others are loading the valises, Chloe and Princess Mechtilda will be making I-wish-we-didn't-have-to-leave-but-the-journey-is-so-long noises at Mrs. Throckmorten. They'll offer to wait and bid farewell to their host personally..."

"...but Mrs. Throckmorten will advise them to hurry while it's still light. She won't expect her husband home until after dark, which gives her several free hours to spread word of the royal visit to her neighbors."

"Exactly." He grinned at Kunigunde. "We won't be fleeing the scene of a crime. We'll have been shooed away in spite of our sincerest protests."

"I'm ready for action. Let's go."

"Costumes first," Tommy said. "Come with me."

"Three miles is too far to flee on foot. Jacob, will you ready the horses?" Graham glanced at Kunigunde. "Astride or sidesaddle?"

Kunigunde looked at Tommy. "Will I be in pantaloons or a gown?"

"*Blend*," Tommy enunciated. She turned to Graham. "*Subtle*."

He nodded obediently. "Astride for me, sidesaddle for her, please."

"I'll go and ready the geldings," Jacob said. "Because of the trees, the path behind the guest house isn't visible from the residences. I'll wait for you there."

In short order, Tommy had Graham indistinguishable from the local farmers, even muddying his shoes for verisimilitude. He looped the canvas satchel across his chest.

Kunigunde wore a simple muslin dress. A wide, floppy bonnet hid her braids and half of her face. Tommy handed her a plain spencer to use instead of her more expensive one. Kunigunde sewed a few small knives to the underside with a single loop of thread for easy snapping, then pinned her father's epaulet above her heart.

"We'll be back soon," Graham told his siblings.

"There's no rush," Chloe reminded him. "Mr. Throckmorten will be gambling until well past nightfall."

Graham smiled. "Not tonight."

Jacob was waiting behind the guest barn with the two horses. Both geldings had been outfitted with the large leather traveling receptacles, in case Kunigunde and Graham needed to pass the pig from one rider to another.

He lifted Kunigunde atop her horse, so as to feel her curves beneath his palms once again. Then stole a kiss on the way up. Two kisses. Only seven short days remained. Five for the return journey, full of many stolen kisses at every moment possible. And then two more at home before her ship sailed.

How he hoped he could convince her not to be on it.

They set out toward the river together. When they reached the water, the riding path was not only wide enough for two horses, it was clear they were far from the first to trot along it.

Er, when *Graham* reached the water, that was.

Kunigunde stopped her horse five yards back.

"Come on," he said. "There's room for both of us."

She didn't move.

He turned his horse toward her. "Kunigunde?"

"Why is it so close?" she stammered. "To the water?"

"Why is the river path...next to the river?"

"It's like standing too close to the railing of a ship. It makes me dizzy, and I..."

"You're afraid," he said softly.

She swallowed. "The ocean took my mother. She fell in, and the weather turned. The current just...They couldn't save her."

"I'm sorry. That's awful." He wished he could help ease her fears. "Anyone would have a horror."

She nodded.

"Do you want to turn back?"

She shook her head.

"Then we must keep going," he said gently. He wished there was another way. "I promise, we're not *that* close to the water. Not close enough to fall in. There's at least two feet between us and..."

Kunigunde looked as though she might pass out. Or vomit.

"It's a river, not the open sea," Graham tried again, coaxingly. "And a shallow one, at that. The Bealbrook isn't more than six or eight feet at its deepest. We could swim across."

"I can't swim."

"All right, well...you won't have to. You're riding Sheepshanks, who is a trained professional. Not only will he keep to the path without straying, but in the event you would want him to cross the river, he could jump it in a single bound." He patted the horse's neck, just above the leather saddlebags. "These two could leap from bank to bank all day if they wanted."

"I don't want him to," she said quickly. "Tell him not to do that."

Graham considered her. His big, strong warrioress's fear of the water was not entirely logical. But then, who had ever reacted to a loved one's death with logic? Instead of seeking safety after his mother's death, Graham had responded by bringing his act out-of-doors, leaping from rooftops instead of wooden beams, every new situation more dangerous than the last.

He could not fault Kunigunde for choosing caution. Or for being afraid of the thing that had taken her mother's life.

"Sheepshanks," Graham said to her horse. "You're to stay on the path at all times. The *inside* path. Charlie and I will take the side nearest the river. Under no circumstances are any of us to venture any closer to the water. Is that understood?"

He made the subtle hand sign that prompted both horses to nod and whinny on cue.

The sound seemed to snap Kunigunde from her trance. Or perhaps it was the promise that Graham—and Sheepshanks—would not allow danger to befall her.

"You're right." She rolled back her shoulders. "I can manage this. I *am* managing this. Here I go, managing with aplomb."

Sheepshanks trotted forward to join Charlie on the riding path.

Graham launched into a steady patter, keeping

Kunigunde's gaze on his rather than on the river beside them. By the time they'd traveled two miles, Kunigunde had...well, not *relaxed*, entirely, but at least seemed more like her normal self.

"I'm a soldier," she assured him, clearly embarrassed he'd witnessed any vulnerability. "I'll be fine."

"I know you will," he answered. "When we arrive at the Durbridge residence, you tether Charlie and Sheepshanks to the trees while I walk up to the house."

Her lips twitched. "Walk? Or shimmy up the side of it?"

He widened his eyes. "I'll slide down the chimney very subtly."

"Perfect. They'll never notice a handsome rogue with—*Look!*" Kunigunde pointed up ahead at a dirt path marked with tall, white wooden posts. "That must be Rose Manor. We're here!"

He grinned at her, his blood already flowing with anticipation.

It was time to steal back the stolen funds.

34

Graham and Kunigunde guided the horses down the path toward the house until they found a clearing where their mounts could be tied to a tree without being visible from the river or from the residence.

He lifted her down, stealing a kiss along the way, then ensured the saddles were snug and ready for a swift departure.

They crept toward the house, keeping to the cover of the six-foot-high hedgerow separating this property from its neighbors, rather than strolling up the dirt path where they might be seen. The brown garments Tommy had chosen for them made them almost invisible in the dappled shadows.

As they drew closer, the ring of rosebushes encircling the house came into view, just as Tommy's maps had indicated. Because it was a crisp, spring day, most of the windows were wide open to let in fresh air. It took no time at all to spot Mr. Throckmorten and Mr. Durbridge, who were smoking cigars, clinking their glasses together, and laughing uproariously.

"In their cups," Graham muttered.

Drunken culls could be a blessing or a curse. They were less likely to think clearly or quickly, but *more* likely to react with violence and without fear.

"Stay here," he whispered to Kunigunde. "I'll enter through an empty room, grab the pot, and jump out a window."

"How can I guard you from so far away?" she whispered back.

Yes. Exactly. Now that they were in place, Graham found he did not wish to put her in jeopardy.

She narrowed her eyes. "If this is some protect-the-helpless-princess tripe, it is *your* handsome chest into which my throwing knives—"

"All right." He took another peek at the house. Kunigunde was right. She had useful talents. If he *didn't* come out that window, she'd need to know why. "Follow me. When we reach the rosebushes, keep low enough to stay out of sight and close enough to hear what happens."

"You'll enter through a window in the next room?"

"I'll enter from the next floor, if I need to. While you're crouching behind the rosebushes, can you still see in their open window?"

She tried it and nodded. "Here is what I will do. As soon as I see you reach the doorway, I'll make a ruckus. Mr. Throckmorten and Mr. Durbridge will rush to the window to see what's happening, leaving the table unattended."

"Perfect. I'll grab the pot and disappear the same way I got in. How will you get away?"

"As you leave the room, I'll wave my arms in front of my face and scream, 'Bee!' That won't be enough for them to discern an accent. Once they realize I'm not a threat, they'll lose interest in me."

"*Run.* They might not notice the missing pot right away, but if they do, they'll give chase."

"Where will you be?"

"Right behind you. I'll meet you at the horses." He dipped his head to give her a searing kiss that left them both breathless. "I'll see you in a minute."

Keeping below the crown of the rosebushes, he made his way around the house until he found the empty dining room. He vaulted over the rosebushes and in through the open window without making a sound. With luck, this would be simple.

He crossed the dining room and hovered to one side of the open door, listening for movement in the corridor.

Nothing.

Satisfied, he strode briskly but quietly toward the gambling parlor. He couldn't risk creeping along and being spied in the act by a maid.

Chuckles and bluster spilled from the open door to the parlor. There was no sense tarrying, but he didn't want the men to spy him before Kunigunde did.

Graham stuck the toe of his boot into the doorway.

Nothing happened.

Of course. Too low. She was peering through the rosebushes. She could not possibly detect movement below the level of the windowsill.

He poked his elbow past the doorjamb.

A horrendous, piercing shriek filled the air.

Chairs scraped and footsteps clattered toward the open window. Unfortunately, it sounded like only one set of feet.

Nothing for it—this was the moment to act.

Graham dashed around the doorframe and into the room. Mr. Throckmorten had abandoned his cards to run to the window, but Mr. Durbridge was still seated at the table, cigar in mouth and whisky in hand.

Mr. Durbridge stared at him in alarm.

Graham rushed forward.

As though expecting a blow, Mr. Durbridge flinched so hard he spilled his whisky and tumbled out of his chair. He left the sticky glass on the ground and leapt to his feet, fists raised in boxing stance.

"There's a woman running toward us," Mr. Throckmorten called.

Kunigunde was heading their way. *Perfect.*

Graham shoved the clay pig into his canvas satchel and hurled it out through the open window, with enough force to carry it all the way to Kunigunde in the middle of the garden.

Or at least, it *would* have done so, if Mr. Throckmorten, turning to see why his friend was not responding, had not stepped right into the flying projectile's path.

Instead of arcing smoothly over the garden, the interrupted pig crashed into his forehead and thunked to the floor on the interior side of the windowsill.

Mr. Throckmorten tumbled flat onto the carpet, out cold, having come face-to-face with his own greed. A hard lesson, indeed.

Graham darted forward to scoop up the pig. Mr. Durbridge's hand grasped the back of his coat. Graham tossed the satchel through the window.

Kunigunde rushed forward to rescue the pig.

"Go!"

Rather than run, she hesitated, clearly unwilling to leave him, not like this.

Graham could not bark explicit orders at her without Mr. Durbridge overhearing the plan. Perhaps if he dove through the window…

Mr. Durbridge grabbed for Graham's other arm. Graham jerked loose, spinning out of the way—but farther from the window and freedom.

Kunigunde slid her hand beneath her spencer.

Her throwing knives. *Shite.* Graham definitely couldn't allow her to commit a capital offense while trying to save him.

As Mr. Durbridge made another attempt to pin him in place, Graham thrust one hand in the air and was almost finished signing *Take horse to Jacob. Give money to princess. Change into uniform!* before he remembered Kunigunde wouldn't understand. He'd attempted to sign to her the day they'd met, to no avail. Why *would* a Balcovian Royal Guardswoman need to know English sign language?

But she pulled her hand away from her throwing knives to make three rapid gestures: *You escape fast.* Then she hugged the pig and took off running.

Once Graham recovered from the surprise that she had understood him, he realized Kunigunde would not be *able* to mount the horse without his aid. Instead, she was running across the garden toward the rear path as fast as she could go with a heavy satchel weighing her down.

He tried to leap forward, but Mr. Durbridge stood in the way—this time, with a pistol in his hand.

Graham held up his palms and froze in place.

The inspector yanked the bellpull hard enough to free the rope and grappled for Graham's arms to tie his wrists together. By now, the servants had heard the bell and would come running. There was little time to act. At this short range, a bullet was bound to find its mark.

At least Kunigunde was on the far side of the garden, well out of harm's way.

He waited until Mr. Durbridge lowered his pistol to tie the loose ends of the rope together. Then Graham dashed forward in a burst of energy. He shook the coil of rope from his wrists as he ran and threw himself through the open window headfirst.

As Graham flew through the air, Mr. Throckmorten, still lying in a heap before the window and thereby blocking Mr. Durbridge's path, moaned for his inspector to come to his aid.

Graham made a somersault before he hit the ground, launching himself upright with one smooth movement. He sprinted away from the house toward the trees. With one hand, he snatched a long white rose from the bushes as he ran.

Twin shouts came from the window, but no report from the pistol. Mr. Throckmorten must still be blocking Mr. Durbridge's path.

Graham didn't pause to look. He was running, leaping, flying through the woods to the waiting horses.

He emerged riding both geldings at once, one foot in each saddle. He needed both hands for the reins, so he clutched the rose between his teeth as he raced Charlie and Sheepshanks past a dumbfounded Mr. Durbridge, who bore grass stains on his breeches.

At the sound of thundering hooves, Mr. Throckmorten poked his bruised head out of the window and goggled at the sight of their thief standing atop two horses at once.

Graham raced past him, rose petals fluttering in his face as he moved both feet onto Charlie. He slid down into his saddle and dropped the reins just in time to scoop up Kunigunde beneath her arms as he galloped past her.

He tumbled her over his lap and onto Sheepshanks's sidesaddle. She grabbed the pommel seconds before both horses smoothly jumped the six-foot-high hedge of rosebushes, blocking them from the men's sight. The startled shouts faded as Graham and Kunigunde cut down the neighbor's walking path toward the river.

Kunigunde dropped the heavy satchel into the saddlebag and grabbed for her loose reins.

The manor house was out of sight behind the trees. For all Mr. Throckmorten and Mr. Durbridge knew, Graham and Kunigunde could have crossed the river by now and gone anywhere.

He gathered his reins with one hand and handed her the pitiful rose with the other. The wind had stolen most of the ivory petals, but it was the thought that counted. A token for the fair maiden Graham loved.

"Anything interesting happen at work today?" he asked innocently.

"Trick circus horses!" She laughed until tears leaked from her eyes. "When I saw you coming... When *they* saw you coming... Why in the crispy crocuses were you standing, instead of riding?"

"I was showing off." He waggled his eyebrows. "Are you impressed?"

"More than impressed." She held the bald rose to her chest, her black eyes shining. "I want you to *teach* me."

35

"*Subtle*," Tommy said, and fell over laughing again.

She and Kuni were changing clothes inside the guesthouse. Tommy was holding a frilly white parasol and wearing an equally frilly white muslin gown sprigged with tiny buds of yellow flowers.

Kuni tried her best not to stare, but Tommy caught one of Kuni's sidelong glances and raised her brows.

"I'm sorry." Kuni's cheeks heated. "I've never seen you..."

"...in a dress before?" Tommy gave a little twirl. "It's not my favorite costume, but our aim is to seem innocuous. Nothing looks more helpless than women."

"Do I *want* to know what your favorite costume is?" Kuni asked.

"There's a right moment for all of them. I'd be partial to Great-Aunt Wynchester, if we weren't trying to hide who we are."

Kuni could only imagine. As much as she wished she could burst into the manufactory and shout that the workers were to receive the money they were owed, the Wynchesters were right. It would be indiscreet.

The original clients were Mr. and Mrs. Goodnight, and it was their home that Kuni, Tommy, and Marjorie were to visit.

While the Wynchesters' drivers were readying the horses, Jacob and Graham were loading the trunks and valises back into the coaches. Philippa, in her mobcap and apron, was checking every nook of the guest chambers to make certain they'd left nothing behind.

Chloe and Elizabeth were in the parlor, taking their reluctant leave of Mrs. Throckmorten. Their hostess was giddy and flattered by the princess's expressed wish to delay her departure. Mrs. Throckmorten was also impatient for her guests to be gone so that she could begin spreading gossip of their visit. She firmly insisted her royal guest make the most of the afternoon light and begin her long journey back to London as soon as her conveyance was ready.

But first, there was a commotion.

Mr. Throckmorten came home unexpectedly early from his standing appointment, raving incoherently. He had been set upon by—well, he wasn't quite sure who. They had materialized out of thin air, flown from windows and stood on horses, and hit him in the head with a pig.

Mrs. Throckmorten was mortified to have her husband's clear inability to hold his drink be on display in front of royalty. She shooed him to bed with a cold compress before he could spoil the princess's good opinion of their family.

Outside, Marjorie dashed up to Tommy and Kunigunde wearing an equally girlish walking dress, embroidered with a band of green ivy beneath the bodice and at the base of the cupped sleeves.

"I'm ready," she said with a smile.

Tommy squinted at her. "You have paint on your nose."

Marjorie swiped at her nose, then glared at her sister. "I didn't *bring* my paints, you beast."

Tommy grinned at her unrepentantly, then turned to Kuni. "You have the spoils of war?"

Kuni lifted the sturdy basket Chloe had given her. "Every penny."

In truth, very few of the coins were pennies. Most were crowns and guineas. The banknotes lay beneath.

Marjorie's eyes sparkled. "Shall we begin?"

They strolled along the side of the road as though they were just three local ladies, out for an afternoon promenade.

Tommy carried pamphlets advertising a charity endeavor and handed them out liberally to anyone they passed along the road.

"This way," she explained, "if anyone remembers us knocking up the Goodnights, they'll think your basket was full of pamphlets, and we were charity ladies begging for donations."

The Goodnights' cottage was smaller than Kuni's private chambers back at the palace, which in turn were smaller than the princess's dressing room. And in this minuscule cottage lived two grandparents, a mother, and soon to be *two* grandchildren.

Tommy rapped on the door, pamphlets in hand.

Mrs. Goodnight answered the knock. "May I help you?"

Marjorie stepped out from behind Tommy and whispered, "It's the Wynchesters."

"Oh!" Mrs. Goodnight stepped back eagerly. "Please come in and make yourselves at home."

She led them to a square table meant for four people, and motioned for them to take their pick of six narrow wooden chairs.

"I'll put on the kettle."

"Please, you needn't fuss with tea." Tommy's voice was gentle. "If you and your husband would join us at the table, we have news we think will interest you. *Good* news."

Mrs. Goodnight's hands fluttered. "He's out in the garden, collecting raspberries. It's Victor's birthday tomorrow, and although he must work like any other day, I thought if I made some warm bread for him and his favorite jam, perhaps his birthday could still be special. But now..."

She pressed her fingers to her throat and hurried from the cottage to find her husband.

Mr. Goodnight rushed into the cottage with his wife on one arm, a bucket of berries on the other, and a face full of hope. "What can be done? What have you heard?"

"Sit, sit." His wife nudged him into a chair. "All right, we're ready. Tell us."

"First," Tommy said, "the 'fines' Mr. Throckmorten took from your daughter-in-law and the final month's wages he withheld from your son are not gone forever. We are returning the full sum to you, today."

Kuni pushed the heavy basket across the table.

Mrs. Goodnight lifted the lid with trembling fingers and gasped. "It's full of coins and banknotes!"

"What?" Her husband lifted the lid to look, then stared at the ladies in confusion. "This is far more than we're owed. This is... I cannot even fathom how much money this must be."

Tommy nodded. "It's not just yours. It's everyone's. The workers at the manufactory. Those who can no longer work, and their families."

"We're hoping you and your daughter-in-law can help determine to whom this money belongs," Marjorie added.

"Of course." Mr. Goodnight's voice was gruff. "We've known these people all our lives and worked by their sides almost as long. We will return the stolen wages to their rightful owners."

Mrs. Goodnight burst into tears. "Adella can now afford to leave the cotton mill until after the baby is born. With proper bedrest...Mother and child will live this time. And Victor will be safe at home until then, too."

She reached across the table and grabbed Tommy, Kuni, and Marjorie's hands in turn, pressing them tight between her trembling fingers.

"*Thank you*," Mrs. Goodnight whispered. "You have answered our most hopeless prayers."

Kuni's throat was suddenly too swollen to respond. All she could do was nod.

Tommy shifted in her seat. "There's more news."

Mr. Goodnight dabbed at his eyes. "More?"

"Mr. Durbridge has not been performing his duties. That is grounds for dismissal and replacement. By the time Adella has given birth, there will be a new inspector."

"Someone kind and responsible who will ensure the workers are treated fairly," Marjorie added. "*We* will ensure the post goes to the right person."

"It's all we wanted." Mrs. Goodnight's voice cracked. "To be treated fairly. To be seen as people."

"What about Mr. Throckmorten?" Mr. Goodnight asked.

"His credibility is about to be destroyed completely," Tommy said. "The Throckmortens believe they opened their home to a Balcovian princess. Mrs. Throckmorten will begin spreading gossip as soon as we leave. Tomorrow morning's newspaper will prove her to be a liar. No one will believe a word from Mr. and Mrs. Throckmorten or Mr. Durbridge after that."

"That is," said Marjorie. "The false princess *did* take a tour of the mill. But perhaps the workers might fail to corroborate that claim?"

Mr. Goodnight patted the basket of reclaimed wages. "They will be honored to collectively forget any such sighting ever occurred."

"In that case..." Tommy rose from her chair. Kuni and Marjorie quickly followed suit. "Our visit to your town is concluded. If you ever need anything else, you know how to find us."

Mrs. Goodnight followed them to the door. "I cannot thank you enough."

Impulsively, she hugged Tommy, then Marjorie, then Kuni, embracing her tight before letting her go.

"God save the Wynchesters," she said to Kuni, her eyes glistening. "You guardian angels have brought hope and joy to so many people who thought they would never feel hope or joy again."

Tommy and Marjorie were all smiles on the walk back, handing out pamphlets with extra glee.

Kuni felt a strange mix of pride and rightness and wonder. The elated clients had taken her for a Wynchester and, for a moment, Kuni had *felt* like one. She had protected those who most needed protection.

She was not wearing her Royal Guard uniform, but a simple dress of yellow muslin. It hadn't mattered. Mrs. Goodnight didn't need Kuni to wear black trousers and a bright amaranth coat to appreciate her efforts. The Wynchester name was as powerful as a royal army.

But it wasn't Kuni's to keep.

36

Five days later, Graham, Kunigunde, and his siblings were at home, seated around a dining table filled with cakes and champagne.

Graham had barely slept during the journey home. When he wasn't conversing with his siblings in the carriage or kissing Kunigunde at every posting inn along the way, he had been writing and dispatching so many letters he feared his quills had permanently dented his finger.

It had been worth it. His connections at every major newspaper and minor scandal sheet had come through exactly as he'd arranged.

The newspapers printed a factual explanation of why England had failed to glimpse the Balcovian royalty (they weren't on the ship) and when they might expect to see the royals (in two months, when Princess Mechtilda and her family arrived for their first visit in decades).

The scandal sheets went one step further, insinuating that a small town outside of Manchester had caught "Caraboo fever." A certain Mrs. T— was claiming a personal acquaintance with a princess who had never left Balcovia. Mr. T— not only spread the same lie, but insisted he and a Mr. D— had witnessed magical footpads manifest from the ether before stealing his pig and dancing atop flying horses.

Graham had embellished the stories slightly differently for each printer, ensuring any attempt on the Throckmortens' part to explain their encounter would sound like one more unlikely version of the same Banbury tale.

While Mr. York and the Duke of Faircliffe were busy doing their part in Parliament, Graham had also preemptively announced a certain Mr. D—'s dishonorable comportment and subsequent dismissal from his post before he had been given any such sack, just to hasten things along.

By the time the Wynchesters arrived home in Islington, their victory was official.

Jacob raised his champagne in the air. "Good riddance to Mr. Durbridge!"

"A wambling, flatulent cabbage who deserves his misfortune," added Kunigunde.

They all clinked glasses in toast to the ousting of a greedy blackguard and the successful return of the laborers' wages. Thanks to Kunigunde, there was even a plaque erected in the heart of Tipford-upon-Bealbrook, dedicated to Ned Goodnight, who had died so heroically, as well as bearing the names of all the other town residents who had lost their lives to the manufactory.

Nothing could bring back a loved one, but their memory could live on. Not just for their children, but for generations.

Even before the champagne cork had popped, Chloe had been vibrating with more good news to share. Due to the Mr. Durbridge scandal, the Duke of Faircliffe and Philippa's father had been able to pass motions taking immediate action to better uphold *existing* laws. Citizens all over the country had been galvanized into submitting complaints about illegal conditions and naming the persons responsible. The House of Commons now had a long and growing list of unscrupulous owners, and unethical or incompetent inspectors to sanction and replace.

Those who had been ignoring abuses until now might not care about the ill treatment of laborers and small children, but they cared very much about their reputations and maintaining a veneer of honor. Mr. Durbridge and the Throckmortens' fall from grace served as a stark warning.

The situation in Tipford-upon-Bealbrook was a precedent the House had no wish to repeat. Faircliffe named Mr. York head of a select committee formed to evaluate all future inspectors and to keep them under Westminster's watchful eye.

The siblings cheered and toasted Parliament. Faircliffe grinned and kissed his wife.

It wasn't *quite* everything the Wynchesters had wanted and hoped for when they'd gathered names for the original petition, but until a new employment act could be passed, at least conditions in cotton mills would improve significantly, all over England.

And Graham had begun several new intelligence journals.

Before this mission, his informants had resided primarily in London. Now, he planned to actively expand his network outside the city, to other places the Wynchesters could be of service.

But tonight, the connections he valued most were right here under this roof.

He set down his champagne and reached under the table to entwine his fingers with Kunigunde's.

Her dark eyes met his.

"I'm glad you went with us." He caressed her soft hand with his thumb. "You were marvelous."

"*You* were marvelous. Villains literally stopped mid-villainy to marvel in wonder at the sight of you."

"What I mean is... You *are* marvelous, Kunigunde. Always. Every day. You needn't wear an ugly bearskin hat to—"

"*Don't*," she said quietly. "You're fulfilling your destiny. Please don't try to dissuade me from mine. Your family is here. Mine is elsewhere. Your home is here. My duty is elsewhere. Can we please celebrate our clients' success without making it about *us*?"

Graham let out a breath and nodded stiffly. Blast it, he *wanted* an "us." He was done with temporary flirtations. He wanted to be a permanent part of Kunigunde's future and for her to be his.

But it seemed he was the only one who did.

37

Kuni did not want to spoil the joy of this celebratory moment by thinking about the future.

She had scant hours left to spend with Graham and his siblings before it was time to board the ship home, and the only emotion she wanted to remember was happiness.

The Wynchester family was every bit as wonderful as Mr. and Mrs. Goodnight had hoped when they'd made the long journey here for the safety of their grandchildren. But Kuni had come to love the Wynchesters for reasons that had nothing to do with their skills in disguise or weaponry or politics.

She loved the way they loved each other.

Kuni hadn't known a family could be like this. A cohesive team who played together and worked together, seamlessly and cheerfully. Loyal, teasing, irreverent, encouraging.

She supposed that was part of what she hungered for in the Royal Guard. Yes, her last words to her father were a vow to bring the same honor to their family and, in doing so, to make him as proud of her as she was of him. But long before that day, Kuni had counted on her inclusion in the Royal Guard to do what her own father could not:

Make them into a family that *acted* like a family.

She and her brothers would fight side by side. Sleep beneath the same roof. See each other every day. They would respect her at last, for they'd have no other choice. She would wear the same uniform, share the same esteemed title. Perhaps then they would even have shared experiences, shared jokes. *Want* to spend their free time with each other.

Of course, she and her brothers would also all be very busy. Fighting, training, protecting. The days would be long but rewarding. Kuni's value wouldn't be in playing dolls with the princess, but guarding Mechtilda's life. What could be more important than that?

It was such an honor to fulfill the de Heusch birthright and continue the chain of Royal Guards. Soon, Kuni would be a respected part of tradition that began a century ago and would continue on for many more. Rather like the monarchy itself. Their futures intertwined and braided together, bringing more freedoms to each subsequent generation.

That was home.

Not here.

This home was a fantasy. A holiday to another land that might as well be another world. She had borrowed this life, this family, this caring, handsome, talented man at her side...but none of it belonged to her.

She belonged in the Balcovian Royal Guard. Princess Mechtilda needed her. Counted on her. Had chosen her.

And Kuni had made a promise to her father.

"Should we open more champagne?" Elizabeth asked.

Tommy tilted the open bottles in search of stray drops. "We already drank two."

"There's nine of us now," Jacob pointed out. "That's barely enough champagne to pour half a glass each time."

Nine of us now.

As if Kuni *had* become part of the *us*.

The longing twisted in her chest, sharp and deep. But the Royal Guard was the "us" she'd been working toward, clawed and battled for, her entire life. An "us" so *us*, they'd sleep in the same barracks, wear the same uniform, be entrusted with guarding the lives of the royal family. Earn the respect of her beloved Balcovia. Inspire little girls everywhere to reach their full potential.

In a matter of weeks, she would *have* all of that. Everything she ever wanted, everything she'd promised her father. And no one could ever take it away from her.

"I'm afraid we won't join you for a third bottle," said the duke. "My wife is tired, and we ought to go home to bed."

Chloe and Faircliffe exchanged meaningful glances.

"Mm-hmm," said Elizabeth. "I believe you're going to bed, but not because you're tired."

Chloe's cheeks were pink, and she did not deny the charge. She and her husband took their leave of their siblings, and exited with eyes only for each other.

"All right," Marjorie said. "One more bottle, and that's it."

Jacob nodded to a footman.

Kuni pushed to her feet. "The hour grows late. I must remove to my chamber as well."

"Probably to pack a valise," Graham said without looking at her.

Kuni had never unpacked it. The guest wardrobe was as empty as the day she arrived. When the time came to leave, there would be no excuses to delay.

She bent to press a kiss to his temple. His soft black curls tickled her face. She wanted to lay her cheek against them and breathe in their clean familiar scent. She bade the family a good night instead.

The footman brought the fresh bottle of champagne just as Kuni was leaving. A *pop* and the explosion of bubbles sounded behind her. The farther she walked away, the more the clinking of glasses and renewed cheers faded.

The party would go on. The Wynchesters would go on. *Graham* would go on.

And so would Kuni.

As she stepped out into the corridor, she touched her father's epaulet. The Royal Guard was not only the aim she'd cherished and worked toward since she was a small girl. It had also been the most important part of her identity for her entire life. The goal and the dream that had saved her from being a lonely and lost little girl.

Without the Royal Guard, she did not know *who* she would be—but it wouldn't be Kuni. She belonged at Princess Mechtilda's side as a new kind of companion. The de Heusch were soldiers—all of them, regardless of sex. Wearing the noble uniform was her destiny and her duty. Just like her forefathers.

Instead of going straight upstairs to her chamber, Kuni crossed into the sitting room and shut the door behind her. She wanted to look around one last time at the communal family space she had shared with the Wynchesters without anyone catching her feeling maudlin.

The ship would leave in twelve hours. She felt seasick already.

Her father's epaulet meant everything to her but was meaningless to Graham. If it weren't for Baron Vanderbean, Graham wouldn't care a button about Balcovia.

None of the Wynchesters would. Just a speck on the map. A speck Kuni had pledged to defend until death.

But Graham *did* care about Kuni.

And she…was in love.

She sat on the sofa she'd first shared with Graham and pressed her hand to her heart. This time, not in search of the epaulet. But to feel the steady beat that had grown within her from the moment Graham Wynchester entered her world and turned it upside-down.

The words he knew how to pen weren't stanzas and romantic couplets, but compendiums of information. Whatever intelligence someone needed, he could provide it. His version of poetry.

Graham wanted to be the thing she needed.

And she could not let him. Not the way he really wished. But she had not meant to hurt him. To allow her anger—and, yes, also her hurt—at his presumption and lack of faith to make her react just as insensitively.

When she had pushed the book away, he had felt as though she were pushing *him* away. And perhaps she *had* been. She'd known then that she could not afford to let him slip behind her shields to the place in her heart where she was still vulnerable and scared.

But nor could she bear to leave without taking some part of him with her. A reminder that once there had been someone who had welcomed her into his arms and his life, without requiring tests to prove herself, or a special rank and uniform.

Someone whose kisses she could still taste on her lips when she closed her eyes. Someone whose shoulder she had felt safe enough to fall asleep against. Someone she would miss perhaps forever. Kuni lowered her shaking hand. Would it be so wrong to at least page through the intelligence he'd longed to share with her? She stood to face the fireplace.

On the back of the far wall rose several bookshelves. The journal she'd declined to even touch was amongst them.

The fire was low, ready to be put out or built up, depending on the whim of the siblings. She took a taper from the basket atop the mantel and lit it at the flames to better scan the rows of carefully compiled albums.

Where would he have placed it?

She remembered the color of the leather, the width of the spine. But there were so many bookcases. Wall after wall of gossip and random facts, here and in the Planning Parlor upstairs. Graham's interests appeared to be voracious and scattered.

What if he were to channel that curiosity, to direct his spies and informants toward specific stratagems? In fact—

Kuni shook her head. What was she doing? Making *plans*, as though she would be here to see them through or have any say in the matter? She hadn't appreciated Graham interfering in *her* business. She would respect him enough to stay out of his.

She turned to a new shelf. Good Lord, how many royal albums could one person collect? Graham knew more about the English king and his sons than they probably knew about themselves.

The book must be in this section, here with all the other albums dedicated to royalty...Ah, here it was! She blew out the taper and returned it to the basket before picking up the book. It was just as she remembered it. Supple brown leather. Spine three centimeters thick.

An unfamiliar marker protruded from the pages. She

opened the book at the spot to find a folded sheet of paper... with her name written on one side.

She opened the paper to read:

Dear Kunigunde,

Most likely, you will never read these words. More importantly, you do not need anyone's help. You are an unstoppable force just as you are.

You are also a fortnight delayed in your mission, through no fault of your own. You chose to help my family, and so many relieved workers, rather than help yourself.

To thank you for that selflessness, I have made a complete and comprehensive copy of the information I will be delivering to my own client. If it helps you in any way, please take any portion of the contents—or the entire book—home with you.

And if my attempt to make up for a small portion of the valuable time you have lost offends or hurts you in any way, then please toss this album directly into the closest fire.

You are the last person I'd wish to hurt. I'd much rather hold you close. I hope you interpret each page of this book as the embrace I mean it to be. Even if you choose not to accept this gift—or me—I shall remain:

Forever yours,
Graham

Heart jittery with emotion, Kuni knelt before the low fire to flip through the pages.

Its contents were everything she could want. Things she hadn't even known she *should* want. Access points and livery, painted by Marjorie. Maps, drawn by Tommy. Dates, histories, interviews, schedules, all collected by Graham and penned in smooth, bold strokes.

He was right. With this book, the royal family could enjoy the best protection and highest level of security of any trip they'd ever taken. And it would all be thanks to…

Graham.

Graham, not Kuni. Graham and the Wynchester siblings.

She drummed her fingers on the album. She knew what he would say if he could see her indecision. What he and his family *had* said, time and again.

That her dogged determination to prove herself got in her own way. The king wasn't collecting his information firsthand, was he? Perfectly capable people delegated tasks. Let Graham help her, just as she'd been helping the Wynchesters. Resourcefulness didn't mean doing everything on one's own. It meant getting the job done, however it needed to happen.

Kuni did not look down at the album he'd made her, but up at all the other albums just like it, tucked in tight against each other from floor to ceiling.

Graham possessed all of this intelligence *because* he wasn't limiting himself to what he could collect on his own. His library was stronger than he could make it on his own because he allowed others to add their voices to it.

The answers she'd been looking for were literally in her hands. As he had pointed out, she *could* have collected much of this reconnaissance by herself, given the time and opportunity. If she hadn't spent twelve of her precious forty days traveling to Manchester and back.

But in the king's eyes, what would show more intrepidity? Reinventing the wheel to prove she could, or acquiring information from the person who had it?

Kuni pushed to her feet with determination. In the end, Graham hadn't forced the book upon her. He'd let *her* decide how best to do her job. And there was only one answer.

She would take the album with her.

Outside in the corridor, she heard the siblings go up the stairs to bed. They must have finished their champagne. The celebration was over.

Kuni strode to the large table where she had caught Graham in the act of creating the original album.

The surface was tidy, though it still contained pencils and ink and paper. She took a sheet and wrote Graham's name across the top. Writing swiftly, she said she would report to the king that the Wynchesters—and Graham in specific—had been an instrumental help to the Balcovian royal family.

Then she slipped the letter into the gap left behind by her missing album.

In the early morning, they would be too busy rushing off to the port for Graham to notice the book's absence. But when he came home, the note would be there for him. He'd know Kuni had not forgotten him, and that the King of Balcovia would remember Graham's name, too.

She pressed the album to her chest. It was for her, but at the same time, it was a gift as temporary as the Wynchester family themselves. Leaving was already difficult. She wouldn't even be able to keep this book to remember Graham by. It would become part of her report.

All she would have left were her memories of the time she came to England, and met a man, and fell in love. Her chest tightened in protest.

What used to scare Kuni most about her impending departure was forcing herself back on a wooden boat floating in water. She was terrified of drowning. The sight of all the water and the knowledge of its deadly currents beneath filled her with panic.

Now what she most dreaded was saying goodbye to Graham. No more adventures together. No more passionate kisses. No more candlelit romantic snacks for two. The next time she faced water, he would not be there with trick horses to help her through.

She leaned her shoulders against the bookcase and wished it was his warm chest that supported her. That was the worst part. Despite her best efforts, she had come to rely on him after all. He had brought out the best in Kuni, even when her fears got in her way.

And they would have to say goodbye.

It would happen soon. At dawn. Each hour, each minute, each second ticked hollowly inside Kuni's chest. She wished she could divide in two. Be in Balcovia as a Royal Guard and here in England with Graham at the same time. It could not be done.

The boat would take her away tomorrow…but they still had tonight.

38

An hour later, Kuni tapped on Graham's door wearing nothing but a night rail.

He answered her knock, tying a soft, leaf-green dressing gown over his nightclothes.

His pupils dilated, and he pulled her into the room. Against his chest, as she'd longed for. Into his arms. Kuni's body trembled. A fire burned behind the grate just a few meters from where they stood, but it was the fire within her that had taken hold.

She had never seen a man in a dressing gown and nightshirt before. Never roamed her greedy hands over every hard plane, memorizing the contours of his back, the muscles of his arms, the width of his shoulders, the feel of his chest.

Kuni tried not to cling to him, but it was impossible to lift her cheek from the warmth of his chest. Impossible to stop breathing in the familiar scent of his skin. Impossible to pull her hands from the dressing gown and the way its silk slid across his tall, masculine form, no longer hidden beneath waistcoat and frock coat and trousers.

His skin was hot through the fabric, warming her in her

own flimsy night rail of pale pink linen. She could feel his defined muscles beneath her palms.

She slid her fingers up the back of his neck and into his hair, lifting her chin to beg him for a kiss.

He did not disappoint her.

His mouth took hers. His hands traced her curves reverently as his tongue plundered hers as though his whole life had been spent waiting for just this moment.

Coupled against him like this, she did not need her hands to feel the hardness of his body. Her breasts pillowed against his chest. His shaft rose to nudge between her thighs, impeded only by insubstantial curtains of linen.

Her body responded at once. Her inner muscles made an involuntary clench of desire, her cleft swelling deliciously in anticipation, ready for his touch.

"Marry me," he rasped. "At least let me court you properly."

"Graham—"

"What if you were *my* princess?" His hands found her buttocks, pressed her to him, so that his shaft pulsed hot against her. "I've spent my life chasing a fairy tale, and you turned out to be real. So much better than my fantasies. I don't want to wake up. I want to live this dream forever, with you. Let me convince you how well we fit together."

Kuni did not need to be convinced. The ache in her heart and the slickness between her legs proved that every part of her brazen body had the same fantasy he did.

But that's all it was. A fantasy.

"You know I'm going home." She tried to make a jest of it. "Besides, I couldn't give you permission if I wanted to. It's Balcovian tradition for the woman's family to grant or deny a suitor's petition. I think we can both imagine what Floris and Reinald would say."

"I don't give a damn about anyone's opinion but yours." He kissed her deeply. "If *you* want me, say the word. I will find a way."

"I can't. You know I can't."

"You mean you won't *let* yourself."

She wasn't abstaining for herself. She was paying back the previous generations and doing her part to fight for the next ones. Becoming the daughter her father had expected her to be.

"You knew I would only be here a short time when we met. How did you think that was going to work out?"

His voice was a growl. "I didn't know it was going to rip my chest apart and rend me in two. If there's no hope for us, then why are you here?"

She rolled her hips against him, letting his shaft rub against her. "I think it's obvious why I'm here."

He groaned and took her mouth again, his hands rough and perfect.

"You're not really asking me to make love to you," he said hoarsely. "It's the champagne."

Her two half glasses of champagne had been well over an hour ago. She'd bathed before knocking. Applied scented cream to her limbs. Chosen the most translucent of her night rails with deliberate care. Felt her body quicken even before she glimpsed his.

"I've wanted this for weeks," she confessed huskily. "Wanted *you*, me, together. But if you think *you're* being influenced by champagne..."

He swung her up in his arms as though she weighed nothing. "Then I guess you're not going anywhere. Not tonight. I've wanted you from the first moment I saw you. I'll give you anything you desire for as long as you let me."

She touched the soft black curls tumbling over his forehead, ran her thumb over the stubble at his jaw. "I've got all night."

"Then let's make the most of it."

39

Graham started to lay Kunigunde on the bed, then thought better of it.

If his remaining time with her was to be counted in hours, he would not waste any of them. She smelled freshly bathed, and felt deliciously soft and warm in his arms. He wanted to feast his eyes and mouth on every inch of her.

Beneath the clinging lawn of her night rail, he could see the outline of her breasts, the brown circles of her nipples, the dark patch between her legs.

But he would begin at her toes.

He set her on her feet next to the bedpost and dropped his knees to the carpet. A pair of pinkish-purple slippers peeked from beneath the long night rail. Expensive royal quality, no doubt. Graham didn't care about the rare color or the fine material. He wanted to expose the first hint of Kunigunde's bare skin beneath.

Kneeling, he slid the slipper from her left foot and bent to press a kiss to the top of each of her toes. Each toe was shorter than the last, making a perfect diagonal line. He mentally added it to the Book of Kunigunde.

Every moment of this night would be etched directly onto his soul.

Off came the second slipper. Five more kisses. He had never known himself to be entranced by pretty feet, and yet here he was on his knees before her. Perhaps the enchantress was Kunigunde. It would not matter what her body looked like. It was *her* he was in love with.

He lifted the hem of her night rail just enough to uncover her slender ankles. He'd never seen such beautiful ankles. He nudged them apart, just enough to dip his head between them. He pressed gentle kisses to the tender skin of her inner ankle, below the bone.

Slowly, he worked his way up her soft skin, one inch at a time. He repeated the row of kisses on the other side. It was the ankles' reward for baring themselves to his eyes, his touch, his mouth. It was *Graham's* reward. He now knew more about her than he had five minutes ago. And with every new inch, he would learn more and more.

Up came the night rail. Beautiful calves, toned and muscled. The calves of a woman who trained with soldiers, who could walk twenty miles if need be or stand still for days at a time. He kissed every inch, all the way around. Her legs spread a little wider to accommodate him. He repaid her with more kisses.

Next came her knees. Was there anything more fetching than the crease at the back of a woman's knee? It fairly begged to be touched, to be tasted. He turned her toward the bed so that he could press his open mouth to her skin and taste her with the tip of his tongue.

"You always smell incredible," he murmured. "Like no other scent I can remember."

Her voice was throaty with passion. "My cream contains the essence of the Balcovian amaranth flower."

Of course it did. But the only essence Graham cared to taste was Kunigunde's.

He kissed his way back to the front of her legs and raised the hem to expose her thighs.

These, too, were toned and strong. Legs that could run, leap, or kick. Legs that could wrap around his hips and lock him to her as he drove his cock deep inside her heat.

He began to kiss her inner thighs. Her own scent was deeper than amaranth flowers. He could smell the musk of her desire. His cock gave a leap of eagerness to explore.

But it was not time for that yet. He was still learning her. Performing reconnaissance with his hands and his mouth.

He lifted her night rail to her hips and nudged her thighs even farther apart.

She teetered on her toes and grabbed for the bedpost. "I don't know how long I can stand like—"

He placed his mouth on her mons and found her clitoris with his tongue.

"I can stand here all night," she blurted out, and leaned against the mattress behind her for balance. "Don't stop."

They were just getting started.

As he licked, he reached around her to cup her perfect arse for just a moment before sliding his fingers into her wetness.

She sucked in a startled gasp. Several gasps.

This night with Kunigunde was already Graham's favorite reconnaissance of all. His mouth, his tongue, his fingers, all working together to discover the secret to unlocking her unique—

Her legs shook, then tightened against him, trapping him in place.

A tiny sound escaped her throat as she climaxed around

his fingers, on his tongue. Only when the pulsations ceased did he continue his path of slow kisses upward to her flat stomach, the dip of her navel, the hint of her ribs.

"Do it now." Her voice was breathy, desperate. "I can't stand to wait."

"You'll have to try." He rose up to take her left nipple into his mouth.

It was stiff and brown and glorious. He held the night rail in his right hand so that he could use the left to play with her other nipple while he suckled. Her breasts were small and high, the perfect handful to cup in his palms.

She fumbled at his waist, managed to untie his dressing gown.

He shook the material from his shoulders and allowed it to fall to the floor. He lifted the night rail up and over her head, flinging the whisper-light material from her body at last.

She took advantage of his motion and yanked his nightshirt up over his thighs, his hips. She sucked in an audible breath at the sight of his shaft. Then she tugged his nightshirt up over his chest and off his body. She gazed at him for a long moment, as if memorizing every part of him.

"Now we're both naked." She gripped both sides of his face and kissed him. "Let's finish this in the bed."

He slid his hands from her arse to her thighs, lifting her easily so that she straddled him. His cock rubbed against her slickness. Right where he had kissed her until she came apart.

Her eyes fluttered upward as though she was not far removed from coming undone again, if he kept up the sensual contact.

Despite the temptation, he would not take her standing up like this, not their first time. He tumbled her onto the bed and climbed atop her. He teased her mons with his fingers until she began to make the little sounds he had learned meant she was close to the edge. Then he quickly positioned himself between her legs.

"This may hurt," he warned, his voice strained from the effort to refrain from plunging inside at once.

"I'm strong." Her desire-glazed eyes held his. "I hope we can do it again in the morning. Before I leave."

God. His hips bucked without conscious thought, and he buried himself inside her wet heat. He froze and held perfectly still to give her a chance to adjust to the new sensations.

Her legs wrapped around him, as strong as he'd imagined. "Is that it? Have we finished already?"

He smiled. "No. There's more."

At first he moved slowly within her, giving her body time to get used to the invasion. When her hips began to match his rhythm, urging him deeper, his strokes grew faster, more urgent.

When he knew he could not hold out much longer, he dipped his hand between them, putting the fresh intelligence he'd gathered to its best use.

She arched her back and shuddered with pleasure a bare moment before he jerked free from her body and spent himself in his hand.

He cleaned with a handkerchief, then bundled her beneath the covers and into his arms, chest to chest, their legs entwined. Tonight, there would be no need for nightclothes. The heat generated between them was more powerful than any fire.

She nestled against him, fitting perfectly against his body.

He held on tight, willing himself not to sleep so that

he could remember her heartbeat against his, the weight of her breasts on his chest, the feel of her silken legs entwined with his. The sigh of contentment that escaped her lips when she fell asleep in his embrace.

How could he drift away when the only place he wanted to be was here, in this bed, holding her?

40

Come morning, Graham left the driver with the carriage and carried Kunigunde's valise up to the dock himself.

It was not nearly as heavy as his heart.

Dawn was streaking brilliantly over the sky. He supposed it must be pretty, but he could not bear to look at it for long. Not when these were the last moments left with Kunigunde.

She'd fallen silent. Possibly because this was goodbye. Probably also due to her abject terror of water. She said she had spent the voyage over in a single cabin, clutching her stomach against the rocking of the waves.

The sky was clear now, but who knew if it would stay that way? It was May. The height of spring. Rain and wind could come at any moment.

"I'll wave to you from the railing," she vowed. Her face was already waxy.

"You don't have to. I'll understand."

"I *will.*" Her voice cracked. "I'll wave until I cannot see the pier anymore."

He nodded. "I'll watch until I can't see the ship."

The river was full of big ships and small water boats ferrying people to and fro. The only vessel Graham cared about was the royal one that would carry Kunigunde away from him.

His siblings had not come to the port with them. There was a new case. A farrier and his brother had arrived last night. The others were still gathering the details.

Graham had never before left his home when a client was inside it, but these were desperate times.

It was his last chance to convince Kunigunde to stay. If not for him yet, then perhaps…

"You would make a good Wynchester," he began.

She looked at him from the corner of her eye but did not answer. Her hand had slipped beneath her spencer, worrying the gold fringe of her father's epaulet.

"And…an impressive Royal Guardswoman," he admitted, voice defeated. "I do not mean to imply otherwise."

"I know."

Conversation had been like this since they'd left the house. Awkward. Stiff. Short. Nothing like the hours they'd spent locked in each other's arms.

He had meant their lovemaking to be soft and tender, but neither of them had shown any restraint. Their mouths had been frantic, their bodies demanding. They'd come together like comets. And then exploded into the dawn.

He'd wished he could float with her forever.

Persuasive arguments to plead his case escaped him. Everything he could think of to say—*They don't need you like I do*, or *England is almost as nice as Balcovia*, or *To the devil with your princess*—sounded desperate and selfish.

But that was how he felt. And he was out of options.

"I know it's important to you," he said, and knew he

shouldn't. "But you don't *have* to join the Royal Guard. I know you and Princess Mechtilda made plans, but it's not like she cannot find someone else to—"

Hurt flashed across her face, her eyes accusing and disappointed.

"It's not important 'to me.' It's *important*. Full stop. I don't just believe in the power of our king. I live the life I lead *because* of the Balcovian monarchy and my great-great-grandfather. He and his wife belonged to the last generation of slaves in my country because the Balcovian government was founded on abolition. Because our king was willing to die to give us a better life."

"And he *would* have died, had your family not intervened." Graham could only imagine how indebted a history like that could make her feel toward both sides. The king who had fought for equality, and each new generation of de Heusch soldiers, trying to fill the shoes of those who had marched before them.

"Yes. Though I have come to realize that the Royal Guard isn't the only post of valor. You and your family are civilian Unroyal Guards and deserve more recognition than you receive."

"We are accustomed to performing—"

"*My* family does good things, too. Marvelous things. Without the Crown, without Balcovia, without the Royal Guard, they would be no one. *I* would be no one. But my forefathers were heroes. I am so proud of them. I want my descendants to be proud of me. I want to inspire the next generations. Is my path less important than yours?"

"That's not what I—"

"This is the destiny I was born to fulfill. I promised my father I would try my best, right before he..." Her voice broke and she swallowed. Her black eyes looked haunted. "What else have I spent my life fighting for? The de Heusch family matters. Soldiers matter. *I* will matter. If you had made the same vow to *your* father—"

"That's not fair," he muttered. His weak protest was a lie, and she knew it.

Graham and his siblings *had* made a deathbed promise to Bean, and they *had* done everything in their power to fulfill it. It had taken over a year, but they had not rested until they'd kept their word.

Of course Kunigunde would feel the same way.

They had reached the end of the pier. Small rowboats and water boats bobbed, packed together in clumps near the shore. Farther out, cargo ships and passenger vessels cruised down the river. Dockworkers rushed hither and yon. Before them, the Balcovian royal ship sat docked and ready. The tip of its gangplank rested mere feet away from them.

He set down her valise. A porter rushed down the long plank to take it.

The footman said something to Kunigunde in Balcovian. Graham recognized her name, but nothing else.

She shook her head and replied in the same language.

The footman nodded and took the valise up the plank.

"I asked him to let the crew and my brothers know I would be returning home with them. He said my brothers were already expecting me. I told him I need another moment with you before I board."

Kunigunde was wearing the canvas bag they'd used when they'd recovered the stolen wages together. She fished inside and pulled out a book.

Graham's breath caught. For the briefest of seconds, he thought…But the color was all wrong. This wasn't the duplicate album he'd made for her. It looked more like the journal he'd seen her writing in since they'd first met.

"Here." She pressed the book into his hands.

His heart leapt in surprise. He started to lift the cover.

"No. Don't open it until I'm gone, please."

He lowered the book. "All right."

An easy promise. What he wanted was not words in a book, but the woman standing in front of him.

A foghorn blasted the air, followed by a cry in Balcovian from up above.

"Twenty minutes." She bit her lip and looked at him as though her heart was breaking, too.

How the devil was *he* supposed to help? *She* was the one who was leaving.

Suddenly, she grabbed his hands and pressed them to her bosom.

"Come with me," she begged impulsively. "Live at the castle. With me. I'll sneak away from the barracks whenever possible, and—"

"I can't." Graham tried and failed to smile. "I didn't pack a trunk."

They both knew it wasn't the reason he wouldn't go. He was needed here. To record all the lives lived, to ensure no one was forgotten, to save anyone in need of rescue.

She dropped his hands and nodded, her eyes not meeting his.

His stomach was hard and small, his heart fluttering. He wanted her. He could have her...at a price he could not pay. But her question gave him hope. It meant she wanted him, too. She was searching for a way for them to stay together...if Graham could only think of one.

There was movement on the gangplank just ahead.

"*Tenslotte*," came a harsh male voice.

"*Zus.*" The answering voice was more amused than angry.

Graham tore his gaze from Kunigunde to see the two Royal Guards he'd helped Kunigunde evade the day they'd first met. Her brothers, Floris and Reinald. Graham wondered which was which. They were both towering and well muscled, with dark brown skin the same color as Kunigunde's, and eyes the same bright black. The angrier-looking brother was taller. A light scar crossed his unshaven jaw. The brother with a smirk flitting at his lips wore his hair cropped close, his visage clean-shaven. His expression was unimpressed.

"I'm Graham Wynchester." He paused. Did they speak English? They had to. They'd come to England to perform reconnaissance. "I wish to formally beg permission to court your sister. I haven't yet worked out how to manage the distance—"

Floris and Reinald looked at each other and burst out laughing.

"No," the clean-shaven one said flatly.

"There's nothing to 'work out,' Englishman," said the other, his tone dismissive. His accent was stronger than Kunigunde's, but his meaning was perfectly clear. "You're not good enough for her."

Kunigunde glared at them. "Mr. Wynchester is Baron Vanderbean's heir."

Her brothers exchanged looks of surprise.

Graham was surprised Kuni had mentioned it, too. He wasn't certain what her unexpected defense meant.

"Well..." Speculation had replaced the look of amusement in the clean-shaven brother's face. "I suppose if he's part of *our* aristocracy..."

Graham's fingers clenched. He did not want to seem

good enough because they believed him Bean's son by blood.

He wanted to be good enough because he was the man in love with their sister.

"Graham, this insufferable beast is Floris de Heusch." She gestured at the clean-shaven brother who had been impressed with Graham's ties to a baron. "And the even worse one is Reinald de Heusch." She gestured at the towering brother with the scar and the stony expression.

Neither man moved.

Graham did not bow, either. He did not know what the customs were in Balcovia, or whether a Royal Guard outranked not-quite-sons of barons.

He supposed it didn't matter. Kunigunde was leaving.

"I'll be back," she told Graham, her voice unsteady. "In sixty days, with the royal family. They'll stay a fortnight, and I'll—"

"You might not do any such thing," Reinald said as if bored. "Upon Her Highness's betrothal, you'll lose the post you are currently shirking."

Kunigunde's eyes flashed. "I don't need the post of companion. When I present myself to the king, he'll let me compete in the trials. Then Mechtilda will petition—"

"And if he *doesn't* let you..." Floris interrupted.

"Which he *won't*," Reinald added with a snort.

"...then you shan't be on any future royal ship, sister." Floris's tone was not cruel, but sympathetic, which somehow made the words all the worse. "You had best say goodbye like you mean it, because this is likely to be your only chance."

Graham and Kunigunde stared at each other.

The foghorn sounded again, followed by another shout in Balcovian.

Reinald raised his brows. "Ten minutes."

"Go." She motioned them toward the gangplank. "I'll be there in a minute. My valise is already onboard. But I cannot say goodbye properly with the two of you looming over our shoulders."

Reinald looked as though he might argue, but Floris tilted his head toward the ship. They ascended the plank without further commentary and turned to peer down from the rail.

It was usually Graham who had the bird's-eye view of his prey. He did not like the reverse sensation at all.

The brothers selected a position so close to Kunigunde and Graham that they could practically jump over the side and land right where they'd been standing before. At least, *Graham* could have done so. Her brothers certainly looked testy enough to try.

Kunigunde glared over her shoulder at her brothers. "*Move.* If you want me to board this ship without my daggers in hand, then give us a moment of privacy."

Floris and Reinald exchanged sour looks, but backed away from the railing until Graham could no longer see them behind the wide brim of Kunigunde's bonnet.

Her eyes met his.

This was goodbye. Mayhap permanently.

He fished for the right words. If indeed there were any. "Kunigunde…"

"Kuni," she corrected him quietly. "Only family calls me Kuni, but you're family now. More than family. I cannot bear to—"

She threw her arms around his neck and kissed him. Not chastely, but as passionately as they'd kissed this morning when they'd coupled before dawn. When each frantic kiss had felt as though it could be the last.

This one really might be.

When she tore her mouth away, Graham felt as though part of his soul had ripped off with the loss. Good. At least she would take that much of him with her.

Kuni reached beneath her spencer and pulled out the gold epaulet.

"I want you to have this." She pinned it to his shoulder with shaking fingers. "This was how my father said goodbye when he did not have the words to convey what was in his heart."

The father who had feared—*correctly*—that he would never return.

A father who had wanted his daughter never to forget that she was loved. Did that mean that she also…

"*Kuni.*" Graham reached for her—

—but she was already turning and gone, racing up the gangplank as the foghorn blasted overhead.

The porter who had taken her valise earlier barely allowed her to step fully on board before drawing up the plank.

That was it. He'd lost her.

She had chosen serving royalty over his love.

Never before had Graham so viscerally wished to dismantle a monarchy. The royals of every country could go and guard themselves off a cliff. They had taken *Kuni*.

She appeared at the railing before him as promised, looking very much like she might be ill over the side. Her brothers flanked her at once. With visible effort, she pulled her panicked eyes from the lapping waves and swung her terrified gaze toward Graham. She was twenty feet away, but the gulf between them would only grow.

He wished she had stayed a few seconds more. He longed to know if she'd really meant the message the epaulet had always symbolized to her. *Love.* His fingers brushed the soft fringe. Could she really love him as he loved her?

She met his eyes and nodded shyly. She peeled one hand away from the railing just long enough to touch her fingers to her heart and lift them to the sky.

His chest tightened and his throat grew dry. He didn't know when she'd learned the Wynchester salute, but it could only mean one thing.

Two things:

She did love him.

And it wasn't enough.

41

Kuni gripped the railing. Her knuckles were pale, her muscles tight and trembling. The ship would sail at any moment.

Panic coursed through her veins. This time, not only due to the choppy water. Seeing Graham on the dock below, six meters and a world away, ripped her in two.

Floris and Reinald hovered at her sides. Guarding her, as they were trained to do. Because females had such delicate sensibilities, one never knew when they might swoon or find themselves in danger.

For once, they were right. Part of her wanted to leap over the railing and into Graham's arms. It was too far—she'd crush him—but the compulsion pulsed just beneath her skin.

He wore her father's epaulet. That was another piece of her, left behind.

Ever since Father's death, his epaulet had never been far from her heart. Now Graham never would be, either. She did not need a token from him to pin to her breast. She carried him with her, inside her soul.

Kuni was certain the only reason his family wasn't with

him now was because they hated her for rejecting their brother. She didn't blame them. They were probably sorry Graham had bothered to come. She could see the hurt on his face. Why would his siblings come all the way to the port to see her off, when they hadn't even waved goodbye to her carriage from their front garden?

"What in the forked spleenwort were you thinking?" Floris chided her.

Reinald looked angry enough for his ears to pop off and cow's-tails to peek out. "*Kissing* a man in broad daylight, as if you've no proper breeding!"

Ah, yes. Kissing Graham goodbye was a far more serious concern than Kuni having stowed away on a guarded ship and successfully eluded their attempts to capture her in order to spend the past forty days on her own in a foreign country performing reconnaissance for their king.

"I told you—" she began.

"Baron's heir or not," Reinald interrupted, "if someone had seen you—"

"Someone who matters," Floris added helpfully. "Someone from Balcovia."

"—you could have been *ruined*."

Or...forced to marry Graham. Kuni's chest thumped. She kept her eyes on him, rather than her brothers. Hearing Balcovian again after all this time made her feel off-kilter. The familiar sounds did not soothe her, but rather increased her sense of dread.

Reinald wasn't finished. "If your royal suitor had any idea what you just did—"

"Juffrouw de Heusch," squealed a familiar voice.

"Ada!" Kuni kept one hand locked around the railing and turned to her lady's maid. "How have you been?"

"Lovely, except when forced to speak to your family—"

Reinald glared at her.

Floris merely looked amused.

"—but the real question is how *you* have been!" Ada looked at her expectantly.

How did Kuni even answer that?

Ada did not give her time to speak. She tried to push Kuni this way and that, scrutinizing her from head to toe as best she could with Kuni's fingers glued to the railing. "I feared you would not get on without me, and look at you! Even your braids are perfect. *How* are your braids perfect?"

"I stayed with the Wynchesters instead of at a hotel. Graham found a maid who knows about hair. And I can dress myself if need be."

Ada blinked. "What is a Wynchester?"

Kuni didn't even know where to begin. Perhaps once her brothers weren't lurking nearby, she'd tell Ada the whole story.

"Come." Ada hooked her arm through Kuni's. "Shall we remove to our cabin so you needn't see the water?"

"No," Kuni said firmly. "I promised to wave goodbye."

The ship lurched.

Kuni yanked her arm from Ada's and wrapped her fingers back around the railing. This was it. The ship was sailing. Her eyes searched for Graham.

Ada muscled Floris aside to stand at Kuni's side. She followed the direction of Kuni's gaze. "Is that...your father's epaulet?"

"That's a Wynchester," Kuni answered softly. "Graham Wynchester. He holds my heart in his hands."

Dockworkers unwound ropes from wooden posts. The ship drifted farther from the port.

Kuni had feared open water ever since her mother's

death. The sea had stolen her mama, and now it was taking Kuni away from Graham. She tried to lift her fingers to wave, but she could not peel her hand from the railing.

Graham wasn't waving either. He was standing there, her book in his hand and her father's epaulet on his chest. All alone.

She would miss his siblings as desperately as she missed Graham. Secret projects with Marjorie, blades with Elizabeth, Parliament with Chloe, costumes with Tommy, the reading circle with Philippa, Jacob's animals. Missions together. Meals together. They might never believe it, but to Kuni it had felt like having a family. A *real* one. Siblings who believed in her, welcomed her, cared about her.

She was leaving them behind, too.

"We have a new cabin," Ada said. "A bigger one. I can ring for whatever food and drink would please you."

"Not now. Go on ahead if you like. I'll meet you there when I'm ready."

Would she ever be ready?

The dockworkers had already quit this pier for the next. There was work to be done. The river was full of boats, and the port bustling with activity.

Kuni couldn't look away from Graham.

She would miss him more than her heart could bear. It was already breaking. Or perhaps it had broken the moment she'd pinned the epaulet to his lapel. And now all that was left were tiny pieces, grinding into each other, turning to dust.

"All right, that's enough," Reinald said. "I don't see what's so wonderful about a Wynchester, when back home you could have—"

"You *wouldn't* see," she said with a sigh. "The Wynchesters are every bit as capable and honorable as the

Royal Guard, and they possess skills you've yet to master. Like *listening*. Like empathy."

Like family.

Like love.

"Now, see here," Reinald began.

Kuni wasn't done. "Do you know where I've been this past fortnight?"

"Playing at surveillance as if you were a Royal Guardsman?" he said in his poor-little-Kuni voice.

She gripped the railing. The wind sprayed cold mist against her face. "No. I journeyed to Tipford-upon-Bealbrook, where I helped the Wynchesters protect hundreds of exploited laborers and tear down the kingdom two greedy men built on the backs of desperate women and children."

Floris blinked. "You what?"

"The knave who was supposed to be guarding them was not. He will now face repercussions. The Wynchesters installed someone they trust to obey the law. Someone with a heart." Her own swelled at the memory. "Workers no longer need toil sixteen-hour days. Small children no longer climb sleepily through dangerous machinery. Lost wages have been restored. And that's just the beginning."

"The beginning of what?"

"They took the case to Parliament," she said with pride. "Because of the Wynchesters, lives are being *saved*. Even the reading circle is preparing a five-point methodology for training future inspectors. They're coordinating with Graham's growing network to find qualified, ethical individuals to replace those who are losing their posts."

The Wynchesters were not the Royal Guards of one specific family, but rather the unhesitating guardians of *every* family that required their help.

"So, no." Kuni kept her gaze on the rough water. "I am not done. I will stand out here as I promised I would and stare at Graham until England is a tiny speck on the horizon. And when that is over, I still will not have time for your lectures. Save your breath and my patience. There's no sense talking about somcthing you'll never understand."

Reinald gave a derisive sniff. "You think defending the defenseless is noble? What do you think Floris and I have been doing for you all these years? You'd be lost without us to guide you. You didn't even notice Prince Philbert's attempts to woo you until we pointed out—"

Perhaps Kuni *could* peel her fingers from the railing.

Just long enough to toss her brothers overboard.

Floris and Reinald loved her, but they did not see her as a full person. They loved her like a pet, to be locked in a cage for its own safety. An eagle with clipped wings inside a golden cage. They thought *she* was a soft, scared little princess to be protected and spoiled and kept from having any thoughts of her own. Much less to be respected on the same level they were.

But she was nobody's princess. She was a warrior who would never stop fighting.

A commotion was visible at the far end of the pier. Two carriages had almost crashed into each other. No...the coaches had arrived together.

Seven figures burst from the two carriages and ran at speed up to the end of the dock. It was Marjorie, Elizabeth, Jacob, Chloe, Faircliffe, Philippa, and Tommy. They crowded around Graham, who pointed in Kuni's direction.

They all turned to look.

The ship was now far enough away for the Wynchesters' faces to be blurry. Or perhaps that was just Kuni's eyes.

Had they come to take Graham away? Bundle him off, rather than let him stand there watching Kuni leave?

Marjorie rushed to the edge of the pier, touched her fingers to her heart, and raised them to the sky.

One by one, all the other Wynchesters followed suit. Not waving goodbye, but letting Kuni know that part of her would always stay with them. Hands to their hearts, fingers to the sky.

42

"Wynchesters," Reinald said in disgust.

Kuni didn't even turn around. "Say one more word against them, and it will be your last."

Floris leaned against the railing, unconcerned about the Wynchesters or the threat of violence against his brother. "Well? Did you learn your lesson?"

She gripped the railing even tighter. The clouds were darkening overhead. Rain would come at any moment. "Lesson about what?"

"You said you spent the past weeks on holiday."

"That's not what I—"

"Obviously you now realize you were not cut out for the life of a Royal Guard and decided to amuse yourself some other way. It's all right, Kuni. Reinald and I always knew you wouldn't be able to gather any useful intelligence. How could you? You're a—"

With one arm wrapped around the railing, Kuni tugged her own extensive journal from her bag and slapped it into Floris's hands, then shoved Graham's meticulously crafted album into Reinald's.

"That's all I had time to gather," Kuni said. "Feel

free to show me *your* little reports when you've finished reading mine."

Her brothers paged through the volumes in shock. Even the violent gusts of wind rocking the ship didn't rattle them as much as the compilations in their hands.

"Holy bog-popple," Floris breathed. "You did all of this yourself?"

"I collected every word of *that* report myself, yes." She nodded toward the other. "Graham Wynchester compiled that one for me."

She returned her gaze to him and his family, her knuckles pale as she gripped the rail. She missed him so much already, it was as though the blades in her spencer had punctured straight through to her heart.

"Your reports. They're..." Reinald didn't finish his sentence.

She ignored him. Her eyes were only for Graham. Besides, there was nothing to find fault with. It would have taken them years and an entire network of informants to gather half as many details as Graham had provided.

Floris said something to Reinald beneath his breath.

Reinald replied in obvious amazement.

Floris tapped one of the journals on Kuni's shoulder. "All right."

She kept hands locked on the railing and her gaze on Graham and his siblings. As much as she would rather be safe in her cabin than exposed out on the railing, the Wynchesters were getting smaller and smaller, and she didn't want to miss a single moment.

"All right, what?" she asked without turning.

"All right, you're right," Floris said. "You've got it under your knee. Your books make our notes look like we never stepped off the boat. This will be the most prepared the Royal Guard has ever been for an international visit. We should have taken you seriously."

"A little late for that," Kuni muttered. Graham and his family were much too small now to make out faces. Just a colorful smudge at the end of a brown pier. The boat was turning around a bend. The sky was dark gray. Soon she would no longer be able to see him at all.

"It isn't too late," Reinald said. "You're not eligible to participate in the men's trials—"

"My report will speak for itself," she said firmly.

"But perhaps we can change that," her brother finished, his voice gruff. "Floris and I have seen you copying the soldiers since you could toddle. Father used to say you learned to march before you learned to talk. But this..."

"It's *good*," her other brother said. "I didn't believe it of you, but Father was right to call you capable and talented."

Reinald made a frustrated sound. "We both underestimated you. Have probably *been* underestimating you for twenty-five years."

"I'm sorry, Kuni," Floris added quietly. "We won't let the king make the same mistake."

"Wh-*what?*" She turned to face them, heart pounding. "*You* will give a personal recommendation? Both of you? The king's two most trusted and decorated Royal Guards?"

"It's in your blood," Reinald said grudgingly. "You'll do our family proud."

Floris gave a crooked smile. "You'll make *Father* proud."

Kuni sucked in a shaky breath and turned back to the railing. Graham was no longer visible. Even the pier was just a memory refracting in muddy water. It was only her and her brothers now. And a shining future as a Royal Guard, protecting Princess Mechtilda.

This was what she had wanted. What she had dreamed of, what she had worked for. It was why she was standing here on this ship, sailing back to Balcovia. With Graham's album and Floris and Reinald's support, her acceptance was no longer in question. On the next voyage, she would be wearing a *real* uniform.

Why, then, did the victory feel so hollow?

She squinted across the water. There were other piers. Countless boats, large and small. Dockworkers. Even some sort of fish market off to the right.

But Graham and his family were gone.

The water had turned as dark as the clouds overhead. It was as though the ship were sailing off at sunset rather than sunrise. The wind picked up next, slicing through Kuni's gown and whipping straight through her heart.

Reinald and Floris were her elder brothers...but no longer Kuni's *only* family. The Wynchesters had taught her that family was more than blood. Family was anywhere you were *treated* like family. Anywhere you were welcomed, and cherished, and loved.

They didn't need her to prove herself better than everyone else. She didn't need to *be* better than anyone else. Being the best possible Kuni was already enough.

Her connections to Princess Mechtilda did not affect the Wynchesters' opinion of her. They viewed everyone as worthy, not just royalty. No wonder they did not understand her desire to spend the next few decades as a Royal Guard to a princess—wherever Mechtilda might be sent.

Was that future still what Kuni wanted?

Loyalty was everything. The question was where her loyalty ought to lie.

To her king? To Princess Mechtilda? To her brothers? To the promise she'd made her father? Or to the family she suspected was still on the pier, watching the big Balcovian royal ship sail away?

A drop of rain slid down her face. Kuni had followed her dreams and achieved them, only to discover they weren't her dreams anymore. They belonged to someone else. Someone she used to be, but no longer was.

She touched the blank space beneath her spencer where her father's epaulet used to be. The distinctive emblem was a symbol, not the goal. Being heroic meant helping those who needed you.

When Father had told Kuni he would support her fight to become a guardswoman after the war, perhaps he didn't mean that the Royal Guard was the only place she would belong. Perhaps he had simply meant for her to *find her place*.

She didn't need a uniform to be important. The Goodnights had taught her that. Kuni had changed their lives because of her actions, not the color of her regimentals.

It was people who didn't have guards that needed guarding the most. People like Mr. and Mrs. Goodnight, like Adella and Victor. *That* was where Kuni could be most useful. Indispensable, even.

Instead of saving one person, she could save many. Not only protecting lives, but changing them for the better.

But only if she stayed.

The heavy clouds overhead could not contain the rain any longer. Dozens of fat droplets fell from the sky and splashed Kuni's cheeks with cold water. The weather was turning. Fear ricocheted through her. She kept her grip on the railing. More drops fell, until the railing was slick with rain. Holding on became harder than ever.

She glanced over her shoulders at her brothers. They were looking at her now, not with condescension, but with respect. As a future colleague. As an equal. As a sister. Could she make this choice?

Staying would mean leaving one family for another.

But Floris and Reinald didn't need her. The king didn't need her. Even Princess Mechtilda didn't need her, personally. The Royal Guard would get on fine without Kuni. Balcovia had thousands of soldiers. There would always be someone to take her place.

The Goodnights had needed the Wynchesters...*and* Kuni. To them, she wasn't replaceable. She was one of them.

Or would be, if she remained in England.

By staying, Kuni would be giving up her home, her status, and life in a royal palace...but she would gain a found family of commoners whose faith in her had never once flagged. And a smart, strong man who loved her and thought her perfect exactly how she was. There was nothing common about that. Kuni was pretty sure the trade would make her the luckiest woman in the world.

The wind howled and waves knocked hard against the side of the ship.

Kuni fought down bile and fished instead for paper and pencil inside her bag. Using one of her journals as a writing surface, she jotted off the most legible note she could while maintaining a one-armed death grip on the railing. She affixed a seal and handed the folded paper to Floris. "I need you to give this to Princess Mechtilda."

Reinald reached for the letter. "Let me see what it says, first."

She knocked his hand away. "That letter belongs to Her

Royal Highness. Your job is to deliver her personal correspondence safely, not violate the princess's privacy."

He nodded, chastened.

"But…why are you giving this to me?" Floris asked. "Can't you just tell her whatever your message is yourself?"

"I won't be there to do so," she told him. "I can't go home and put on a uniform when my home is here, no uniform required. Not anymore. I'm retiring my old dream to live a new and better one."

The ship gave another lurch as the rain poured down harder.

"I don't think you are," said Reinald. "This ship has already sailed. Unless you want to jump overboard and swim?"

43

Graham watched the large ship grow small, his stomach sinking more as each new wave pushed Kuni a little farther away.

He hoped she was all right. The wind had picked up, turning the water choppy. The air was thick with falling rain. Visibility diminished by the second.

Graham couldn't see Kuni's face anymore. He couldn't even see her outline. But he knew where she was because he hadn't looked away, not for even a second.

"It's . . . all right to be sad," Marjorie said hesitantly.

"Stop it." He was doing his best to keep his face blank and his emotions locked deep inside.

"It's all right to hurt," she added, softer.

"*Stop it.*"

He could not deal with them being kind to him. Supportive. Understanding. He could remain stoic just as long as no one put the feelings he was trying to hide into words.

"You can go back home if you want," he told them without tearing his gaze from the receding royal ship. "While your umbrellas still hold."

"And you?"

"I'm going to watch until the ship is completely gone."

Perhaps *then* he'd be ready to walk away.

Perhaps.

"Then we stay," said Marjorie.

The siblings' umbrellas were open now, huddled close to form a protective barrier between them and the sky.

Graham didn't want an umbrella. He needed Kuni.

Jacob smiled despite the rain. "She made the Wynchester salute."

"I taught her," Chloe said with pride.

Graham hadn't thought she would do it back. While the boat was anchored was one thing, but rocking in a storm... Kuni must have been terrified. But she'd been brave enough to return the gesture anyway. He knew she was still there at the railing. Fighting panic. For him.

"Did I see her brothers with her?" Marjorie asked.

"Charming fellows," Graham muttered. "They said she might not return, no matter what her wishes."

"Not return!" Elizabeth said in surprise. "Why not?"

"According to her brothers, the probability of her becoming a Guardswoman is doubtful at best. She'll have lost her post and her status on this trip. Without a royal connection, she won't be accompanying the royal family anywhere."

No one could think of anything to say.

"She's afraid of the water," he added inanely, as if *that* were the obstacle keeping them apart. "She can't swim."

Even if she *could* swim, no one in their right mind would attempt such folly in water this rough. It was a good thing Kuni was in a large, sturdy ship and not a light, tiny water boat.

No, it was a *bad* thing. He didn't want her on *any* boat.

He wanted her here, in his arms, forever. But it was not what Kuni wanted. The sea was taking her away.

The same sick panic Kuni felt on the open sea was how Graham felt inside, too.

"*I* would make a handsome Royal Guardsman," Tommy said to Philippa. "And there is no chance in hell Prinny would appoint me to the position."

Graham stopped listening to his family.

Kuni didn't want him enough to stay. Had never seriously considered him as a possibility. She had been planning to leave from the moment they met, and in the end, nothing she'd seen or experienced could tempt her to choose love.

Nothing Graham had shared with her, not himself, his soul, his family, his life, his body—none of it had changed her mind.

If he was honest, what could he offer her?

Something like: *Relinquish your raison d'être, your family, your friends, your home, your dreams, your legacy, your castle, your palace, your prince who wishes to court you, your close ties with a princess, your promise to your father...and stay here with me, far away from everything you cherish most, for no other reason than because I love you?*

It did not sound like much of a bargain.

Life as a scandalous Wynchester in semi-fashionable Islington would be a far cry from the respect, riches, and high social status she enjoyed in bucolic Balcovia.

England didn't contain any of the people or places she was used to. There was a different language, different food, different customs. Including many terrible ones. Slavery still being legal throughout the rest of the Empire, for example. Many aristocrats here owned plantations and human people elsewhere. It was not a good trade.

Graham would have loved to see where Bean came from and would leap at the chance for a short holiday. But like Kuni, he could never abandon his siblings. Nor could he turn his back on the good works the Wynchesters did here, where they were needed, just to coddle himself like a royal somewhere else where life was easy. He hadn't been able to save his mother. He'd be damned if he failed to help anyone else who needed him.

"Fake Princess Mechtilda wouldn't need an umbrella," Elizabeth said, deadpan. "Her neck ruffle is wide enough to shelter an entire village."

Graham wished he could share in the humor.

Much as the Throckmortens had treated the false princess, Graham supposed he had viewed royals the same way he'd hated to be seen in the circus: as entertainment, as a show, as a farcical drama to go and gawk at and be near, but never to think of as people.

From everything Kuni had said about Princess Mechtilda's lack of independence, being royal did not sound as marvelous as Graham had once imagined. Of course he wouldn't mind the palaces, and the prestige, and the luxury... but at the cost of his free will?

Bean had not dictated the siblings' lives. Nor did London's high society possess any hold over them. There were no vouchers to Almack's for the Wynchesters, but they could do and live as they pleased. There were no rigid roles to undertake, no pomp and circumstance to adhere to, no forced marriages for strategic political alliances, regardless of one's personal interest.

Graham was free to love anyone he pleased.

And he'd chosen the one person he could not keep.

Although Kuni's brothers did not seem to understand their sister, she'd grown up with Princess Mechtilda. The princess had spent years aiding and abetting Kuni's wish to train with the soldiers so that they would be together forever. Why leave such a staunch, understanding friend?

And then there was that damnable prince.

He wished she hadn't told him the scoundrel's name. He didn't want to know anything about Prince Philbert or obsess about all the things royalty could offer Kuni that a mere Wynchester could not. All the things Balcovia could offer that England could not.

As far as Graham was concerned, Kuni was everything he'd been looking for. But the fairy tale was over. All he could do was watch her leave.

The ship sailed around a bend. That was it. Kuni was gone.

He felt the loss deep in his soul. He no longer wished to be a long-lost prince. He wanted to be chosen for himself. To be acceptable, just as he was. To offer everything he had, and have it be enough.

"I'm sorry," Faircliffe murmured.

Graham nodded, but could not speak. He was still staring at the spot where he'd last seen the ship. *Should* he have gone with Kuni, when she asked? Was that his one chance at love, and he'd let it sail away?

"Is that your poetry album?" Jacob asked quietly. "You tried to give it to her, and she wouldn't take it?"

"No, it's..." Graham didn't know *what* it was. He lowered his eyes from the empty horizon. Kuni couldn't see him now, anyway. He opened the journal to the first page.

BALCOVIAN ENCYCLOPEDIA
FOR GRAHAM & FAMILY
FROM KUNI, WITH LOVE

A little choking sound escaped his throat. He turned the pages, slowly, then faster.

List after glorious list of the provinces, the shires, the towns. Names and descriptions of important people. Royalty and aristocracy, past and present. The name of the head cook in the royal castle. Ada, Kuni's lady's maid. The genealogy of Kuni's family, as far back as she knew it. What her father had looked like. The sound of her mother's laughter.

Menus. A disclaimer that Kuni had never actually tried to cook anything, so there were no recipes to accompany the dishes. Little drawings to show how it looked fresh from the oven, or how courses were arranged during royal feasts.

The history of Balcovia. What those same lands had been like under Dutch rule. What the citizens had fought to achieve. How the abolitionists and the duke who became Balcovia's first king relinquished their share in the Dutch East India Company in exchange for independence. How it hadn't been quite that simple, and many lives were lost.

"It's an encyclopedia of Balcovia," he said in wonder.

Maps. Where the major rivers were. How to find the Winter Castle, the Summer Palace. A schematic drawing of Kuni's private chambers. The location of her bed. Where she lay her head upon the pillow.

It was every question he'd ever had, answered. Questions he hadn't even thought to ask yet. The amateur drawings and uneven lines only made him adore the encyclopedia all the more.

Kuni had done this with no help. For Graham.

He remembered the ink smudges on her fingers and closed his eyes. She had been making *him* a poetry album all along. Information *he* wanted. Her story, and the history of her people.

Something to remember her by.

"May I see?" Marjorie asked.

He didn't want to let it go, but forced himself to hand over the encyclopedia.

The other siblings crowded around Marjorie's shoulders.

"Ha!" Elizabeth pointed at a page. "It's a ceremonial formation of Royal Guards. I'd like to challenge every one of them to a sword fight."

Marjorie turned the page. "Oh, it's Princess Mechtilda's family tree!"

Graham did not even look. He'd just waved goodbye to the only princess that would ever matter to him.

"The rain," Chloe said. "It's easing."

Marjorie poked an arm out from under her umbrella to test the weather. "What's that?"

Graham glanced at the book. "It looks like a list of seasonal fruits and vegetables."

"No." Jacob tapped his shoulder. *"That."*

Graham squinted down the Thames. Visibility was rotten, but yes, he could see *something*. Coming toward them was a little gray speck, growing bigger by the second, rising and falling with the waves.

"It's a water boat," Tommy said excitedly. "I think…I think…"

Graham rushed to the edge of the pier, sliding on the slick surface. The tips of his boots teetered on the last wooden plank. He leaned into the wind, squinting against the rain, and did not breathe until the gray smudge came into focus.

It *was* a water boat. A small, rocking vessel containing a tall, familiar valise and a woman wearing a traveling dress of Balcovian amaranth.

Graham's heart banged in joyful disbelief.

When she drew close enough for him to discern Kuni's face clearly, he saw her hands gripped a ring-shaped life buoy to her chest, and her eyes were shut tight. She looked absolutely terrified.

Kuni peeled open one eye in time to see them all watching her approach. She gave a woozy-looking smile, touched her hand to where her heart would be if a circular float weren't plastered to her chest, and lifted her fingers to the sky.

Graham's siblings burst out in cheers and shouts.

When the water boat finally reached the pier, the boatman helped a still-shaking Kuni up onto the wet dock. The life buoy fell from her fingers. Faircliffe dashed over to rescue the buoy and give the boatman a vail for his service.

Kuni stumbled forward, sliding on the slippery planks. She threw herself into Graham's arms, clinging to him even more tightly than she had done to the lifebuoy.

When at last she lifted her head, she swiped at her cheeks with the back of her hands and turned toward his siblings.

"Wynchester family." Her voice cracked. "May I please have your permission to court your brother Graham?"

"We cannot grant it," said Marjorie. "Graham's life is his own. You had better ask *him* if he would like that or not."

44

Kuni's stomach lurched as though her feet were still in the rickety boat and not standing on the solid dock.

Semi-solid. She could see the turbulent river between the pier's sodden wooden slats. It was how *she* felt. The illusion of being strong and whole, but with tumult churning beneath the façade if you took a close enough look.

She'd made it back to the port. Alive. Dripping wet. But that was only the first step.

When she'd thrown herself into Graham's embrace, he had…not truly embraced her. His arms had come up reflexively, but his body had been stiff. As though to say, *I watched you sail away. How do I know you won't do it again?*

She would have to show him that nothing mattered more to her than him. That she had risked her life in that tiny boat because the only life she wanted to live was one spent with Graham.

"I think you missed your ride," Marjorie offered when the silence wore on.

Kuni kept her eyes on Graham. "I meant to miss it."

The wind whipped through his hair, tossing his curls asunder. His brown eyes remained fixed on hers.

"When will the next ship come?" Elizabeth asked.

"Two months," Kuni replied.

"But... isn't that *after* the trials where your king chooses his new crop of Royal Guardsmen?" Tommy asked.

Yes. Yes, it was.

"I'll miss it," Kuni answered. "And the next ship, too. Only royals and their staff will be allowed on board."

Elizabeth leaned on her sword stick. "Did... your brothers say you were unlikely to be chosen as a guard?"

"They said I would definitely be chosen. Floris and Reinald offered to sponsor me themselves."

"They *did*?" Chloe said in surprise. "Graham said..."

"That they would not support me? No, not at first. But when they saw the thoroughness of my report, as well as the album Graham put together—"

His face lit up. "You took the copy?"

"I did. His Royal Highness, the King of Balcovia, shall be informed that the Wynchester family was instrumental in this mission and that Graham Wynchester in particular is owed a debt of gratitude."

"You took the album," Graham repeated. He looked as though he might float away with happiness.

Marjorie and the others lowered their umbrellas. "Are you going to try for the Guard next year instead?"

Kuni shook her head. "All my life, nothing was more important than serving my king as an honored member of the Royal Guard, just as my family has done for generations. And then I met you. You showed me all the different ways to guard others with honor."

She placed her trembling hands in Graham's. "It is *you* whom I have disappointed. I'm sorry I did not accept your help when I could have. I'm sorry I packed my valise and said goodbye. I'm sorry I boarded the ship, and I'm sorry I left. But regardless of whether there's any hope for a second chance, I'm *not* sorry I came back to try."

She lifted their joined hands and stepped close.

"I love you, Graham Wynchester. I would sail the entire world twice over to be with you. No king of any kingdom can command my heart, which belongs only to you. Let me give you all of me, and spend the rest of my life by your side. If you don't want 'forever' yet, we could try for two months to see—"

He hauled her against his body. "I want forever."

Before she could reply, he covered her mouth with his.

The rest of the discussion was not with words, but with kisses. The stroke of his tongue against hers, the feel of his strong arms wrapped around her.

The Wynchester siblings cheered.

Kuni held on to Graham as tight as she could. This was the first kiss of forevermore. A kiss of hope and joy and completeness. Of finding her place, here in his arms. Of their fairy tale, coming true. Of a future worth fighting for.

"I love you," he said, when at last he ripped his mouth from hers. "I'm not certain even forever will be long enough, but we can begin with that and continue on from there. You don't have my heart, Kuni. You *are* my heart. And I would love for you to be my wife."

"I would love that, too." She kissed him again.

More cheers erupted around them.

"Kunigunde is a Wynchester!" Marjorie shouted.

"Not yet." Elizabeth unsheathed her rain-speckled sword stick. "We agreed when Philippa joined our family that we would add ceremonial flair to the moment of official acceptance."

"*Did* we agree to that?" Jacob said doubtfully. "Or was it something *you* said whilst holding a knife, and no one chose that particular moment to disagree?"

"*Knees*," Elizabeth commanded Kuni without remorse.

Without hesitation, Kuni sank to her knees on the wet wooden dock. This was the opposite of being rejected, of being not enough. This was being welcomed with open arms. Being *wanted*. It felt every bit as momentous as becoming a knight in a royal accolade.

Despite the strong wind, the blade did not wobble in Elizabeth's hands.

Kuni was about to become part of the one family who had never doubted her. Who had loved her even as she sailed away…and loved her even more when she sailed back home to them.

Elizabeth brought her rapier down on Kuni's right shoulder. "By the power vested in me by…*me*—"

"Cut her, and I'll kill you," Graham growled.

"Cut her braids, and *she'll* kill you," Marjorie added.

Elizabeth ignored them. "I hereby dub you…" She lifted the rapier and brought it down on Kuni's left shoulder. "…an official…full-blooded…Wynchester!"

The siblings clapped as though Kuni had been knighted by the queen.

As soon as Elizabeth sheathed her sword, Graham pulled Kuni up and back into his embrace for another kiss.

"Congratulations," he said between kisses. "You're stuck with us."

She grinned at him. "There's nowhere else I'd rather be."

Epilogue

Two months later

One would not suppose that the neighborhood of Islington was merely *semi*-fashionable from the quantity and quality of the many carriages cluttering the Wynchester property and stretching along both sides of the street in front of it.

The wedding ceremony had been a small, family-only affair, but the wedding *breakfast* that followed was already the best, loudest, happiest, most chaotic, and most memorable celebration Graham had ever seen unfold between these walls.

This, despite the fact he kept forgetting to pay any attention to his guests. How could he, when he was busy gathering Kuni in his arms to steal kiss after kiss at every possible opportunity?

She was resplendent in a flowing gown with skirts of rich pinkish-purple Balcovian amaranth, embellished with three rows of freshly picked white roses along the flounced skirts, and a white silk bodice. Glistening teardrop pearls were sewn to the golden ribbon traveling beneath her bosom. All the women present exclaimed that they had never seen a more beautiful bride or a more stunning gown.

Graham smoothed the epaulet on his lapel. It was a twin to the one beneath Kuni's bodice. Pinning them had felt just as momentous as exchanging rings. Now that the ceremony was through, Graham was ready for the next step. He calculated how many more cakes he would have to eat before he could politely whisk Kuni upstairs to divest her of her pretty dress and make love to his gorgeous wife.

As a matter of fact, he was perilously close to whisking her upstairs *im*politely, royal guests be damned.

In addition to providing Kuni with a wedding dress and bejeweled tiara, the princess had brought Kuni's belongings from Balcovia and arranged for all of her fellow companions—the friends Kuni had grown up with—to come along on this journey in order to attend the wedding celebration.

At the moment, Princess Mechtilda was conversing with Chloe and Faircliffe in the middle of the largest salon. She had been delighted by the preemptive portrait Marjorie had painted of Graham bowing to Her Royal Highness, and had not only suggested they reenact the image in exactly the spot depicted, but had even bowed *back* to Graham in return.

Marjorie already promised to paint *that* scene next.

Kuni's brothers were currently inspecting the sideboards. It was a grand buffet, fit for a king...or a pauper. There was something for everyone. Even Balcovians.

Floris devoured several meat pies and returned for more. Reinald had discovered a weakness for oatcakes and refused to stray far from the tray. This unorthodox visit would not only appear in the gossip columns of tomorrow's London newspapers, Graham suspected it would become legend back in Balcovia as well.

The royal guests had brought gifts for the entire

Wynchester family. A large trunk full of expensive amaranth—paint for Marjorie, dye for Tommy. Another trunk full of books—a Balcovian illustrated manuscript for Philippa, and an enormous collection of political essays and parliamentary transcripts for Chloe and Faircliffe. A sword forged by the royal blacksmith for Elizabeth. And for Jacob, several translated volumes from the most celebrated Balcovian poets.

Graham didn't want anything but Kuni. As far as he was concerned, she was the best thing Balcovia had ever created. No gift on earth could surpass Kuni's love.

Princess Mechtilda had surprised him by anticipating this perspective. Her gift for him was a trunk full of spectacularly gilded, blank albums, in which to chronicle his married adventures with Kuni—and any equally dashing and rebellious children, the princess added with a wink.

All the Wynchester family's friends were also present, including the two dozen members of Philippa's reading circle, who had spent the past few months educating themselves on the history of Balcovia and its dialect. Several of the bluestockings were currently charming the regimentals off all the Royal Guards present—and perhaps even one of the companions.

This time, it was Kuni who wrapped her arms about Graham's neck and drew him to her for a passionate kiss.

"I'm glad you meddled your way into my life that first day," she teased.

"I'm glad you daggered your way into my heart," he replied, and gave her another kiss.

They were so immersed in their loving talk and accompanying kisses, that at first they did not register Princess Mechtilda addressing the entire Wynchester family.

"...personally invite you to Balcovia for a winter

holiday," she was saying. "My father has granted me full permission. You will be my honored guests and stay for as many weeks as you'd like in our humble palace."

"It's not humble," Kuni murmured in Graham's ear. "Even the water closets are dazzlingly lavish."

He could barely hear her above the buzzing in his brain at his family being hosted by no less than the royal family.

"Can I take my canvases and paints?" Marjorie asked.

"You can if you like," the princess responded. "Or we can provide you with supplies and a studio, and send you home with trunks containing your creations."

Graham thought Marjorie was going to swoon on the spot.

"Can I fence with your soldiers?" Elizabeth asked, brandishing her new sword as though the princess might have forgotten its presence.

All the Royal Guards ran over at once, blades drawn.

Her Royal Highness laughed and waved them back. "You can do as you please. My home shall be your home for the duration of your visit."

"Can I—" Jacob began.

Mr. Randall appeared in the open doorway, his impeccable appearance marred only by a few cake crumbs in his cravat. "Pardon the interruption. You have a visitor."

Their friends and loved ones were already present... which could only mean one thing.

A new case.

"If you'll excuse us, Your Highness," Graham said to the princess, then strode over to the butler. "Who has arrived?"

"A Mrs. Lachlan. Out of desperation, she was forced to sell her great-grandmother's pendant in order to keep her home, only to be paid...with these." Mr. Randall handed him a small stack of guineas.

Graham flipped through them, counting in his head as he went. "Is it not enough coin?"

Marjorie appeared at his shoulder and snatched the guineas from his hand.

"They're *not* coins," she breathed. "These are *forgeries*."

"Bloody good ones." Jacob took them from her and let out a slow whistle. "As good as Marjorie could have done herself."

"Take that back," Marjorie said hotly. "If *I'd* done it, I wouldn't have been caught."

"This forger has not been caught either, I'm afraid," said Mr. Randall. "That is why Mrs. Lachlan is here. She has no usable money, and soon will have no home. Her landlord has granted her one week's amnesty. She is hoping—"

"Accepted." Marjorie plucked a false coin from Jacob's hands and glowered at it. "Art is meant to improve lives, not ruin them. These forgeries are insult on top of injury. I will find who did this, and I will destroy him."

"Where is our client now?" Graham asked the butler.

"In the sitting room."

Kuni laced her fingers with Graham's. "Then let's get started."

Eyes narrowed, Marjorie muttered to herself as she glared at the guineas.

All nine Wynchesters slipped away from the celebration to meet their new client...leaving the royal princess behind.

Kuni grabbed a tray of hot pies on the way.

Don't miss
Marjorie's story in

My Rogue to Ruin

Coming in
Fall 2023

About the Author

Erica Ridley is a *New York Times* and *USA Today* bestselling author of witty, feel-good historical romance novels, including *The Duke Heist*, first in the Wild Wynchesters romps starring caper-committing siblings. Other fan-favorite series, The Dukes of War, Rogues to Riches, and The 12 Dukes of Christmas, feature roguish peers and dashing war heroes amid the splendor and madness of Regency England. When not reading or writing romances, Erica can be found eating couscous in Morocco, zip-lining through rainforests in Costa Rica, or getting hopelessly lost in the middle of Budapest.

You can learn more at:

EricaRidley.com
Twitter @EricaRidley
Facebook.com/EricaRidley
Instagram @EricaRidley

Fall in love with more enchanting historical romances from Forever featuring matchmaking, disguises, and second chances!

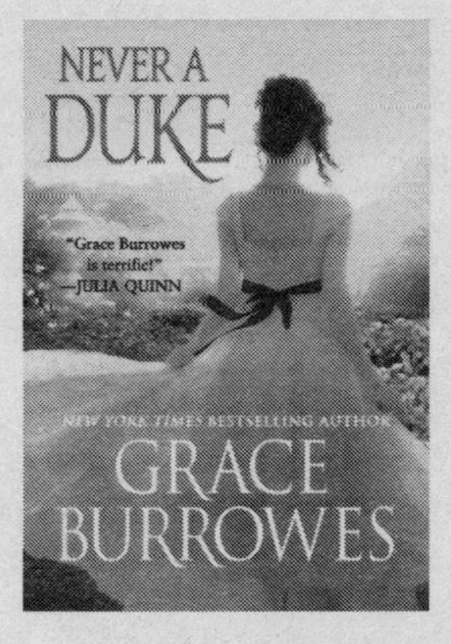

NEVER A DUKE
by Grace Burrowes

Polite society still whispers about Ned Wentworth's questionable past. Precisely because of Ned's connections in low places, Lady Rosalind Kinwood approaches him to help her find a lady's maid who has disappeared. As the investigation becomes more dangerous, Ned and Rosalind will have to risk everything—including their hearts—if they are to share the happily ever after that Mayfair's matchmakers have begrudged them both.

Follow @ReadForeverPub on Twitter and join the conversation using #ReadForever

THE PERKS OF LOVING A WALLFLOWER
by Erica Ridley

As a master of disguise, Thomasina Wynchester can be a polite young lady—or a bawdy old man. Anything to solve the case—which this time requires masquerading as a charming baron. But Tommy's beautiful new client turns out to be the reserved, high-born bluestocking Miss Philippa York. with whom she's secretly smitten. As they decode clues and begin to fall for each other in the process, the mission—as well as their hearts—will be at stake…

THE HELLION AND THE HERO
by Emily Sullivan

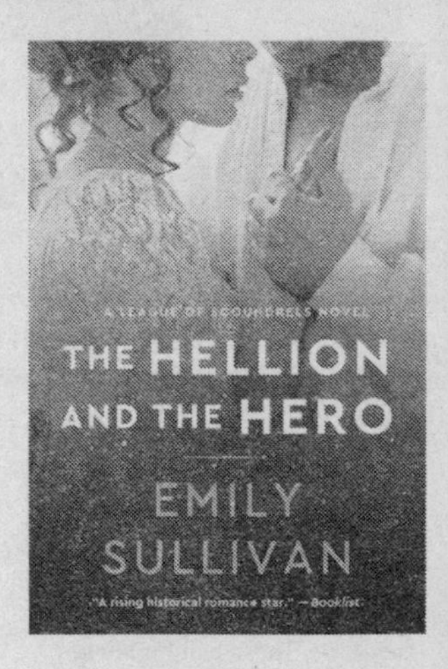

Lady Georgiana Arlington has always done what was best for her family—even marrying a man she didn't love. Her husband's death has left her bolder—a hellion, some would say. When a mysterious enemy jeopardizes her livelihood, only one person can help: the man she left heartbroken years before. Once a penniless fortune hunter, Captain Henry Harris is now a decorated hero who could have his choice of women. Fate has given Georgie a second chance, but is it too late to finally follow her heart?

Discover bonus content and more on read-forever.com

Connect with us at
Facebook.com/ReadForeverPub

DUKES DO IT BETTER
by Bethany Bennett

Lady Emma Hardwick has been living a lie—one that allows her to keep her son and give him the loving home she'd never had. But now her journal, the one place she'd indulged in the truth, has been stolen. Whoever has it holds the power to bring the life she's carefully built crumbling down. With her past threatening everything she holds dear, the only person she can trust is the dangerously handsome, tattooed navy captain with whom she dared to spend one carefree night.

HOW TO DECEIVE A DUKE
by Samara Parish

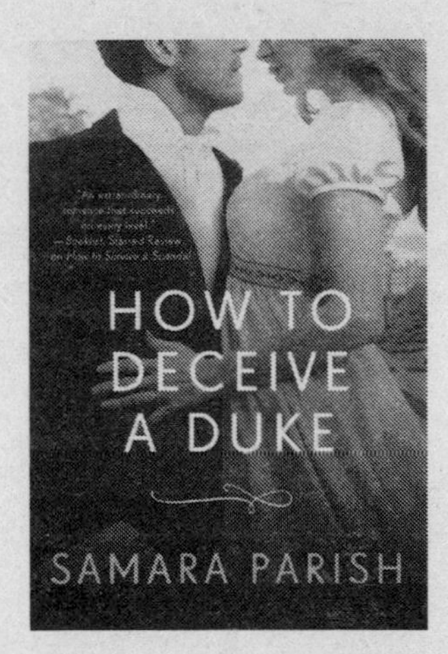

Engineer Fiona McTavish has come to London under the guise of Finley McTavish for one purpose—to find a distributor for her new invention. But when her plans go awry and she's arrested at a protest, the only person who can help is her ex-lover, Edward, Duke of Wildeforde. Only bailing "Finley" out of jail comes at a cost: She must live under his roof. The sparks from their passionate affair many years before are quick to rekindle. But when Finley becomes wanted for treason, will Edward protect her—or his heart?

Find more great reads on Instagram with @ReadForeverPub

SAY YOU'LL BE MY LADY
by Kate Pembrooke

Lady Serena Wynter doesn't mind flirting with a bit of scandal—she's determined to ignore Society's strictures and live life on her own terms. But there is one man who stirs her deepest emotions, one who's irresistibly handsome, and too honorable for his own good…Charles Townshend isn't immune to the attraction between them, but a shocking family secret prevents him from acting on his desires. Only Lady Serena doesn't intend to let his propriety stand in the way of a mutually satisfying dalliance.

SEVEN NIGHTS IN A ROGUE'S BED
by Anna Campbell

Desperate to protect her only family, Sidonie Forsythe has agreed to pay her sister's debt to the notorious, scarred scoundrel dwelling within Castle Craven. But without any wealth, she's prepared to compensate him however possible—even if it means seduction. Yet instead of a monster, Sidonie encounters a man with a vulnerable soul, one that could be destroyed by the dark secret Sidonie carries. When dangerous enemies gather at the gates, can the fragile love blooming between the beauty and the beast survive?